The

False

Prince

The False Prince

Fall Of A King: Book One

James Fuller

Irwin Publishing, Geneva, Illinois

Copyright © 2012 by James Fuller

Published and distributed in the United States by:
Irwin Publishing, 480 Cannon Drive, Geneva IL
60134

ISBN: 978 -1470013134

First Printing 2012
Printed in the United States of America

Contents

Acknowledgements

First and foremost, I must thank my beautiful wife, Nicolette. Without her support, understanding and criticism, this book may not ever have seen the light of day. Adam Romano and Jason Pearson, you both have been there from day one, listening to me ramble on and on about this story. Your hints and advice helped make this book. Last but not least, I thank my mother. You've always believed in me and encouraged me to settle for nothing but my dreams, thank you.

Prologue

The sky was alight with dim, yet vividly vibrant scarlet and amber hues. The colors slowly darkened and changed tones the further the sun slipped behind the imposing mountains. Silently a petite, hooded figure glided through the dense overgrowth of jungle. She constantly looked over her shoulder expecting someone to be there - awaiting to be glimpsed before they struck. If she were caught in this act of bitter betrayal, her death would be instant - regardless of her stature.

A light breeze slithered carelessly through the many obstacles the jungle floor offered in idle resistance. A hint of smoke lingered within it, reassuring her that she was heading in the right direction, and was not far now from her target.

Moistened eyes glanced down at the cloth bundle she held firmly to her chest, yet more gently than anything she had ever held before. Milky white eyes peered back curiously at her. The white would only last a few days before their true color would take over. She knew they would be a vibrant green, much like her own.

The figure halted once the campfire was in view through the entanglement of vines and branches and the murmurs of men and women could be overheard. It was as she had prayed for - a small group of poor traveling merchants and entertainers. They would do perfectly - there were Wizards among them, and she could sense them. They would be able to help - they would do what was right...she hoped. Though her options at this point were limited, this was all she had and it outweighed the latter by worlds.

A tiny hand found its way out from beneath the folds of the soft material and gripped a smooth finger. Her heart halted for several moments from the unfathomed emotions that nearly overwhelmed her. Unspoken words fell from her tears, absorbing into the dark brown cloth.

"I love you my sweet child. I swear to you it is true." The figure whispered softly placing the bundle onto the ground. The child let out a small worried whine at leaving its mother's warm, loving arms.

"It will be okay my darling, I promise." The figure cooed gently, placing a kiss on the infant's forehead. "May you one day forgive me my son." Slowly she melted away into the darkness, leaving the helpless bundle alone.

"We are making great time Master Ursa, thanks to you and your friend Master Samuel." The camp cook said, stirring the large pot of rabbit stew cooking over the campfire. "I must thank you again for coming with us - these woods are not safe at the best of times, with the savages, highwaymen, Shyroni and all."

The tall Wizard did not even seem to notice the man's words. Not out of disrespect, but because his attention was drawn elsewhere. Ursa's eyes gazed off into the thick entanglement of the jungle and his ears tingled as he focused them on something nearby.

"Master Ursa what is it?" Samuel asked, coming to stand beside him. "Is something wrong?" Master Samuel's hand instinctively reached for his short sword at his hip, through habit more than necessity since he had The Gift.

"Shhhhhh!" Ursa commanded, not even turning to look at his friend. "Do you hear that?" he whispered.

Samuel cupped his ears with his hands and listened. "What is that noise? It sounds almost like a baby crying. But that cannot be right - not out here at this late an hour."

Ursa nodded his agreement and started off into the thickness, towards the noise with haste. Several steps into the jungle and darkness sapped what luminosity the campfire and moon provided. Without thought, a small flame erupted from Ursa's palm, pushing back the gloom. With each step he took, the cries became louder and more frightened. Soon Ursa was staring down at the abandoned, white eyed, wailing bundle.

"What in the nine hells is a baby doing out here alone?" The camp cook - who had followed Ursa - said dumbfounded.

Ursa leaned down and scooped up the Gifted child in his long arms - almost instantly the baby's cries calmed. Ursa stared hard into the baby's ashen eyes and the bond was almost immediate. "It was deserted here not too long ago, on purpose."

"But why would anyone do that?" The cook asked still confused searching the growth for any sign of movement.

"This child has The Gift - the parents must not have wanted the ridicule and harassment that follows when having a Gifted child." Ursa replied, checking the sex of the child.

"I cannot wait for a time, when The Gifted are treated with the respect they deserve as people like any others," the cook muttered back as he began leading the way back to their camp.

"So what are you going to do with the child?" Samuel asked, once they had returned to the camp.

Ursa placed the child down on the back of one of the wagons and everyone gathered around. He thought long and hard for several moments before answering. "I shall raise the child myself."

"Are you sure? There is an orphanage in the next town. His eyes will have gone normal by then - no one will ever know." Another of the men blurted out, more harshly than he meant too.

"He was abandoned once already by the ones who were meant to love him the most. I do not have the heart to do something as callous to him again. I will raise him as my own and when his Gift is ready I will train him in the ways of Wizardry," Ursa said, his heart already warmed to the child.

"What will you name him?" One of the women asked, coming over to ogle the baby.

"I have always liked the name Meath." Ursa replied back, a slight smile creasing his lips.

"Tis a strong name indeed Master Ursa." The woman cooed as she tickled the baby's feet. "I do not understand how anyone could desert their own blood like that, it is absolutely horrible."

Most of the group went back to what they had been doing before the commotion started. But Ursa stood there staring down at the baby boy with a smile. "I will not abandon you, for I too know the hurt of such an act."

"I knew you would do what was right, Wizard." The figure whispered to herself, from deep in the darkness of the woods. She told herself to keep going and not to look back, but when the cries of her child had ceased she had to make sure he was safe. She could just make out what everyone was saying - her heart warmed when she heard the Wizard was going to raise the child. She made sure she

would remember his name forever - Ursa and the name her son had been given.
 Meath....

1

"You all have been selected for your unique, exceptional talents," the man in black shouted arrogantly for all to hear. He paced the length of hundreds of people, resentfully silent and kneeling unwillingly before him.

"You all will have a part in history this very night," he roared with eager enthusiasm, but he was the only one enthused... the large crowd was there against their will - held by shackles, and gags.

"Do not fear my Gifted friends - I shall never forget you or rather The Gifts that you will...provide me," he called maliciously with a heartless grin. His eyes glistened with a sadistic anticipation of what was to come.

"You are all aiding in a glorious cause.... My cause.... My divine destiny!" Vanity dripped from his every word as he threw his tattooed arms up high in the air with such authority the sky answered to his call. Lightning exploded throughout the empty heavens and thunder quaked the earth for miles

He began chanting in a rhythmic, forgotten language and with each word the crowd howled louder - in such raw agony that it could have awakened the dead from their eternal slumber. Their very essence was extracted from the unwilling bodies and surged reluctantly into the man in black. He stood, laughing callously up at the heavens, as he grew stronger with each essence he consumed.

Meath woke in a cold sweat. His long brown hair was matted to his head, his breathing erratic. His heart was hammering hard in his broad chest and he could feel his pulse in his ears, his forehead. After a few moments, his vivid green eyes cleared from the sleep and

dizziness to refocus upon his window. Judging by the darkness outside, the sun would not rise for an hour or more.

I have got to stop having these bloody nightmares. What is my problem? He groaned restlessly, running his hands through his thick shaggy hair. He knew there was no point trying to sleep again - he would only toss and turn and he knew better than to be late for another one of Ursa's lessons.

Ursa was like a father to Meath. He had come across Meath discarded in the woods as a baby and had taken him in as his own, and given him a life no orphan had the right to dream of. Though their relationship was not typical of father and son, it was still a better life than what would have befallen Meath otherwise.

After a few moments of catching his breath, Meath crawled out of bed making sure to step on the bearskin rug and not the cold, stone floor. He had killed the bear in his seventeenth year as a test of his bravery - and a stupid bet with his friends - and it had almost cost him his life. With a gesture of his hand and a solitary thought the candles in his room came flickering to life. The flames sputtered and swayed in the room's slight breeze, which made the shadows dance across the bare stone walls.

Meath glanced around, as if expecting to find something or someone in there with him. He looked from left to right - starting at his large wooden door and then moving across to his desk and bathtub past his large brass mirror and oak armoire to his window. Satisfied with finding nothing, he walked over to his mirror to have a look at himself. His hand traced the thick scar on his left shoulder where the bear had left a reminder of how close he had been to losing more than just a bet.

Meath was nearing his twentieth year, though his build and size - along with his facial features - made him look several years older. His muscles were tightly toned from years of the severe training as a soldier - something he had finished only a summer before. All the hard physical labor Ursa had made him do while growing up had readied for that level of training. Ursa had called it "character building", though Meath was sure they were just chores to keep him out of the Wizard's way while he worked.

It was in those years in the army that Meath had made many of his friends. They had all been brought there as boys and after a few hard years of training and a handful of battles, they left as warriors. Many of his companions were stationed in the castle as guards, or in the army based near the Kingdom to stop any of the barbarian raiding parties from the east in the jungle wastelands. When Meath had graduated as a full-fledged soldier at eighteen, he had returned to Drako Castle to begin new training. As a Wizard, under the study of Master Ursa.

Not just anyone could become a Wizard - they had to be born with The Gift. When a child with The Gift was born their eyes were pure white with no pupils. After a few days they would turn ordinary ,their Gifts sealed away until their bodies had matured and their minds developed sufficiently to control them. For most, it took until their seventeenth or eighteenth year before their minds could begin to control their Gifts with clarity. In some cases children could access them in times of necessity or distress, but they usually died in the process or shortly after, for The Gift could do immense damage to both body and mind if one did not know how to control it.

It took great discipline to utilize The Gift and overuse would deplete the body and mind of strength and often it took days to regain it. Most people feared magic and anything they did not comprehend - they would slay their children or abandon them somewhere when they discovered they had been born with The Gift.

In Zandor - the neighboring Kingdom - anyone with The Gift was put to death. The people of Zandor believed The Gift to be the work of The Keeper, but in Draco Kingdom - thanks to Ursa and many other Gifted - they were finding that those with The Gift could be used for the greater good of everyone.

For the last ten years, the majority of the people in Draco Kingdom had accepted The Gifted, or at least tolerated them. Their ability to heal wounds, sicknesses and their rare Gifts of the elements and unknown were a great aid in the wars and battles they had had with the Savages in the wasteland and other rivals.

The process had been slow because many parents were too ashamed to admit their child was born with The Gift and their bloodline might somehow be tainted. They feared what others might think or say - but there were now a few places throughout Draco Kingdom that were trying to instruct those with The Gift. It seemed fewer than ever were born with The Gift, or perhaps they would not come forth and admit that they were Gifted for fear of being judged and ridiculed or even hunted down. Even the King and his Lords had taken in several of the strongest Wizards into their castles. For reasons of both a show of goodwill to the people that there was nothing to fear and to be able to have their abilities on hand should they be needed.

It was rumored that there were secret cults that found others with The Gift and trained them to use their powers in such ways that only the Gods should know.

After looking over himself and washing his face, Meath grabbed his dark brown woolen robe and threw it on. As it slid down his body he felt the weight and warmth of it embrace him, almost like armor. Though he would rather be in his buckskin pants and vest than his new Wizard's robe, he knew that after his day's studies and training he could go back to his regular clothes. Next, he grabbed his belt - which had to be put on just right for all the pouches and pockets of herbs and potions to be ready at hand.

Meath finished dressing and felt the grip of hunger assault his gut. He took one last look out the window and saw the first few rays of the sun coming over the tops of the mountains. He knew the cooks would be getting up and lighting the ovens and it would be a while before they had something fresh to eat, but he was not going to wait. He decided to go now and see what he could stumble upon for breakfast. Before closing the thick wooden door, he waved his hand again and the candles flickered out, leaving small wafts of smoke billowing upward a few feet, before dissipating.

As he made his way through the castle's long, open stone hallways he noticed a lot more activity than normal. At this hour of the morning, there were usually only a few guards and a handful of servants about. But now the hallways were occupied with servants running everywhere looking to be in a stern hustling rush.

As he walked through the halls, side-stepping through people, he could not help but glance at every wall hanging he passed. There were colourful drapes and paintings of faraway lands and of beasts that only the bravest of men went seeking. Ursa had told him stories as a child of each portrait and had explained what they were and where they were found to the best of his knowledge. Ursa's stories were always long and full of detail and when he told them he seemed to bring them to life - as if you were really there, no matter how many times you heard them.

Meath stopped for a moment and admired his favourite hanging as he had a hundred times before. It was of a large, rare, winged lizard, with a hideous maw of sharp teeth and thick scales as strong as some men's armour. The beast clung to a jagged rock with its clawed feet, its leathery wings stretched out nearly as far as they could go as it arched forward, its maw open for its attack on the brave warrior who stood before it with nothing but a wooden shield and an obsidian-tipped spear. After a moment, Meath continued down the hallway - the picture had always inspired excitement and awe in him. As a child, he had often asked Ursa where such beasts lived, but Ursa had told him they had died out long ago.

Before Meath knew it, he was down the stairs and coming around the corner to the castle's kitchen. He could hear Maxwell - the head chef - barking out instructions to his kitchen staff and the cacophony of pots being banged around and people shouting the names of ingredients needed to prepare the morning meal.

Strange, the kitchen shouldn't be this hectic in the morning, he thought to himself.

The kitchen was one of the largest rooms in the castle. It had to be, to feed the vast amount of people who lived there. On the distant wall were huge granite ovens that baked and cooked the massive amounts of breads and meats. There were large wooden tables and shelves all around the giant room, which housed countless cookware items. Beside the great ovens was the door to the slaughter room. Butchers worked in the small room, cutting and preparing the many different types of meat for the cooks and the cold cellars.

"Maxwell, what is going on in here? What is the rush this morning?" Meath interrupted a heavy set man, while he moved out of the way of several passing servants carrying heavy armloads of supplies. The plump cook turned around to face him. His apron was covered in flour, mixed in with bits of other food he had been working with and he looked exhausted and a little frustrated.

"Meath what are you doing up? You are never up this early - are you ill?" he asked, before turning to bark orders off to people in the room and watched them long enough to see that they were off to do as he had told.

"I could not sleep very well again. Nowplease, answer my question, what is going on?" Meath yelled again trying to drown out the many sounds around him and the voices of so many - it was hard to believe one could understand anyone else in there.

Maxwell almost burst out laughing. "You mean to tell me you have not heard? Well it does not surprise me I guess, since you never pay any attention to what folks are saying anyway. The King's daughter - Princess Nicolette - is returning by mid-morning and the King is having a feast this evening. We have been up all night preparing for her arrival, and if we fall behind the King will have my neck in a rope. So I really must leave you now and see to some things." He ran his thick hand through his blonde, greasy hair, smiled tiredly and then hurried away into the thick mass of people and food, barking orders loudly as he went.

Meath knew the King would not harm Maxwell in any way, as the two had been friends for countless years. The King was as kind-hearted a man as Meath had ever known. He had even let Ursa bring Meath into the castle and be schooled and trained in things only nobles or wealthy merchants could put their children through.

Meath's mind drifted back to what Maxwell had said about the Princess coming back to Draco Castle. He wondered how he could have possibly missed hearing about that. This was huge. He smiled at the thought of Princess Nicolette's return. He had not seen the Princess in several long months and his heart warmed at the thought at seeing her again. He had not realized how much he had missed her until hearing her name and knowing he would be able to see her soon.

"You make a better pillar than a doorway Meath!" One of Maxwell's kitchen staff grumbled at him, slightly annoyed because Meath was in his way.

Meath snapped back to reality and apologized to the man. Without getting in anyone else's way, he managed to attain a chunk of freshly baked flat bread and some dried deer meat along with a small flagon of honey milk. *A fine breakfast indeed*, he thought with a small grin. He got out of there as fast as he could, before someone thought he looked like a good candidate for helping with something, as he so often did.

Meath started back to his room to eat. Now the castle was reeling with even more activity and he did not want to get in the way again. When he had reached his room and closed the door , where it was silent enough that he could hear himself think again. He pondered the news he had just heard and could not believe he had not heard it sooner. He thought back to the last week and tried to recall anything or anyone who would have clued him into it. He had been so absorbed lately with his training and progress that he guessed he must have missed all the talk and commotion about the Princess' return.

"So the Princess is returning for a visit." Meath whispered to himself as he ate. The last time he saw Princess Nicolette was at the spring renewal festival when all of the Lords, Ladies, merchants, and wealthy families came to Draco Castle to celebrate the beginning of a new year. It was a weeklong festival of dancing, eating, and games - drinking, gambling and best of all, the Warrior's Challenge. The best soldiers, warriors and championstested their strength, bravery, skills and honour in hard challenges and then finally one-on-one combat with dull blunted weapons to pick the year's finest warrior.

Meath had not been able to spend as much time as he would have liked with Nicolette. They were both older now and had greater commitments to the lives they were to have. They had grown up together in the castle and had been best friends, together as often as they could - which as they grew older became harder to do. As they matured, that friendship had only grown stronger and even more intimate. Several difficult moments had occurred and a few had been discovered, when firm scoldings had ensued.

He only saw her several times a year now, since her mother had died several years previously. Now when she came home, she spent most of her time with her father or with the Ladies of the castle. Meath could understand that, and though it was not like they did not spend time together, it was not the same as before, though how could he expect it to be. They had both grown up so much over the last few years and had done and seen so much that was so different. They were not children anymore. Things were different between them now as there were more thoughts and feelings than there ever were before. But they had been told several times that those feelings could not transpire... friendship was all that could be.

Meath gulped down the last of the bread and meat and went to the window. The sun was now just about half way out from behind the lush, dark green mountaintops and it was almost time for him to be in Ursa's study for his lessons. He turned to grab the last of the things he would need, when there was a knock at his door.

"Come in," Meath called out and Ursa walked in. His lengthy, ashen hair was as it forever was, straight down his back and held together with a black string near the end. Not a hair appeared out of place and his white robe seemed to glimmer like the sun in the dim room. Though the man was nearing his seventieth year, he still managed to get around better than most half his age and he only looked like he was entering his fiftieth year.

Ursa was one of the most powerful Wizards in Draco Kingdom, which was believed to be why he was still so agile and full of energy. But even his powers were restricted. There were only a few Wizards in Draco Kingdom who could equal Ursa's skills and only a smaller handful who were rumoured to be able to outdo him, though it had never been demonstrated.

"Ah, I see you are already out of bed, good, good then. So I take it you have finally heard the news, yes?" Ursa spoke in a tone that sounded as if he was eager as he cleared the distance from the door to Meath in a few strides of his long, lanky legs.

"Yes, I have heard that Princess Nicolette is returning," Meath said as he yawned and stretched his arms, trying not to tip the old man off that he was actually excited himself to see her again.

"Have you been taking that tea I gave you to assist your sleep?" Ursa said already knowing the answer. "No matter, lose sleep if that is what you want, but I will accept no blunders in your studies because of it. But that is not the point," he finished, almost too rapidly for Meath to understand. "The Princess is not just coming back, she is coming back to be wed to Prince Berrit of Zandor in several weeks. All of the royal families from Zandor will be here soon, for the wedding," Ursa said..

Meath could feel the blood in his face drain out, making him feel cold and clammy - his stomach twisted at the thought of the Princess getting married. He knew she was well past the age that most were married and it really should not come as a surprise, but it did.

"Meath!" Ursa spoke snapping Meath out of his thoughts. "Are you all right boy? You appear like you have just seen a spirit," Ursa said as he blinked, then chuckled.

"I am fine." Meath lied, trying to compose himself.

"She is a Princess, Meath. You cannot persist with this puppy love. I tried to advise you that it would never work back when I first noticed this predicament. You should have known better by now," Ursa told him compassionately.

"I know…. I just thought that…I do not know. I am fine and happy for her." Meath rambled, still lost in the moment.

"You will marry one day I am sure of it, but until that day you have far more important concerns, like your studies," Ursa told him gesturing to the door.

"Your Highness, it is but a few more miles to Draco City. I sent a rider to tell them of our arrival and he has returned with good news - they are ready for us. Your room and a warm bath will be made ready for when you arrive." The large bearded soldier said as he rode up beside her carriage.

"Thank you Rift - it will be good to be home again." The Princess replied as she pulled the hood of her deep blue traveling cloak back, letting her long brown hair sparkle in the light from the small window.

"It has been too many months since I have seen my homeland as well your Highness. It will be good to be back. I wonder how much has changed since the last time we were there," Rift said, a grin fashioned on his face as he considered the things he would enjoy while they were back. "It will be good to see your father and everyone again," he said cheerfully.

Nicolette smiled. "Yes it will be good to see the old bear again," she replied with a chuckle, "and Lord Tundal and Lord Dagon as well."

Ever since she could remember, Rift had been there for her; watching out for her and protecting her when she needed it. The deep scar across his chin was scarcely noticeable anymore, nor were his many others. When she was a child, she remembered calling him names and running from him trying to hide because he frightened her. Now she had grown fond of the man, and found his rough features comforting. Although he was a fierce warrior who had killed countless, she knew the man within. He was more of a gentleman than he ever let on.

The Captain was oath-bound to her, until his death. He had been her mother's champion before she had died, and on her deathbed Queen Lavira had made the Captain pledge a blood-oath that he would defend Nicolette from any harm 'til he took his final breath.

After her mother's death from a mysterious illness- when Nicolette was in her fourteenth year - her father had sent her away to be raised in Dragon's Cove where her Aunt Jewel and her husband Lord Marcus resided. Dragon's Cove was on the coast of Draco Kingdom, to the west. Her father knew he could not raise her the way she should be raised - to be a Lady - without her mother. King Borrack did not have it in him to take another wife, and only a woman could raise a girl to be a proper Lady and a Princess - and one day a Queen. He had too much to deal with at the time - with wars and his Kingdom's affairs - to give his daughter the time she would require from him.

It had been a fortnight's ride with a group this large, but a solitary rider, with little sleep, could have made it in four days. The risk of killing a few horses from exhaustion was certain though. With a personal royal escort of five hundred of Dragon Cove's finest, battle-hardened soldiers, the expedition was slow going.

As they traveled along the road to the castle Nicolette felt the overwhelming joy of being back in her homeland. In Dragon's Cove you could see a great distance, for the land had few hills and the timberland was not as dense as here in the jungle. Once they had crossed the mighty Sheeva River, every step brought them into a thick, dense jungle where the eyes could not begin to grasp all the colours and hues that were surrounding them.

As she looked out the window of her carriage into the deep growth of the forest, she watched some monkeys playing in the trees. Some of them watched the large group that pace by - certain to keep their distance and stay out of harm's way.

Nicolette envied the primates, for they lived in peace and sovereignty and could do as they wished - with no responsibilities. She sighed at the thought of what had brought her back home after all these years. Soon she would be wed to Prince Berrit of Zandor. He was a man she had only ever met a few times in her life. He was handsome, but she remembered that he lacked everything else she had hoped for in the man she would wed. He reminded her of a serpent - one who was prepared to do anything to better himself, no matter what the cost. Also, being he was Zandorian, made him bull-headed and ruthless. She had begged and pleaded with her father to find another suitor, but he had insisted that it had to be Prince Berrit. With their marriage, the two Kingdoms could finally work collectively to rid themselves of the Barbarian tribes that threatened both lands. They could also come to an accord on those with The Gift and finally end their Kingdoms' never-ending quarrel. The fate of her soon-to-be land and citizens counted on this marriage, being that she was the only pure blood of the royal line of King Borrack and Queen Lavira...there was no one else.

After Nicolette was born her mother had been left barren and could no longer conceive children. Her father - being madly in love with his Queen - never took a mistress to his bed to get another heir. Even when her mother had died, Borrack had never taken another wife, even though many had urged him to for the sake of the Kingdom. He had always claimed he would when the time was right.

"I cannot wait until we are finally done with this boring trip." Tami, her cousin said with a very irritated sniff as she took her eyes from one of the side windows.

"I just wish father were here. He always knows how to make the trip seem shorter with all his stories," replied her younger sister Avril.

Tami ignored her and looked over to Nicolette. "What is the matter with you today? You have hardly said anything since we broke camp this morning." She spoke in that same flat, annoyed tone she always used when she was vexed - which seemed to be most of the time.

Nicolette turned her attention from the window for the first time in hours. "I just have a lot on my mind, I'm sorry. I did not mean to be rude."

"I bet you cannot wait to see Prince Berrit. I hear he is the most handsome and fearless man in Zandor - nothing scares him." Avril chatted to Nicolette with wide eyes of excitement for her. "I cannot wait 'til I get married. I hope I am as lucky as you." Avril said, still wide-eyed with childish excitement.

Tami laughed. "No man will ever want to marry you; you are too ugly and aggravating."

"Will too! You're the one who will never get married because you are too mean." Avril shot back as she stuck out her tongue at her older sister.

Nicolette turned back to the window while the two sisters - whom she had spent a great deal of her life with - argued back and forth as always. Normally she would try to stop them, but right now she just could not bring herself to care. All she could think about was what her life with her new husband was going to be like. Maybe it would not be that bad, maybe Prince Berrit would be all that she had hoped for in a man. Maybe she would be able to learn to love him as so many others had told her she would.

She hated the thought of having to learn to love someone. Love was meant to happen and be as magical as in the songs the bards always sung. Yet she had seldom met anyone who had wed someone whom they had fallen in love with. She knew what love was and knew she would not ever get the chance to wed the man she had fallen for. She had known years before, and yet still had allowed those feelings to grow.

She wondered if Meath was even still in Draco Kingdom. It had been a while since they had last seen one another and even then it had been awkward and different between them. Last she had heard he had finished his training as a soldier and since he had been born with The Gift, he would have started his training as a Wizard. She was sure he would have found someone by now - being in his twentieth year, a fully trained soldier, and now a trainee Wizard.

Once Ursa retired from the King's services, Meath would take his place as Draco Castle's Wizard. Nicolette hoped he had found someone nice who would give him everything he needed and deserved. Someone beautiful and caring, who would treasure him for his quirks and flaws.

"Hey, you still in there?" Tami waved her hand in front of Nicolette's face trying to get her attention.

"Make ready your Highness…we are almost in Draco City. It looks like all of the citizens in the city have come to welcome you home," Rift said as he rode past her towards the front of her carriage. He would see to it that no one got in their way or delayed them and he needed to bark final orders to his men. His men held their banner up high, waving in the warm breeze and marched in perfect formation as they had learned to do.

Nicolette looked out her window, to see the gathering of people who had come to welcome her back with cheers and whistles. Though they had not even reached the actual city limits, she was surprised that there were more people gathered here than she would ever have expected. As she rode past them she tossed out copper coins, mixed in with the occasional silver and gold coin and rare spices to those who were swift enough to grab them. Nicolette wondered if they had truly come out to see her arrive or to see what handouts might be given. She did not mind all that much either way - she knew the folks on the outer limits of the city were but poor families and farmers. The thought that she had just helped them - even with as little as a copper coin - made her smile.

As the soldiers, wagons and carriages made their way through the now crowded streets of the city toward the castle; she could not help but notice how much the city had transformed. It had been several months since she had last been there, and now the buildings seemed newer and larger than before. She could not believe how different things looked in that time and how many more people now seemed to be living in the city. Before long all she could hear was the people chanting her name and asking for the Creator to show her favour with many years of happiness and to bear many healthy sons.

As she neared the castle parapet, she remembered back to when she was a little girl, and her father would come home from war or from a trip. She and her friends would stand on the wall above the gates and watch him ride in with his troops. Now, others were on the wall watching her arrive. Nicolette could see the small children up there pointing her way and waving. She almost expected to see Meath up there, but knew he was not - she had to stop herself from looking.

Before long they were within the ramparts of the castle and only a few moments away from the enormous front entrance of the grand feasting hall. Her father, his advisors, Lords and Ladies and people of high favour to the Kingdom were waiting for her. To her, there seemed to be many more than she remembered.

The driver pulled up as close as he dared... doing his best to avoid stirring dust up in the direction of the King and his guests. Rift helped the Princess out of the carriage and onto solid ground, and then Nicolette made her way toward her father's open arms and wide smile.

Ursa was one of the King's closest friends and a key advisor, so he had been summoned to be there for the arrival of the Princess. Since Meath was his apprentice, he stood at the doors of the feasting hall waiting to see his old friend - the future Queen of Draco Kingdom.

Meath watched as the stagecoach - bearing the Princess' royal colors of bright blue and gold - pulled up to where they all stood. He watched as the familiar man who he knew to be Captain Rift - the Princess' champion - got down off his horse. He opened the dusty stagecoach door and provided his hand to help her down. Meath's eyes grew wider as he saw the tall, slender, womanly figure step down to the ground and start toward them.

"If you remain staring at the Princess like that, my boy, you are going to discover your head on the chopping block." Ursa whispered without even looking at Meath.

Meath shook his head and tried to regain his composure. He could not help but stare. The Princess' beauty never ceased to take his breath away. This was not the same girl for whom he had once stolen a full basket of her favourite candy apples from Maxwell - or the girl he had shared his first kiss with back when they were both not more than ten years old. She was the most beautiful creature he had ever laid his eyes on.

"My darling daughter - you are looking more like your mother every time I see you. How was your trip? I heard you had trouble with that cursed river again. You are not hurt, are you?" King Borrack asked as he embraced his daughter and held her for a long moment. His eyes began to tear up a bit.

"The trip was lovely, Father. I almost forgot how beautiful this countryside is, and how fresh the air tastes," the Princess replied. Through the long embrace, she glanced over to where Meath stood. Their eyes met but she promptly looked away.

"Where are Lady Jewel, Lord Marcus and Mathu?" Borrack replied withdrawing from a lingering hug. He did notice Jewel and Marcus had sent their lovely (yet irritating) daughters along. More than anything else they seemed to be more interested in barking orders at their servants - demanding which of their things should be brought up to their rooms first.

"They were not able to make the trip as Lord Marcus has come down with the fever and were not well enough to travel." The Princess spoke in grief-tinged tones. Everyone knew that the few who came down with the fever rarely recovered - those who did were never the same. "But they do send their love and respects and even some of their fine brandy that you like so much, Father," Nicolette added with a smile.

"That is such a shame. I was so looking forward to seeing them both again. I do hope he will be okay. After the wedding if I can find the time I will travel down to see him." Borrack said. "Well, let us not talk of such things now. No daughter of mine is going to look and smell like that while she is staying in my castle. Take your maidens up to your room where there is a bath and fresh clothing waiting for you. I will have a servant bring your things up to your room and when you are ready we will feast until we burst. I just might sample some of that brandy you have brought along." With that said the King walked back into the massive hall where the feast was to be held.

2

As fashionably late guests filtered into the grand feasting hall, their noses were greeted with a dozen mouth-watering aromas. From cooked meats, to more pastries than anyone could hope to sample in one evening, to the variety of sweet meats that littered each table filled the air with invitation. Plenty of wine, mead, and ale kegs were tapped - placed never far from hand, so that no one would go thirsty throughout the long festive evening.

Servants swarmed the massive hall, keeping each table stocked with fresh food and empty of dirty tableware and food waste. They were so proficient at their tasks that no one ever noticed a mess for long

The Grand Table - which seated near a hundred - ran over half the width of the hall. It was set at the far end, while other smaller tables were set up lengthwise down the sides of the hall, leaving the middle open for the various entertainments the night held. Already bards were singing their enchanting tunes and epic fables of true love and heroic wars to all those who gathered round. Exotic dancers flaunted their alluring performances throughout the hall and earned the tips they received for their tempting arts. Fire breathers, sword jugglers and many more acts filled the center of the hall, making sure that everyone had something to their tastes.

The walls were decorated with all of Draco Kingdom's flags, banners, beautiful scenic tapestries and paintings. The artwork showed pictures of all the Kings, Queens, Lords and Ladies that Draco Kingdom had ever had. King Borrack's most trophy hung above his painting for display - the bronze sword and horned battle helm of Azazel. The King himself had slain the Barbarian leader a few years ago on the battlefield in single combat, altering the fate of the war.

The people had gathered outside the castle wall and overflowed into the streets of Draco City. They drank and danced ceaselessly to the jumble of music that flowed hypnotically through the city. The people were having their own celebration for the return of the Princess, and it well matched that of those inside.

At the beginning of the celebration, the seating was meticulously arranged by Borrack's planners. But now that most had had their fill of the delectable food and plenty of drink had flowed between their lips, no one stayed seated for long. Guest's mingled with each other in migrating groups, or danced and sang aloud with the bards, adding more gusto to the melody.

"This is a fine turnout - it is all for you my daughter!" King Borrack roared, as he swayed in his seat. He was trying not to appear too drunk, though everyone knew he was well past that stage. "I am glad to have you home again. You have become a beautiful woman and shall make a fine wife... "he slurred. "Your mother would be proud."

"I completely and fully agree... I think?" Lord Dagon slurred, as he too seemed to be having a difficult time keeping his balance in his chair and maintaining a steady tone in his voice. His two sons, Ethan and Leonard, were no better off.

"I have not had this much merriment or ale since I was married," Lord Tundal hollered as he slapped Raven's back and made Drandor's champion spill his drink all over his lap.

Raven stood up, doing well to hide his own awkward, drunkenness. "You my good sir have spilled my mead - what man would I be if I did not challenge you after such an act," he bellowed out while steadying himself on the rear of his own chair.

The cluster at that end of the table went silent, watching while the rest of the gathering continued with their merriment.

"Well Raven, my fine man. I, being a man of...of...of honour shall accept your challenge!" Tundal stammered out to him as he stood from his own chair.

"Oh dear - not this again, Tundal. You cannot be serious, not tonight," his beautiful wife Tora begged him, as she looked for support from the others in her vicinity.

"I am sorry, my wife. I must defend my...my...well you know that word I am thinking of," Tundal replied, meeting Raven's determined stare with one of his own.

"King Borrack, will you not stop this foolishness before it gets out of hand?" Tora begged, giving him a half-annoyed and half-pleading look.

"I am sorry my Lady but I cannot. This is between these two drunken fools," the King said with a chuckle. Tora just sighed and started talking to Lady Angelina, trying hard to ignore her drunken husband.

Lord Dagon stood between the two men. "Well let us have it then you two. Raven, my good man, I have known Tundal my whole life and he is going to have his drink…drank and pissed out before you even get past the foam in your cup!" Dagon roared for all to hear and laughs sprang up from all around them as the crowd cheered the two men on.

"Well Raven - let us get you demise over with," Tundal slurred with a wink to his good friend, who by now could not hide his own smile. He started to chuckle about it all.

"May the best man win!" Raven winked back, slammed his mead to his lips, and drank for all he was worth. He knew he had already lost before he heard Tundal's cup hit the table. Everyone cheered, but he finished his brew just the same.

The two belched and clasped hands - more to keep each other upright than anything else, as the mead went straight to their heads.

Raven slumped back into his chair. "I shall beat you one of these days!"

"Father…I do not feel well!" Thoron moaned, as he fell to the floor and vomited on himself…and all over the floor around him.

"That is what happens, my boy, when you drink too much!" Tundal cheered as he watched his wife Tora and his daughter Salvira carry the drunken child away to clean him up. A servant ran over to clean the boy's mess from the floor before anyone else saw it - or slipped. No one seemed to notice. They were all having too good a time and Lord Tundal's boy had not been the first to vomit, nor would he be the last this night.

"Halpas, my good friend, where be your beautiful wife Nora and that strapping young lad of yours?" Dagon asked with a slur.

"They are visiting family up north," Halpas replied shortly.

"Will they make it back for the wedding?" Dagon asked.

"I'm afraid not," The King's champion said, his eyes wandering the room.

"A shame, I had my personal blacksmith craft him a fine hunting knife and I was hoping to give it to the boy," Dagon slurred again. "I feel so bad for missing his last birthday. Alas, I shall have to make another trip down here to give it to him myself once he returns."

"You could always leave it with me. I will let him know it is from you." Halpas replied, a small hint of aggravation in his tone. "Then you do not worry about making another trip."

Dagon eyed him curiously, not sure if he was truly hearing his old friend correctly or if it was the alcohol distorting his perception. "Well you will have to remind me another day when I am not so...so...well...drunk you see," Dagon laughed, deciding to drop it.

A duo of bards promenaded up to them through the crowd and began playing a harp and lute. They sang about an old war in which King Borrack, Halpas and a few others at the table had fought against the Barbarian's previous leader, Azazel. The group went silent and listened to the magnificent tale of how Borrack exterminated the heartless beast in single combat and turned the tide of the war with a massive blow of his mighty sword.

"If I would have known that all it would take to shut them up was a bard to sing that tale, I would have had it happen an hour ago," Lady Angelina remarked to Nicolette and the other ladies around the table. They all shared a laugh.

While the bards sung their tale and the men quieted down - the ladies were able to commence their talk and gossip.

"Master Ursa, was Meath not going to be here this evening?" The Princess asked the Wizard, ignoring her father and the other party-goers drunken behaviour. "It has been a while since we last saw each other. I figured he would be here so that we might catch up on our lives."

"Yes - that is a little strange. He appeared happy to hear of your return this morning. I am sure he is around somewhere - no doubt making a fool out of himself. Or trying to impress a girl with that thing he calls charm," the Wizard said with a chuckle, as he glanced around the room trying to spot Meath for her. He gave up shortly after, shaking his head to the young Princess with a look that said he was unable to see Meath.

"Well, I think I will go get some fresh air and see if I can find him. He cannot be far off," she replied as she stood up and made her way through the crowd of people who were dancing and singing all round. She knew no one would notice her being gone for some time. No one, except Ursa, had even looked up to watch her as she left.

Meath took another long, hard swallow of the dark honey brew. He knew this would be his final mug of the night - he had already drunk more than his fill and was feeling its influence well enough. He knew that if he had any more, he would not rise tomorrow without painful consequence. He looked down at the small engraving on the thick branch of his childhood climbing tree and sighed. Ursa was right. Even as a child, Meath knew it was just a delusion and could never happen ... now, he could not help but experience the sting of truth. He wondered if he would ever find someone else who he would care as much about - someone who could make him smile like she did.

He had passed up numerous opportunities to become familiar with other girls while growing up. He could not help but feel foolish now for trying to hold onto lost hopes and dreams. Meath knew that once the Princess and Prince Berrit were married, he would have to continually observe them together. Scowling, Meath thought he might depart and go back to the army. Somewhere far away where he could forget her and all of this, but he knew Ursa and the King would never permit it. No - Meath knew he had to stay and conclude his training, and accept his fate as Draco Castle's future Wizard. He would inherit Ursa's place one day - when Ursa grew old or died. Meath could hardly believe Ursa would ever die - the man never seemed to age or slow down. He finished off the last of the ale in his mug and dropped it to the soft earth. Then he made his way down the tree - slowly, to accommodate for the effects of the ale.

Nicolette wandered through the less used hallways of the castle, so as not to be seen by numerous people who might wish to stop and congratulate her. Fortunately, everyone she passed was too excited or too drunk to take up too much of her time and she made her way through the castle to the north-west end.

She had a funny feeling that she knew where Meath might be this night. She had already checked his quarters and the kitchen, knowing he used to go there and speak with Maxwell. However, Maxwell had not seen him since the morning. That left only one place - the Royal Garden where, as children they had exhausted many of their fun-filled days...growing up and playing games. It had also been where they first met, when her father had finally accepted Ursa's request for audience on behalf of The Gifted.

She walked out into the garden beneath the clear night sky and looked around as so many wonderful memories flooded back to her. She walked down one of the well-kept paths toward the west end corner where, as children they claimed it as their own.

"I thought I might find you out here." A soft, gentle, voice said from behind him. As Meath twisted to look, his hand fell short of the branch he had intended to grasp and he fell the last few feet to the ground with a hard thud and a groan. Meath lifted his head to see who had caused him to fall. He heard a memorable laugh, and knew - right away - who it was.

"I thought after all these years you would have figured out how to finally climb down from there," the Princess giggled.

"Well - it helps when people do not creep up on you while you are doing so." Meath groaned as he stood up and dusted himself off. He looked up at her and their eyes locked. In the short moments they shared, it seemed all the time they had spent separately faded away. As if a day had not past since they had seen one another.

"You look as lovely as ever, your Highness." Meath managed to stammer out, and kicked himself knowing she did not like it when he called her by her title.

"Meath you know you do not need to call me by my title. You, of all people, should know that by now," she replied, sounding nearly hurt that he would address her so. "I was hoping we would be able to speak about old times. Why are you out here and not at the banquet?" She asked but already knew the answer. She could feel the awkwardness in the air.

"I…I just could not bear to see you yet." Meath replied, struggling with the urge to go to her.

"You know there has not been a day gone by that I did not think about thee," she said, as they closed the gap between them and coming together in a long embrace.

"Nor I," he whispered just loud enough for her to hear.

They pulled away to an arm's length and gazed into each other's moistened eyes. For what seemed like an eternity, they just stared into each other, knowing and feeling everything the other one sought to say. Slowly their lips came together and entangled in an ardent kiss.

In that moment, his mind brought him back to when last they had seen each other, months ago at the spring renewal festival….

…They had been invited casually to go on a hunting excursion with Lord Dagon, his champion Jarroth, and several others. Meath had been sure the invitation was just a kind gesture, but they had accepted nonetheless. During a mid-afternoon break, Meath and Nicolette had wandered off to collect pheasant eggs in the woods while the meal was being prepared and the two stags Dagon had shot down were being cleaned.

They were not interested on collecting any eggs - collecting instead, a few moments alone. He had told her he loved her - it was the first time he had ever voiced the words, though he was well aware that she knew. She had smiled up at him and returned the words - they had kissed deeply and time had stood still until they had nearly been caught.

"We cannot do this," Nicolette whispered pulling back from the passionate embrace - as if not trusting her own arms to be free, she wrapped them around herself. Her eyes dropped toward the soft earth, afraid to look up at him.

"I know, but I…" Meath whispered struggling with his inner feelings as he took a step forward but quickly retreated.

Nicolette finally lifted her eyes to his again, tears cascading to her cheeks. "I am to be married soon. I have too…we have to stop this. We can no longer do whatever this is Meath," she sobbed.

Meath's own eyes welled up. "I know, I know. I just wish…" He stopped, knowing anything he said would only make it worse for both of them.

"I should go," Nicolette said, wiping the tears from her eyes. She turned to leave and stopped. Everything in her being told her to keep going, yet her heart would not let her. "Meath, I will always love…" Before she could finish Meath turned her around and their lips met again.

"Get off of her you soiled, flea-infested dog!" Rift bellowed as he ran toward them with his dagger drawn and ready. "How dare you take advantage of the Princess in this way!" he barked, as he tore her away and put a good distance between the two.

"No, Rift. It is not what you believe..." Nicolette said in a panic.

"Highness, I have been around long enough to know what that was! I made an oath to your Mother to keep you away from dogs like that one." The Captain spoke in tones that made the hairs on Meath's neck stand on end. Still, he did not budge an inch - he just stood there staring at Nicolette. "Besides, your father sent me out to find you...He would like a word with you." With that, Rift took her hand and led her back in the direction of the party. Nicolette looked over her shoulder and met Meath's eyes once more, mouthing "I am sorry" before she was out of view.

Meath stood there for some time before finally returning to his room, but not before he made a few stops along the way to replenish his mead mug. He drained the mug just as swiftly as he filled it, trying hard to drown the confusion, hurt, and sorrow that now consumed his mind and heart. He needed to find rest this night but his thoughts assaulted him, no matter how hard he tried to stop them.

"So this is how it is to end - we should have known better than to rekindle our love," he whispered bitterly, hating himself for not listening to Ursa years before. Finally, he fell into a drunken stupor.

For the next several days, the castle was alive with constant activity, as preparations for the royal wedding were paramount. All attention was focused on the massive event - the King wanted everything to be of the finest quality and of exquisite taste and spared no expense to see it so.

Meath exhausted himself with his studies, trying hard to bury his frustrations.

Ursa was more than eager to spend the additional hours each day with him. He taught him several new potions and even a few new techniques with the elemental aspect of his Gift. Ursa knew the motives behind Meath putting in so much extra time so suddenly. To help keep his thoughts elsewhere, he did his best to teach Meath things he sought to learn. It also gave Ursa a little more time with Draco's other apprentice Wizard, Keithen. It was rare for a Wizard - even one as experienced as Ursa to take on two apprentices. To train one with The Gift, it took so much time and focus to learn how to stimulate each individual, for everyone was different in their learning and perception.

Keithen was the scrawny, fair-haired bastard son of one of the servant women. The father was an unknown soldier who had died before Keithen had been born. After Ursa has befriended King Borrack and had offered his services to the good of Draco, the mother had come forward begging the King to allow Ursa to teach her son the arts of The Gift. The King had been reluctant for the deceit the woman had shown in hiding the truth. However, Ursa had educated him on the benefits of having more Wizards in his arsenal, and the King had seen reason and agreed.

Keithen had been raised in the servants' quarters of the castle and had spent his life as a pot scrubber for Maxwell until it was time for his training. Only because Ursa had requested it for his training, had Keithen been allowed to learn to read and write.

Ursa spent the majority of his time with Meath, for Meath was like his son and his first apprentice - he had showed great talent in his skills so early. Though Ursa felt terrible that he could not spend that sort of time with Keithen, there just was not enough time in the day to train both equally. Though Ursa did his best to accommodate Keithen well, he searched for another Wizard to take him as their apprentice.

"Focus!" Ursa commanded Meath.

"I am trying!" Meath growled back tensely as he focused on the basin of water - his fingers no more than an inch away from the smooth surface.

"Picture ice forming on the surface," Ursa said sternly. "Centre your Gift as if you were summoning fire, but will it frozen."

"I can feel it." Meath proclaimed enthusiastically as a thin layer of ice formed under his fingertips and slowly crept its way across the span of the basin.

Keithen looked up from his studies and could not help but watch eagerly and enviously. How he wished he was learning the things Meath was instead of sitting there reading theory.

"Exceptional!" Ursa said proudly. "Though after your tenth try, I would expect so. Now freeze the basin all the way through," he added strictly. "And if you do not mind, do it quickly. I have other things to tend to this day."

Meath cracked a smile. He knew the old Wizard was just hazing him, trying to motivate the best way he knew how. Nevertheless, even in the old man's stern words, Meath could still hear the approval.

"Anytime now if you would like," Ursa mocked, as he sorted through several piles of parchments on the table, not looking up at Meath. "Do not worry Keithen about what Meath is doing, back to your studies. Finish that reading today and if I have time, I will teach you a new potion."

Keithen sighed and lower his eyes back to the parchments in front of him. Potions and theory were all Ursa ever taught him. Ursa had once asked him to summon Wizard's fire, but that had turned out badly for one of the bookshelves in the room.

Meath turned his attention to the basin again and began focusing his Gift when Rift entered the room.

"Master Ursa, His Majesty would like to see you," Rift spoke, standing just inside the doorway.

The sound of Rift's voice heated Meath's blood. His eyes squinted into a loathing glare. His Gift surge forth with the aid of his anger and the basin of water began to freeze and was not long until it was frozen solid. But it did not stop there. Frost and ice formed on the outside of the basin and cascaded down to the stone floor around it. The ice persistently consumed several places of the floor, growing thicker with each heartbeat.

"Enough!" Ursa ordered, knowing Meath would freeze the room solid if not stopped.

Meath balled his hands into fists and pulled them to his side, halting the ice from conquering any more of the stone. His breaths were deep and edgy.

Keithen's eyes could not help but leave his papers again at Meath's bitter display of his Gift.

"Next time Rift, I would appreciate it if you waited for the lesson to be over before interrupting," Ursa spoke calmly.

Rift stood up straight and cleared his throat. "I will remember that for next time. The King is in the library."

"You may tell the King I will be there straight away - my lesson is nearly finished." Ursa replied going back to his papers. Ursa waited several moments after the door was closed before speaking. "How many times have I told you not to intergrate emotions into your studies?"

Meath exhaled deeply, "I know, I am sorry."

"You can do immense harm to yourself in doing so. Your broken heart is no reason to break your mind," Ursa scolded. "I am going to go see what the King wants. Clean up your mess," Ursa told him, handing him a chisel and hammer. "I will know if you use your Gift at all, and Keithen do not help him." With that, he walked out of the room.

With Ursa's lessons and the late nights he spent in the warrior's den helping prepare fresh soldiers, he was able to occupy his mind to some extent. He had volunteered his time to help train the new recruits in hand-to-hand and weapons combat. Not really for them, but for himself - it helped him take his frustrations out on something inanimate. But practice was over for the night and now Meath sat alone in his room staring at the candle flames dancing in the chilly draft that nearly always ran through the castle. It was the last night before the arrival of the Royal families from Zandor. He had not even seen Nicolette in the last few days. The last he had heard, they were having troubles with her wedding gown and she was holed up in her room with a handful of seamstresses.

Meath knew there was nothing he could do to impede what was going to come, even if there was a way they would never get away with it. It would only make matters worse and he knew he had to let it go...let *her* go. It was foolish - it had always been foolish and now they were paying for it.

He clenched his fists tightly and glared irately at the flames of the candles as if they had done him this remorseless wrong. The flames grew brighter and more zealous with each passing second until they almost reached the roof. Then he slammed his fist against his wooden bed frame - the candles erupted, sizzling wax splattering everywhere, although none came his way.

After only moments in the gloom, Meath conjured a flame on the palm of his hand. Though he could feel the violent heat that came off the flame, it did not burn him - it was part of him. A Wizard's fire would not burn that which yields it - though curiously enough, the other elements could still do the caster harm.

As he stared into the flame, it began to grow and form into an almost liquid ball that was soon larger than his head. The fire went from a natural yellowy-orange, to a deep red with an almost clear white external layer. Meath knew he should not merge his emotions into his castings, but he could not help it. With a swift throw, the blistering orb shot out his window and into the night sky where it dispersed within a few hundred feet. He sat there staring off into the dark for nearly an hour. Finally, there was a light rap at his door, shaking him out of his contemplation.

As he lit the one candle that had survived his wrath, his door creaked open and a slender form wrapped in a black cloak slipped in and taking care to confirm that no one had seen or followed, the dark figure promptly shut the door. Though the light of one candle was not enough to see well, Meath knew who had come into his room and his heart felt as if it would cease beating. Nicolette turned to him and pulled off the hood of her cloak and her auburn hair streamed down the sides of her face. Her light brown eyes glistened in the frail light as she looked at him.

"I had to see you again. I could not stay away any longer." Nicolette whispered as she made her way to him. Meath could tell she had been crying - even in the faint glow, he could see her eyes were crimson and swollen.

"If we are caught like this again we might not be as fortunate as last time. This is treason... it will be my head and your honour now. We are not children anymore - we will not be shown sympathy," Meath whispered back, as he placed his arms around her. She rested her head on his shoulder. He did not really worry because he wanted her more than anything he had ever dreamed and death would be a sweet liberation to living life without her.

"Then my life they would also have to seize, for I do not think I can do this Meath." She wept, pressing herself harder into him. "I do not want to marry him Meath, but there is nothing I can do. The fate of my kingdom and our people depend on it. I do not want this kind of responsibility - I just want to be common." She wept even harder.

They held each other in silence for a long time with neither needing to speak a word. Both could tell what the other was thinking and both knew they could do nothing to alter the outcome. Before either one knew it, they were asleep in each other's arms.

They both woke with a start and lay in panic as the door flew open to Meath's quarters. The tall, commanding figure of Ursa stood looming over them. His eyes were not livid, as they feared they would find them. Instead, they were overflowing with concern and knowing what would have happened if anyone else had found them.

"Foolish children, do you not know what would ensue if someone else found you like this? Meath, I told you this could not be!" Ursa paced the room in a rush and was more aggravated than Meath had ever seen before. "It is time for you to get back to your room, Highness, before anyone notices you are absent. Like the very conclusion-jumping Champion of yours, who would very gladly skin alive my dim-witted apprentice here." Ursa said calming himself a little.

"You will not inform anyone about this, will you Master Ursa?" Nicolette feared what he would say as she straightened her garments.

"I will shield your secret, but I warn you now, do not let this happen again. If it had been any other who had come through that door, you would not be so blessed. If anyone finds out about this, it is treason for us all!" Ursa was infuriated that she even thought it necessary to ask as he rushed her toward the door. He watched for an instant to make sure it was safe for her to leave and once she was gone and he had closed the door, he turned to Meath with a deep scowl.

"What are you trying to do you fool - get yourself killed? You cannot just have the King's daughter come and spend the night in your bed. What were you thinking? Have you utterly lost your mind you half-wit? I cannot believe you would do such an imprudent thing," Ursa blared as quietly as he could, but with enough effort to show his frustrations.

Meath tried to clarify as he too straightened his attire. "Nothing even happened, we just..."

"That is not the point, fool. She is a Princess, and you are not a Prince or even of noble blood - she is betrothed to another. Do you know what would occur if it had been anyone else who had come through that door? If the King's knights did not run you through straight away, you would certainly be as good as dead. Now what good would that do you? I have not even mentioned that the Princess's reputation would be destroyed along with the chance finally to unite Zandor and Draco - bringing an end to our great King's royal bloodline. Who would want to marry our fair Princess if she were not untainted? Did you not stop to think that what you were doing would affect more than just your minuscule world? What you were doing would affect us all and your little heartbreak is the least of any of this," Ursa barked angrily.

Meath glanced toward his window and bit his lip for he knew better than to quarrel with the Wizard. He also knew Ursa was correct. Meath then noticed it was still moderately dark out, "How did you know she was here?"

"I had need of you early this day - the Prince, along with the other royals from Zandor, will be here by midday and the King has asked me to arrange a grand show for the wedding. We cannot afford any mistakes. Now get dressed...we have much to do before the day is done," Ursa said as he calmed himself fully.

The trumpets sounded as the large group from Zandor made their way through the city toward the castle. Many in the city hurried off to acknowledge their new allies, while others muttered curses and threats under their breath. The two Kingdoms had only coalesced long enough for the common ambition of ridding both countries of the Barbarians - more often than not, they were at war. It was well known that on either side not everyone welcomed this alliance. Both sides knew if they were to conquer the savages, they had to unite forces.

Once again, the castle was in a fluster making room for the thousand men and women who had come from the south for the wedding. As the group flooded into the courtyard, they all made way for the royal carriages so they could get as close to their welcome committee as possible. Since those from the south did not yet approve of those with The Gift, Ursa and Meath were not asked to be there.

King Borrack, Nicolette, Tundal, Dagon, their wives and children and the daughters from Dragon's Cove were present along with only the most prestigious families, and a hundred servants awaited the Royal Family from Zandor. Many more folks were there in the distance or watching from the castle parapet and windows.

The commotion and talking stopped as King Dante and his beautiful Queen - Glenelle - were assisted from their finely decorated carriage.

"How did you fare on your journey?" King Borrack asked after everyone had climbed out and all were making their way toward him and the others.

"It would have been a lot smoother if you had kept your roads up rather than letting them get riddled with holes and fallen trees," Prince Berrit answered with an attitude that showed his disappointment as he looked down at his dusty traveling garments, his cheeks flustered with anger. His younger brother Kayrel shook his head in conformity.

"Mind your tongue Berrit or I will...," his mother, Queen Glenelle snapped - she was all smiles as she was greeted by the others.

"The trip was long and wearing, but I had forgotten how beautiful the countryside is. Makes me wish I would have taken over this country when I might have had the opportunity," Dante joked as the two Kings embraced. Though the two kings had never gotten along well, they did their best to put on a good illusion for those around them. "This must be my future daughter-in-law," Dante said as he took Nicolette's hand in his, kissed the top of it, and smiled up at her with approval. "My son, she will make you a fine wife. There is none more beautiful than this little flower I see here before me," he boasted with satisfaction as he looked back to his son, who was still dusting off his traveling clothes. He seemed to be more concerned about that than looking up to see the woman he was to marry. When he was finished, his eyes met hers and he was transfixed by what he saw. A malicious grin formed on his face, but no one seemed to notice.

When Nicolette saw the look he had given her, it sent a quiver up her spine. She felt like running, but she stood her ground as the Prince, who was several winters older than she walked toward her. He was holding out a fine golden necklace with a hefty pendant encrusted with diamonds and rubies. It surely was worth more than most common folk could make in a lifetime.

"This is but a small Gift for my future bride. There will be many more where this came from after we have wed, my dear," Berrit said in a manner that made Nicolette's stomach twist and turn in disgust. He leaned in and kissed her palm - his tongue flicked her wrist, nearly making her cry out. It happened so fast that no one apart from Nicolette noticed. After composing herself, she thanking him and sanctioning him to put the bauble around her neck. The stroke of his hand was like the touch of death, sending more shivers down her spine. She hid it well - only Berrit seemed to take it in, his grin widening.

For several minutes, everyone made polite conversation about the trip or how their families and lands were doing. They also spoke about how one another were fairing against the hordes of Barbarians and how excited they all were about the wedding, as hollow a truth as it was.

"Well I am sure, after your long journey, you all would take pleasure in a warm bath and then some refreshments. A hardy feast awaits you, followed by an even better sleep. Tomorrow we shall start on the treaty, and final wedding plans," King Borrack declared while he greeted the rest of his new guests and then ordered servants to go and help with everyone's things.

After half a fortnight, near every concern each Kingdom brought forth had been discussed and a suitable resolution had been established, some through heated debate, where others were easily resolved with little to no anguish. Trade routes had been prepared, soldier training placement had been agreed upon, so that each Kingdom's troops would be well versed in both countries terrain for better tactical purposes. Even where the Prince and Princess would reside had been decided. All that remained was the topic of The Gifted, which everyone had hoped to ignore.

"We have accomplished much this day," King Borrack pronounced after the newest decree had been passed around to be signed by all in attendance. "We do have but one more matter to discuss, it being the gravest, and likely the most heated and animated. I fear the hour has already grown late and we are all in high spirits this evening, so wherefore sully that good vibe. I suggest we wait until tomorrow before the final topic of our treaty is discussed at length." A chorus of agreement from everyone followed. "But before we all end for the night, I have an announcement that I would like to share with you all." Borrack stood from his chair, his mouth opened as if to say something, then shut again as he struggled to find the right words.

"Come now, surely you have not lost thought already." King Dante chuckled in jest.

"This be a first," Tundal spoke up. "Our Mighty King be tongue-tied?" Again, all shared a laugh as the jest.

"Yes, it is a first," Borrack replied with a wide smile. "But only because the topic is so significant. It has been many years since Queen Lavira passed away, and much time has passed for ample grieving, even for an old fool such as me. Now that our Kingdoms have found peace and my only daughter to be married away, it has stirred much emotion and turmoil inside me. It is time that I take another wife to bear me an heir to my throne."

The room erupted into joyous cheers and congratulations as wine cups raised in toast to the magnificent news.

"Gratitude my friends," King Borrack said as he waved them to silence. "It is long overdue. Now let us find our beds, for tomorrow is sure to be a trying day indeed."

It was not long before the library emptied - until just Borrack, Ursa and Dagon remained.

"This is glorious news my friend." Dagon said clasping hands with Borrack. "We all have been waiting a long time to hear these words."

Borrack smiled, "I know my friend. Forgive a foolish old man for his weaknesses."

"Nonsense, old man you may be - but foolish? Never." Dagon winked and left.

"Well what have you?" Borrack asked, seeing Ursa looking at him in surprise.

"I am not sure I understand my King." Ursa replied, doing well to hide his smile.

"Do not play coy with me Wizard!" King Borrack laughed. "I have known you long enough to know when thoughts dance in that mind of yours."

Ursa smiled, "I am just pleased with your news. It warms my heart knowing you will finally try for an heir."

Borrack smiled half-heartedly, "Well my friend I will not live forever. Now let us retire to our rooms, tomorrow's negotiations I fear will not be pleasant."

It was a humid night with a fresh, sweet-smelling breeze - Nicolette sat alone in the royal garden by their tree. She wished Meath would happen by with a way to make everything work to their advantage, but she knew there was none. She knew it was wise that he was not around. She would have to learn to love another and disregard what they had. She sighed and selected a blue rose from the bush beside the bench. It smelled so sweet, but did little to calm her soul.

She took one last glance at their tree and got up, gradually making her way back to find her bed. As she walked, Nicolette heard voices coming from behind a large cluster of fruit trees not far from the path. She thought it was odd for anyone to be out this late in the royal garden so she went to witness who it was. Silently, she walked up to a large apple tree that over-looked where the people stood - she peered out and saw three dark figures standing together, hooded in black.

"Once I am married to that wench of a Princess we can finally rid ourselves of Borrack and Ursa. Then I will formulate a way to dispose of my darling new wife - as she will be of no use to us when I am the new King of Draco Kingdom." A voice - which was not Prince Berrit's - said with a sinister chuckle behind it.

"We will have to keep a close eye on that Wizard, Ursa. He is no fool and he is crafty enough to cause us difficulty if he catches on. It may be best if we make him... depart... sooner than we had planned." The woman spoke in a smooth voice tipped with venom.

"We shall dispose of him soon enough, my love. He and the others here with The Gift shall make fine treats and soon none shall stand in the way of what we were destined to achieve," the first voice said.

"As long as we keep to the plan, we shall have all we want," the third person said - his voice rough and edgy.

Nicolette recognized the second man's voice, but could not put a face to it.

"Yes, but of course we will," the female agreed in a snide tone.

"Do not dare get sarcastic with me. I have the most to lose here because of you two!" the second man growled furiously.

"Yet you have an enormous gain as well." The other replied casually. "Do not forget about that."

"Do not get coy with me asshole, I am only helping you because you..." His voice trailed off in frustration.

"I could kill them if you would prefer?" The female voice cooed maliciously. "But I promise you it will be slowly."

"You bitch!" The man raged taking a step toward her.

"Careful now, we would not want things to get out of hand. Besides, there could be more possibilities for you, if you allow them." The first man remarked shrewdly.

"I am already betraying my kingdom," he hissed back. "When this is over, I never want to see your faces again."

"Nor your own I am sure." The first man teased.

"Awe, and here I thought we could all be friends," the female mocked.

"You repulse me!" he growled violently.

"Mind your tongue, lest you make me cut it out!" the leader of the trio hissed. "The plan is how I say it is and your family will be returned to you when your usefulness has expired."

What Nicolette had just heard caused her to stumble back as panic coursed through her body like fire. She was about to turn when a hand went over her mouth - she went rigid and almost fainted.

"It is I, Highness." The old Wizard whispered as he turned her around to face him and then gradually led her away from where they stood.

"Ursa, we must warn my father. There are…" The Wizard cut her off.

"Yes, I know my child - there is vile evil at work here tonight. We must tell the King at once," He whispered searching the vicinity for any indication that anyone had caught on to them. "Stay close to me and do as I say."

Silently, they made their way through the castle's numerous hallways and chambers, avoiding the midnight patrols and anyone else who was about at this hour, wary of who they should trust. When they reached the King's chambers, they burst through the doors of the vast room to warn him. Once they were in the room, Ursa lit the candles with barely a thought, and the King woke in panic.

"What is going on here!" he muttered, rubbing the sleep from his eyes to see who had barged into his room.

"Majesty, there are those who conspire against you in the castle this night!" Ursa informed as he made his way to where the King was getting out of his bed.

"What? Are you sure? Who are they?" The King questioned as he pulled on his robe.

"We do not know father, but they said they were going to kill you and then me. He spoke like Prince Berrit, but it was not his voice." Nicolette cried.

"There are three who plot your demise - maybe more - but I have not uncovered who they are. I was about to confront them when I took note of the Princess and thought it better to get her away. We need to sound the alarm and flush these assassins out!" Ursa told him. Just then, Halpas entered the room. His sword was drawn and he was breathing hard.

"What is going on in here? Is everything all right your Majesty?" Halpas said through long, hard breaths - as if he had run a long way even though his room was not far down the hall.

"Halpas, I am relieved to see you. There seem to be traitors amongst us who plot my death and that of my daughter. Search the castle for anyone out of their rooms and bring me Prince Berrit and the rest of those Zandorian bastards so we can resolve this once and for all. Alert all the guards. I want this castle locked down tight until this is solved," the King ordered. "I will take no chances!"

"I am so sorry…my friend," said Halpas, a flash of metal crossed the room and imbedded itself deep into the King's throat, the tip jutting out the back of his neck. Borrack's eyes went wide - pain and treachery sliding across his face as his hands grabbed the dagger buried in his neck. Thick, dark crimson blood drained over the top of his fingers as he fell to the ground gurgling for a breath he would never find.

Ursa hurled his hands out toward the traitor and a molten column of fire flew with a roar and hit Halpas square in the torso. He erupted into flames with a cry of agony and was dead before his blackened corpse hit the stone.

"Father!" Nicolette shrieked as she ran to his aid, but she knew there was nothing she could do to save him. "Ursa, help him, please!" She cried cradling her father's limp head.

"I had not anticipated this." A man said as he walked into the room. He was clothed all in black and had the cold look of death himself. His skin was tanned, and his eyes were bright, vibrant green.

"You foul fiend!" Ursa yelled viciously. He tossed a massive ball of energy toward the man but it battered an unseen barrier around him and dispersed into nothing more than sparks. Ursa's eyes went wide.

"It will require more skill than that to be rid of me, Wizard." The man laughed, and with a tilt of his hand. A brutal wave of power sent Ursa soaring back into a sculpture of Queen Lavira that the King kept in his room.

Crying over her father's limp body, Nicolette burst out, "Why are you doing this?" as she staring up at the man with terror and loathing.

"What is the matter Princess; do you not recognize your soon-to-be husband?" As the man spoke the words, his features altered and twisted into Prince Berrit. Both Nicolette and Ursa gasped at what they had just witnessed. "I had other plans for you Wizard, but I guess you killing the King, Halpas and the Princess will have to do as my story." The false prince said with a devious grin.

"No one will ever believe you!" Ursa rose to his feet slowly trying to think of some way to spirit the Princess to safety. His eyes glanced down at the King, and Ursa knew it was already too late to save him.

"Just watch and see!" The man said as he closed the distance to where the Princess sat.

Ursa instinctively called upon his Gift and cast a dense air torrent the man had not been expecting. He flew back hard into the wall beside the King's bed and crashed through the bedside stand and to the floor. The attack knocked the wind from his lungs and his eyes almost rolled into the back of his head.

"Run Highness, get out of here!" Ursa yelled as he summoned the spell once more, pushing the intruder harder against the wall with nearly bone-crushing force. "You shall pay for your crimes!"

No sooner had he spoken the words than did he notice the false prince's hand point his way, vicious fire forming from his fingertips. Ursa knew there would be no way he would avoid being struck down if he did not flee.

Ursa quickly bolted from the room to find the Princess hunched down in the hallway crying. "Quickly girl, we must move!" He grabbed her arm and pulled her along, knowing the enemy would not stay down for long.

Moments after, three guards billowed into the King's room organized for a fight.

"What has happened here?" One of the young soldiers demanded as they entered the room and saw the body of their King - and what was left of Halpas lying on the floor.

"That cursed Wizard Ursa has killed the King and abducted the Princess." Prince Berrit bellowed as he tried to get up, but the Wizard's attack had caused more damage to him than he had thought. "Halpas and I tried to prevent him, but he used his wickedness against us." The Prince howled as he caught his breath and tried to get to his feet once more.

"What are you talking about? Ursa would do no such thing and what are you doing in the King's room? You are behind this I bet you Zandorian filth!" Before the soldier could finish, an arc of lightning seared through him and his companions, killing them almost instantaneously.

"Foolish pawns! Why could you not believe me?" The false Prince muttered crawling over beside King Borrack's body. "Someone please help! Please god help!" He cried, terror-stricken, hunching over the body.

"What is going on in here?" Another soldier yelled as he arrived at the room with a small army of men behind him.

"Ursa has gone mad! He is trying to frame me by bringing me here and killing the King." Berrit tried again, needing his explanation to work before his plans simply dissolved. "Halpas and those others caught him in action and tried to stop him. He destroyed them and escaped."

"What? Are you sure?" they asked, not sure what to make of the situation.

"Hurry, you fools! He has abducted my future wife, and your future Queen!" He screamed dramatically at the soldiers, prompting them into action. "A hundred gold to whomever brings him to justice!"

"Sound the alarm! Master Ursa has killed the King and taken the Princess!" One of the soldiers screamed to the men who had finally responded to all of the commotion. Once they had heard the news, they fled to spread the word and stop Ursa from escaping with little question.

The false prince knew the news would spread, and eventually it would be worded right and all would believe. He wiped his bloodied hands on his shirt for more effect. "Not how I had planned it, but innovation had always been on my side."

"What are we to do now?" Nicolette sobbed as she tried to calm her breathing and stop the tears that flooded down her cheeks.

"We must get to Meath at once- he will not be safe for long, and they will try to get me through him. Then we must flee the castle," Ursa whispered as he made sure the next chamber was clear for them to go through.

"Where will we go? What will we do?" she cried as if it mattered - anywhere would be better than here. Her entire life had just taken a plunge into chaos and she was trying to contain the anxiety that was devastating her. The world was spinning and she had to force herself to focus solely on Ursa to keep herself from collapsing.

"I do not know yet, your Highness, but I promise you, I will keep you safe until this is resolved. You have my word," Ursa responded hastily as they scurried down the corridor toward Meath's room. As they turned the corner, there stood a lone guard searching for them.

"Why would you do this Ursa? How could you? Those Zandorians are right about those with The Gift after all. How could you betray us? After everything the King has done for you and your kind," the guard cried out, his eyes burning with confusion.

"I did no such thing!" Ursa replied. "You need to help us out of the castle - it is not safe for us here now!"

The guard's face showed his confusion, "Why is it not safe, unless it is true! Why are you holding the Princess's hand so tightly?" His eyes grew wide as he accepted this conclusion. "You let her go! Princess, are you all right?"

Nicolette tried to speak and tell the guard that she was all right, but could not - her voice froze in her throat as she was overwhelmed by all that was happening and nearly fainted.

Without another word, the guard charged forward, his spear tip heading straight for Ursa's chest. The guard was thrown from his feet as a concussion of air hit him, sending him and his weapon to the floor in a heap, where he struggled to draw breath before blacking out.

It had taken longer to arrive at Meath's room than Ursa had wanted, but to evade being caught - and dodge more confused men - they had to be exceedingly careful. He had had to employ his powers more than once along the way to deceive or silence the guards and now most of the castle had heard the lies that the false prince was telling. The guards would be looking for them everywhere. Ursa burst into Meath's quarters with the Princess in tow. "There is no time for that now! You must get your things - we must depart quickly!" Ursa ordered, urgency consumed his words as he stormed by Meath, leaving Nicolette near the door.

"What is going on?" Meath stammered out, as his meditation was broken.

"There is no time to explain that now. The King has been murdered and we must get out of here now or we will definitely be joining him." Ursa replied as he grabbed some of Meath's things and threw them at him. Meath's heart skipped a beat at the thought of the King being murdered and his adrenaline stirred him from his weary state.

The three ran down toward the kitchen. The guards were searching high and low for them and Ursa did not want to kill anyone he did not need to…but if they were caught by a large number, he doubted that would leave him much choice. They were just men following orders - they did not know the truth, nor would they likely listen to it.

They were steps away from rounding a corner when a guard leaped out swinging his sword at head level, looking for a quick kill, Ursa saw the man too late to escape unscathed. The tip of the blade sliced into Ursa's collarbone and shoulder as he rolled his body backward avoiding the deathblow. The attack off balanced him and he fell to the ground in a heap, blood seeping quickly from the deep wound onto the floor beside him.

"NO!" Meath cried out and he barrelled into the guard, crashing him hard into the stone wall, causing him to drop his shortsword. A knee was fast to ensue well his abdomen was exposed and another until Meath finally let go and stumbled backward. The guard took a step forward, his hand balled into a fist ready to strike. Meath ignored the spreading pain in his abdomen and launched himself forward, his own fist leading the way relentlessly. He connected with the man's jaw sending him back into the wall and slumping to the floor.

Meath ran to Ursa's side. "Ursa, Ursa talk to me," Meath cried afraid to move the old man."

Ursa rolled over to face him, not in as dire a state as Meath has expected. "Meath look out!"

Meath turned back to the guard who was charging full force toward him, dagger in hand. Instinct took over and he met the guard's charge. Meath sidestepped the midsized man's wild swing with the dagger and caught his arm with a twist, dropping both man and dagger to the ground. An arrow skipped off the stone wall inches away from Meath and his attention turned to the two bowmen down the hall taking aim. Someone grabbed Meath's shirt and pulled him back, around the corner before the next assault was released. Meath span around and came face-to-face with Ursa.

"We do not have time for that now - come on!" Ursa said flatly, and they ran down the rest of the hallway and through the door leading to the stairwell.

Ursa pushed the thick wooden doors shut - placing his palms on the smooth wood.

"I thought you were..." Meath started to say. "How did you?"

"Silence!" Ursa shot back to him and he inhaled deeply and concentrated again on the door. The wood crackled and snapped as it shifted and expanded as frost coated the door in ice, freezing the frame solid, making opening it impossible for some time.

"To answer your questions - I healed myself while you were distracting that guard," Ursa said, looking at the tear in his blood-soaked robe. "Now let us keep moving before our fortune runs out." Men were already trying to break down the frozen door from the other side with their weapons.

When they at last reached the kitchen, it was still dark and vacant. Ursa produced a small flame in his hand, so they could see where they were going. They went for the side door of the kitchen leading to the stable yard where Ursa hoped they could find horses to make their escape. There was no way they could get far enough, fast enough, on foot.

"What is going on?" The thick accent of Maxwell came from behind them. They turned to see him standing there, holding a giant meat clever in one hand. Once he saw who it was, he planted the weapon into one of the nearby tables. "Meath...Ursa, what is going on here?" The chef asked in a voice displaying dissatisfaction toward people in his kitchen at this late hour. Suddenly his eyes widened when he realized who was with them. "I am so sorry Highness, I did not know you were here. I meant no disrespect." The chubby chef apologized as he bowed his head up and down.

"Maxwell, we need to get out of the castle. Now!" Meath said, just loud enough for the man to hear and comprehend something was wrong in his tone.

"Why?" He replied with a look of surprise as he reached for his weapon again.

"There is no time for that," Ursa cut in. "Just know that what you will later hear is not how things actually occurred. Are there any horses nearby that are ready to set out?"

"What are you talking about?" He started, but stopped short, for Ursa's look was harsh. "Well aye, of course. The evening patrol horses are being fed out back as we speak." Maxwell looked around as if something was going to leap out at him at any instant.

"Good." Ursa said flat out. "For your own protection, I would advise you go back to your bed Maxwell, and pretend none of this happened." Ursa called back to him as the three ran to the door. They left Maxwell standing in the kitchen scratching his head in puzzlement. Not being one to disbelieve Ursa, Maxwell was swiftly on his way back to bed.

They ran through the stable yard without being seen and found the horses Maxwell had said would be there. As they mounted the beasts, soldiers on the wall caught sight of them.

"There they are!" one of them yelled.

"Stop them!"

They spurred the horses and galloped off toward the gates at full speed. A cluster of men from both Kingdoms stood their ground waiting to stop them - but no one from up above had yet begun to seal the gate.

Ursa spurred his horse hard, both his hands alive with a violent maelstrom of air. The arms of several soldiers were cocked back, ready to throw their spears when Ursa released the surge of power into the cluster of men. The blast of air tore the soldiers from their feet, throwing them violently aside to the hard-packed earth.

They rode down the faintly lit city streets as swiftly as the horses would go, scattering a handful of homeless beggars who did not wish to be trampled.

The three of them made it several miles from the city before they were forced to slow their pace. The horses were luminous with sweat and needed to rest.

"Would someone mind telling me what just happened? How was King Borrack murdered? Who? Why?" Meath asked frantically, not able to restrain it any longer. He looked to both Ursa and the Princess for some sort of response.

Ursa began explaining what he and the Princess had witnessed in the garden. Next, he told of what had unfolded in the King's bedchamber and at last how they had made it to his quarters.

Nicolette sat on her mare, staring off into the trees. Her emotions did not appear to work at all. She just stared off into the night sky blankly, her mind vacant and her body numb.

"You mean to tell me the man from my dreams is Prince Berrit?" Meath uttered an oath, as he shook his head in disbelief.

"No, I am guessing the Prince is dead and has been for a time. As for your dreams, I would not leap to such conclusions. We do not have time to shape this all out yet," Ursa said as he watched the road behind them. "It will not be long before they pick up our trail."

"Where will we go - what will we do?" Nicolette asked again, coming back into the conversation. She fought back the tears that consumed her. Her mind began to come back to life her grief besieging her.

"We will set out to your Uncle Marcus. He is the only one who has yet to be misinformed of the true murderer of the King. We should be able to make it there before the rumours do if we make haste and stay ahead of the hearsay," The Wizard replied with a sigh of sorrow for the girl.

She had been through more catastrophes in the last hour than in all of her life. He knew it was far from over and he did not know what help Lord Marcus would be, but it was the only safe place he could think of. The only place they could find help. "We must stop and take care of the band of soldiers that will be coming for us," Ursa said unsympathetically as he dismounted his black and white spotted mare. He started to look through the saddlebags for provisions that they might require and discarded what they did not. They needed to ease the load for the horses. "We will not make it far with the armies of Draco and Zandor looking for us," he continued, his attitude harsh, angrily throwing some mouldy fruit to the ground.

"What are we going to do to stop them? We cannot just kill them. Some of them are our friends! We must inform them of what is going on - then we will not have to run," Meath exclaimed as he also searched his horse's saddlebags for effects that might be of use.

"We will do as we must!" Ursa snapped back dangerously. "They are men led by deception and lies and they want their Princess back, along with whatever bounty they were promised. They will not be concerned in hearing our side of the tale. I am not trying to be cruel or insensitive, but I am willing to do whatever is essential for our survival! If we die, no one will know the truth and then what will happen?" Ursa finished as he placed his head in his hands. He had already used a great deal of his powers throughout the day to escape and feared he would not have a sufficient amount left to conclude the task at hand. "I am sure many of those coming for us will not be our own soldiers, but those from Zandor - they are almost fearless when hunting The Gifted and will show us no mercy."

"Once we prove to them that she is all right and you were not trying to abduct her, they will pay attention." Meath said as he took a swallow of water from the skin he had found on his stallion. It was as if he were trying to persuade himself, more than them.

"They will listen, if I tell them," Nicolette finally cut in as Meath handed her the water and nodded his head in agreement.

"Maybe you are right, Highness, but we need to be prepared for them if they do not." Ursa wished it would be that straight forward as he pulled a jewelled sword from its hiding place in the saddle. He handed it to Meath, who held it in his hands for a moment, getting a feel for the blade. It was heavier than he was used to, but it would have to do if things went badly. He looked to Ursa solemnly and could hear his words over and over in his head; *I am willing to do whatever is essential for our survival.* His eyes drifted to Nicolette who was trying hard to flake off the dried blood on her hands and arms—the blood of the King, her father—as she fought to remain composed. His attention went back to the sword, his jaw firmed. He would do what was necessary for her survival.

They waited on the path for the advancing search party - Meath counted each man who came into view. There were thirty; most were Zandorian soldiers armed to the teeth with full body armour, swords, spears and bows.

"It is all right Princess - you will be in safe hands soon. If you Wizards yield now you will be granted a swift death. If you resist, I assure you, you will suffer indefinitely!" The Captain yelled, as he and his men dismounted from their steeds. They drew their weapons and bowstrings were pulled back tightly and notched.

"You do not understand! Things are not as they seem! They did not kill my father. Prince Berrit did!" Nicolette screamed back. She was trying to find the right words to persuade them, but it all seemed to come out too fast to make any sense.

"What is it going to be Wizard?" The Captain yelled, ignoring the Princess's plea.

"It would not matter I fear," Ursa called back. "You have already made up your mind of the outcome."

The Captain's grin was malicious as he pulled his full helm over his head. He raised his sword and signalled his men to attack, and they charged with a battle roar.

Ursa raised both his arms high, towards the sky, and bolts of arcing energy exploded from his fingertips with a thunderous crackle, tearing through the chests of the flanking men. They dropped to the earth, riddled with gaping holes that allowed their entrails to seep out from their charred bodies into the dirt.

Meath let loose an inferno of flames that engulfed a trio of soldiers as they ran toward him. They dropped, screaming to the ground, frantically rolling around as their skin blistered and melted from their faces as the Wizard's fire feasted. He met another warrior with a fierce forward thrust of his sword, slipping through the Zandorian defensives. It punctured through the man's chest plate and protruded out his back, while yet another enemy sword just missed cleaving his arm. Meath put his boot to the dying man's chest and tore the blade out, to meet the new attacker with a savage slash to the throat. Blood sprayed across his face. Battle lust had overtaken him and now death was all he could see. His training had come back to him full force and instinct mixed with his adrenaline. Meath twisted just in time to see another soldier swinging his sword at him. As their swords met with a loud metal ring, Meath pushed the man back and discharged a bolt of pure energy from his palm sending the man flying back into the dirt, smouldering in a ragged heap.

The five bowmen had difficulty aiming with all of the fighting, but at last, an opportunity came. While he was preoccupied, all five fired at Ursa, eager to bring the great Wizard down quickly. Ursa had seen the attack coming from the corner of his eye. Both hands thrust outward, one toward his original attacker who charged at him with his lance levelled, his other pointing palm out toward the looming missiles that were just released from their strings. Two currents of wind erupted from Ursa's palms - one slamming violently into the torso of a charging threat, sending the man plummeting back a dozen paces to the ground, twisted in a painful mound. The second met the arrow assault scattering them off course and into two of the oncoming soldiers wounding them severely.

Ursa fell to his knees, feeling his powers weakening dangerously. His hands hit the earth and he released a wall of fire that tore from the dirt a dozen paces in front of him and caught another group of men who were engulfed by the unruly inferno. They tried to run but only made it steps before the air was consumed from their lungs and they dropped to the earth in a frenzy to hold onto life that ended moments later.

Meath moved just in time to miss the fiery columns that erupted from the earth. Just then, a man who he had not noticed plunged a spear into his thigh and he fell with a howl. Meath stared up at the large warrior whose spear was prepared to take his life - he watched the man's eyes go wide and a trickle of blood spurt from his mouth. The man fell to the earth trembling, Meath looked up and there stood Nicolette with a short sword held tightly in her shuddering hands. And then everything went black...

"They are too powerful. Retreat!" The last of the men ran to their horses and galloped off into the mist as fast as they could.

"They will send more after us and we might not be so lucky next time. We need time to regain our strength - let us make haste!" Ursa said as he got to his feet with more than a little effort. He looked over to where Nicolette and Meath were and saw the Princess cradling him in her arms, crying.

"I do not know what happened, he just blacked out." Nicolette cried as she held him tighter, ignoring the blood that was staining her blue cloak. It already had been stained with much blood this night.

"He is not used to conjuring that much power in one day. He will be fine in a few hours. Now bind off his wound and help me put him on his horse - we must go now!" Ursa said as the two of them lifted Meath. They rode off down the dark, misty road leaving the dead and dying men strewn behind them.

3

"What do you mean they got away?" Prince Berrit screamed slamming his fist into the table, his face flared bright red in anger, "you incompetent mules!"

The tension and frustration in the library could be felt like a torrential rain in the jungle. Everyone of note in the castle had been summoned there shortly after news of their escape became known.

"Relax my son - they will not make it far, not with two full companies after them," King Dante said to his aggravated son, and then turned back to the small group of soldier who had faced the Wizards and retreated. "As for all of you, ten lashings a piece for your cowardice!"

"This does not make sense. Why would Ursa do something like this? There must be something missing," Lord Dagon questioned, looking around the room as if expecting answers.

"If that bastard so much as harms one hair on her head, I will see him beaten, skinned and left for the buzzards," Berrit howled at all those in the room while he paced back and forth, from one end of the table to the other.

"Who is the other one with Ursa?" Dante asked, looking to Lord Tundal for an explanation.

"Meath is Ursa's adopted son - also his apprentice - though his training in The Gift started not more than a few seasons ago. However, he was first trained as a soldier in Drandor's infantry. I recall he did quite well in his training, several of my Captains had nothing but positive things to say about him," Tundal replied calmly, though he was anything but.

King Dante pondered Tundal's words before speaking. "So you taught a tainted heathen how to use a blade as well?" Dante grunted his dissatisfaction. "It would appear to me like he is just as dangerous of a threat as Ursa."

"I still do not understand why they would do something like this. What reasons would they have for abducting the Princess?" Dagon bellowed out. "There must be some mistake… There has to be! Ursa and Borrack were good friends - he would never have done this in his own mind, ever! Ursa is a good man and a good friend to all who reside in Draco I cannot believe these accusations." He slammed his fist on top of the table. "Something is amiss!"

Berrit turned to face Dagon with an imperious sneer. "Oh, believe me, my good Lord Dagon," Berrit hissed. "It was Ursa. That fiend came into my room with the Princess, cast some sort of curse on me that stole my freewill and made us go to the King's room with him! We could not talk or scream for help. Believe me, I tried with every ounce of strength I had, and I'm sure the Princess did too!" He bellowed, storming around the room recounting his horrifying experience to everyone yet again.

Berrit was sure to keep his story exactly the same as before, for any mistakes could ruin everything. "That Wizard murdered King Borrack as he tried to reason with him for the safety of his daughter and those in the castle. Then he told me he was going to frame me for both the King's death and that of the Princess. He was about to use his cursed evil to make me murder the poor, grief-stricken Princess. That is when Halpas tried to intervene." Berrit stopped at the table and downed a cup of wine while everyone sat breathlessly, waiting to hear the full tale. "Then more guards showed up to help, and he massacred them too, without a moment of remorse. He realized he was going to be caught if he stayed any longer and grabbed the Princess and ran off with her, leaving me alone in the room in hopes I would be framed. He knew because I am Zandorian that you would blame me before him and that would give him ample time to escape if he needed." He said the last part of the story with melancholy, as he sat down in his chair. "He did not support this treaty! He loathes Zandorians with a passion because of our views on his kind. He refuses to let our Kingdoms unite…at any cost, and you wonder why we are so reluctant to accept them."

"We will find her my son - just stay composed," Dante said while patting his son's back.

"This is just proof that The Gifted are cursed beasts!" Zefer, Lord of Samel, blared out in rage at the whole situation.

"It still does not make any sense at all," Tundal replied bitterly, his eyes glaring across the room towards Berrit, recounting his tale in his head for any flaws. He did not believe him, he could not believe him and yet there was no proof otherwise.

"You doubt me!" Berrit screamed across the table. "Who else could have massacred those men like that? If it were me, I would have had to use a blade not vile sorcery!"

"There are many witnesses that saw Ursa and Meath attacking our own men to get out of the castle with the Princess," Dagon said, though everyone could tell it pained him immensely to do so.

"It was like he was possessed," a Draco soldier said, his face still pale as he recounted what he saw. "Ursa did not think twice to unleash his abilities against me... I...I tried to confront him and the Princess in the hall. The Princess looked like she was fighting something - you know, on the inside - trying to talk, but could not, you know? That is when I knew something was really wrong, so I attacked and he hit me with his magic....almost killed me. I hit the wall so hard."

"Possessed you say?" Berrit questioned and the soldier nodded, "and the Princess could not talk to you?"

"Ay, it appeared so, yes," the soldier replied.

King Dante dismissed the soldiers after hearing each of their accounts. "Words from your own men claim truth to what my son has said."

"It is still too much to fathom. Something is missing. Ursa would not have just done something like this," Dagon muttered bitterly, though he could not deny the words of the soldiers who were there.

"Whatever the cause or reasons Ursa has, the truth remains, King Borrack is dead, and Ursa and his apprentice have fled from the castle with a reluctant Princess," Dante said to those in the room. "Treachery is afoot - one way or another. They need to be found and Princess Nicolette needs to be returned - only she will have the full truth of what happened." Reluctant murmurs of agreement filtered through the room.

"Thank you for joining us Rift," Lord Tundal said to Rift when he entered the library. "What news do you have?"

"I searched the Kings quarters and found nothing to discount anything that has been said," Rift replied. "Though I found nothing to fully credit it either."

"Where were you?" Berrit yelled, storming right up to Rift. "Where were you when she needed you? You are supposed to be her Champion...to protect her from harm! That is your sole duty in life and you were nowhere to be found!" Berrit hissed, mere inches from the larger man's face. "Now she is in the clutches of those heathens!

She would have been safer in the Keeper's hands himself!" Berrit knew his words were like venom to the Champion - he needed them to be. He needed Rift to be angry enough to kill Ursa without question.

Prince Berrit's words hit Rift hard - he grimaced noticeably from the truth of them. Nevertheless, he held his ground, squaring his shoulders. "I shall be leaving shortly - I will bring her back safely. Nothing will hinder me from achieving this."

Berrit looked him hard in the eyes - he could see the man's rage at his failure and his need for redemption. "What if you have to kill them to get her?"

Rifts jaw firmed. "I said nothing will hinder me!" He growled back.

"Make haste then Rift," Tundal said. "Bring the Princess back to us, and Ursa and Meath if you can - if not, at least bring back the truth."

Rift nodded in determination and took his leave, stalking out of the room, the Prince's words echoing in his mind, adding fuel to each step.

"He would be better off to bring back their heads," Berrit muttered bitterly. "I swear, if they hurt her…"

King Dante rested his meaty hand on his sons shoulder again. "We will get her back, and they would not be foolish enough to harm her," his father tried to reassure him. "She is their only leverage in this madness."

"I knew we should never have trusted those beasts. They should all have been killed long ago," Bartan, Lord of Laquaco Cove muttered, folding his arms and glared straight ahead is disgust.

"We cannot judge all those with The Gift because of the actions of two," Tundal barked back. "We still do not know what the motives are or why they are doing this. They could very well have a perfectly good reason of which we are unaware."

"When will you people see it? They are the work of the Keeper and can never be trusted," Lord Zefer spat. "Two of your so-called most "trusted" and "honest" Gifted just murdered your beloved King and abducted his only bloodline, to stop this treaty. How much more evidence do you need? You own men witnessed him doing so, with the Princess in tow, lest I forget."

"It has been a long night and there is nothing further we can do. Let us return to our beds and try to get what sleep we can this night,"

King Dante cut in, seeing that the situation was about to escalate. "Tomorrow we will know more and the Princess hopefully will be returned safely and we can begin moving on from this tragedy."

"I do not trust that Berrit. Ursa would never do this," Dagon whispered to Tundal, as they both knelt down in front of the altar in the castle's cathedral. A thousand candles burned brightly all around them in honour of the dead king, bathing the grand room in a prismatic glow.

"I do not believe he would either, but one can never know for sure," Tundal sighed.

"You do not believe that little whelp, do you?" Dagon said in shock, trying to keep his voice lowered.

"I did not say I believed him, but what if he is telling the truth. There is so much proof against Ursa. Maybe Ursa has been planning this for a long time. Some say he can see into the future." Tundal looked around to see if anyone was listening, but there was no one close. "Maybe he was just waiting for the right time to strike."

"Listen to yourself! This is not some common street urchin. This is our trusted friend. What does he have to gain from this? He is now a wanted man. If it was riches he wanted, he could just have easily robbed the treasury. But he would not - Ursa has never had much need for money and if he ever needed anything Borrack would have granted him the funds without question," The Lord of Mandrake said trying to keep his voice down. "Ursa is just as trustworthy as you or I. There must be something missing from the story."

"I do not know my friend, but let us keep our ears and eyes open. If one of those Zandorians is behind this, I will personally whip their flesh from their bones," Tundal said rising off his knees and patted his friend on the back in reassurance.

Nicolette gripped Meath's hand tightly, wishing with everything she had that he would come around. Under the thick canopy of jungle, very little starlight filtered through - leaving it in near utter darkness. She could just make out Ursa's form resting against a thick jauari tree. He had told her to try to sleep when they had moved off the main road to rest, that he would stay awake and stand watch - but she was sure the old Wizard had fallen asleep. She had not heard him move since he had sat down some time ago. All she could hear was the eerie night sounds of the jungle, making her heart beat quicker - she had no idea if the sounds were trees groaning in protest of their imposing weight or if a nocturnal predator was stalking in for the kill. All she knew was she would not be able to find sleep out here.

Nicolette tightened her grip on the dagger Ursa had given her whenever she heard voices from the main road. She knew there were search parties, looking for them. This had been the third time she had heard a group pass by. She was sure the last team had found them when she saw a man's silhouette rummaging in the overgrowth holding a torch high. Thankfully, he had given up before he had gone any further or they would have been discovered. Ursa had assured her he had covered their trail adequately, and it would be near impossible to see in the night.

Before the great Wizard had sat down to rest he had healed Meath's leg wound, knowing it would become infected and fester quickly out here in the humid jungle. Meath had begun to show signs of a fever by the time they had stopped, but now as Nicolette felt his head, it was no longer hot and clammy - showing the fever had passed quickly.

Abruptly, Meath's eyes shot open, panic flooding through him. He leaped to his feet desperately, searching for his sword - or any other weapon that might be within reach. Then he saw Nicolette looking up at him and he fell to his knees. The throbbing in his leg finally hit him, adding to the agony in his head. His skull was hammering so hard it made his vision blur and his stomach turn so violently, he had to turn and retch on the ground.

"It is all right Meath, we are safe," Nicolette whispered as she helped him back to where he had slept only moments before.

"My head is killing me, what happened?" He mumbled rubbing his temples, trying to ease the throbbing.

"Ursa said that you blacked out from using too much of your Gift," she explained. "I have never seen anyone use The Gift to kill," she shivered remembering the cries of the men who had died.

"I have never experienced anything like that before. I have never before killed with my powers. I knew I would one day, but..." He trailed off staring into the shadowy growth of the jungle. Vivid flashes of what had happened came back to him. He had fought in several battles before and had killed with a blade, but using his Gift was so much more personal and violent.

Even in the darkness, Nicolette could tell he was struggling with what had happened. "You did what you had to Meath. There was no other way."

"I know. I just wish they would have listened to us! This whole situation is just so unbelievable."

"Ursa wanted me to give this to you when you awoke," Nicolette said, remembering the vial Ursa had given her.

Meath took the vial, broke the wax seal around its cork stopper, and sniffed at its contents. "I do not think so." He put the foul smelling vial down beside him. "I will be fine… I just need this pounding in my head to end."

"That is what the mixture is for, you adamant fool," said the prevailing voice of the one who had made it. Both their eyes went straight to where the old Wizard sat. He was staring at Meath, shaking his head in frustrated irritation. "I am astounded we are not dead with you two talking so loudly. Surely the soldiers could have effortlessly discovered us at any time with you two giving our position away with your babbling," Ursa said sharply, as he stood up and stretched his weary bones. He was still feeling drained even after several hours of meditation, but knew they better get moving now that Meath had regained consciousness.

"Drink up Meath - we have to get moving. We will have to stay off the main roads and exploit some of the lesser used paths and tracks. There will be fewer individuals to notice us, for surely the rumours have travelled faster than we have this night," Ursa said, going to where he had tied the horses. He knew all roads would be patrolled by soldiers, but at least this way there would less risk of being spotted by citizens. The longer they waited, the harder safe travel would be.

Meath picked up the vial again and held it for a few moments. He looked at it with a sour look on his face and then put the beaker to his lips, drinking the thick, green liquid as fast as he could.

"That is vile - worse than the stuff you gave me to help me sleep!" Meath coughed trying not to gag the pungent tasting potion back up. "You think you would try to make your potions taste a little better after all these years."

"Why? I never tire of seeing that expression on people's faces." Ursa smiled back. "Now keep your voice down."

"You are a cruel old man, you know that?" Meath stood up and noticed the pain in his head was already subsiding. Unfortunately, he could now feel the intense burning from the force-healed wound in his leg.

"How are you feeling, Master Ursa?" Nicolette asked as she went toward the horses with the blankets they had used during the night.

"I am fine Highness - a little weary but I will manage just fine...and please, call me Ursa. That title always makes me sound older than I care to believe." He winked, handing her one of the water skins.

"You may also call me by my name and not my title," she said, after taking a large gulp of the stale water. The events of the night and lack of any sleep made her gaunt and pale.

"I will try to do that, my dear but I am old and set in my ways remember?" Ursa replied. "Meath, what is taking you so long? We have no time to waste."

"My leg hurts!" Meath snarled back, as quietly as he could. When he tried to go faster, he stumbled and fell - the muscles knotting up in his thigh. Quickly Nicolette went to his aid, letting him use her for support.

"Your leg is just stiff and your mind believes it is worse than it is. You know how wounds work when they have been force-healed," Ursa explained. He patted his horse's strong neck, being sure it was calm before he tried to lead in anywhere in the dark. He looked back at Meath and the Princess and could not help but smile at the affection the two possessed for each other. Even at such a dire time as this, he could see it...it could never happen between the two, but Ursa always wished it could have.

They slowly led their horses out of the dense growth in silence and onto the road that they had abandoned hours before. The horses seemed eager to be out of the confinements of the growth and out in the open once more. The small amount they had been able to graze seemed to have been enough to perk the beasts, though without proper feed and water, they would not last the hard day ahead.

"A few miles up the road is a three-way junction, one that leads south-west to Drikis City, one, west to Darnan, and the other northwest to Sheeva City. We will take the northwest fork. There is an old hunter's trail that cuts through near Darnan. It will be the safest way to get there without the inconvenience of exposing ourselves much," Ursa explained. "Hopefully it will also confuse those who are following us as to our destination."

"They will have a road block at the junction," Meath told him, knowing the protocol that would be used to impede them.

"Yes there will be, I am sure of it. We will find a way around it. I do not want to have to kill anymore misled men," Ursa sighed. "There has been far too much blood spilt, and I fear there will be much more before this is resolved."

They travelled as fast as they dared through the morning dawn - Meath's eyes kept darting from side to side and then behind them, making sure no one was coming. It bothered him that they had not passed or even seen any other travelers. It gave him an eerie feeling inside, as if someone was watching them. He knew regular travelers would be light today. The roadblocks would deter a lot from traveling if they believe there was danger about, or if they had something else to hide. Chances were though, if they were seen by anyone it would be trouble.

Meath looked over at Nicolette and saw she was looking back at him. He could not help but admire how strong she had been through all of this. For he and Ursa this was easier-they had been trained and were prepared for battle, fear and betrayal. Nicolette was not. She was a Princess and should never have been put through anything like this.

Twice they had to stop and hide in the growth of the jungle as travellers passed by - both times talk of what had happened carried to their hiding places. Ursa's face became grim each time, before travelling on when the coast was clear.

"We need to stop," Meath called forward to Ursa, who was already slowing his horse.

"What is it?" Nicolette asked, worry edging her words.

"The roadblock is just up and around that next bend. We will have to lose the horses and cut through the jungle to get around them safely." Ursa dismounted.

"There might be hidden sentries off the road in the woods," Meath told them. "We will have to keep alert."

"Bring the horses over here," Ursa said, cooing his horse down into a laying position behind a large section of dense ferns and trees. He poured a yellow powder into his water skin and shook it well, then gave the horses each their share. "It would not serve us well to have royal guard horses grazing around."

"What is that?" Nicolette asked, pointing to the water skin.

"It will make them sleep for several hours," Ursa replied, "more than enough time for us to be long away from here."

Silently as they could, they crept through the jungle several hundred paces from the road so that they would not be seen or heard. They stopped every so often to listen for any indication that they had been caught.

Meath eyed everything like a starving hawk. Any movement or change of shadow and he was aware of it. His hands tightly gripped the handle of the jewelled, sword so hard his knuckles were white. They were half-way past the roadblock and could vaguely hear the murmurs of the many soldiers on the road.

"We have to stop and take a break...my leg is killing me," Meath whispered finally. He did not want to have to rest, but the pain in his leg was causing him to stumble and they could not afford to be heard. They stopped and hunched down close together.

"I have not seen any signs of hidden sentries," Ursa whispered not taking his eyes from the overgrowth.

"Me neither," Meath replied massaging his sore leg hard. "But that does not mean they are not there."

After a few more moments, Meath stood up and indicated he was ready to continue. They started slipping through the dense ferns and vines again, when Meath noticed a overgrown root sticking out of the earth. He was about to warn Nicolette but he was too late. She cried out instinctively as she lost balance and crashed forward - rustling and breaking branches as she went to the ground. Ursa and Meath stopped immediately their senses perking for any notion that they had been discovered.

Meath heard a distant crunch from behind them and knew a sentry was coming to investigate. "Someone is coming!" He whispered urgently helping Nicolette up. She looked up, her eyes glistening with apologies.

They picked up their speed and trudged hastily through the thick jungle, still doing their best to keep silent. However, Meath knew they would not be able to avoid a confrontation. "Slow down but keep going. I will catch up," he instructed them.

"What? Are you daft?" Ursa cursed softly turning to glare at him but it was already too late - Meath had turned off their course and was already gone.

"Where is he? What is he going to do?" Nicolette cried softly looking from where Meath had just been to Ursa.

"He is being a soldier," Ursa grunted, pulling her along, their pace slower, just as Meath had told them.

Meath watched as the sentry stalked within a stone's throw behind Ursa and Nicolette. He was camouflaged fully from head to toe and blended well with his surroundings, which was why they did not see him before. His steps were precise and swift as he closed the gap on his targets. He held a crossbow steadily in his hands, a bolt locked and loaded as he tried to get a clear shot, but he was still too far off. At his side was a short sword and several large throwing knifes.

Meath slowly moved in behind the sentry, mimicking his enemy's every movement. He knew he had to be quick and accurate in his attack - he had to kill him silently so he would not have a chance to make any sound and alert the others.

The sentry stopped again and began to take aim - Meath knew he had only heartbeats to act. He sprung forward at full speed, his sword aimed for the sentry's heart. He lunged forward for the kill but the sentry rolled off to the side in a burst of speed. Meath then realized he had been baited - the sentry had always known he was behind him. Meath tried to recover his steps but he was already too far committed to stop, and he plummeted down in a sideways roll coming up on his knees. He turned just in time to see the sentry levelling his crossbow for his chest. Instinctually, Meath released his Gift and flames consumed the crossbow's cord before he could pull the trigger. It snapped loudly, licking the sentry's face deeply, but if he felt it, it did not show.

The sentry exploded forward, daggers emerging out of nowhere into his hands. Meath could not rise to his feet before the sentry was on him. Daggers flashed and sliced, frantically trying to bite into Meath's flesh. Meath fell backwards, barely avoiding his throat being slashed by the wild, violent swings. He kicked his feet hard, smashing into the enemy's knees, tripping him forward. Meath got one of his legs up fast enough and slammed it as hard as he could into the sentry's chest, cracking ribs and knocking the wind from his lungs while launching him backwards.

Meath was on his feet and on top of the sentry, raining fists down hard before he had a chance to recuperate, dazing the man even further. For a split second from the corner of his eye, Meath saw the glint of light reflecting off steel. But before he could act, the blade bit into his shoulder. His hand wrenched the knife from his shoulder and he stabbed down immediately hoping to end one of his threats. The sentry regained his senses and grabbed a hold of Meath's hands, halting the attack. Meath pushed down with all his weight trying to overpower him, but the sentry held strong. Meath knew he had only moments before the other sentry was upon him and then he would be in trouble. He forced his Gift into the dagger, heating it to blistering temperature within an instant. The sentry could not take it any longer. The dagger pierced through his heart scorching and blackening the skin around the immediately fatal wound with a pungent hiss.

Before Meath could react, the other sentry exploded from the overgrowth. His foot connected solidly with Meath's ribs, hurling him off the dead man and into the trunk of a tree. Meath coughed and gasped desperately for air as he tried to push himself up so he could defend himself before it was hopeless. He turned his head so he could see the next attack and was surprised at what he saw. The sentry was standing there crossbow levelled, the kill there for the taking at any moment.

"Tell me it is not true Meath!" The sentry said, his posture softening only slightly.

"What?" Meath coughed out agonizingly, not comprehending what was happening and why he recognized the voice.

"Tell me the rumours are not true Meath! Tell me you did not kill the King and kidnap the Princess!" The soldier towered over him and cried out frustrated. "Tell me so I do not have to…kill the man who once saved my life!"

At once Meath knew who the sentry was.

His name was Stewart - he was younger than Meath and had been trained in Drandor alongside him. They had been in separate squads

that trained together frequently. It had been on their first serious
excursion out as freshly trained soldiers. Both squads were sent out
to investigate one of the towns near Lake Lajuen, near the border of
Zandor. There had been countless reports of Barbarian raiding
parties, attacking the town and caravan supply wagons going in and
out for months.

They had met up with a small caravan heading to the town and
disguised themselves as fellow travellers. Most of the soldiers hid in
the wagons out of sight so not to give their true numbers away, in the
hope of luring out the enemy. Drawing out the enemy - they did - but
they had not been ready for them. They had still been two days ride
away from the town and had stopped for the night on the side of the
road near the river. Many of the soldiers had befriended the caravan
merchants who were more than willing to share their wines and ale
with them for the extra protection. Many of the soldiers had
overindulged in the generous offer that night, completely unaware
they were being watched.

Meath had been part of a sentry squad that was to protect their
flanks for half the night. Along with him in the squad had been a fine
soldier named Tyler, who was well on his way to becoming a
Captain. Then there was a giant brute of a fellow, who they had
nicknamed the Sandman. His sheer size and fierce looks had made
several of his training partners black out from anxiety before they
had ever stepped into the training square. Then there had been
Stewart. He had come from a rich family of respected sailors and
soldiers, his parents expected him to follow suit.

It had almost been the end of their shift when the unruly attack
ensued. The four of them had just met back up at their checkpoint
after surveying their designated surroundings one last time. Everyone
reported a dead night, which had made them overconfident and
careless on their trek back. They had been a mile from the camp
when they were ambushed - they had missed all the signs. The pure
tranquillity of the night had dulled their sense of danger. The vivid
stillness of night creatures and insects should have been their first
clue that something was wrong, but it had not.

They made small talk as they hiked back to camp - which had
given their numbers and location away effortlessly. They had
stopped for a few moments to catch their breath, when a barrage of
arrows mutely hailed down on them from the darkness. It had caught
them all bitterly by surprise. Any chance they had to mount a proper

defence was taken hastily from them by the time the last arrow struck the earth. Tyler was dead - half a dozen arrows had laid him to the dirt before they had even realized they were in peril. The Sandman had taken two arrows, one in his thigh another in his side, but still stood firm and ready with his twin headed battle-axe. Stewart too had been hit in the thigh - the wickedly crafted arrow had severed a part of an artery and he was bleeding profusely. Luck had been on Meath's side for he was the one who had been chosen to carry the supply pack - it had stopped three arrows from penetrating his back.

The rain of arrows ceased and they went back to back as several savages melted out of nowhere - their crude, tarnished weapons hungry for blood. They knew they were dangerously outnumbered and if they did not act quickly, death was imminent. Retreat was their only option for survival and the survival of those back at camp. Several of the savages plundered Tyler's corpse for anything worth pilfering, while the others were left to deal with the three ambushed soldiers.

Tyler had been the Sandman's best friend and watching the enemy maul and disrespect his body had enraged him. He broke rank like a charging bull, yelling for Meath and Stewart to run back to camp to warn the others - his blades leading the way in wild, vicious swings of defiance. Meath had to fight the urge to stay and die fighting like his friend, but he refused to let the Sandman and Tyler die in vain. They bolted through the trees - the distraught cries of the Sandman who bought them as much time as his life could fuelling their steps.

Meath had known by the amount of blood Stewart was losing, that he would not be able to keep up for long. Meath forced him on, putting his arm around him, half-pulling, and half carrying him until finally, Stewart collapsed. Meath refused to leave another comrade behind and did something on pure instinct for survival. Something Ursa had warned him never to do.

Meath forced a stick into Stewart's mouth and told him to bite down, as he tore the arrow from his leg. His hands covered the deep wound as he urged the unknown power that he knew was hidden inside of him to come out before it was too late. But nothing happened - he was about to give up when he heard the shouts of the enemy not far in the distance. Panic and fear overwhelmed him, but in those moments, his Gift surged through him and released into Stewart's leg. The fatal wound began to close and heal slowly by means neither one of them really could fathom. With a newfound strength and will, they made it to the camp just in time to warn them.

"Stewart I swear to you it is not true!" Meath gasped pushing himself up onto his knees.

"How can I believe you Meath when here you are?" Stewart cried, his crossbow shaking in his hands.

"On my honour, I promise you it is not true!" Meath said imploringly to his old comrade - he knew Stewart was reliving that moment too.

Stewart glared hard at Meath for several long moments fighting some unseen inner battle, until finally the crossbow lowered to the ground. "I owe you my life Meath, and I feared I would never get the chance to repay it."

"Ursa no!" Meath cried out just in time to stop the Wizard from smashing a thick branch over Stewart's head.

Stewart spun around to level his crossbow at the unexpected assailants that had appeared behind him, but a sharp surged of air tore the weapon from his hands and off into the growth.

"Treachery!" Stewart cried looking back at Meath as if betrayed.

"No, what Meath said is true," Nicolette said drawing Stewart's stare her way. "They did not kill my father."

"Stewart…Ken, are you all right in there?" A voice called from the road.

Stewart looked hard at the three of them, again fighting some unseen skirmish from within. "I believe you…now run! I will lead them astray," he told them running off towards the road. "They're getting away. This way!" Stewart yelled leading the others the opposite way into the jungle.

"Let us not waste our good fortune!" Ursa said again leading the way.

They hiked through the jungle for a handful of hours before finally feeling confident enough to venture out onto the road again. It appeared as if Stewart had been able to lead the soldiers astray.

Ursa marched over to Meath and cuffed him upside the head. "Heroicness does not become you! Are you trying to get us all killed?"

"What?" Meath blurted out dumbfounded. "I saved our lives!"

"You almost got yourself killed! You need to stop thinking like a brute soldier and start using your wits," Ursa snapped looking at the moist blood oozing from Meath's shoulder. "Another wound, hardly surprising!" his tone carrying a father's worry.

"It was my fault we were almost caught," Nicolette intervened, shocked by Ursa's outburst. "I am sorry."

Ursa stopped his eruption and let out a long exasperated sigh. "What is done is done - it matters not anymore. We are all alive. Now let me heal that before it gets infected and I have to remove the whole arm." Ursa placed a palm onto Meath's shoulder and let his Gift flow through him into the wound. His outburst had been more a father's concern than anything else - he knew Meath had most likely saved their lives. "We are not far from the trail we must make haste and get off this road."

"They were here, all three of them, Sir," The tracker said over his shoulder to Rift tracing his hands over the footprints on the ground.

"How long ago damn it!" Rift yelled while looking down at the man from his horse.

"They came through here a few hours ago, I would say. From the looks of their tracks, they are heading northwest to Sheeva City. It seems foolish though, they must know the news would have reached there by now and that getting in would be impossible. Not to mention it is a long way to go without supplies and horses." The tracker mounted his horse and waited for new orders. "If Sheeva City is where they're headed and they're still on foot, we should be able to overtake them before the sun sets."

"Believe me, nothing is impossible for Ursa. He is a cunning man and very well connected. But why would they take her there? It does not make any sense - where are they going?" Rift said aloud while he pondered what to do. "Are you sure you know nothing else?" He asked the battered sentry who had engaged them.

"They passed right by Ken and myself. If they were going anywhere else I would figure they would have tried to slip by on the other side of the road," the sentry replied.

"Did you hear them discussing anything, anything at all?" Rift pressed with a stern look.

"No sir, they were dead quiet, we only heard them because her Highness tripped and cried out," he answered.

"Was she restrained?" Shahariel asked.

"No sir - it was very peculiar if you ask me," Stewart replied awkwardly. "But then again she was most likely scared out of her wits and knew better than to resist."

"You are lucky to be alive...you might have ended up like your friend here," Shahariel said pointing to the unfortunate sentry, who had a charred dagger protruding from his chest.

"I was sadly outmatched, but would have died for the cause all the same," Stewart sighed, looking down at the other sentry whom he had known for years.

"Good job soldier," Rift muttered walking out of the woods and back onto the road. "As for the rest of you..." he began, but stopped when he saw a pair of riders coming hard from the west.

"Rift, we found their tracks a few miles up ahead. They travelled northwest for a time but turned off onto a hunters trail, which leads back toward Darnan," One of the riders blurted out as he jumped from his horse, almost too fast to catch his feet underneath him.

"Shahariel, you come with me. I might need you to find their tracks again and it will be much faster with just the two of us. The rest of you follow as fast as you can. Darnan is as far as they will go!" Rift ordered leaping onto his horse and spurring it into a hard run.

Stewart watched the group ride off around the bend and cursed under his breath. "Sorry Meath, I tried."

"What did you say Stewart?" A patrolman asked while swatting as a bug.

"I just said I hope they catch those bastards." He lied, still watching as the dust settled.

"They will - they will," the man replied.

Meath neared the group of soldiers guarding the entrance to Darnan and dread encircled his insides. He could not help but wish Ursa was with them, but the Wizard was already waiting on the other side of the barricade in the town somewhere. It had appeared so effortless watching Ursa go through. The guards hardly seem to pay the Wizard much notice, as they were not looking for a simple old beggar drifting by himself. Ursa had rubbed dirt along his arms, face and even in his hair, giving him a mangy, vagrant look. Then he had used one of the dusty horse blankets that they had taken from the horses as a cloak to hide his dirty white robes

Ursa had played the part so flawlessly; the hump back, the limp, even begging the guards for a few coins. Meath shook his head. He had to concentrate and play his part just as convincingly, if not more so. The guards were looking for the Princess and she was with him, huddled right beside him.

He looked at Nicolette and could tell she was just as nervous as he was. He knew, as well as she, that if this did not go precisely as planned they would likely never see each other again. He gave her a reassuring look, though he did not quite believe it yet himself. He stole one last glance at her as they came to a halt in front of a large, clean-shaven soldier.

"Remove your hoods!" The soldier commanded. He stood his ground in front of them with his hand lazily on the hilt of his sword.

"What is the meaning of this?" Meath asked cautiously. "We have done nothing wrong."

"I said, remove your hood, or I will remove it for you! I am not in the mood for insolence," The man sneered, a fierce tone behind his words.

"All right, no need for violence," Meath said, pulling the blanket off his head. The soldier glared at him for a moment then looked over to Nicolette who still had not removed the blanket from around her head.

"I said take it off! This is the last time I will ask," The man barked, taking a step closer to Nicolette. She slowly pulled the blanket down and let her scarlet hair fall down her back. The soldier stared at her hard for a moment, "what is your name?"

Nicolette's eyes shimmered with anxiety. They had not thought any need of false names and she was so terrified she could not calm her thoughts long enough to think of one.

Meath noticed her delay and knew every second counted. "I am afraid my poor sister is a mute sir," Meath blurted out nervously. "She got bit by a spider when she was younger. Our parents could not afford the potion to counteract the poison in time and she lost her voice. Her hearing is not too good either," he added cleverly.

The guard looked her in the eyes for several moments then turned back to Meath. "I did not ask for your life story - what is her name?"

"Her name is Victoria, sir," Meath replied, saying the first name that came to his tongue. Meath was almost certain they were about to be discovered and wished Ursa had not made him throw his sword away.

The man stood back and looked at both of them as if contemplating their story. "What brings you to Darnan?" He asked dourly.

"Well sir...we are..." Meath mumbled out trying to think of a reason. "...are travelling to each town and city in hopes to find a physician or Wizard who might know of a cure for her muteness," he managed.

"Then I would suggest you go and see Mister Todward, he is the best physician in town and if he cannot, I am sure he would know of someone who can," the guard told him, a hint of compassion edging into his voice.

"Thank you - may the Creator shine on you with many blessings sir," Meath praised in thanks.

"A pretty little thing like that must have had the voice of an angel - it would be a shame for no one to ever hear it again," the guard replied respectfully falling fully for the ruse. He stepped aside and waved the other men out of the way so they could pass. Meath and Nicolette made their way through the mass of soldiers that formed the roadblock.

"That was too close," Meath whispered after they were out of hearing range. He looked over his shoulder and was glad to see none of the guards showed any signs of suspicion toward them.

"I cannot believe that worked," Nicolette replied, pulling her hood back on.

"I was sure we were done for. I have to say, the red hair was a good idea. I think it saved our lives," Meath replied with a long sigh of relief.

"Of course it was," Ursa said from behind them. "Follow me at a distance and make sure no one sees us together, Meath, good job." With that, he turned down a side road between two small houses, all the while keeping up his begging as he went.

Meath had a difficult time following the aged Wizard. Ursa looked so much like all the other beggars in the fading light and even had the gait perfected. More than once, Meath and Nicolette lost view of him and each time, after only a few moments, he would emerge behind them again scolding him.

"We are almost there. Keep your eyes open and do not lose sight of me again," Ursa muttered, clearly irritated.

They followed Ursa through several more alleyways until he finally came to a stop in front of a large gated off mansion. Ursa waved the doorman over, once Meath and Nicolette had caught up to him.

"It is late - what do you want? We do not give to beggars. Go bother someone else," the short, black-haired man said, waving his hand in dismissal when he neared the gate.

"We are not your regular beggars," Ursa said lifting his hood back.

"Master Ursa! I am so sorry for my insolence. I did not know it was you or else I would never have…" The man stammered apologetically.

"There is no need for that Adhar. Just open the gate and bring us to Master Saktas. It is of dire urgency," Ursa urged the man while he scanned the streets behind them.

"Yes, right away Master Ursa," Adhar replied. He ushered them in quickly and locked the gates again, doing a final check for any peering eyes. Satisfied there was none, they moved on towards the mansion.

They followed Adhar down the well-maintained, hedged path to the main doors. Nicolette could not help but stare in awe at what she saw. Every bush and tree in the yard was cut and flawlessly fashioned into animals of all species and poses. Even in the growing darkness, Nicolette could tell the grounds around the mansion were lush and vibrant with exotic flora.

Adhar led them up the granite stairs and through the large oak doors - the soft fragrance of roses filled the air upon entering.

"Wait here, I will go and locate the Master and tell him of your arrival. I am sure he will be very pleased to know you are here," Adhar said quickly bowing before leaving the room.

Meath and Nicolette sat down on one of the entrances many davenports, while Ursa stood pacing the area as they waited.

"I will finally be able to meet Saktas," Meath said. Ursa had talked highly of the man all Meath's life and had several times gone off to meet him - sometimes in secret, sometimes just for a visit.

"You have met him before, though you were just a boy then," Ursa replied, admiring a festive painting on the wall.

"Why have I not met him again then?" Meath asked with a raised eyebrow.

"I did not want you falling under any of his influences." Ursa cracked a smile as if recalling something particular.

"Like what?" Meath asked, his interest aroused.

"He has a certain way with the curiosity and gallantries of the young," Ursa said softly.

"I recall my father talking about Master Saktas before. He is a well-respected merchant in Draco. When my mother died, it was Saktas who found the great sculptor - Zomen - to create the statues of her that my father treasured so dearly," Nicolette said getting up and wandering around the room, looking at all the different art pieces.

"Yes, that would have been I," A husky voice said as a man came through the doublewide doorway that Adhar had disappeared through.

All three of them turned to see the tall, older man who stood before them. He was dressed in the finest of silk clothing that had been tailored to fit his large frame.

"Ursa, my old friend, it is good to see you," Saktas said, clearing the gap between them to clasp hands.

"This is not a social call Saktas, but a matter of ominous urgency," Ursa responded his features turning gravely serious.

"I assumed as much old friend. I hear it is because of you that all these soldiers are in Darnan. The rumour has it you murdered King Borrack and kidnapped his daughter." Saktas laughed knowing better than to believe what he had been told. "I guess this young lady over here is the beautiful Princess Nicolette?" Nicolette took her hood off so he could see her face. "You are even more beautiful than the rumours say. Nice touch getting her past the guards with that red hair. What did you use? Ruby berry?" Saktas asked with a wide smile on his face knowing the ploy well. Meath and Nicolette nodded in unison.

"It is true that the King has been murdered, but not by my hand. There is great evil in Draco and I fear the worst kind of outcome," Ursa said, tone critical.

"I see. Let us not talk of such things here…we should go to where we can talk in private. First - you three must be famished and all of you are in need of a bath," Saktas said, realizing the situation was far worse than he had expected. "You are safe here - take your time. There will be plenty of time to discuss everything at length this night."

"Captain Rift, what brings you here?" The soldier asked, walking over to greet him with a salute.

"Where are they?" Rift yelled jumping from his horse and throwing the reins to another man who was standing there.

"They have not come by this way sir, or we would have surely sent word of it," the man replied apprehensively.

"What? You halfwit, they are here in Darnan! How could you not have seen them? They could not have made it over the walls so that means they came through one of the roadblocks either on this side or the other!" Rift roared, shoving the man violently to the earth.

"I do not understand sir - we have not seen anyone to match their description and no one in a group of three that even came close," the man cried up at him.

"Well they must have fooled you - I know they are here somewhere," Rift snarled, walking past the soldier shouting orders to the other men, who had now gathered to see what the commotion was.

"What is going on here?" The commanding officer barked as he rode from the town to the gather of men who had formed at the gates.

"The assassins are here in Darnan, you insolent fool! You were given one easy task and you could not even do it," Rift bellowed marching up to him.

"How do you know this for sure?" The officer asked, still not sure of what to make of the situation. He knew Rift's reputation and did not want to be on the man's bad side if rumours held true.

"We followed them here by their tracks, you flea ridden whoreson!" Shahariel hissed out coming to stand by Rift.

"Search this entire town and its outskirts. Leave nothing untouched. Search every home, every street, every alley, and every man, woman and child. They are here somewhere and we will not let them get any farther, do you hear me!" Rift yelled so all the men could hear him. "We stop them here…a thousand in gold to whomever brings them to me!"

Nicolette relaxed in the large, elaborately designed brass tub in the astonishing room she has been shown to. She traced her fingers over the etched grapevine pattern that framed the rim and down the outer sides to the ankles of the tub. The interknit design was faultless and flowed so naturally. Nicolette wondered how its creator could have engraved it so precisely without being in the core of a vineyard when he did so - even then it would have been a feat. She laid herself back against the warmed metal and slid herself down into the steaming, juniper-scented water until her head was beneath its embrace. Her eyes opened and she watched the red colouring in her hair bleed out, diluting itself in the already murky water.

She dried herself off on the linen towels that had been laid out for her. How good it felt to be clean again, yet some of the filth felt like it remained. Her eyes glanced back at the crimson hued water and she had to wonder how much of that was blood.

Her father's blood, the Zandorian soldier she had killed to save Meath's life, and Meath's blood had gotten on her too. So much blood had been spilled in a day…so much innocent blood. She did not even realize it but her eyes were moist with tears as she relived every vivid moment of the night before.

Nicolette looked at the lavish bed in the room and wanted nothing more than lay down on it for a while. She knew if she did, she would fall fast asleep as soon as her head hit the pillow. She was so tired - yet somehow she had the strength to stay awake.

A servant came and collected them after they had bathed and changed into the new attire left out for them. They met in Saktas' private meeting quarters, where an expansive spread of food and drink was laid out for them to indulge in.

"I hope the clothes all fit, if it had been earlier in the day that I found you at my steps I could have had a seamstress do anything needed, but alas on such short notice there is only so much even I can do," Saktas said to Nicolette and Meath as they were showed into his luxurious study, Ursa following behind them. "And of course Ursa always keeps a change of clothes in his room," he added with a hardy chuckle. "Eat...I am sure you are famished."

"How did you...?" Meath started to ask.

"The clothes?" Saktas laughed. "You and my son share the same taste in apparel it would seem and luckily enough are of the same build."

They ate their fill of delicate meats, cheeses and exotic fruits while Ursa explained to Saktas the tale they had been through since they left Draco castle. He went on to tell of how they had managed to escape and finally made it to Darnan.

"My word, I have to say you three have been through an awful lot since last night," Saktas said getting up from his chair and walked over to the stone fireplace to empty his hornpipe. "I am sorry to hear that your father is dead, Princess. He was a great man...one of the greatest I ever had the privilege of knowing," he said as he bowed his head and placed his hands on the mantel. His gaze dropped to stare into the burning embers. "How can I help you Ursa?" Saktas asked turning around to face them. "Name it and if it is within my powers, I shall see it done."

"We need an army so we can march in there and kill that bastard, Prince Berrit, or whoever he really is," Meath replied animatedly. "Assassins, several of them would work to!" Excitement filtered into Saktas eyes at the thought.

Ursa glanced over to Meath and rolled his eyes. "We need you to go to Draco and tell Lord Tundal and Lord Dagon the truth of this matter," Ursa said, ignoring Meath's outburst. "But it must be you that goes and talks to them. They know you and know you can be trusted."

"That is it? You do not want me to kill this man - this fake Prince Berrit?" Saktas asked in confusion. He walked back to his seat and poured himself a mug of wine.

"No, Saktas. This impostor is most powerful with the Gift - he is like no other I have ever encountered and I fear he would not make it that easy. If you were caught trying or even succeeding in assassinating him before anyone knows the truth, you will find yourself hanging from the gallows. Let the Lords know the truth, from there a better plan can be thought up. There is at least one other who is wrapped up in this plot, but there may be more…we need to find them as well," Ursa said solemnly.

"I see my friend - your words are wise as always. I will see to it they hear it from my own mouth and from there we will do what is necessary," Saktas agreed. "Where will you go then? You are more than welcome to stay here in my home until this is all resolved."

"That is a kind offer, but one we must decline," Ursa replied and Saktas cocked an eyebrow in question. "I must ensure Princess Nicolette's safety until this is all resolved. There are too many eyes looking and too many ears listening for us to be safe here I am afraid. A reward of a thousand gold coins is far more than enough to tempt even the strongest willed men."

"Very true my friend, very true," Saktas concurred. "Then where will you go?"

"Dragons Cove - the Princess will be safe there with her Aunt Jewel and Uncle Marcus until this is resolved. It is far enough away that rumours will be slow and we will be protected," Ursa explained, finishing his meal and filled his mug with cold, fresh water. He wanted no wine to drink, as he needed all his wits about him.

"Wise plan, but if all goes my way, the problem will be resolved long before you reach Dragon's Cove," Saktas laughed confidently.

"Then you may send word for us on the swiftest horse," Ursa told him.

"It shall be done. On the morrow before the first rays peek the sky, I shall be off," Saktas confirmed. "Tonight you get as much rest as you can and tomorrow whenever you're ready I will have Adhar take you to the escape tunnel out of the city with any supplies you may need."

"Master Saktas," Adhar interrupted as he ran into the room unexpectedly. "There is a mob of soldiers at the gates demanding to be let in!"

"What? What do they want?" Saktas asked urgently, standing up.

"They say they are here to search the house. They know Master Ursa and the others are here in the town," Adhar blurted out while trying to catch his breath. "They have orders to search everything!"

"I see. Take Ursa, and the others to the escape tunnel and I will go and deal with the guards," Saktas ordered turning to Ursa. "Well my old friend, it seems that our visit has been cut short, as always. I will go to Draco and do as you have asked of me. Just promise me you will keep the Princess safe until this is all settled. We do not need those damn Zandorians ruling our country!"

"I will, my friend and thank you for everything," Ursa promised. They clasped hands again before the three followed Adhar down several halls and stairways to the far west wing of the mansion and into the house's immense cellar.

Saktas had exquisite tastes in all aspects and brought back the rarest and most exotic of flavours wherever he went. He had a wall of wines and ales from half the world away, barrels and sacks of every spice, and dried fruits he could get his hands on. Money was never an issue for Saktas; he had many different investments and dealings in everything, though some he would never admit to.

"Over here!" Adhar called to them stopping in front of a large wooden crate pressed securely against the stone wall. He pulled hard on the front of the crate, prying it open to reveal a ladder that led downward into the earth. "The master presumed your visit may be cut short and had me prepare a few things to help on your journey," he added grabbing several items from beside the crate.

Adhar handed Ursa a large pouch of coins and a pack full of provisions, which Ursa passed to Meath to carry. Saktas had always helped Ursa out when he had needed it, and he needed it now more than ever. Adhar held the ladder while Ursa climbed down into the darkness that waited. Adhar then paused for a moment as he fiddled with something in the large sack. "My Master wanted you to have this. It was for his son, but after he went missing, the master did not have the heart to part with it. You reminded the master of his son, he believes the sword must have been meant for you to wield." Adhar handed Meath an oddly shaped sword that felt much lighter than any sword Meath had ever held before.

"Please give him my thanks," Meath said then began his decent down into the void.

"And for you, your Highness, my Master wanted me to give you this. He found it on one of his adventures not too long ago." Adhar handed her a small hand-held crossbow, with a leather pouch full of small bolts. "The four black bolts are tipped with a rare, deadly poison, so please be very careful with them."

"Thank you," Nicolette said taking the weapon and bolts and attaching them to the leather belt she had been given when she had changed clothes.

"What do you want at such a late hour? How dare you disrupt my home and trash my property!" Saktas raged.

"I am sorry Master Saktas, but we have our orders to search everywhere in Darnan. There is reason to believe the assailants and the Princess our here in town," the commander replied.

"Those you seek are not here in my home. I would not harbour such criminals. Who do you think I am?" Saktas snapped at the soldiers who now infested his yard. They had not waited for the gate to be opened - they simply tore it down and started their search.

"We will replace your gate of course, Master Saktas," the soldier said sending his men into the house. "But you can understand our urgency about the matter. Word is, you and Ursa are good friends and he has even stayed here in your house many a time. So forgive me for the harsh treatment, but I have my orders."

"I cannot believe this. You should know me better than that. Yes it is true Ursa and I are friends - but if he has committed treason as the rumours imply, then he is no friend of mine!" Saktas proclaimed bitterly. "Your brutes better not break anything that you cannot afford to replace," Saktas added as he crossed his arms angrily.

After a few minutes, one of the soldiers ran out carrying the Princesses' bloody, ripped nightdress. Behind him followed most of the others that had entered his house with a few other articles of clothing from the others and pushing out a female servant. "Sir, sir, we caught this servant trying to hide these upstairs!"

"What is this, Lord Saktas? It appears you have lied to us," the soldier said, drawing his sword and pointing it at Saktas' throat. "You two, arrest him. The rest of you continue to search the house and the surrounding area. They may still be in there hiding." He mounted his horse while Saktas was forced to follow him, restrained and tethered to the horse.

"What about her?" One of the men yelled to the commander before he rode off.

"She is a traitor to the throne - hang her!" he called back callously.

Saktas turned his head to see his servant being dragged kicking and screaming towards one of the large trees in his yard, a noose already was being prepared.

"Captain Rift, this man knows where the Princess is. We found her nightdress in his house and other signs that they were here," the commander announced eagerly as he rode up to where Rift and the tracker sat eating and threw Saktas to the ground in front of them.

Rift jumped to his feet, knocking over a small table that was in front of him. He ran to Saktas and heaved the man impatiently at his feet.

"Where are they?" Rift blared out, as he shook the man like a rag doll. "Where? I demand that you tell me!"

"I do not know what you are talking about," Saktas bellowed back. He tried his best to stand his ground through the violent shaking.

"Do not play dumb with me, you worm. Tell me what I want to know and I will spare your life," Rift yelled, punching him in the guts before letting him drop to the ground.

"I told you I do not know what you are talking about," Saktas coughed out.

"Why do I recognise you traitor?" Rift growled. "What is your name?"

"You know well of me Rift," Saktas said pushing himself up.

"His name is Saktas - he is a very well-known merchant," one of the soldiers intervened.

Rift thought for a moment, recalling the name. "Yes I know of you - well respected with King Borrack and good friend to his killer, and makes me wonder if you had anything to do with the assassination."

"You are out of your mind, Borrack and I..." he started but was silenced when Rift's fist connected with his jaw.

"King Borrack, to you swine!" Rift hissed. "Now stop playing coy with me. Where are they?"

"I do not know what you are talking about," Saktas held his ground, his voice firm - he knew there was no way out of this.

Rift flared red. "Fine, if that is how you want it, bring me a rope. You will die a traitor's death, you vermin," he snarled as he kicked Saktas in the face knocking him back to the ground and the men around cheered.

"What are you all standing around for? They are in the town - now find them and bring them to me," Rift ordered to the soldiers.

"Well? Will you not spare your own life and tell me where they are? Or would you rather..." Rift stopped his sentence and looked from the rope back to Saktas.

"Death does not scare me and neither do you," Saktas spat at him, knowing his fate already was sealed.

"You will regret that you foolish bastard!" Rift hissed.

"I regret nothing," Saktas answered, standing to his feet with pride as he awaited his death. "But one day you will for your mistake."

An imposing labyrinth of conquering roots reigned absolute throughout the dark, humid tunnel. Roots of all kinds had forced their way through every crack and knot in the sturdy boards that encased the passageway, rupturing or tearing them clean from the corridor sides in several locations as they continued their conquest. Each breath the group took was thick and bogged their lungs, leaving their mouths filmed with pungent, stale mildew.

Adhar led the way with torch in one hand and a sinister shaped hatchet in the other. With sharp, fluent swings, he cut an easier path through the dense, entangled web that obstructed their journey. The trio awkwardly followed behind, twisting and turning their bodies so they could maneuver around the mesh of roots that reached out for them. Trying to stay as close to the soft light of the torch as possible, for the tunnel had an eerie gloom to it; they bunched up together, standing on one another's feet or robes. Ominous sounds of wooden planks - being disrupted and violated by the weight of the world above - echoed drearily down the never-ending channel. Several small, murky pools had accumulated along the seams of the soggy floorboards which could soak up no more of the drips that bombarded them from the rooftop, making the floor slick with an algae film.

As they hurried through as best they could, Meath had to give Saktas credit for being as well prepared as he seemingly was. However, in his kind of business one could never be too well prepared. The tunnel was propped with sturdy wooded beams and they had been encased entirely in quality wooden boards. Though, after the apparent decades the tunnel had remained, nature was taking its toll. It must have cost a fortune to build and even more to keep those many workers who built it quiet. However, from what he had gathered of Saktas, the man was well adapted to proving payment in all forms of the word. So he was sure the workers were all paid fairly - in their own way - and would take the secret to their graves, if that had not been where they had been placed after the work had finished. Meath shook the thought from his head - he knew Ursa would not befriend a ruthless murderer.

Nicolette held tightly to Meath's hand. She never had liked the dark, or the things that might dwell within it. Every now and then, he would look back at her and give her a reassuring smile. It raised her spirits a little more every time he did. She was glad he was with her, and knew he would not leave her side. He never did when things went sour and she needed someone. Like at the Spring Renewal Festival many years ago when they were still nothing more than children.

It had been halfway through the annual fortnight long festival - the sun had just set in the west and a long night of drinking, dancing and celebrating a new year was ensuing. Nicolette and Meath had spent the day at the fair, watching all the spectacular magic shows, plays, archery challenges and the many other performances that were of worth. Let alone the many hours they spent at the gaming booths playing darts, bobbing for apples, egg toss, sack racing and many more games that they played every day of the festival.

They were almost never apart - King Borrack had always joked around, saying Meath was more like the Princess's Champion than Rift. They were sitting off to the sides nibbling on some sweet meats watching everyone dancing and enjoying themselves. The Princess' Royal guards had been a dozen feet away, chatting up with several ladies - but their eyes drifted back to where the Princess sat every couple of minutes.

Victor - the son of a very wealthy silk merchant - approached them pompously. Victor was a handful of years older than Meath and a respectable size larger. He was arrogant, egotistic, and most fell for his superficial charm, mostly to be in good favor with his father in hopes for some form of personal gain. He had asked her to dance with him, but she had refused - her legs were tired and she did not want anything to do with him.

Victor was not used to being turned down and the snarl that spread across his face displayed it. He almost walked away, but his pride just would not allow it to end there. He swung back to face them, a new fortitude set in his jaw and posture as he grabbed the Princess' hand and pulled her to her feet unwillingly, dragging her toward the dancing.

She tried to pull away, but his grip was too firm. She remembered the confusing thoughts that flooded her mind when she turned back to look at Meath, only to find he was not there anymore. Where could he have gone? She was about to yell out for help when she realized she was no longer being pulled along against her will and that her intimidating capture no longer grasped her wrist. She turned to see what had happened and realized Meath had not abandoned her – instead he now stood his ground in front of them, not allowing Victor to pass by. She was sure she would remember the exchange of words that followed, until her dying days.

"How dare you step in my way, you little orphaned bastard!" Victor cursed at him. "Remove yourself before I do it for you!"

"She said no - leave her alone!" Meath barked back, his hands balled into tight fists.

"What do you plan on doing?" Victor laughed, seeing Meath's knuckles turning white. "You going to fight me, you little freak of nature? Do not make me laugh." He tried to push Meath aside but Meath refused to budge and slapped away his arms.

Victor's face flared red and he charged Meath in blind rage. Meath's fist was ready and collided hard with Victor's jaw, stunning him in his place. An instant later, his own fists flew wildly, battering Meath to the ground. Meath had done his best to defend against the overpowering blows of the much larger boy, but he was losing.

Nicolette had tried to push Victor off Meath before he could kick him anymore. But Victor easily swatted her aside. She had cried out in pain and crashed into the bench that she and Meath had been sharing. Murmurs and gasps from the crowd alerted the Royal escorts to the events that were unfolding outside of their notice. That cry had triggered a newfound strength in Meath and he kicked his own legs out smashing bitterly into Victor's shins dropping him to the ground beside him. Like a cornered dog fighting for its very life Meath dove on top of Victor, enraged fists raining down hard.

Meath's victory was short-lived, as by now all those around were fully aware of the drama and two of the guards were pulling Meath off Victor. Another took care of the Princess. Had it not been for a few onlookers who had witnessed the full event, several lashings would have been dealt out to Meath for attacking someone of such higher class. Instead, Victor was forced to apologize in front of everyone that evening - to King Borrack, for disrupting the festival and not honoring his daughter. Next to Princess Nicolette, for ignoring her decision and forgetting his place, and worst of all, he had to thank Meath for defeating him so that he had not been able to worsen his mistake further.

"Meath!" Nicolette cried out, tightening her grip on his hand pulling him to a stop.

"What is it?" he asked turning to see what the problem was. He realized it was just a large black spider crawling on her shoulder. "Hold still ... it is okay. This will only take a second," he assured her pulling out his dagger and flicking it to the ground. She exhaled loudly, hugging him tightly.

"Thank you - you have always been good at saving me from those things." She shivered at the thought of the creepy arachnid that crawled off into the consuming darkness.

"Hurry up - we do not have all night," Ursa called back to them. He had stopped a few feet in front of them to see what was holding them up, and was now waiting impatiently.

For most of the way, everyone was silent - listening for intruders from behind, talking echoed bleakly off the damp planked walls but traveled forever down the passageway. The tunnel seemed to go on incessantly as Meath counted each board they passed by. They had been walking for what seemed an endless time, when Meath finally broke the silence.

"How much farther until we are out of this foul smelling place?" he asked, spitting out the tainted saliva residue that had coated his tongue.

"Should not be far now," was all Adhar said, not slowing his pace. His demeanor was as though the tunnel were no different from being outside in the fresh air.

Almost on cue, they came to a large root enmeshed square room, and the torchlight pushed the darkness back into the corners revealing several other passages.

"Stay here a moment," Adhar motioned to them while he walked over to the far tunnel on the right and went in several feet. There was a soft click and he returned. "It is safe to go down the far left tunnel now...you go alone from here. I must get back. You are only a few thousand paces from the exit," he told them.

"Thank you, Adhar. I will never forget this, and tell Saktas I owe him," Ursa said.

"You will be a half mile from the road to the north. There will be a small path that will take you most of the way," Adhar explained handing the hatchet to Meath, whom swung it several times to get the feeling of it. "May the Creator guild your footsteps and simplify your quest." Adhar bowed to them before leaving.

Meath lead the way with the hatchet, cutting the easiest path through the throng of roots he could for the others to follow. Though many of the roots were far thicker here than they had been back at the beginning of the compound. He was thrilled when he realized the wall had diminished the torchlight's path and ladder that now stood in front of them.

The opening at the peak of the ladder came out of a hefty old stump that lay in the middle of the dense jungle. As soon as they were out, they all filled their lungs with the fresh, sweet night air. Though they had all bathed only hours before, they felt grimier than they had before they had arrived at Sakar's.

"I did not know how much longer I could have taken that smell." Meath coughed, taking in another deep breath, clearing his lungs of the heavy feeling, before stretching his arm and shoulder. Clearing the path had been harder than he had expected and he had to wonder how Adhar had done it for so long without slowing or complaint.

"We will not be stopping to rest tonight. We must keep going and get as far away as we can. That was too close back there," Ursa explained, glad to be out on the surface again. "We will rest come morning."

Meath pulled his new sword out of its sheath to examine it. It was the most striking sword he had ever laid his eyes on. The blade was long; it arched ever so slightly outward for half the blade, then it flared upward to a furious point. The sword was only sharp on the front side and was made from the uppermost quality of steel. The hilt was an unusual design and one Meath had never seen before. The guard was crafted into the blade itself and not the handle like most. Two steel claws jutted out from near the bottom of the blade at different distances, strategically placed for defecting and stopping enemy blows. The handle itself was made of a solid wood, one that Meath did not recognize. It was angled vaguely downward, and was large enough to place both your hands on yet it was light enough that he could swing it with one with ease.

Never in Meath's life had he seen a better weapon, nor did he think he would ever hold one that matched its beauty and power. The sword felt so right in his hands as he swung it. The swings were so flawless and fluent it was almost as if it was an extension of his arm. Meath knew that crafting such a sword must have taken months. It was made of the finest materials, only the most talented of blacksmith's could have forged such a piece, and only the deepest of pockets could have afforded it.

Ursa stretched his lengthy limbs one last time before beginning to lead the way down the dark path, not wanting to waste any more time. Meath and Nicolette followed close behind - the jungle was a dreadful place to be alone at night. You never knew what might be stalking around or what snake you might stir. The path had not been used in a long time and had become vastly overgrown. A few times, they had to stop and search for where the path continued.

Nicolette found Meath's hand again and their fingers intertwined contentedly. She felt protected when she held his hand and she loved the way it made her feel. Even in the deep jungle in the dead of night, when death could find them from any direction, she felt safe.

It was not long before they had reached the road and Ursa stopped them once again so they could catch their breaths. They had traveled quickly through the woods and had luckily avoided any beast that might be lurking about.

"We will rest for a few moments but not long - without horses, travel is going to be dreadfully slow. We will stay close to the side of the road in case we need to hide. Trust no one, and try not to be seen. Anyone traveling will surely be looking for us or have heard the rumors," Ursa said, pulling off his water skin and taking a drink before handing it to the others.

"It sure is humid tonight," Meath moaned, wiping the sweat from his brow and fighting away the bugs.

"I wonder what is happening back in Darnan," Nicolette speculated aloud.

"Saktas has gotten out of worse in his days." Ursa untied the black lace that held his long hair in a ponytail and let his hair free. "We should get moving."

They traveled long into the night and more than once had to hide from passing patrols. Meath could tell that Nicolette was beginning to tire. She held onto his arm for support and was having difficulty keeping up. He knew she was not accustomed to all this traveling on foot, but they had no choice but to keep moving. Even Meath was beginning to stumble - it had been a while since his days in the army, and since he had traveled this hard.

Daybreak came and the trio found temporary shelter under a rocky overhang from a small hillside. The shelter was far enough off the main road that Ursa doubt anyone would know about it or be able to see or hear them. Meath covered the opening with large leafy branches to help camouflage them and keep the heat of the day out so they could get some sleep.

As much as Ursa wanted to keep travelling, he knew they needed sleep. During the day was the best time for them to sleep and be off the roads. This was the time people travelled and the more they exposed themselves the more likely they would be caught.

They ate sparingly, not knowing how long their small supply of food would have to last. They slept into the better part of the day. When they woke, they ate a small meal and began making slow progress through the jungle's dense growth in the fading light of day. Once it was nearer to dusk, they ventured onto the road again for faster travel.

"We will stop here so the Princess can catch her breath," Ursa called back. He turned around and realized he was a fair distance ahead of them. Since they had gone back onto the road, they had made good progress, and had not needed to hide from sight.

"I am okay - I can keep going," Nicolette said weakly, her feet dragging across the ground.

"We will stop anyway. I am not as young as I used to be and I need to rest my weary bones," Ursa replied.

They had not rested long before all three went dead silent, straining their ears to the night.

"Quick, get into the trees, someone is coming!" Ursa whispered urgently.

"Do you really think that what everyone is saying is true?" said a male voice that Meath thought he recognized.

"Of course not, you dolt. Meath would never have a part in treason. Do you even listen to yourself when you talk?" Another male voice boomed in defense.

"But why else would it all have happened. People just do not make up stories like that, and Meath always did have a thing for the Princess, you know. He always used to talk about her and such," The first voice spoke again and now Meath knew for sure.

"How could you ever think something like that of our friend?" Zehava growled as he slapped Dahak across the head, catching him off-guard. "Smarten up, Dahak. We know Meath better than most and I say something fishy is going on here with this whole thing. The story and facts do not add up, or even make sense for that matter. Something is wrong with it all."

"Ouch. Why do you always do that? It hurts, ya know," Dahak whined, rubbing his head from the light blow he had received.

"Good, that is the point." Zehava laughed looking over at his friend who was still complaining.

"You are probably right. Meath would not have done such things," Dahak agreed with his friend. "Though it has been a year since we have seen him, a lot could have happened to change him."

"It is okay. They are friends of mine - they will help us." Meath whispered to Ursa climbing out from his hiding place and back onto the road. He stood in the middle, waving his arms slowly.

"Stop you fool!" Ursa called trying to grab him, but missed.

"Sweet phantom mother!" Zehava yelled pulling back on the reins stopping the horses just shy of Meath. Both men goggled, before turning to look at one another.

"Please do not kill us Meath. We are your friends, remember?" Dahak whimpered finally, as he hid behind his arms and peered out to see what might be coming his way.

"I am not going to hurt you Dahak. How did you ever make it into the army with a girly scream like that?" Meath teased. Zehava jumped down from the wagon and clasped his arm.

"Meath, are you a sight for sore eyes! Please tell me that what they're saying is not true - you had no part in the King's death did you?" he asked, but was almost afraid to hear the answer.

"Of course not, Zehava!" Meath said, looking into his friends eyes to assure him.

"Well, we may as well go and join them," Ursa groaned, shaking his head.

"It is a trap - get down!" Dahak yelled again bailing off the side of the wagon taking cover behind the horses.

Zehava looked over to his friend and shook his head. "Will you relax? You are worse than my little sister."

Dahak slowly made his way around to where they stood. He was still feeling uneasy but tried not to appear so by standing a little taller. "Sorry about that Meath, but with what everyone has been saying you just start to believe it, ya know," He said with his head down, not wanting to look his friend in the eyes.

Both Zehava and Dahak's eyes focused on the Princess in both awe and admiration. "Your Highness," they both said with a slight bow of their heads in respect.

Nicolette was almost taken aback by the formalities. Though she was the Princess of the Kingdom and soon to be Queen, the last few days she had almost felt normal, as if her status meant nothing. All she could do was nod her head in greeting, but for the two soldiers that was more than enough.

"So what the heck is going on?" Zehava finally said, not being able to hold it in any longer. "In the last few days the whole country has gone ballistic and everyone is searching for you."

"It is a long story; one better told when we are not all standing here in plain sight for someone to find us," Ursa said urgently as he scanned the road and woods.

"Oh! Of course, climb in the back, there is plenty of room. No one will check back there." Zehava jumped back up to where he had been sitting and waited for everyone to get in so that they could start moving.

Once everyone was seated and ready, Ursa explained what had transpired the last few days. By the time the story was done, Nicolette was fast asleep on one of the wooden crates. She was using Meath's leg as a pillow and one of the hemp tarps as a blanket.

"Well, that all makes more sense than the rest of the rumors," Dahak said once the story was told, still feeling a little dumb for how he had reacted.

"It all sounds so unreal. I cannot believe what is happening. What is going to happen with everything now?" Zehava asked, shaking his head in disbelief.

Ursa sighed. "I wish I knew. Our best chance is to get to Dragon's Cove before the news travels that far. We have to hope that Saktas tells the other Lords what really happened."

Dahak slapped Zehava's shoulder. "You had better tell him."

Zehava sighed and looked back at Ursa. "Saktas will not be telling the Lords anything."

"Why not - what happened?" Ursa said staring hard at the young man waiting for a response.

"Well, we just came from Darnan after picking up some cargo. They found your old clothes when they searched his house. He refused to tell them where you were so he was branded a traitor - they hanged him," Zehava managed to explain.

Ursa's expression went blank in defeat. He rested his back against the wagon's side - a deep sigh escaped his lips as he shut his eyes and went still.

"Is he going to be okay?" Dahak asked waving his hand in front of the Wizard's face.

They rode in silence for a long while. No one seemed to know what to say. The news of his friend's death had hit the old Wizard hard, or maybe it was the fact that the plan Ursa had hoped to set up had crumbled before it had even had a chance to begin.

"So what have you two been up to since I last saw you?" Meath asked trying to lighten the mood a little. His eyes drifted to Ursa from time to time to see if he had come around, though Meath was sure he was deep in meditation.

"Not a heck of a lot when I think about it; just moving supplies for the army. We are taking this down to the Sheeva River Camp 'cause there has been large amounts of barbarian attacks down there. They are going to try to go in and end the threat before it gets too far out of hand," Zehava answered.

"I figured you two would be right in the midst of all the action by now," Meath responded confused.

"We were stationed in one of the eastern posts near Mandrake for several months. But all soldiers must serve their time as transporters for three months every couple of years," Zehava informed him. "There was not much action going on the eastern boarder so we decided to serve our time now." He paused, looking at the reigns in his hands, before brightening. "So are you a Wizard yet?" Zehava asked, his eyes glistening with excitement. Dahak perked up with the topic change.

Meath chuckled, remembering the last few weeks he had served with his friends before heading back to Draco Castle, to begin his training. They had appeared to be more excited about it than he had been. "Well, I know more about it now than I did when we were together last - though I still have much training to receive before I could class myself a Wizard."

"You should show us something," Dahak said wide eyed with excitement, "anything!"

"Ya, I have only ever heard stories of what people with The Gift can do; I have never seen it firsthand yet," Zehava piped in excited to see some of Meath's Wizardry.

Meath looked over at Ursa who still had his eyes closed and had not moved or responded in any way. Meath though about it for several long moments, but could not see the harm in it. "I guess there is no harm in that."

He held out his hand flat and almost immediately, a small ashen orb formed in the middle of his palm. Though Meath could have formed the fireball in full and cast it within a heartbeat, he wanted his friends to get the full visual effect. Slowly, he supplied more of his innate influence into the orb and soon vibrant yellows, oranges and reds swirled and danced within the molten sphere. His friends sat there staring into the flames with their mouths hanging as far down as they could go. Meath grinned seeing his friend's reactions, glad this was what they had wanted to see.

"What are you doing you damned fool!" Ursa snapped. The orb of flames that had rested in Meath's hand wavered and hissed at being disrupted and bellowed upward just missing the canopy of the wagon before it dispersed. The sudden commotion in the wagon woke Nicolette. "I told you not to waste your powers, and what do I find you doing, showing off in front of your friends like some cheap jester. By the Creators grace, do you not realize what kind of chaos we are in? We cannot afford to waste any strength or advantage we have got!" Ursa bellowed in anger. "Our world is crumbling around us and you are doing party tricks. I thought I taught you better."

Meath let out an angry sigh at himself. "I...I am sorry," was all he could say.

"He did not mean anything by it Master Ursa," Dahak said trying to help. The Wizard turned his attention onto Dahak, glaring at him sternly.

"I hate to interfere but I can see the fires of Tarel ahead," Zehava said hoping not to anger Ursa anymore.

"Good, can you get us in without being caught?" Ursa asked sliding back behind a crate, forgetting the situation that had happened only moments ago.

Zehava smiled. "Of course we can. They will not look in here, I know everyone."

"Good. Once we are in, take us somewhere where no one will be around. We cannot be seen at any cost, and I mean that," Ursa said covering his head with one of the tarps.

Zehava pulled the wagon up to the guards post at the entrance of Tarel, where three guards were waiting for them on the road, while several others were around at different points of advantage. A hint of worry coursed up his spine at the thought of what would happen if they were caught, but he quickly pushed that aside, knowing they could not afford failure.

"Evening gentleman," Zehava greeted the three in front of him with a smile, glad to see a face among them he knew well.

"Zehava, Dahak, I figured it was you two," The young guard said. "It has been long time my friends."

"That it has been Hyde - that it has," Zehava replied, climbing from the wagon and clasping hands with his friend.

"You are late!" A large, burly soldier barked out, less friendly. "Why?"

Zehava's façade changed with the tone in the guard's voice and he knew the true test here.

"Do you know what kind of problems are over in Darnan?" Dahak announced before Zehava had a chance. " Princess Nicolette has been kidnapped by two Wizards and they thought they had tracked them to Darnan. They were tearing through everything and detained us while they did so. No one was allowed to leave until everything was searched."

"Ya, we did hear - that is why there is more security around," Hyde spoke, motioning to all the extra guards around.

The large guard eyed them suspiciously. "Well, we have also been given the order to search everything that comes in or out."

"You have got to be kidding. Do you know how many times we have been stopped and searched since we left Darnan?" Zehava groaned, irritated. His heart beating faster with every second, his sword arm tingled with anticipation and yet he did not really know if he could pull a weapon on his comrades.

"Oh leave them alone - we do not have to search army wagons," Hyde snapped back.

"Everything that comes in and out!" the guard barked. "Those were the orders."

"Well search away then, but we are heading to the tavern for a few mugs of ale and something to eat. So when you are done with your search, you can bring the wagon to the stables and tend to the horses," Zehava replied casually.

"You will go nowhere," the guard snapped taking an aggressive step forward.

"Enough!" Hyde barked out. "Zehava, Dahak, go to the stables - and I will deal with this."

"You are the boss Hyde," Dahak replied, jumping back onto the wagon with Zehava and slowly pulling into the town.

Zehava could hear vague parts of the argument that was occurring behind them now. "That was close," Zehava whispered.

Zehava pulled the wagon up to one of the less used stables, still feeling unsteady after the encounter with the guards. He motioned for Dahak to ensure the area was free of wandering eyes. Dahak returned several moments later saying the coast was clear.

"I had better tell the Stable Master that we are here so he does not come snooping around later." Zehava informed them, he was about to leave but Ursa stopped him and grabbed a silver from his pouch and handing it to Zehava.

"Tell him you will be bringing ladies around tonight and would like some privacy, 'til morning," Ursa said with a wink. Zehava smiled and nodded his understanding.

Meath helped Dahak tend to the horses once the barn doors had been secured. They got the feed and water trough ready and let the horses have their fill. Nicolette stretched and walked around in the barn to rid her legs of their stiffness. For once since their escape from Draco Castle, it felt like they were reasonably safe.

Soon Zehava was back with the okay that the stable master would let them have their privacy in the top loft, with no questions asked, as long as they did not burn the place to the ground.

"We must leave early - the sooner and the fewer eyes around the better," Ursa told the two soldiers, who he knew would be sleeping in the barracks so no one would think anything odd.

"We will be here before the sun comes up. But we had better go check into our quarters. If we are not there, someone might come looking for us. Like a certain guard looking to cause trouble." Zehava said with a roll of his eyes.

When the two were out of sight, Ursa turned to Meath. "Are you sure they can be trusted?"

Meath looked hurt that Ursa would say such a thing. "I would not have climbed out and stopped them if I did not know they could be trusted. We all trained together and fought together - they are as trustworthy as you would ever find." Ursa just nodded his head in understanding.

"We had better get some sleep. Tomorrow will come fast and trouble may come faster." Ursa yawned holding the ladder for Nicolette and Meath to climb up into the loft above.

The sun's rays had just started to break through the darkness from behind the towering mountains and the mist was beginning to lift from the earth's warm embrace. The air had a sweet smell, from the light rainfall they had had during the night. Ursa got up, walked over to the window in the center of the barn's loft, and looked out at the small farming town. Only a few people were up feeding their livestock this early.

Ursa sighed in frustration. He truly wondered if going to Dragon's Cove was the right answer. It had seemed the only answer at the time he made the decision. He hoped that once they were there, Lord Marcus would help them find a way to overcome the false Wizard Prince and all his treachery. He had already lost two of his good friends and he did not want to jeopardize anyone else's life, but he feared many more lives would be lost before this was over.

Meath woke to the smell of straw and dust. He opened his eyes to see that Nicolette had closed the gap between them sometime during the night and was now sleeping nearer to him. He smiled - she looked so relaxed and at peace, something he had not seen in her for the last few days. Meath slowly got up and moved off the stack of hay they had used for beds, making sure not to wake her. He knew they would have to leave soon and he would have to wake her, but he wanted her to have this peace for as long as she could.

Meath looked toward the window and saw Ursa looking back at him with a half-smile, on his face. He did not know what to make of it, as it was a look Ursa had never given before. "What is that look for?" Meath asked as he stretched and walked over to him. Ursa just turned and looked back out at the town and breathed in deeply. "Answer me, what was that look for?"

"You know, when I first found you out in the woods alone, I swore I would do everything in my power to give you the life you deserved. The life so many Gifted children never get - a life I myself never got." Ursa turned and smiled at Meath. "I know I have not been much in the way of a father to you in the sense that most fathers are with their sons. I believe that stems from my own lack of a father, but I have tried the best way I know how."

"I know that," Meath replied, taken aback by Ursa's emotional conversation. "You have always done right by me - do not think otherwise."

Ursa looked back to where Princess Nicolette slept. "I knew from the first day, when King Borrack first agreed to meet with us, that you two would grow to care deeply for one another." He turned back to the window and sighed. "I even once brought the idea to the King's attention of marriage; he even entertained the idea for a while. The thought of a warrior king with The Gift was intriguing to him. Yet he knew the people would never allow it, not this soon. Then of course bloodline...or rather lack of it." Ursa sighed again.

Meath stared at Ursa in utter shock. "Why did you not tell me of this sooner?"

"I did not want to make it any harder for you than I knew it would already be."

"Then why tell me now?"

Ursa looked back to Meath. "I wanted you to know that I did attempt it, as foolish as it was, I did attempt it."

Meath's eyes glistened with tears. "You should have told me sooner, maybe there would have been something I could have done too..."

Ursa held up his hand cutting Meath short. "No Meath - that is one of the reasons I did not inform you. There is no way that you two will be able to fulfill this childhood fantasy." Ursa grimaced in remorse at watching Meath's facial expression change from one of joy to hurt. "It is not written in the stars for you my boy, and for that I am truly sorry. But you will find another and know these feelings again."

They stood there in silence overlooking the small farming town from the barn window. A mix of emotions stirred in the air between them.

"When this is over and all settles down, can we do some travelling and get away for a while?" Meath asked watching a farmer tend to his livestock.

Ursa thought about it for a moment, he knew why Meath had asked such a question. "I think we could, yes. It might be good for the both of us to get away." Ursa turned his eyes back to the town and saw Zehava and Dahak strolling toward the barn. "It is time."

Ursa started toward the trap door to the loft. He removed the lock and opened it. Dahak peered in for a moment. "Okay, we are ready to go."

"Excellent, keep the barn doors closed until we are hidden inside the wagon," Ursa reminded him.

"Will do sir…I mean Master Ursa," Dahak answered and hurried down the ladder.

Meath watched Nicolette sleep for a few moments, so many emotions playing on his mind. He looked over to Ursa who was partway down the ladder already and knew he was right. "It is time to go," He whispered, waking her up softly.

Nicolette smiled up at him - she had almost forgotten they were running for their lives. "What is it?" she asked, seeing the grin on his face.

Meath reached forward, pulled several pieces of straw from her hair, and showed her, his grin only going wider.

"Well your hair's no better," she laughed back at him.

As they had hoped for, with the town mostly still asleep they had no trouble leaving. The guards at the west gates did nothing but nod their sleepy heads and open the gate to let them out.

It was not long, until the group was making good time down the road toward the river. It was not more than half a day's ride until they would reach the river crossing, though none of them knew yet how they were going to make it across without being seen.

There was only one way to cross the Sheeva River safely in this area. The river's current was violent and unpredictable, making travel across it dangerous and life-threatening. It spanned a thousand paces across in most places and thirty deep. A pulley system had been created, several ropes were anchored to each bank and large sturdy rafts had been built and attached to the ropes. Once a raft was loaded its users could pull it across with a guide rope.

Meath stared out the back of the wagon and watched as they passed by trees. He noticed they were slowly becoming less dense and of a different species, the closer they got to the Sheeva River. Even the wildlife had started to change to hardwood creatures.

Dahak reached into one of the leather bags on the side of the wagon and pulled out half a loaf of bread and a block of goats' cheese, which he cut up and handed out to everyone.

"It is not a lot, but it will have to do until we get somewhere where we can get more supplies. I did not get a chance to get any rations this morning in our hurry. Maybe we can get something at the Sheeva River's encampment, though I highly doubt it. I am guessing we are going to try to get through there as fast as we can," he said, enjoying his meal.

"So how do we plan on crossing the Sheeva River without being seen?" Zehava asked.

"Once you get us to the camp you will do as you were ordered to do and deliver these supplies. The three of us will find a way across on our own," Ursa replied sternly.

"What do you mean? You need us!" Zehava argued in retort.

"We could use their help. The more of us there are, the better our odds if we run into trouble again," Meath added.

"The more of us there are, the harder it will be to hide and slip by unnoticed." Ursa countered.

"Ya, I think Master Ursa is right.... Uh...we should just let them out a bit before we get there and do our job Zehava," Dahak added agreeing with Ursa.

"No way! I am sick of this delivery boy job. Besides this is as much our problem as it is yours! She is my future Queen and I will be damned if I am not going to protect her in her time of need," Zehava barked back.

Ursa looked squarely into his eyes and spoke sternly. "You will do as you are told, understand?"

"No - I will not back down Ursa! This is just as much my Kingdom and my problem, as it is yours!" Zehava fumed. "She is my Queen. Fate brought us together for a reason and I will be damned if

I will be treated like a child. You are going to need all the help you can get."

"He is right - he has every right to help save his Kingdom. That is what he was trained to do," Meath put in, stopping Ursa from saying anything else.

"Maybe it would be wise to have the extra help." Nicolette finally added, beginning to feel overwhelmed again. Everyone was still for a minute, in quiet consideration.

"Do you smell that?" Ursa asked quieting everyone.

Meath smelled the air deeply. "Almost smells like smoke."

"Not almost, that is smoke," Ursa replied, his eyes scanning the tree line around them.

"We are not far from the encampment - it is most likely just cook fires." Dahak said calmly, not seeing what the big deal was.

"We are too far away to be able to smell cook fires," Zehava said, drawing his sword and resting it beside him, which prompted Dahak to do the same.

"Look!" Nicolette exclaimed pointing to the sky through the break in the trees where black smoke bellowed up.

"The encampment must be under attack," Dahak cried out.

"We must help them," Zehava said, about to slap the reins down on the horses.

"Do not charge in," Ursa ordered, drawing a confused look from Zehava. "We have with us the Princess. We will not risk danger to her foolishly."

"But the camp needs us!" Zehava bellowed out, his instinct nearly overwhelming him.

"Do you really believe our small number will make a difference if the camp is being overrun?" Ursa countered. "Go in slowly and be prepared to turn the wagon and run." Zehava nodded his head in understanding.

Nicolette gripped a small crossbow in one hand, and her dagger in the other, as fear started to overtake her again. She wondered if this is what people felt like when they rushed into battle.

Meath noticed Nicolette's hard grip on her weapons and tried to ease her mind with a half-hearted smile, but he knew that it probably would not help. The closer they got to the camp, the more intense the stench of smoke and death became.

They stopped the wagon just outside of the encampment log walls. The gate had been burnt down from a constant volley of pitch and burning projectiles. A horde of half-charred, butchered bodies lay all around where the front gates once stood. The bodies were of both the defenders and attackers. Meaht looked over one, and saw crude weapons, and scraps of leather....Barbarians.

The Barbarians had sacrificed many warriors to take down the gates. There were ten dead savages for every Draco soldier.

Nicolette gasped in terror when she climbed out and witnessed the slaughter - it made her stomach turn. She tried to fight back the urge to vomit, but could not hold it for long and retched on the ground.

"We are too late," Dahak coughed. The smoke and stench of burnt flesh was overwhelming.

Slowly they crept into the camp, their weapons drawn and ready, but the place was a barren wasteland of death. The only thing that moved was the smoke as it slowly drifted up into the sky, being whisked away by the light breeze. Even the ravens and other scavenger birds had not shown up yet for the feast that awaited them.

"Meath, Zehava, go check out the north side and see if anyone is alive. Try to help if you can. The others will come with me to the south. Do not linger long," Ursa said, his eyes taking in the gruesome scene around them.

Meath and Zehava walked through the burnt debris and down the crimson-pooled streets, toward the north side of the camp. Appendages and whole corpses littered the encampment. As they got further into the camp, it became apparent that most of the soldiers had been killed and now the citizens and farmers had defended the camp with their lives. Men lay dead with farming equipment and makeshift weapons gripped tightly in their hands. Meath and Zehava stopped several times to check bodies that had not been butchered or disemboweled for signs of life.

"This is...this is...madness!" Zehava muttered dropping to the ground and vomiting. His head spun and his legs weak. Even in the many battles he had seen, he had never witnessed anything like this.

"Who could do such a thing?" Was all Meath could mutter out.

It took several moments before they continued down the barren, scarlet-soaked road, being careful not to step on the gore that littered the ground. They followed the path that led to the far end, but they both knew there was no one left alive. They kept going however, in hopes of finding one person that had been able to hide.

"I cannot believe this. Why...how could they have broken through? There were more than a two hundred trained men at this camp."

"We had better get back. Maybe the others have found someone and know something more," Meath said, trying to not look too hard at any given spot for long.

They had started on their way back when Zehava suddenly fell to his knees, his hand went to his neck, "what the...?"

"What is it?" Meath asked turning around to see if his friend was all right.

"Run damn it...ruuuu - -" was all Zehava could manage before he crumpled to the ground in a heap a small wooden dart sticking out of his neck.

"Damn it!" Meath muttered, another dart hissed out of nowhere and caught him in the shoulder. Meath tore the dart out and tried to run but his legs had already gone numb and he too fell to the ground in a heap and into blackness.

5

Ursa leaned down and felt the footprint in the soft earth - it was fresh and deeper than the others they had found. Ursa knew that meant they were carrying something heavy - like the bodies of Meath and Zehava.

When Meath and Zehava had not come back, Ursa and the others had gone looking for them. They had searched frantically for any sign of where they were or could have been taken. It was not until Dahak had found a small wooden dart tipped with a potent sedative that Ursa knew what had happened. They had been taken for information or for slaves.

Finding fresh tracks had been nearly impossible - the carnage and chaos in and around the camp distorted any hope of finding a true set. But Ursa had been persistent for the rest of the day and even into the night searching for the right signs, until he was sure he had found the right tracks.

"We will rest for the remainder of the night and begin following these tracks at first light." Ursa told Nicolette and Dahak who had been waiting eagerly for his plan. He had no idea if they were even still alive, or how many enemies they would find, he did not care. His son needed him, and he would find him.

Meath woke. His face was on the cold earth, his hands bound firmly behind his back. He shifted to one side awkwardly and managed to sit up. The drug was still flowing through his veins, making him sway a little - so many thoughts assaulted him and swirled in his head. His sight was hazy and vague, disorienting his senses and nauseating his insides. He shut his eyes, head falling backwards and connecting with something solid - it kept him upright and for that, he ignored the throb of pain. The whole world felt like it was twisting and spiraling out of control.

"Nicolette!" Meath moaned, barely loud enough for him to hear. The sound of his own words seemed to help pull him out of his bewilderment. He opened his eyes again and put all the energy he could into focusing them. He saw Zehava laying a few paces away, obviously still unconscious from the drug's potent influence. Meath gradually took in his surroundings for the first time. They were in an undersized, barred cell located in what appeared to be a larger wooden barn-like building with many other cells like theirs. Everything they had with them had been taken away. Only their clothes remained.

Meath sat there for a long time breathing deeply trying to overcome the drug's effects, before moving again.

"Zehava, wake up!" Meath urged, crawling to his friend on his knees, trying hard to keep his balance. "Zehava, you need to wake up!"

Zehava moaned and started to come around. "What… Where are we?" His groaned weakly and slowly sat up.

Meath could tell his friend was going through the same process he had and gave him several moments for him to clear his head, kneeling patiently at his side

"What is going on?" Zehava managed his eyes open again, eyes darting to take in the scene.

"We must have been captured," Meath whispered. He did not know who might be in the dark room with them, and he did not want to find out until they had fortified themselves considerably.

Meath closed his eyes, concentrated hard on summoning his Gift, before burning through the leather straps that held his hands. Then, he quickly untied his friend while keeping an eye out in case anyone was approaching.

"What is the plan?" Zehava asked rubbing his wrists working the blood back into his hands.

The cell roof was just high enough for Meath to stand up straight. He went over to the thick bamboo bars and looked around. There seemed to be many cells just like theirs, but he could not make out if anyone was in them. The barn reeked of human waste and mould, from various sources throughout. The ground was covered with straw and long dried grasses that had spilled out from the cages.

"They have housed us like animals," Meath whispered, loud enough for Zehava to hear.

"What have we gotten ourselves into?" Zehava said coming up to stand by Meath. "Do you think the others are in here?"

The question got Meath's mind racing, though he doubt a handful of leftover scouts would have been able to overpower Ursa. "Ursa? Dahak? Nicolette?" Meath called out as loud as he dared. The two waited for an answer but there was none.

Zehava grabbed the bamboo bars and tested their strength. "Not going to be able to break them."

Meath grabbed the bars with both hands, and closed his eyes tapping into his innate ability. The wood started to smoke as he burnt them from under his hands, with a firm pull, the two sturdy shafts broke and black ash sifted to the earth.

"I wish I could do that! Think of all the things we could have done back when we were training," Zehava said in awe.

Within heartbeats of being out, Zehava had already found a long, sturdy bamboo pole. He swung it in the air a few times to gain a feel for it. "It does not beat steel but it's better than nothing."

Meath smirked at his friend's new found enthusiasm and was glad he had such a reliable companion at his side. They had been through a lot back in the army - they knew each other's abilities well.

Meath looked around finding only a large knotted branch that was used for beating the dirt from animal hides. "Well, it is no sword, but it should work well enough to help us out of here," Meath said with a sigh at the lack of luck they had gotten.

"I would not try… no escape, if I was you," a raspy voice said from one of the cells in the far dark corner.

Both Meath and Zehava swung around, their makeshift weapons held high, stunned that anyone else was there. They walked over to the cell the voice had come from and looked in at the feeble life form inside.

The man inside was bone thin, his leathery skin sagged from his tiny frame. His ribcage and backbones protruded through what little flesh covered them. Scars plagued his body, crisscrossing each other in more places than not. Years of torture and torment by rod and lash had inflicted them. His hair had thinned to nothing more than a handful of long strands that were misplaced across his head. All he wore was a tattered piece of cloth that was tied around his waist to cover his groin.

"Are you ok?" Meath asked - he knew the question was absurd but it was habit.

The man turned his attention from the ground to face them. His eyes were dark and sunken deep within his skull. "Fine... me fine," he stuttered back awkwardly.

Zehava took another step forward. "What is your name?"

The caged man shifted several inches closer to the bars. "My name... Ke...no, no, NO...lies... LIES! No name no name. Me no allowed...name.... NOT worth...no.... NO...worth..." He cried out confused and frustrated as he fidgeted with something on the floor.

Meath and Zehava listened for a long moment making sure the distraught outburst had not been noticed.

"How long have you been here?" Zehava asked.

"Many moons...many winters..." he mumbled, averting his eyes back to the ground of his cell.

"Come with us, we can free you from this place," Meath told him, grabbing the bars of the cell.

"NOOOOO!" he screeched terrified, diving back into the far corner whimpering. "No disobey... no try again... no."

Meath and Zehava glanced at each other wide eyed in dismay.

"What did they do to him?" Zehava whispered in utter disgust.

"They broke his spirit." Meath whispered back.

Zehava took several steps back from the cell, his eyes glistening with fear of what their future might hold. "I would rather die...than become...like that."

"That will not be us. We will get out of here," Meath snapped back at him, gripping his club tighter.

"You will not make it... stay here better...leave barn only bring pain... only pain..." The man mumbled from his corner rocking back and forth. "Work... obey... no pain... no pain..."

"I will be no one's slave!" Zehava barked louder than he meant to.

"Enough of this... he made his choice long ago. Let us get out of here. There is nothing we can do for him," Meath said, taking his eyes from the cell.

"You will see...no escape...only pain..." he muttered at them, crawling further back into the corner of his cell.

"Shut up already!" Meath hissed back causing the man to whimper and rock all the harder.

They went to the doors of the barn and peered out the small cracks in the wood. Three barbarians stood idly about twenty paces away - cruel looking spears and axes loose at their sides. Beyond the barbarians was what looked to be a small village. Meath counted everyone he saw in his limited view... women and children included. Barbarians trained their women to fight alongside them, so their numbers were much greater in times of need.

"I only see five," he whispered. "There has got to be more than that."

"This might prove harder than we thought," Zehava whispered back.

"If we stay together and kill fast I think we can make it. Once we get to those trees over there we just run for our lives and stay together; we should be able to lose them in the jungle," Meath said pointing to the thick growth of the jungle closest to them.

Zehava looked back towards the cell with the man in it and took a deep breath before looking back at the door. "It is now or never."

Meath kicked the large barn door open and before the barbarians turned to see the escaping duo, he called upon his Gift. A liquid ball of flame erupted from his outreached arm and collided into the chest of nearest savage, igniting his flesh like dry tinder. He dropped to the earth hoping to suffocate the flames that cracked and blistered his flesh eagerly. The other two savages hooted and hollered in battle frenzy and charged them.

Zehava ducked under a wild swing from one of the savages, seeing an opening, he smashed his pole into the back of the enemy's legs, dropping the savage hard to his knees. Zehava reversed direction with a twist and connected with the man's skull enough to stun him. Zehava lunged forward knocking the savage over backwards. Quickly Zehava braced the bamboo pole over the savage's throat and pressed down with all his weight. The savage's hands grabbed the pole and tried to push it off so he could draw a breath, but Zehava was unrelenting. Pushing down with all his strength he felt the windpipe crush and the savage go limp.

Meath was still engaged with the other guard. He could tell the barbarian had many seasons of fighting behind him, but by his lazy spear thrusts, Meath knew the man underestimated him. The moment finally came when Meath saw an opportunity in his defense and took it with a great swing. Meath's club exploded into the savage's face, shattering jaw and cheekbone and dropping the savage to the dirt. With the immediate threat removed, the two quickly moved on.

They crept along the sides of several large thatched and wooden buildings, slowly making their way closer to the tree line. They knew that someone would be coming to see what all the noise was about and their time was very limited.

They came around the corner and were about to bolt for cover behind the next hut, when they were spotted. A barbarian exited the hut they were running for, crying out for help in his native tongue when he saw them.

Meath noticed the savage was not armed - taking full advantage, he charged forward. The barbarian took a step forward before he too realized he was empty-handed. He turned to run back into the hut to retrieve his weapon, but Meath showed no mercy in the savage's misfortune. His club smashed into the barbarian's ribcage with bone splintering force, dropping him on all fours gasping for air. Meath brought the club down hard on top of the savage's head.

"Meath, they know we are missing!" Zehava said catching up to his friend.

"We are almost there." He could already hear the cries of alarm sprouting up all over the camp - their chances of escape were dwindling with every heartbeat.

They ran towards the tree line but stopped short when they cleared the last set of huts. There in front of them stood dozens of barbarians with bows and arrows notched and pointed straight at them. Beyond them was at least twice that number, training with the weapons they had stolen from the dead soldiers back at the river encampment. For a few moments, there was silence, as the barbarians almost seemed startled.

"This is not good!" Zehava said gripping the bamboo pole hard in his hands, not sure of his next move. He licked his lips and looked to Meath.

"No, I think this would be where we give up," Meath said back to him.

"I cannot end up like that guy back there Meath - I would rather die right now."

"There is still a chance we can make it out of this later. Do not give up now," Meath whispered back and they both lowered their weapons slowly, hoping not to startle the bowmen.

One of the barbarians walked out from the group yelling at them in a language neither Meath nor Zehava could understand. He had a fierce appearance and the aura of a leader.

"You think they are going to kill us?" Zehava asked, following the man's finger and went to his knees.

"I think they would have done that already."

"I will not be a slave Meath," Zehava said to him, his voice full of fear.

"Do not give up hope yet," Meath told him, though his eyes did not stray from the massive barbarian who marched towards them.

He screamed down at them picking up Meath's club and raised it high into the air bellowing out something neither understood. He turned to his men and said something regarding Meath's chosen weapon and they all shared a laugh. He turned back to them; his eyes glistening with loathing. With one mighty swing, it all went black for both of them…

Meath came around faintly; he felt himself being dropped hard, to the ground. He tried to open his eyes but they were heavily blurred - the light that assaulted him felt like daggers and he recoiled. His head was pounding violently as he slipped in and out of consciousness. The only thing that kept pulling him back was the voices he could hear around him. He could not understand who they were or what they were saying. He was sure it was in a language that was not his own, but he honestly could not tell. He tried to force himself alert but the vicious pulsing that surrounded his head kept dragging him back down. He felt his arms tingle and move. With all the strength he could muster, he rolled over onto his side and almost lost consciousness again. The voices stopped - he could hear shuffling getting closer to him. He opened his eyes again only to see a dark figure moving toward him. He tried to focus on the figure but suddenly pain erupted through his guts and he curled into a tight ball, coughing grimly and collapsed.

Zehava sat in the cell beside the one he and Meath had escaped from earlier. He had woken a while ago - surprised to find he was not dead and wondering where they had taken Meath. He feared for his friend and his mind played on those fears while he sat in silence. *Had they killed Meath because he had The Gift and was a dangerous threat? Had Meath died from the club to the head? Or maybe Meath had already awakened and they were interrogating him?* So many possibilities and none of them seemed to have a good outcome.

He groaned as his stomach grumbled with hunger. It was becoming dark outside and Zehava questioned himself even more if Meath was even still alive.

Zehava wondered if he should try to escape again, though he doubted he would be able to. The bars of the cells were strong and even if he could get out, the result would likely be the same or worse. Though death was more appealing to him than becoming a slave. He could not make a rash decision until he knew if Meath was still alive or not.

"I told you.... I told you...never make it," the man in the far cell rambled out.

Zehava had almost forgotten about him and was surprised he had not heard him earlier.

"See... see... me was right... me right, you wrong..." He cackled out as if it were an immense achievement for him.

"Yea?" Zehava eyes narrowed dangerously. "Silence you vermin - crawl back to where you came from!"

The man shifted uneasily and shuffled back several inches to the darker side of his cell mumbling to himself. Zehava was in no mood for the man's lunacy.

Zehava sat there in silence for what seemed like forever. He found it hard to believe that the crazed man had once possibly been normal. He found it petrifying that one's spirit could be broken down to that point. What horrific things had they done to be able to destroy all hope? What terrified him most was the thought of that becoming him. Impossible he told himself. He would not succumb to such a fate, ever.

Zehava cursed under his breath and his head banged up against the back of the bars. "Do you know where they would have taken my friend?" The man ignored him as he continued to converse to himself.

"I am sorry I yelled at you - I am just having a really, really bad day," Zehava exasperated, trying to hold back his anger. He needed answers and information and the crazed man was the only one he had. "Please, do you not want someone to talk with? To be your friend?" The man looked back at him seeming to understand and to take interest in him again.

"Me like talk…. Me like talk," he finally replied crawling back closer to the bars.

"Good, me too. Do you know where they took my friend?"

"He magic…" he mumbled. "They will…take…"

"Yes he has The Gift. They will take what?" Zehava probed.

The man rocked back and forth and scratched his head as if deep in thought. "Magic… they take… they keep…"

"Who will take his magic?" Zehava asked intently, worry for his friend growing.

"High Priest take…make stronger…dark practice…pain…much pain…" He rocked harder, his tone almost a whimper.

"What about Meath? What will happen to him?"

The man moved as close to the bars as he could and stared gravely at Zehava. "Death…death will come… death will…will take him…away."

"Of course!" Zehava muttered to himself bitterly. "Do you know when?"

He just shook his head back and forth as he rocked.

"What about me? What will happen to me?" Zehava asked almost defeated.

"No kill… work… no kill…" He replied enthusiastically. "Me work… no die… me work. You work… no die…"

Zehava sat back against the bars of his cell and put his head between his knees. "Slavery… just what I wanted."

Zehava sat contemplating the information he had gotten for some time - not liking any of it. Not all of the information was useless - Meath was alive, at least for now. That gave him some hope, staving off the more defeatist thoughts.

"Where are the other slaves?" Zehava asked, wondering why the cells were not full since they had just overtaken the river encampment.

"All gone… no more…" he stammered. "Just me… now you too…"

"But there were others?" He pushed for more.

"Men and girls… trade… bad men… trade… no want me," the man whimpered.

Just then, the doors to the barn opened and a girl slipped in with a large steaming pot and two clay bowls. The man in the other cell shrieked joyfully and bounded around his cramped cell like a dog happy to see its master.

The girl put the pot and bowls down and began lighting several torches placed in the wall brackets. Soon the place had an orange glow of faint light. She picked up the pot and bowls and set them down again, this time closer to the cells. She was slender; her muscles were toned and smooth to her petite frame, Zehava guessed she was younger than he was by a few years. She wore a simple buckskin skirt that hung halfway down to her knees. It had a high slit up the right leg, to stop constriction and provide flexibility without hindering the wearer. Her top was of the same material. It had a single strap over one shoulder to hold it in place and stopped just shy of her navel. Her hair was a bright auburn ...straight and smooth, it fell halfway down her back.

She dipped one of the bowls into the pot and filled it with the thick stew inside. By now, the aroma had wound its way over and found Zehava. His stomach growled its reminder that it was hungry - so loud in fact, the girl heard and looked up at him. Her eyes caught his and held for a long moment as if intrigued by him. She quickly glanced away, back to the floor, as if she had realized she was staring.

She brought the filled bowl to the crazed man and handed it to him. He took it gratefully and began scooping handfuls of it into his mouth, not caring that it was hot. She watched him for a while, a heartrending gaze on her face in the dim glow of the barn. Zehava found that strange and looked harder to make sure he was seeing the look it appeared to be.

The girl went back to the pot of stew and filled the other bowl slowly, almost unsure of her safety. Her eyes came up and met his again and this time Zehava knew it was not intrigue he had seen before, but sympathy. She averted her eyes again as she brought the stew to his cell. She held the bowl out to him, her eyes avoiding his, but he did not take it. She held the bowl closer to the cell and shook it lightly prompting him to take it, but still he made no move to receive it.

"Why do you not take?" She asked awkwardly, shifting on her feet trying hard not to meet his gaze. He was surprised to find she spoke his language and her accent was not as barbarian as he would have guessed.

"You are not like them," Zehava said moving closer to the bars to get a better look at her. Her skin and hair was more diluted then most of her race and her features not nearly as sharp.

She shifted back uncomfortably several steps. "I am not like them?"

"Your voice, it is so soft and peaceful, not forceful and hoarse like most of your kind. Your eyes are so compassionate and..." he trailed off for a moment, seeing her eyes in the light now. "...and a vibrant blue."

"I am a half breed!" she growled, with more than a little acid in her tone. She put the bowl down by his cell, tired of holding it for him and walked back to the pot of stew.

Zehava knew half-breeds amount the savages were rare. They were an overly proud race and spawning with another race was deemed loathsome and tainted their bloodline. "What is your name?"

She stopped and slowly turned her attention back to him. "Why? My name is of no value to you...slave."

That word hit him hard and resentment flashed in his eyes briefly. Her tone had no conviction behind it - she was merely using it in hopes to silence him. "I did not ask it for value. I just enjoy knowing who I am talking to."

The half-breed eyed him suspiciously, taking a few steps closer to him again. "You are not like most men. You are strange."

"PLEASE more... more eat... more eat..." the broken man cried out and he banged his bowl against the floor.

She went and filled his bowl again then came back to Zehava's cell. "If I give name, you eat?"

Zehava found this too uncanny and it only raised his curiosity about her. "Deal," he said, picking up the bowl of warm stew.

"Name is Shania." A quick smirk crossed her lips, but vanished just as fast.

"My name is Zehava." He put the bowl to his lips and began pouring the mild tasting stew into his mouth. Though it was plain, it stopped the cramps in his stomach.

She filled his bowl again once he was done. An awkward silence followed. She stood there as if waiting for more conversation or maybe just for him to finish with the bowl so she could take her leave.

"What is going to happen to me?" Zehava asked bluntly.

Her eyes shifted uneasily. "I...I not know..."

Fair enough, he thought to himself. She was almost a slave herself, so why would she know. He could tell the question had bothered her, possibly even scared her. What trouble might she get into for telling him anything like that? "So what do you do here, besides feed the slaves?" He asked, the last part rolling bitterly off his tongue.

Before she could answer, the barn doors opened abruptly. A large, imposing barbarian stood towering in the doorway. "Shania! What is taking you so long?" he barked sourly in broken tongues. The crazed man in the cell screeched in terror, tossing his long emptied bowl by the pot and curling up in the corner of his cell, rocking and muttering.

Shania quickly snatched the still full bowl from Zehava and backed away from the cells to the half-empty pot. "I...I...I am sorry...father.... I was leaving...now."

The bulky barbarian walked over to her, his demeanor hard and furious with each step. "Were they giving you trouble?" he growled when he reached her, his eyes burning full of hatred.

Zehava could tell by his movements that he was under the influence of liquor. The way Shania shuddered at his presence he knew she was afraid to death of her father.

"No...no father.... I was..." she started to say, but the meaty grip of her father's hand clenched over her jaw and mouth cruelly.

"I told you to hurry, and you disobeyed!" he hissed down at her, his thick fingers digging into her cheeks. He pushed her away and with the same motion, his hand connected hard across her face.

She hit the ground knocking the stew pot over, her hand instinctively covering where she had been slapped. Tears rolled freely down her cheeks as she trembled, but not from pain, from the fear of what might come next. "Forgive me...father.... It will not happen again..."

He was breathing hard, almost labored breaths of exertion. "Go ready my food," he ordered her - his tone gritty with annoyance his attention shifting toward the crazed cries and mumbles in the cell. Shania got to her feet and bolted out of the barn without looking back.

Zehava watched the barbarian lurch over to the crazed man's cell and grab the bars and shake them violently. The broken man inside cried out, afraid of what might come next.

"You wretched piece of filth, shut up!" He spat angrily. He grabbed a thick branch that lay on the ground and was about to open the cell door. Zehava moved forward on impulse wanting to help the man. The barbarian noticed the moment and his eyes turned on him. "What?" He barked walking over to Zehava's cell. "You want to do something?"

Zehava just stared hard at him. He wanted nothing more than to reach out and strangle him. Though he doubted he would be able to do so, his neck was thick and he stood almost a foot taller than Zehava.

The barbarian grinned broadly as he watched Zehava's face twitching involuntarily, as he tried to restrain his temper. "Your fate will be worse than his," he pointed to the crazed man, "much worse."

Zehava spat down at the barbarian's feet in defiance. The savage's hand dived between the bars and grabbed Zehava's shirt and pulled him hard, into the bars. Zehava tried to pull back but the savage's strength outmatched his own and his head smashed violently into the bars.

"I will break you, vermin!" the barbarian snarled, yanking Zehava's face and body against the bamboo repeatedly.

Zehava tried to find his bearings as he was battered viciously. Finally, the battering stopped and Zehava opened his eyes again to see a meaty fist coming towards him. It connected hard with his jaw, knocking him backward to the ground, dazed.

"You will learn your place soon enough, slave," the barbarian grumbled, kicking dirt in at Zehava then exited the barn.

Zehava pulled himself up, using the bars for support. He rubbed his jaw and was glad to see he had not lost any teeth from the assault.

Meath woke again but did not find himself on the cold dirt floor as he expected. He lifted his head, surprised to find that most of the pain had subsided, though some still pulsed in his sides and he was sure he had cracked some ribs. He tried to move his arms but he could not feel them - anxiety shot through him and pulled him out of the dreamy stupor, he blinked several times before he realized he was upright. He looked up and saw his hands suspended him above the ground. They were tied to a large wooden beam in the center of a large hut. He tried to move his arms again, but they had gone numb from lack of circulation.

He looked around for Zehava, wondering if his friend shared the same dangling fate, but there was no one with him. The room was almost completely bare other than a large wooden table in one corner, which was covered with hide, and a burning fire pit a dozen paces from where Meath hung. There was a small hole in the center of the roof that allowed the fresh air in and smoke to travel out. He hung right above the ground; looking down he noticed there was white powder circle all around him.

Meath has no idea how long he had been out for, or how long he had been hanging from the ceiling. All he knew was dusk was fast approaching by the dimming light outside.

"If they think I am going to hang here all night they have another thing coming." Meath said to himself tapping into his innate abilities to burn the leather cords holding him to the roof beam. A sharp pain coursed through his entire body like Wizard's fire was flowing through his veins. His screams could have awakened the dead. The pain lasted several long moments and he almost slipped into unconsciousness from the intensity - it left him disoriented and his body convulsing.

"You will find your powers no good to you now, Wizard. That circle ensures it." A man said, very calmly as he walked into the hut.

The barbarian was tall and slender wearing a brown leather loincloth with a large white tiger skin draped over his back.

Meath pulled himself out of his pain-induced stupor to focus on the man in front of him. "What is going on? What have you done to me? Where is my friend?" Meath yelled, but he was too weak to have any conviction.

"Your friend is of no concern to you now. You should be much more concerned about yourself. As for your question about what is going on, you have The Gift. I want it!" the man said with a hiss.

Meath laughed at the man, impertinence drawing back some more strength. "You are a fool - that is impossible."

The man looked him in the eyes with a deadly, sure smile. "I assure you, it can be done, and of course you will not survive the ordeal."

"Who are you, you maniac?" Meath questioned trying to keep his tone in check and not give away the fact that he was truly terrified.

The man paced the room not sure of whether he should answer the question or not. "I am one who should not be taken lightly boy."

"What, are you afraid to tell me your name? You are pathetic!" Meath spat at him.

"The one hanging from the roof, powerless, calls me pathetic - how ironic." The man laughed walking just outside of the white circle.

The gleam in Meath's eyes gave him away he knew. He kicked his legs up hard trying to score a hit at the enemy who stood before him. The man just sidestepped with a mocking laugh, watching Meath swing back and forth. It had been a mistake - the leather straps had tightened from the effort, cut into his wrists even more, and caused his shoulders to blossom in an agonised frenzy of burning and pulling pain. Meath cried out again.

"What is in a name to a dead man, anyway? If you must know, I am High Priest Kinor of the Blood Lotus tribe," he laughed, amused by Meath's pathetic attempt.

Kinor walked over to the table and pulled a bone knife and small clay bowl out from under the hide. He came back over to Meath and snarled, slamming a sharp fist into Meath's abdomen, knocking the wind from his lungs. He grabbed hold of Meath's leg and cut deeply into the back of his calf. Meath cursed through his coughing and wheezing. The blood soaked through Meath's leather pants and started to drip towards the ground and into the small bowl Kinor had placed there.

"You bastard! When I get down from here, I am going to kill you!" Meath spat.

"Well, I hate to leave since things are just getting amusing, but I must prepare for the ceremony that will be taking place in two days." The Shaman laughed picking up the bowl of blood and left the hut, without as much as a glance back at Meath.

Meath hung from the beam, his mind racing. As long as he was in this circle, there was nothing he could do. The hours went past, the last of the sunlight faded away, and his thoughts brought him to Nicolette. He wondered if she was okay. He knew Ursa would not let any harm come to her, but the ache in his heart from not knowing grew by the minute. He wondered where they were and if they were going to try to save them. Or did they think that he and Zehava were dead and were just continuing to Dragon's Cove. He shook his head. He could not lose hope, for hope was all he had now.

The cut on his leg bled for a long time until it had scabbed over. He had lost a lot of blood and now the dirt floor below him was stained with it. He tried to force circulation into his arms by flexing them and moving his fingers, but is seemed an insurmountable task, it did give him something to concentrate on aside from his grueling fate ahead.

Zehava had all but exhausted himself in his quest to free himself from his prison. The bars were just too thick and well set in the wooden frame. He had tested every bar top to bottom, but it was no use; his cell was built well for its purpose. He had thought to try to pick the lock that held the door shut, but he could find nothing in or around his cell that would work. Defeated, he sat back down.

He could hear the light breathing from the crazed man to his side. He had thought to try to make conversation with him again, but knew he was asleep and did not have the heart to wake him. The man's dreams were most likely the only joy he had left in his life.

Zehava slowly closed his eyes, and was moments away from sleep's embrace when the sound of the barn door opening stirred him. There was no torchlight following the figure in. The figure was cautious and checked to see they had not been seen entering the barn. Zehava's adrenaline surged as he got to his feet.

"Meath, I am over here!" he whispered as softly as he could, though his enthusiasm was easily detected. "I never thought I was going to see you again."

The figure stopped and looked his way for a brief moment before moving to the center on the barn and kneeled down. Zehava's heart sank at the realization that it was not Meath coming to rescue him. He heard the spilt pot being moved and knew who it was.

"Shania is that you?" he whispered.

She stopped what she was doing and seemed to ponder if she should respond. "Yes...I cannot talk. I must go."

"Are you all right?" He could tell there was something wrong, her voice was faint and somber.

Shania stopped her pursuit to the door. "Why would you care?"

"I am not really sure," Zehava admitted. still remorseful, "maybe because, you and me have something in common."

He heard her disbelieving chuckle in response. "How do you mean?"

"We are both slaves, we both have had our freedom taken from us," he replied.

She stormed up to his cell, holding her face inches away. "I never had freedom - I was born a slave!" she barked, her voice crackling with anger.

Zehava looked closer; the left side of her face was bruised and swollen badly. He moved closer to where she stood, his eyes never leaving hers. "It does not have to be like this you know - I can help you."

"You know nothing," she replied, tears welling up in her eyes.

"I know this is not how life was meant to be," he assured her. "And is not how it has to be. Help my friend and me escape and we will take you with us. You can start your life anew." Zehava saw the twinkle of hope in her eyes at the notion, as fast as it came it faded back to despair.

"My fate is sealed..." she whispered, her eyes falling to the floor. "...Your fate will be no better. They will break you, like him." She pointed to the crazed man who was still soundly asleep. "Or sell you."

"I will never be like him, ever!" Zehava proclaimed sternly.

"Then they will kill you," she told him solemnly.

Zehava felt helplessness sinking in, he had hoped she would see the truth in his words and fight for it, but her spirit had been crushed. "Then release me. Tell me where they are keeping my friend and give me the chance to escape, with or without you."

"You will be massacred before you ever made it to the ceremonial hut."

"At least I will die like a man," he shot back, more angrily than he had intended.

"What is your world like?" she asked, her eyes finally leaving the floor to meet his again. They were full of a forbidden hope.

"It is not like this," he told her, "nothing like this."

Slowly her hands rose up to touch the lock that contained him. A small sliver of metal was gripped tightly in her trim fingers as she pondered her actions one last time.

Zehava's eyes were wide with anticipation. He had not expected this at all ... he had no idea how he was going to be able to free Meath and survive. That part did not matter; he would be free. He licked his lips as she slid the metal into the lock and maneuvered it around until a soft click sounded out, and the lock fell to the floor.

"Thank you," he said, as he opened the cell door to freedom and a gloomy shroud seem to drop from his shoulders.

Shania grabbed his arm and turned him toward her, her expression torn between hope and helplessness. "Take me with you, I beg you…!"

"Ye filthy little wretch!" slurred a deep angry voice from behind.

Shania knew who it was before she even turned around.

"I should have feed ye to the wolves the day you dropped from the womb of that whore!" her father slurred again.

"Father…I was…just…" Shania stuttered terrified.

"Do not dare call me that ye wench. I know what you were trying!" he barked, pulling a malicious whip from his belt.

"No please… no… no…" Shania cried out at the sight of the cruel weapon, knowing its bite.

Zehava snarled and charged, his fist balled tightly, hoping to get to the brute before he could put the weapon to work. But the barbarian was ready for him. Before Zehava could get there, the tip of the whip stung him across the right shoulder and chest, slicing through his light leather shirt and into his flesh. The snap knocked Zehava off balance and he stumbled. He heard the sharp unyielding crack of the whip again and felt a biting pain across his thighs. His legs buckled and he crashed to the floor.

"NOOO!" Shania cried, knowing they were both dead if she did not act. Without thinking, she charged forward and latched onto her father's arm before he could rain down another brutal assault.

"You wench!" he screamed at her. His fist connected solidly with her already swollen face and her grip loosened. He heaved his arm free and backhanded her hard, sending her sprawling to the ground. Swinging his whip back and took aim at Shania. "I am done with you wretched girl! You have caused me nothing but shame."

Zehava lifted himself on all fours just in time to see the tip of the whip slither to a stop just in front him. He lunged forward and grabbed it just as the savage was about to unleash his fury upon his half-breed daughter. Zehava pulled back hard as the barbarian swung, nearly dislocated the savages' shoulder.

Zehava got to his feet, rushed the barbarian, and landed a hard punch, crushing the barbarian's nose flat to his face. He stumbled back a step and Zehava pressed on not wanting to lose his advantage.

He launched several more staggered blows hoping to keep his enemy off balance and defending. He caught movement by the door and knew it was too late when three armed barbarians entered the barn wondering what the ruckus was. When they realized what was happening, they leveled their weapons Zehava's way. He stopped his attack and backed away with a curse.

"You okay?" asked one of the new arrivals with a thick accent.

"What happened?" Another questioned, while he slapped the flat of his sword against Zehava's knees forcing him to the ground.

The barbarian wiped the blood from his broken nose. "The new slave was trying to escape with some help," he replied, turning back to regard his daughter who was on her feet, her eyes on the floor. "Take her to my hut and watch her until I return." He turned back to Zehava with a glare filled with malice. "I have unfinished business with this one!"

"We will stay outside in case you need us," one of the barbarians told him - the other grabbed a hold of Shania. She went with him willingly, knowing if she struggled, it would be worse.

Zehava's mind was blank - his chance of escape had dwindled away before it had ever truly begun. He knew if he tried anything now the man would kill him, though he had to wonder if that was his plan now anyway.

The man stared long and hard at Zehava with an icy, dark glare. It seemed like forever before he moved towards Zehava. He felt a lump well up in his throat when the man let the slack from the whip hit the dirt floor.

"Well slave, it looks like I came in at just the right time." His tone was so cold that it made Zehava's heart stutter right there and then.

Zehava just stared at the barbarian in defeat. There was nothing for him to do anymore. He looked over to the crazed man. He could see him rocking back and forth muttering to himself again, trying to ignore what was happening, hoping the man would kill him. Zehava got to his feet knowing it would enrage the barbarian, and it did. *Die well Zehava, die well*, he told himself, seeing the whip flail back.

Zehava flinched as the first blow caught him across the leg and tore through his leather pants into his flesh. Still, he stood his ground, proud and firm. A second snap left its malicious stain across a forearm. A third and fourth tasted his chest with its fierce sting. Zehava gasped, trying to block out the pain.

Time seemed to stand still - the only sound was the sinful crack of the whip and the heavy breathing of his attacker. Zehava did not even know when he had fallen to the earth, but the cold dirt felt good on his skin.

Each time the whip found Zehava and licked another part of his tender flesh, he clenched his teeth, tears escaping his tightly closed eyes. Never in his whole life could he remember being in so much pain or being so afraid. All he could do was curl up on the floor and hide his head while the enraged man whipped him mercilessly.

Zehava did not even notice that the man had stopped hitting him, his body had become so cold and numb. He lay there in a puddle of blood and tears and stared blankly at the flies that buzzed around to feed on it.

"Get in here now," the vile barbarian called to the others outside. "Put him in his cell and watch him."

The two savages looked at the bloody mess on the floor that had once been a proud man. "Why need watching? He go nowhere. Be dead before sunrise."

"Do not argue!" he barked, leaving the slave barn heading to his hut where his daughter waited, the whip still in hand.

It seemed like hours had passed before he had the strength and courage to move. He was afraid the man might still be watching him, though he had left long ago. Zehava dragged himself into the far corner of his cell, curled into a tight ball, and whimpered himself to sleep.

Shania crept around the barbarian camp stealthy as a shadow in the fading night. Her two curved twin blades in hand at the ready. Dried blood still flaked off the finely crafted weapons, though she ignored that resolutely. She had found the blades a handful of years back - in a pile of supplies her brethren had returned with, after taking out a military supply caravan. She had kept the remarkable weapons hidden. Had her father found them, he would have surely beaten her nearly to death - as he had on several occasions when he had thought her hiding something.

Shania had trained many hours with these blades in secret. She would sneak out of the camps when the warriors were off pillaging or hunting and her father had gone with them. She had watched the warriors train and practice with their weapons and had learned from observing them and then rehearsing the sequences later. On several occasions, she had trained on the corpses of animals and even dead slaves, by hanging them up and running drills on hitting the body's kill points. She had even improved several of the attacks to compensate for her smaller size and strength.

Shania had gone willingly enough with the barbarian back to her hut and she had known before she left the barn what she would do. The man had never expected it and had not even seen it coming. She had granted him a quick death - more out of necessity than respect.

She had thought of escaping the camp then, but knew she would not make it far once her father returned and had seen what she had done. The whole tribe would go after her. Plus, she felt compelled to help the man back in the barn, Zehava, had been his name. He had been kind to her and talked to her as if she was an equal, something she had never had before. Almost like a friend, in truth he was the closest thing she had known to a friend. She had been forbidden to play with the other children growing up; she was not of pure blood.

Shania had waited for her father to return. She knew he would beat her to death. When he had entered the hut, he had not even noticed the body off to the side. His eyes were instead transfixed on the weapon-wielding figure that stood in the middle of room. They had stared long and hard at each other - a lifetime of unspoken hatred spread from her eyes into his. Then, he had just grinned at her patronizingly, until his eyes drifted off to the side where the corpse of her guard lay. His eyes had immediately snapped back to her, her intent clear to him now.

He dropped the slack of the whip to the earth and gritted his teeth. He had not even cocked the whip back before Shania had let loose one of her deadly blades, and followed its course in fast pursuit. Her blade hit true, half the blade's length implanted into his chest. He had not even realized a blade pierced him before Shania was there - her other blade quick to work. A downward slash severed thumb and first two fingers on his weapon hand. Before he could scream, a tightly balled fist connected with his windpipe, stealing his voice. She brought her free blade around low, cutting deep into his thighs, dropping him to his knees. He uttered several curses, before she had ended his wrath forever.

Shania had collected a pack full of things before she made her way back toward the slave barn. She had to make sure he was still alive before she made her next choice.

Shania could hear talking from inside the slave barn and knew the two others were still inside. That gave her hope that he still lived.

She moved to the back of the barn where she knew of several loose boards that she could dislodge silently. A moment later, she was in the barn behind several empty cells. She could see the two guards sitting on stumps around a supply crate, gambling with cruelly carved bone dies.

Shania maneuvered through the cells and crates to Zehava's cell. She almost gasped aloud when she saw the sight before her - she was sure he was dead. She was about to leave when she noticed the rise and fall of his chest. She watched long and hard before making her decision. His breathing was weak but she knew he was not on his deathbed, at least not yet.

She moved through the shadows, back around the way she had come, getting as close to the guards as possible. Though they were still a good dozen paces away, she knew these two men well, through stories she had heard. They were both remarkable fighters and had won the respect of many tribal members for their prowess. It eased her mind a little when she noticed several empty ale jugs beside them. Their postures were sluggish and their coordination was careless.

Shania knew if she acted quickly, she could do it - but if she faltered and they had a chance to react she would be doomed.

She had only ever killed once before this night. Two winters ago, a prisoner, a boy about her age who her tribe had taken from a farmhouse. One night out of some sadistic lust, her father had decided to pit the two against each other. The tribe had forced them both into the middle of the village and surrounded them in a tight circle so there was no escape. She and the boy had been given a dagger and both a separate promise. The boy, if he could kill her, would be set free and for Shania she would finally win the respect of the tribe. Something she had yearned for her whole life; a chance to finally lift the shame. They had both taken the promise to heart as they circled each other, the firmly gripped blades in their hands, and a statement of their intent. Wagers were placed and hoots and howls ensued as the bloodthirsty crowed encouraged the scrap.

It had not been until after she murdered the boy that she learned the promises had been hollow. Shaking her head, she steeled herself and then crouched. She took a deep breath to center herself before she dashed out stealthily towards her targets.

The two barbarians swayed in their seats and slurred making their bets before the die were thrown. All was silent as they waited for the cubes to stop and reveal their marks to prove the winner of the round. The savage on the far side roared in victory as the die landed in his favor. He looked to his champion, continuing his gloating. But his mirth was cut short when he noticed the blood spilling out of his wide-eyed partner's mouth and the two glossy scarlet blades that penetrated through his chest.

It took him several moments to realize what was happening, but when he saw the two crimson fangs disappear and his friend crumble to the earth revealing the assailant, he knew the danger that revealed itself to him. He shot to his feet and reached for his battle-axe , which rested against the crate. But Shania was the quicker. Her left blade sliced clean through muscle, sinew and bone, leaving the savage's outstretched arm on the crate. He stumbled back in shock at seeing the bleeding stump, almost tripping over his seat. Shania was fast to act, leaping over the crate with cat-like agility. Her feet touched the ground and she bolted forward, sinking both blades deep into flesh before he could act further. With his remaining hand, he grabbed Shania's throat and squeezed, hoping to take his killer to the afterlife with him. But his strength was dwindling with each second, his grip now slackening. With one final twist of her weapons, a concluding gasp escaped his mouth and he slumped forward.

Zehava awoke with a moan as something soft and wet touched one of his fresh wounds. Tears welled up in his eyes, as he feared the sight of who was there with him.

"It is okay. I am not going to hurt you," the familiar voice whispered to him, she stroked his blood-soaked hair back and cleaned the wounds on his back and legs. "I cannot believe you alive." She whispered again helping him sit up and start to remove his tattered shirt. Zehava moaned in pain as the shirt pulled free of the wounds it had dried to, re-opening many of them.

"I am sorry it hurts - but I must clean them, or they will fester." She spoke so softly and gently that Zehava imagined it must be what an angel would sound like at death.

"I did not scream," he said. His head began to spin again and he fought to stay conscious.

"I know," she whispered back. She knew that warriors prided themselves on never screaming or begging for mercy when at the hands of an enemy, no matter the pain they were put through. She almost thought it odd that he would hold onto that throughout the ordeal. She had witnessed many of his race, who had so easily given up and begged for mercy or a quick death.

It seemed like it took her forever to clean all his wounds, but once she was done she applied a sweet smelling paste to them. The paste made the wounds tingle and took a little of the sting out of them by numbing them.

She laid him back down, rested his head in her lap, and fed him more of the stew she had brought in her pack to help him get regain his strength. Shania knew he was in no shape to escape that night. He had lost a lot of blood and could barely move. His wounds needed time to close and his focus to come back.

Between mouthfuls, he spoke to her. It took more strength than he though mere words ever could. "Why are you helping me?"

"I do not know," she paused. "I never met anyone like you, and since I first see you I felt connection." Shania stayed silent for a while. "When I look into your eyes I see something I never see before." She tried to stop herself from being caught up in the thoughts that were racing through her mind. "Instinct tell me to trust you."

"I must get out of here," Zehava groaned, trying to sit up, but when he could not, he let his head fall back into her lap.

"You in no shape to escape tonight." Shania replied, trying to think of what to do next. She could not stay within the camp through the following day. The bodies of her father and the three warriors would be discovered.

"Find my friend and free him, he will be able to help," Zehava whispered.

She went silent for a time as she caressed his head with her soft touch. "I be back tomorrow night, and we escape," she told him getting up. "If not here by the full of night," she paused. "Then me dead."

"I cannot leave without my friend," Zehava moaned rolling over to look at her. All she did was nod - her head and then scurried into the darkness, leaving him alone again.

Meath had tried to sleep but could not. His arms ached and his stomach would not let up, while the cut in his leg throbbed. He had no idea what was going to happen and that truly frightened him. What if what the Shaman had said was true? It did not really matter; he knew he was dead either way. He had prayed to the Creator to make sure Nicolette stayed safe. He had prayed for her before he had prayed for Zehava or even himself. He knew he would never see her again.

He had not attempted to use his Gift again, because of what had happened the first time. He never wanted to feel that kind of pain again, and he knew trying would not help. Meath wondered if Ursa knew that such a circle of powers even existed.

Meath looked up through the small hole in the very center of the hut and saw that it was still quite dark out. He had never felt as helpless in his whole life, than he did at that moment. Meath looked up at the hole in the roof again and saw someone looking down at him. He thought it might be Death coming to take him away.

"Who is there?" Meath whispered.

"Shhh." The figure whispered back as it climbed in through the hole and onto the beam above him.

"Who are you?" Meath asked. The slender figure came closer and he could see it was a barbarian girl, her face badly bruised.

"My name, Shania. Will be killed if found here," she whispered back to him, her eyes never stopped scanning the room.

Meath could see her urgency. "What are you doing here?" He could see from her expression she was fighting with her words.

"Me help your friend escape tomorrow night," she paused. "I cannot help you. If escape tonight me could, but not tomorrow."

"Then we will leave tonight!" Meath whispered back eagerly, a new hope filling him.

She shook her head down at him. "He no travel tonight, badly hurt."

"What happened to him?"

"Me tried to help him, got caught. He was punished," Shania whispered down, sorrow in her tone.

"Cut me down and take me too him. We will leave tonight," Meath stammered to her. "All three of us, I can carry him."

The girl seemed to consider his words carefully. She looked up through the hole in the roof. Day was fast approaching. "Not enough time."

"What?" Meath cried up at her louder than he should have. "You cannot be serious. You cannot just leave me."

"Not enough time. Too many awake soon; never make it," she told him directly.

"I do not have until tomorrow night. I need to be cut down tonight or I am dead," he begged her.

She looked down at him again, nothing but remorse in her eyes. "Me can get him out tomorrow night. You, me can do nothing for, me sorry."

"Please cut me down…. You cannot leave me here," Meath begged, knowing this was his one chance and he did not want it to slip away. He looked down at the white powder circle interfering with his Gift. "Just break the white circle for me and I will do the rest!" he urged, looking back up, but it was already too late. She was already gone from sight. He could hear her light footsteps on the roof and then… silence again. He cursed under his breath.

6

Meath watched the sunlight invade the shadows as it slowly spilled over the rim of the hut's chimney. It had been an hour or so since his encounter with the barbarian girl. He had been so angry with her for leaving him there, but in the several minutes after she left, he heard the activity of the stirring camp. She had been right; they would never have been able to make it out alive. He cursed again to the emptiness.

He had tried to keep blood flow in his arms, but it seemed unimportant now. What good would his arms be? He was not getting down alive. This would be his last day on earth he had to accept that. He cursed again, this time at himself. How could he give up? His heart still beat and his lungs still drew breath.

Meath looked up through the hole in the roof and wished he could feel the warmth of the sun that beamed through on his skin. It was touching his tied hands, but he could not feel. He forced his fingers to move slowly at first, then faster and harder clenching his hands into fists, feeling the full burn of blood pumping through them again.

The sun had been up for a while when Kinor finally returned to the hut. He carried a small bag - Meath could only assume that he would be using for the ceremony.

Meath glared hard at the Shaman; bitter hate emitting from his eyes with vicious intent. But the Shaman did not notice. He had not even gazed at Meath yet, as if he had no interest in him whatsoever. Meath found it odd and that angered him more.

Finally, the Shaman looked over to Meath with a tranquil gaze. "Ah, you are still awake. Sleep well?" he asked with a sardonic grin.

Meath bit back his rage that almost slipped from his mouth. He was not about to give the Shaman any satisfaction to his jabs. But the twisting of Meath's lips seemed to be enough for the Shaman.

Meath watched him walk over to the small table and pull the hide off, revealing what was underneath. There were small and large iron knives - some curved, and some as small and as thin as they possibly could be without breaking when cutting into flesh. Beside them were eight metal symbols attached to long metal rods. Meath knew what those were for and he could feel his body start to sweat.

Kinor began to pull small pouches of herbs and powders from his bag, placing them on the table. Once he was done, he called in his savage tongue to someone outside. A large brute came into the hut. Over his shoulder, he carried a slender, elderly man. The brute regarded Meath for a moment, and then with a snarl, looked to Kinor for direction.

"Anywhere!" Kinor snapped aggravated, "then start the fire!" The brute dropped the man to the earth hard and went outside to grab some wood.

Meath watched the man on the ground, he was out cold, several bruises riddled his face and his robes were stained with blood. His robes...Meath's eyes widened, the man on the ground was a Wizard too.

"You two share the same fate," Kinor said, seeing the question in Meath's eyes. "It was so very convenient for my men to come across another true Wizard."

"You are a mad man!" Meath hissed.

Kinor chuckled patronizingly. "Maybe, but soon I will be more than the Creator Himself."

The large brute came back, started a fire in the pit, and waited for his next task.

"Tie him up beside our friend." Kinor ordered, he placed one of the metal symbols into the coals and sprinkled one of the pouches of herbs on the fire.

Meath's heart began to pound in his chest, watching the metal brand heat up, but a slight movement from the old man pulled his attention away. The brute had the old man over one shoulder as he walked over to the beam. His eyes opened quickly to survey the scene and met Meath's for a second.

The old man pushed himself upright in one sudden movement, catching the brute off guard enough that he released his hold on him. Before the Wizard's feet hit the ground, spikes of ice formed off the palms of his hands and he slammed them hard into the brute's oversized chest. With one last surge of will before death sealed his fate, the barbarian swatted the old man hard.

The Wizard crashed to the earth, momentarily stunned from the blow. He lifted his head to see his hand a reach away from the white powder that encircled Meath. He moved his hand out to break the spell that restricted Meath's Gift, but his hand was stopped. A thorny vine tore from the earth entangling it, pulling his arm down violently into the earth up to his elbow, dislocating his shoulder and breaking his forearm.

The Wizard cried out in anguish trying to pull his arm free, but the ground refused to release its prisoner. He shot his free hand up, several small ice shards had already formed in his palm and released with a violent flow of air.

Kinor was ready, with a single thought, a prevailing concussion of air met the lethal assault, scattering the ice blades around the hut. Several of the pieces cut into the old Wizard's defenseless body. Before the Wizard could muster another attack, Kinor launched his own.

"You like ice?" He hissed bitterly, hurling two solid ice orbs at the exposed Wizard. The orbs hit his chest hard, cracking bones one after the other.

Meath hung there helplessly. His blood pumped furiously as he lurched and pulled on his restraints, wanting nothing more than to help the old Wizard who was being battered by the frozen rocks.

Kinor grabbed a handful of white hair and pulled the tattered Wizard up to look him in the eyes. "Was it worth it?" he asked coldly.

The Wizard lifted his hand toward Kinor in defiance. Kinor's face quivered in fury. He grabbed the Wizards arm and released his Gift.

The Wizard howled and thrashed in agony, frost and ice began consuming the length of his arm to his shoulder. Kinor released his arm and it fell to the earth stiff and unmoving. The man's wails continued until Kinor's hand covered his mouth. The Wizard thrashed and convulsed wildly and Meath could smell burnt flesh.

Kinor released his handful of hair and the Wizard fell to the ground, exhausted and silent. Though he still was screaming, only a muffled sound escaped the melted, blistered flesh where his mouth had been.

A lean warrior entered the hut, his eyes darting this way and that, taking in the scene. Kinor's head snapped over to him. "What do you want?"

The warrior's eyes locked with the Shaman's and Meath could see fear in his eyes. He held up his hand and showed the Shaman a bloodied whip. The warrior said something in his native tongue and Kinor's eyes widened.

"Are you sure?"

The warrior nodded his head and said something again that Meath did not understand.

"Find her and bring her to me!" Kinor left the hut and several minutes later two large savages came in and dragged the corpse of their comrade away.

Meath looked down at the old Wizard and wished he had something to say, but there was nothing. The man looked back up at him with regret and apology in his eyes. Meath nodded his understanding. "It is not your fault, you tried."

Kinor entered the hut once again, one of the large warriors in tow. He grabbed the red-hot brand from the fire. "It is a shame you will not feel this!" He pressed it down into the palm of the defiant Wizard's icy arm. Kinor walked back to the table and grabbed a new brand and placed it in the fire.

Meath eyed the Shaman attentively, his adrenaline renewing his strength and will. His eyes narrowed on the sword that hung at the hip of the warrior, his sword. The impressive blade looked small and out of place on such a large man.

"Watch and witness for it will be your turn soon," Kinor growled, clearly annoyed of how things had gone.

Meath lurched forward, his face twitching with anger and hate. He was about to speak when Kinor cut him off.

"What? Hmm, what are you going to do?" he taunted. "Even if you could use your Gift, you are no match for me." As he spoke, the ground rippled underneath him and a platform of steps emerged from the earth all the way up to the edge of the white circle that contained Meath, until he was eye level with him. "I have taken The Gifts of a dozen Masters and a hundred whelps like you, and with each one I grow stronger!"

Meath could smell his breath and a wicked smirk curled across his lips as he spat into his face. Meath embraced the moment and kicked his legs up hard. Kinor did not have time to react and he was knocked off his earthly pillar.

"Stronger maybe, but not smarter," Meath spat again, a defiant smile spreading across his lips.

Kinor scrambled to his feet, his face flush with rage. "You wretch!" he screamed, flames erupting from his outstretched arms.

Meath flinched back as he saw the ravenous flames rush towards him. At least this way he would be killed before the Shaman could steal his Gift. Meath could feel the intense heat from the fire all around him, but no flames licked his flesh. His eyes slowly opened, the heat stinging them. The fury of fire crackled and raged all around him, but did not penetrate the circle. It was as if a wall was stopping the flames from entering. Soon after, the flames dispersed into nothingness.

"Your time will come!" Kinor hissed, grabbing the brand from the fire pit and walked over to the battered Wizard on the ground. The earth shifted and rose exposing the Wizard's frayed, broken arm. He pressed the brand into the palm hard. The old Wizard tried to pull away but did not have the strength to resist effectively. "Bring me a knife and a goblet," Kinor commanded to the warrior who stood dumbfounded in the hut. He was fast to act, lest he anger the Shaman any more than he was.

The Shaman took the blade and ran it across the old Wizard's cheek, freeing the warm blood he was after. He held the cup under the old man's jaw and collected the stream until he was satisfied with the amount.

Meath's stomach turned, watching the Shaman drink every crimson drop from the wooden goblet. His eyes drifted to the brand mark in the Wizards palm and he tried to make out what it was.

"They are the Keeper's symbols. I am sure you have heard of them, 'Hate, Lies, Murder, Devastation, Greed, and finally Death'," the Shaman intervened. "It is His will that makes it all possible, but you will see that soon enough. You will get to watch this one die and give his Gift to me, and then you will give me your Gift."

Meath lurched forward again, his teeth gritted in anger, which only brought a smile to the Shaman's face. He grabbed another one of the brands and placed it into the flames.

Meath's attention turned back to the old Wizard, the earth was rising up with him on it. Vicious vines sprouted around him, latching on and entangling the poor man tightly. As the vines moved and consumed his body, their sharp thorns cut and tore into his flesh. Meath could hear the muffled wails of the Wizard and he prayed the lack of air would kill him before anything else. Only his feet remained uncovered by the thatch work of crimson wet vines.

Meath watched the Shaman burn two more symbols into the man, one on each of his feet. It was sickening to watch the Shaman work, his face was void of anything but satisfaction in his inflictions.

The bloody vines unraveled back to where they had come, leaving behind their lacerated, near-dead victim. Meath could not even tell if the man was still breathing. He hoped for his sake he was not.

The Shaman seemed to notice this too. "Cannot have you die, yet," the Shaman mused. The blood-soaked earthly table shifted forward, rippling the ground as it came to the call of its master. The Shaman place his hand on the Wizard's chest and several of the deep gashes closed as they were force-healed. Kinor turned back to the fire pit and grasped the next symbol. The earthen podium lifted from the back, sitting the Wizard almost upright. Kinor waved the warrior over and the brute tore the tattered robes off, leaving him naked. The brand pressed hard into his chest with a hiss.

Meath could not help but get lost in the splendor and ease of the Shaman's Gift. He was so fluent and motionless, it was almost impossible to tell when or if the Shaman was summoning his Gift. The pure magnitude of his powers was baffling. Meath had to wonder just how powerful the Shaman really was, for his powers had to outmatch that of Ursa's.

The Wizard slumped weakly in his earthly chair - as if on cue the vines returned and slithered tightly around his neck, holding him in place. His hands shot up to grip the choking vines but they were already entangled and going nowhere. He kicked and thrashed futilely. His air was being cut off and his face began turning purple.

Kinor lifted the final symbol up and pressed it hard into the Wizard's forehead. The Wizard's eyes rolled back into his head, he began to thrash and spasm artificially. Several of his restraints snapped from the unnatural force he seemed to now possess. His screams were muffled at first by the melted scab where his lips had once been. Soon the wails broke free, tearing through their cauterized cage with deafening tones from an unholy source.

Finally, the Wizard's body collapsed and went limp. The Shaman slashed the Wizard's throat and filled his wooden goblet again with blood, and drank it hastily. He dropped the cup to the floor his face and body began convulsing uncontrollably. His muscles pulsed and contorted freakishly on his skinny frame. The veins in his arms twisted and bulged, as if full of maggots and worms trying to break free.

The Shaman dropped to his knees in what appeared to be agony. The temperature in the hut dropped substantially, so each exhaled breath was fully visible in plumes. The flames of the fire died down and wavered out, leaving the hut a gloom narrowed dark.

Meath's eyes widened tremendously - the dead Wizard's body went rigid and the muscles snapped taunt. His mouth jolted open so wide the jawbones cracked, leaving his maw gaping. An eerie, disturbing howl escaped, sending a shiver up Meath's spine.

Kinor crawled nearer to the dead Wizard - he was breathing hard, labored exhalations as he waited eagerly. The howl stopped and a wraithlike vapor hesitantly ascended from the body. It pulsed and radiated a raw aura of power, causing the large warrior to stumble back out of the hut in retreat.

Meath was so caught up in the moment; he had to remind himself to breathe. The aura fought bitterly as it descended down toward the waiting Shaman. Unholy light flashed in a fury and the still air of the hut pulsated in defiance at the aberrant act that was occurring. Slowly the Shaman absorbed the translucent essence, until there was nothing left.

Kinor collapsed to the ground in exhaustion, his breathing so shallow and weak his chest did not rise. Meath wondered if the event that he had just witnessed had killed the Shaman - he could only hope.

Much time passed and still the Shaman did not move, but finally the large warrior who had run off entered the room apprehensively. Seeing the Shaman face down on the ground seemed to ease the warrior's mind. He came in, collected the dead, naked Wizard, and carried him out.

Meath was sure the Shaman was dead, and had to wonder what was going to happen to him now. But a slight movement of dust under the Shaman's lips alerted Meath. He was not dead. Slowly his breathing strengthened and his chest began to rise and fall noticeably.

Meath had watched the Shaman slowly drag himself up onto the earthy chair he had summoned during the murder of the old Wizard. He could barely keep himself upright. Meath wondered if he even knew where he was.

Meath clenched his fists again to keep the feeling in them. He could not stand the waiting any longer and knew if there was any hope of him getting out alive, he had to try again. He pulled himself up and grabbed a few inches above where the rope was tied to his hands. His arms and shoulders bugled in strain and exhaustion. The beam that held him creaked with the new movement. Once the weight was off, he could feel the rope loosen slightly around his wrists. He moved his hand up another inch and tried to loosen the knots that bound him, but it was too late. Fatigue overwhelmed him as sharp stabs of pain besieged his shoulders and back as the muscles knotted and spasmed. His grip loosened and he fell. The rope pulled taunt, digging into his flesh as his wrists took the brunt of the strain. He cried out in pain, feeling the fresh, warm blood stream down his arms.

"Still trying?" the Shaman asked, sarcasm thick in his weak voice. "Your Gift is mine - your life is already over."

"You son of a bitch!" Meath spat.

"She was worse than that," the Shaman chuckled.

Meath concentrated his Gift again on the leather ropes that bound him. Hoping, praying for some miracle. Again, agonizing pain spiked through his entire body like wildfire. Meath lapsed into semi-conciousness.

"The young are so foolish." Kinor took a long hard swallow from a water sack.

Meath's eyes refocused as he regained most of his senses. He gritted his teeth and unleashed his Gift again. His body convulsed violently from the inner assault. Vomit and blood trickled out his mouth and onto the dirt floor.

"What is the matter with you?" the Shaman asked, his attention turning to Meath, who was summoning his Gift again and again. "How dare you try to rob me of your powers!" He jumped to his feet, but did not make it more than a few steps before he collapsed from disorientation and weakness. Quickly, he called out in his native tongue and the large warrior came running in and surveyed the scene. "Stop him!"

Meath was about to summon his Gift again when a sudden burst of pain erupted in his midsection, stealing his breath. He wondered if his insides had exploded. He figured his brain would shut down or his heart would stop first. But this would kill him all the same. His victory would be bittersweet....

The smell of cooking meat wafted up and making his nose tingle. He could not place the scent … meat? He was sure it had to be exotic. He knew he had smelled it before, but where? He wracked his mind trying to remember, but his head hurt. A constant thumping pulsed through his skull - he was sure his ears would pop and his eyeballs would burst soon. Battle scenes flashed vividly in his mind. Towns and villages slaughtered and destroyed. Left in ruins, smoldering fires, waiting for the scavengers to come and do their job. Smoldering fires? Why did that stand out in his mind? The odor of burning meat assaulted his senses again. Flesh, human flesh was the smell. Yes, he was sure of it now; he had smelled it a dozen times before in battle. But why now, had he fallen in battle? Had the scenes he had so vividly seen been his last moments? A sharp stringing feeling engulfed his right foot and then was accompanied by the burning flesh scent again. It was him! He was burning!

Meath's eyes shot open frantically, and he kicked his right foot hard, hoping to free it from the fire that was consuming it. His foot connected hard with something, but it moved from his force. Slowly his eyes focused - he was in a hut. There were two men in the room with him - a large fierce man standing a dozen paces away looking angry, and a skinny frail man lying confused on the floor. No not confused, that was not the look, annoyed, yes that was it. He held in his hands a metal pole with a strange symbol attached to it - it was red hot. Then Meath remembered, it all flooded back to him.

"I was hoping you would come to and not miss your own death," Kinor hissed, wiping the blood from his nose.

The large warrior rushed over, helped the Shaman back to his feet, and stayed close in case he stumbled again.

Meath's head pounded - a thousand war drums all going off at once. His vision blurred horribly from the increasing pain shooting through his entire body. Nausea and exhaustion battered him like a club as he fought to keep his head up. He vomited what little he still had left in him and it dripped down his chest and legs to the earth.

Kinor motioned to the large warrior to grab the next brand and bring it to him as he tried to keep his balance. The warrior placed the metal brand in the Shaman's ready hand who stumbled as the weight of it nearly sent him off balance. The warrior walked over to Meath and grabbed his legs tightly in a bear hug, squeezing them so hard Meath thought they would break. The brand pressed hard against the bottom of his left foot. Meath tried to pull his legs free and fight it, but his body did not respond. A loud hiss and a slight tingling sensation spread up his leg.

The Shaman dropped the brand to the ground, not waiting to waste any unnecessary energy. He stumbled backward and would have fallen had the warrior not been fast to react and catch him in time. The Shaman lowered himself to the ground, in a half-sitting half-laying position while the next symbol was placed in the fire.

"It will all be over soon," the Shaman coughed out, his voice weak.

Meath just glared down at him bitterly. A small trickle of blood and saliva escaped the corners of his mouth. He tried to summon his Gift once more, but he did not have the strength, or the concentration to do so. He would wait for it - he would stare death in the eyes. He just had to hold on a little longer and then it would be over with. Two more symbols and his fate would be sealed.

Meath grinned to himself looking up through the chimney, it was almost dark outside already. Zehava would be escaping soon with the savage girl, if he had not already. Meath hoped he was already gone and far away. He would be travelling to Dragon's Cove to meet up with the others. Then they would be able to strike back at the false Prince. Nicolette would be able to start her life again. He could feel several tears stream down his swollen cheeks. He would never see her again. The thought tugged hard at his heart. But then, he would not be there to confuse her anymore. It was foolish for them to think they could be together; this was just fate's way of proving it. He just wished he could see her beautiful face one last time and tell her he loved her. He had always loved her, from their very first meeting in her father's garden....

"Hey!" A voice barked out at him. Meath's eyes opened again to see the Shaman wobbling in front of him, his balance still shaky and weak. "Stay with me, we are almost done."

At first, all Meath could hear was the hissing of blistering hot metal on flesh over his heart, then came that smell again accompanied by a fierce stinging on his chest. His breathing was shallow and labored - he fought the urge to cry out. He refused to give the Shaman the satisfaction. He was glad Nicolette would not see what was done to him here. It would be too much for her. His death alone would be so much for her to bear after all those she loved had already been killed.

Greed - that was the symbol that scarred his chest now. Only one more symbol to go, Death. It would be all over after that. His body itched and quivered from the inside, as if unseen parasites were moving through him. His nerves all pulsed together. He could not determine if it was pain he was now feeling or not. No, not pain - he knew pain. This was different, some queer sensation that he could not even begin to describe.

Zehava woke with a gasp of agony. He had rolled over in his sleep and several pieces of straw had assaulted his wounds like needles. Slowly he rolled over and pulled the sharp grass out of his oozing wounds. The urge to just roll back over and let weariness overtake him into slumber again played in his mind. His muscles were stiffening and sore. If he were going to be able to escape without being useless, he would have to start moving his body.

Zehava pushed himself up slowly, trying not to break open the fresh scabs. He grabbed his cell bars firmly in both hands; he took deep hard breaths pulling himself up to standing position. Had his hands not been gripping the bars, his knees would surely have buckled. "Ata boy Zehava," he whispered to himself.

"You alive, you still alive!" The crazed man screeched aloud, bounding in his cell.

Zehava had forgotten all about the other prisoner and the sudden outburst from him startled Zehava. He fell backwards - his hands grabbed the bars at the last moment, halting his crash, but only for a second. The weight of his body snapped his arms taunt, forcing him to flex his muscles to support the weight. Several of his scabs cracked and tore open - the pain was too much, his grip released and he crashed to the floor. Zehava buried his mouth into his arm to muffle his cries of agony.

"Me sowwie, me sowwie!" the crazed man cried out bouncing around his cell. "No mean...hurt...no mean hurt!" He pushed his head tightly against his cell bars eyeing Zehava benevolently.

Zehava centered his breathing and forced the pain back. He wanted to yell and scream, but it was not the man's fault. "I am ok."

"You…you no…no mad?" the man whimpered, watching Zehava push himself back up.

"I am fine, really," Zehava replied through gritted teeth, resting up against the bars. Many of his wounds were bleeding and oozing now - he used the last of the salve Shania had left for him.

"Good, you are still alive," Shania whispered, unlocking his cell.

Shania's sudden presence startled Zehava. He had not even heard her or anything for that matter. She helped him to his feet and walked him out of the cell.

"No escape…no, no, no, no…" the distraught man squealed shrilly, "pain, more pain…"

"Shhh," Shania walked over to his cell and bent to him. He came to her waiting hand like a dog to its master. "You stay silent," she cooed to him, dropping several pieces of cooked meat into his lap. He grabbed the meat and scurried off to the far side of his cage, hording it.

"You got my things?" Zehava said picking up his sword. It seemed a lot heavier than he remembered. The cold wooden handle felt good in his hand - it soon warmed under it as he strapped it back to its rightful place on his hip.

"Personal possessions lift spirit," she replied, picking up the large leather backpack she had brought with her. "Man needs weapon to survive."

"Hopefully, we will not need to use them." Zehava looked around but did not see any of Meath's things. "Where is Meath?" he asked her.

Shania's stare dropped down, trying to avoid his eyes, as she thought of what to say. She had not had much time to think about what she was going to tell him and now that the time was here, she was feeling guilty.

"What is going on? Where is he?" Zehava stammered out, taking an uneasy step toward her. She flinched back.

"I…I coul—" she stuttered, her eyes locked with his now. The look he was giving her cut her very soul. "I could not save him."

"What do you mean you could not save him? Where is he? Is he still alive?" he barked, grabbing her by the shoulder, out of frustration and to help steady himself.

"He is with the Shaman - I could not free him. Would have been caught, everyone die," Shania explained, her eyes welling up with moisture.

"Is he still alive?" Zehava shouted, louder than he had intended. Shania's eyed the ground again nervously. "Not for long."

"Where is he?" he growled.

"Large hut, at the far end of the village."

He pushed her away hard as he stumbled for the large barn doors.

"You never make it - they kill you!" she cried out to him. "Your friend might already be dead. We can make it, you and me. Two lives for one."

"He would not leave me behind if there was a chance I was still alive," he barked back, drawing his sword.

"They kill you before you make it to him." She ran to his side and pulled on his arm.

Zehava yanked his arm from hers with a snarl; several more wounds opened. He continued his way to the door before he stumbled and collapsed to the ground. He let out a loud curse as he pushed himself back up, using his sword for support. His anger fuelling him now.

"No go, no go!" the man cried from his corner again.

"SHUT UP!" Zehava hissed back and the man curled into a ball whimpering.

Zehava took several deep breaths, gathering his wits and will to move. He looked back to Shania. Her eyes were glimering and confused. "True friendship is so much more than life and death."

He pushed open the barn doors almost falling over as he did so. He stumbled forward, the tip of his sword cutting a thin line into the dirt beside him. He could see activity all around him from the corners of his eyes, but no one seemed to take notice of him. One foot in front of the other, he forced himself on - toward the hut.

The cool night air helped clear his head, but also nipped at his oozing wounds. His breaths were labored as he fought through the pain of walking. He did not care anymore - he knew he was going to die. He accepted it.

Attentions were piqued as the feeble warrior staggered pitifully across the village. A crowd gathered in his pathway towards the hut. Warriors, children and women, watched him, pointing and laughing.

Zehava stopped a dozen yards away from the crowd, wondering why they had not cut him down already. *I will not be taken prisoner again*, he promised himself. He lifted his blade and tried to form his stance. Blood from his open wounds ran freely down his arms and legs, dotting the ground beneath him.

The group all broke into a howling laughter when they watched the wounded warrior lift his sword. One of the warriors stepped out and challenged him, grabbing a small dagger from one of the children. He turned to the crowd and said something as he pointed to the dagger. They all laughed aloud. He turned back to Zehava and mocked his pathetic threat, by raising the small dagger in the air. The group of savages howled all the louder.

Zehava clenched his teeth - he wanted to die with dignity. He tightened his grip on his sword. His nostrils flared in defiance, as he went forward to meet his challenger.

The camp grew suddenly bright behind the clustered group of barbarians. Two massive spheres of fire assaulted the tightly formed group, bursting on contact. Flames erupted and tasted all those within its range. By the time it was over, many bodies lay unmoving and blackened, while many more still tried futilely to quench the hungry fire's appetite by rolling on the ground frantically. The group pushed and battered each other aside, showing no remorse for anyone but themselves.

The blast caused Zehava to falter and hit the ground hard. The brute who had challenged him now ran toward him maliciously with his dagger held high. Zehava lifted his head up, disoriented and stunned at the scene unfolding around him. He saw the charge and knew he could not stop it. He stared into the savage's fierce eyes and the man jerked suddenly, stumbled, and crumbled to the earth in a heap, two arrows protruding out his back.

Zehava strained his eyes trying to make sense of what was happening. The savages were scrambling all over, pushing each other to the ground trying to escape the attack. He swore he saw Dahak break from the tree line dropping a bow and charge into the midst of his terrified enemy.

Zehava felt a hand on his shoulder, he looked up and Shania began pulling him away from the battle that was unfolding.

Ursa lifted up his arms and powerful arcs of energy escaped, striking another large group of savages who were frantically searching the scene for answers. The arcs tore through their targets, leaving charred gaping holes in their stunned dying victims. Others stared down in disbelief at the blacken stumps where a limb had once been.

Nicolette stood beside Ursa, dagger gripped tightly in one hand and the small crossbow Adhar had given her in the other. She aimed the small but powerful weapon into the scattering enemy, trying to pick a target, but she was shaking hard. Ursa had told her only to fire when she had a sure shot. The string released, sending the small but deadly bolt flying. It struck an unsuspecting savage in the spine with enough force to sever it. The brute fell to the ground sprawling, no longer in control of his legs. He had not crawled far before Dahak finished him with a downward thrust of his blade.

Ursa summoned another ball of flame, casting it at a small group of archers that were establishing a formation by one of the huts. They had notched their wicked arrows to fire back at the intruders. Their eyes widened with terror when the Wizard's fire closed the gap in a heartbeat. They did not even have time to cry out before the flaming sphere overwhelmed them in a aberrant inferno.

Dahak ran straight ahead into the throng, slashing and hacking the disoriented enemy before they could defend themselves. Blood soaked his arms and legs as he opened a savage's bowel with a fierce swing. He had never been so focused or scared in his entire life. In the army, he had never been in the front lines of an attack. He had always been in the backlines finishing off the wounded. He had not the nerve or the skill to lead a charge. Now he did not care, he wanted his friends back.

Dahak swung his sword low, avoiding a barbarian's high shield and biting deeply into his thighs nicking bone and crippling his target. He turned just in time to see a duo of savages charge him, their spears leveled. Without thinking, he hurled his sword end over end at the charge - it embedded with a cracking thud into an attacker's chest ending that threat. He barely was able to sidestep the other's mad thrust for his midsection. Instinctively he pulled his dagger and stabbed deep into the enemy's exposed side, slipping through ribs and into the lungs.

Dahak pulled his bloody knife out with a twist, gore poured freely from the fatal wound. The savage tried to crawl away between coughing fits as his lungs filled up with blood. He quickly picked up the fallen man's spear and threw it at another charging barbarian. The spear missed its target and the man continued toward him with his axe in hand, yelling a savage war cry. Dahak froze, closing his eyes and held his breath as he realized his time had finally come. Most warriors wanted to see their death coming. Dahak did not.

A lifetime seemed to pass before Dahak had the courage to open his eyes again - the man laid dead a few paces in front of him, a small bolt sticking out his side. Dahak wasted no time retrieving his sword - he pried it quickly out of the gurgling enemy's chest. His hands gripped in tightly and he drew a deep breath and charged forward again. The enemy was becoming more organized and Dahak realized he was taking more than his fair share of cuts and gashes. His attacks were more forced and labored as he began to tire.

"What is going on out there?" Kinor staggered, gripping the final brand tightly. "Go find out!" he hissed to the large warrior in the room with him. The Shaman snarled at the inconvenient timing of the distraction. He stared at Meath, his chest raising and falling from his deep labored breaths. Sweat streaked down his weary face and trickled fat drops from his pointy chin.

Meath's head hung - lack of strength made him kitten-weak. His body tingled and pulsated with strange, unnatural energy. He was not sure if it was death approaching or his Gift preparing to leave him. Either way, he was not able to do anything about it. He though he heard screams outside, but was not certain he was hearing anything at all.

The warrior rushed in moments later. "The camp is under attack!"

"By whom?" the Shaman cried in shock, almost dropping the metal brand to the ground.

"A powerful Wizard is laying waste to our army - he must be leading an army in retaliation to the river settlement," the warrior cried out, drawing Meath's sword from his hip and guarding the door, expecting an attack.

The Shaman growled in frustration, lifting the last symbol up to Meath's head. He held it there for a long moment, his facial expressions twisting with inner turmoil. He cursed, angrily lowering the symbol. "We need to leave - I am too weak to fight off a powerful Wizard and his army."

When no reply came, he turned his attention to the door, his helper was on his knees gasping for air, his hands trying to grasp the tiny bolt embedded in his chest but his hands seemed not to want to cooperate. A girl stood in the doorway fumbling with another bolt as she tried to reload. Her gaze darted toward the Shaman then back toward her crossbow.

"You little wench!" the Shaman hissed, finding a new dose of strength, he hurled the metal brand her way. The metal bar smashed into her legs, she cried out and her finger pulled the trigger of her crossbow, the awkwardly placed bolt fired, scoring a deep grazing hit to the Shaman's shoulder. He hissed in pain. Clearing the distance, he backhanded her to the ground. He was about to strangle the life from her when a quake shook the hut - he heard screams of death from outside and knew he did not have a moment to waste. "We will meet again." He disappeared from the doorway.

Meath hung from the beam and had to force himself not to black out while he looked down at the female on the ground. He recognized her from somewhere, but he could not place where. He could not keep his thoughts together long enough as his world fazed in and out of blackness. He wished he could go to her and help her up, but he could not move - he could not even feel his body anymore.

"Meath!" she cried weakly pulling herself off the ground. "What have they done to you?" She ran to him, repulsed by the sight in front of her. His body was battered and limp - bruises and blood covered most of his torso. Cuts and burns riddled his flesh.

Nicolette grabbed his sword that the dead warrior had dropped and cut through the leather ropes that had held him to the beam for the last day and a half. He fell to the earth with a crash, and lay there, motionless. Nicolette lifted his head and cradled it in her lap crying, believing he was already dead. *Are we too late?* She thought to herself.

Ursa and Dahak soon ran into the hut and saw Nicolette holding Meath's limp body. Ursa's eyes focused on the white sand circle that she was lying in and cursed under his breath.

"Are we too late?" Dahak cried, also thinking Meath was already lost. His eyes shot back to the door, making sure the enemy were not aware they had disappeared.

Ursa ran over to Meath, being careful not to go inside the circle, and felt for a pulse. "No, he is still alive, barely. We need to go now - we cannot stay a moment longer."

"What about Zehava?" Dahak cried, turning his attention from the door to Ursa.

Ursa was just about to speak when a savage girl burst into the room, knocking the distracted Dahak to the ground hard. Dahak scrambled backward holding his sword up. Ursa was about to unleash a deadly assault when she spoke.

"No kill me, me help, come with me, me help!" She blurted out frantically licking her lips, her eyes moistened with fear and uncertainty.

Dahak got to his feet, the tip of his blade not leaving her. "What do I do?"

"Please, other friend is waiting. We have horses," she replied, fearing for her life as she looked outside again. Dahak looked out the door and saw Zehava swaying like a branch in the wind on one of the horses.

"She is not lying, Zehava's out there!" he assured Ursa and Nicolette with a confused smile.

"We do not have time to question our luck. Grab Meath - we have outstayed our welcome," Ursa ordered, he went outside and unleashed several more attacks on the burning camp.

They had only been in the village for a few moments and it already looked like two armies had clashed in a full-scale war. Huts and buildings were collapsing under themselves as flames gutted them. Blackened, broken bodies scattered the scene all around them, as still most of the enemy had no idea what was going on. They searched for the enemy army, which they believed to be attacking or fled for their lives into the dense jungle.

Dahak used one of the fallen savages as a step to help him throw Meath's limp body onto a horse. Ursa finished another violent attack then mounted on the horse in front of Nicolette.

The young savage girl was already mounted behind Zehava. He looked just as bloodied and beaten as Meath did. He had no shirt on and Dahak could see the whip marks and bruises that scorned his body.

"Follow me!" the girl yelled, spurring her horse into a full gallop wasting no time. They did so without question. Dahak rode along with Meath so he could keep him on the horse.

They followed the savage girl down a path that was just wide enough for a horse. Two barbarians rode hard after them in pursuit. They were able to make easy time catching up with less weight on their beasts.

"We have trouble behind us!" Dahak yelled to Ursa holding on frantically to Meath's bouncing, limp body almost losing him several times.

Ursa quickly turned and looked back. He was already weak from using a great deal of his Gift; he did not want to waste any more than he had to. He knew he still had to heal Meath and Zehava. He aimed his arm back to the oncoming warriors - they were yards away, weapons ready.

A torrent of solid air tore the first warrior from his horse, a handful of horse's mane thick in his hand. He sailed through the air like a twig into the savage behind him, toppling man and beast into a mangled heap.

"I think we finally lost them," Dahak murmured tiredly, coming back from scarching the area. Most of his wounds had closed over with fresh scabs and only a handful would require any attention at all.

The group had almost ridden their horses to death before finding a spot where they could hide safely for the night. Though they doubted the barbarians would pursue them any longer. They would be busy putting out the fires and organizing what was left of their camp.

The small party all sat around the two wounded members while Ursa worked what energy he had left to heal them. He sat between the two young men, his hands placed flat on their chests. His breaths were deep and ridged he concentrated his mind fully. He knew this would weaken him to a point of self-harm. But he had no choice. The hairs on his neck stood on end as he forced his energy down his arms into the two men. Slowly, the cuts and burns on both men`s bodies began to mend and close right before the others' eyes. Ursa's body began quaking uncontrollably as he forced his mind harder to continue, knowing the repercussions. The wounds began to heal slower as his powers weakened. The smaller wounds had closed entirely and the scars now faded. The larger wounds were closed over and dwindling into themselves, slower and slower. Ursa's eyes rolled into the back of his head as his mind wavered in and out of consciousness. The wounds stopped healing and the great Wizard crumbled to the ground.

"Ursa!" Nicolette cried out going to the old Wizard.

Shania eyes widened in panic at the fallen Wizard. "What happened to him?"

"He must have used all he could," Nicolette replied, pushing the Wizard over so he was on his back. He looked weak and fragile - sweat drenched his long white hair. His facial lines seemed to be much more defined than she remembered. His eyes were sunken into his skull and his lips were ashen. She looked over to Meath - most of his wounds had healed completely, and only one remained. A deep fleshy burn above his heart, it was still blistered and fresh and had not been healed in any way. "What were they doing to him?" Tears welled up in her eyes.

Shania looked up at her. "The Divine Shaman, Kinor, was stealing his magic." She reached into her leather pack and pulled out a small clay container and started applying a white paste to Zehava's few remaining wounds. None of them were bad anymore. But one could never be too careful in the jungle - infections and parasites could fester the smallest wound.

"Are they going to be all right?" Dahak knelt down beside the three downed companions. "They look like they are going to..." He cut himself off not wanting to say the word, but he finished in his head, "...die"

"I do not know," Nicolette sobbed, fear shading her face at the possibility that everything might not be okay.

Dahak saw the worry on her face. He wished he could think of something positive to say in reassurance, but he could not think of anything. In truth, he was just as worried. He retrieved the horse blankets and covered the three unconscious companions. Before he sat down again, he scanned the area thoroughly. If they were ambushed now, they were dead.

"Why did you help us?" Nicolette asked, her glistening eyes searching Shania's.

"I...I...do not know," she confessed, meeting Nicolette's eyes with confusion. "Something inside soul said to."

Dahak and Nicolette exchanged glances full of uncertainly. Neither knew what to make of this strange new companion.

They all sat silently for several long moments, a certain awkwardness in the air. Dahak could tell she was a half-breed and had to guess her life with her people had not been an easy one. Her accent was there, but her English was surprisingly good. Dahak rubbed his arms flaking off the dried blood. He noticed many of his wounds were still bleeding slowly and were deep.

"Highness, you should get some sleep," Dahak said. "I will stand watch tonight."

Nicolette could hardly keep her eyes open anymore. They had only gotten a few hours of sleep the night before. Ursa had insisted, knowing they would not be of any help to Meath and Zehava if they were not alert.

She smiled tiredly at him and nodded. "I guess you are right."

Dahak and Shania sat there, an awkward silence hovering in the air. Dahak fidgeted around, flaking more dried blood off his body, finding all his serious wounds. He could not help but steal quick glimpses of the savage girl. She was surprisingly attractive. Her features were smooth and soft and her frame was petite but toned. Unlike full-blooded barbarian woman, whose features were hard and sharp and their build bulky like a man, she had a touch of the ethereal and soft about her. Even in the faint light of the moon through the canopy of trees, he could see her striking sapphire eyes. They pierced through the obscurity almost like that of a jungle cat.

"Me can help with wounds," Shania said timidly, noticing him staring at her.

Dahak's eyes shot to the ground and his cheeks flushed with embarrassment. "I...um.... I would...um...thanks," he stuttered.

Shania poured some water from one of the skins onto a rag and began wiping the dirt and blood off him. Most of his wounds were nicks and small cuts, but he also had some deep lacerations across his arms and back.

"Ouch! Damn it," Dahak growled as she cleaned out the deepest wounds.

"Almost done," Shania told him. Once she had finished cleaning them, she applied the same white paste that she had on Zehava, to help stop infections and to help ease the pain.

"Thank you. I had better go stand guard. You should get some sleep too," his eyes trying their best to avoid hers.

Dahak watched the camp from a distance. He realized though, that if they were attacked during the night, they would all likely be killed. He stood with his back against a large tree staring off into the night, thoughts of the battle flooded back to him. He could not believe it had all happened, and that he had survived, that any of them had. It was all so much, so intense, so alive and so fulfilling. As he remembered the night's events, his adrenaline began pumping into his system again, helping him stay alert and awake.

7

Two hardened riders rode past the group of armed soldiers with a nod. They were piling bodies in two separate heaps - the Sheeva camp defenders in one, the enemy in the other. Draco's soldiers refused to burn the bodies of their enemies with those of their own. The defender's bodies would be cremated first - in belief that the enemy dead would have to watch them ascend to the afterlife before them.

The riders pasted under the still smoldering, blackened gateway. Their horse's hooves already tainted with thick blood and gore from the soiled earth. Once they were inside the walls, the smell of death was no longer just a lingering odor in the air, but an overwhelming stench that made even the veteran soldier's stomachs queasy.

The small contingent of soldiers had not been there long. Already cleanup was well under way. The remaining fires had been quenched, the unstable buildings were being torn down and the bodies were being collected.

"What happened here?" Rift jumped down from his tanned stallion.

The firm faced Captain turned to meet his questioner. His eyes lightening a little from their impassive state. "Rift, what brings you out here?" the Captain asked. "No matter - that is none of my business. What does it look like happened? The encampment was slaughtered. How, we do not really know. Looks like they simply were overrun, by wave after wave of enemy warriors. From the bodies we have found it was a collective effort from a handful of tribes." The Captain sighed in frustration. "Their weapon reserves were low. A new consignment was on its way; it must have gotten here too late." He pointed over to the supply wagon that rested in the middle of the encampment.

"The supplies were here?" Rift asked.

"They were here when we arrived." The Captain ran his dirt-stained hands through his damp hair.

"Where are the soldiers who were with the wagon?" Rift inquired, watching a group of soldiers load severed limbs into a large wagon. Thick blood dripped from the ceases of the wagon and onto the already crimson dirt.

"Killed maybe? Ran off perhaps," the Captain shrugged his shoulders as if it did not matter.

Rift looked to Shahariel with a nod and the tracker went to the wagon to search it.

The Captain raised his eyebrow with intrigue. "So I guess the rumors are true then?"

Rift nodded back to him grimly, confirming the Captain's unspoken question.

"Figures, our Kingdom is at its weakest with the death of our King and these bastards decide to start working out their differences." the Captain muttered bitterly.

"She was there," Shahariel said coming back. In one hand, he held several long brown strains of hair. "I found it stuck to one of the wooden crates. It is her hair."

The Captain wrinkled his face curiously. "How can you be sure? It could be anyone's hair." The tracker put the hair under the Captain's nose, "Lavender?"

"In one of the rooms back in Darnan, the tub was still full of warm water with lavender oils in it," Shahariel replied. "It was her."

The Captain took a step back, shaking his head in disbelief. "I do not know how you trackers do it."

"What you thinking?" the tracker asked, seeing Rift deep in thought.

"I will need to look at all the bodies," Rift told the Captain grimly.

King Borrack's funeral pyre burned steadily well into the fourth day. It would burn for another five before being allowed to burn out as was customary. Nine full days and nights, his pyre would be fuelled to burn so his smoke could ascend to the highest level of

Paradise beside the Creator in the afterlife. If the flames were to die out before the ninth day, their great King's soul would be forced to spend eternity on a lower level of Paradise.

 A constant crowd of people milled about the area, paying their respects to their fallen king, throwing small tokens of herbs or crafted items into the flames to help fuel him on his ascension.

Lord Tundal and Lord Dagon sat watching the burning flames from their podium along with the Zandorian King and his Lords. Every day and night that the pyre burned, they were out there for the time of the sun and moons highest setting in the sky. It was a time of silence, where their prayers and memories of the fallen king reigned ultimate in their minds and ascended to the afterlife with the plummets of smoke that carried their king and friend.

Tundal grimaced as he tried to concentrate on joyful memories of his dear friend, but he could not. His mind was filled with frustration as he was sure was everyone else's. Reports had been filtering in the last several days of towns and small army posts being overrun and massacred by large barbarian tribes. Most of the places had been abandoned after the attacks but the most important places had been kept for their strategic values, leaving much to wonder. The barbarians only ever kept places they overran when preparing for war.

Worse still, Princess Nicolette had yet to be found - no reports had come back to them of her whereabouts. Rumors of that night's episodes had been impossible to contain and now most of the country had heard some vague tale of what had transpired. Some believed it and called for the death or banishment of anyone with The Gift again. Others believed it to be the treachery of the Zandorians and wanted full-scale war. None of this helped the already trying situation.

"Let us get inside my friend and deal with what is on all our minds." Lord Dagon said, drawing Tundal out of his deep thoughts.

Tundal smiled solemnly at his friend. "We cannot avoid it forever I suppose."

The Lords moved across the courtyard, some made small talk others just stared off in contemplation of the overwhelming problem ahead of them. Dante, the Zandorian King had extended his and his Lords' help in this time of need, extending their stay as long as they could in helping strategize a feasible plan. King Dante's hope was also that in that time the Princess would be found and returned safely. A new time would have to chosen for the wedding - if the wedding was even to still take place. It was yet another thing that would need to be dealt with.

"My Lords..." A young, burly soldier called out to them.

"What is it?" Dagon asked, turning to regard the man with the other Lords.

"Sorry to intrude but a man is here - he says he is the sole survivor of the north east boarder encampment. He says he has dire news that he needs to report to you." The soldier reported.

"Not another one," Zefer, Lord of Samuel moaned. "They all have the same story to tell."

"Bring him to us and let him speak." Tundal nodded to the soldier who gestured to the two soldiers holding up a ragged figure.

The haggard farmer was helped over. The man was so weak he could barely shuffle his feet fast enough to keep up with the soldiers who helped him along.

The man's clothes were in near complete shreds as they hung desperately to his flaccid half-starved frame. Dried blood and mud stained what frayed material was left. Only a small hint of grey rimmed the edge of his collar, at one point in time it might have been cotton - clean, white. His face was pale, his eyes sunken deep in his skull from exhaustion and trauma.

"Bring this poor man some fresh water!" Tundal ordered, surprised the man was still alive. "What happened?" Tundal asked the farmer, who had the full attention of the group.

The man's eyes darted around too each of the Lords' faces nervously. "It was...horrible.... I have never seen anything like it." He began reliving the moment. "It happened so fast - we did not have time to get a defense together. It would not have helped us anyways." The man stopped, almost afraid to continue.

"See, just like the rest," Zefer sighed, folding his arms.

The man's eyes went wide. "No, no you do not understand..." He stammered uncontrollably. "...their Gifted have...have come forth again!"

"What!" Everyone blurted out at once, a cold uncomfortable tension cascaded through the group.

"No, impossible - you are mistaken!" Andras, Lord of Besha bellowed out. "Their Priests and Priestesses have not been seen since..." But he was cut short by the farmer's bold voice.

"I watched the earth split open and vines sprout out and entangle and tear through my friends and family, crushing them and pulling them down into the depths of the earth itself." He paused, his lips trembling at the memory. "The very earth that we walk upon swallowed them whole, leaving not a trace that they ever existed!" The farmer's eyes stared blankly at the Lord who had berated him. "Every time I close my eyes I relive that moment!" the man bellowed out, pulling his arms from the soldiers who helped him stand. "I wish I would have stayed and died with my wife and son, but I knew someone had to warn of what was coming!" The man collapsed to the ground, his outburst sapping what little strength he had left.

"Take him to a room where he can get some rest. Have food and a bath waiting for him when he awakens," Tundal told the two guards who picked the ragged framer up and carried him away.

The Lords, King Dante and Prince Berrit quickly made their way back to the library to discuss the news they had just heard - not wishing to discuss such things in the open.

Tundal sat down at the grand table - the room was dead silent as everyone contemplated the dire report. He ran both hands through his hair in frustration. This was the worst news they could have received at this time.

Lord Dagon slammed his fists down hard and burst out, "We must act, now! We cannot just stand by and watch as our country falls into the hands of these monsters!"

"We have to find them first," Lord Bartan replied, looking down at the hide map covering the table. "They seem to be moving their camps every few days. They must be grouping up with other tribes when they are ready to attack. Single tribes should not be able do this kind of damage, regardless if a few of their Priests and Priestesses have come forth again."

"We need to stop all this talk and send all our armies further out to root these bastards out!" Dante's youngest son, Prince Kayreil barked.

"We cannot divide the armies little brother, until we know what we are up against," Prince Berrit finally spoke. "If forces are run too thin, and their Tainted have returned, then when the time comes, we may not have enough soldiers to stop them," Prince Berrit warned.

Prince Berrit's situation was awkward - he had been arranged to married King Borrack's daughter, Princess Nicolette. But with the

King dead and the Princess absconded, he was left in an uncomfortable limbo.

"Who is to say they are up to anything other than the usual raids and pillaging?" Lord Andras asked, still not sure about the whole situation.

"Andras is right - they have made attacks similar to these in the past. We are dealing with mindless savages and they have just gotten lucky in attacking your weakest points. They have yet to take anything of great value and there is no solid proof that their Priests have returned," Lord Zefer replied.

"Nothing of great value? I should cut out your tongue for that! Hundreds of my countrymen have been slaughtered by these mindless savages," Dagon growled angrily. "So do not tell me we have lost nothing of value."

"Most of them have been nothing more than farmers and peasants," Edroth said carelessly with a roll of his eyes.

Ethan nearly jumped from his seat in rage. "Here in Draco we value a man's life beyond the size of his coin purse!"

Dagon grabbed his son's arm and pulled him back down to his seat, but gave him an approving smirk. "We also value a man's word," Dagon put in. "There may not be any solid proof that the barbarians Priests and Priestesses have joined the fighting. But that does not mean you ignore the possibility of it being true. One man's word could mean the difference of winning a war or losing it."

"Very true Dagon," King Dante replied. "We cannot underestimate the enemy, but neither should we assume the worst at this time. We should send scouts out to confirm what we have heard. From there we will be better able to asset the situation."

"Should we not alert the kingdom of the possible threat?" Mathu asked. "So they can be prepared if the sort does happen."

"No Mathu, sadly,"that would not be a wise choice of action," Tundal replied. "We do not want the kingdom in a panic. With King Borrack's death shocking the country and the rumors of the Princess's kidnapping leaking out, we are in dire condition as is. A shock such as that would be sure to create immense disorder."

"You may be too young Mathu, to remember the last time the barbarian Gifted unified together with their warriors," Dagon said.

"I…I have heard the stories, but yes… I was too young," Mathu replied with no more than a whisper.

"It was a horrible time - one that we thought we would never make it through." King Dante shuddered at the memory.

"And we would not have, had it not been for Ursa coming forth for the Gifted and working with King Borrack..." Dagon added.

"And look what that demonic heathen has done now!" Lord Zefer hissed.

"Likely a plan of his from the very beginning," Prince Berrit added coldly.

"We are not going to do this again!" King Dante cut in before any more turmoil could ensue. "We will be leaving in two days' time back to Zandor... to ensure the safety of our own kingdom. If the barbarians are attacking in force then we need to be there to crush their efforts. If by some curse in our fate their Gifted have committed to the fight again, then that is an even greater reason to return home. With King Borrack dead and no heir to replace him..." he paused and shook his head, "Lord Tundal...you are the most likely to take rule of Draco until the Princess has returned...or her body is found. Then when the time is allowed and Draco is safe from threat once again we will commence with the treaty and... the wedding."

"And if the Princess is no longer with us?" Tundal asked, though it pained him to do so.

"Both our countries require peace - if we are to prosper and push back the savages, a treaty is a must," King Dante answered promptly.

"What if you the Princess is returned to us safely and we decide to call off the wedding?" Lord Dagon added defensively.

Dante sighed and his features softened. "We will cross that bridge if we come to it. My son has offered to stay here to assist and give what help he can offer with his three hundred warrior escort, until all is under control." Several murmurs ensued, but soon diminished.

"We welcome Prince Berrit and what aid he may lend to our cause," Tundal replied, as graciously as he could. "But he must know that his status gives him no political powers here." Berrit nodded his understanding.

"I will leave a squad of Zandor's personal Sintu," King Dante added.

"We do not need - nor want - the Sintu involved," Dagon stated, irritation still looming in his words.

"No one is more experienced in battling The Gifted than the Sintu!" Lord Zefer barked out.

"If it is true and the Priests and Priestesses have returned, then the Sintu will aid you greatly," Lord Andras explained.

"We have several Wizards nearby who will come to our aid if we need them," Dagon snapped back.

"What if they have taken the side of Ursa?" Zefer remarked, crossing his arms as if in some form of victory.

"We will cross that bridge if we come to it!" Dagon hissed snidely.

"Messengers have already been sent out to ask for their council," Lord Tundal interrupted.

"What!" King Dante and Prince Berrit both gasped together.

"I sent word for them yesterday afternoon," Tundal explained to them, his tone unwavering.

"You did not think to inform us?" Prince Berrit asked barely concealed anger edging his tone.

"I have just informed you," Tundal remarked as if it did not matter.

"Do you not think it would have been wise to seek everyone's council on the matter?" King Dante asked irritation on the tip of his words.

"Had I thought that, I would have," Tundal replied firmly.

"We might be in a war with these demonic heathens and you have invited them here?" Zefer argued.

"There is no reason to believe that we are at war with them," Tundal shot back calmly.

"Are you daft?" Zefer hissed almost raising to his feet. "Clearly you have been touched with madness!"

"No, my good Lord Zefer, I am not daft nor have I been touched with madness!" Tundal barked. "I am not about to let King Borrack's reign with them be so easily dismissed, when the facts have yet to be fully determined!"

"Do as you see fit then with these devils, Lord Tundal," He said sternly. "But walk with a step of caution around them I beg of you."

"How can you sanction this?" Zefer hissed out at his king.

King Dante turned a dangerous eye on the outburst from his Lord. "You forget your place Lord Zefer! This is not Zandor, hence why Zandorian laws are moot on such topics."

"How many of these Gifted 'friends' have you invited here?" Prince Berrit asked, cold irritation spreading through his voice.

"We know of twenty two who live within a five day ride of us," Tundal answered. "They have been called upon before. Though several more may be accompanying them, most Wizards take on an apprentice or know of other Gifted individuals who have yet to reveal themselves."

"How strong are these, Wizards?" Berrit asked coyly. "Are they as powerful as Ursa was rumored to be?"

"It has never been tested, nor does that matter," Dagon piped in. "Wizards have their strengths and weaknesses like average men. Their abilities will aid us greatly in this catastrophic time, if they so choose to aid us."

Prince Berrit licked his lips pondering his next words carefully. "I would like to meet these Wizards in person when they arrive. We must not take any chances - they might secretly be our enemy."

Tundal nodded his head in agreement, more just to avoid argument. "We will greet them in full, with a side of caution."

A ruckus in the antechamber drew all eyes to the doorway. Within moments, an exhausted rider exploded through the doors. His face was pale and sunken in from lack of nutrition and dehydration.

"My Lords. My Lords!" The man wheezed out. "I have just come from Mandrake!" he coughed, putting his hand on one of the many bookshelves to steady himself. "A large group of barbarians are gathered a day's march west of the castle." He coughed and almost lost his balance. "They look like they are going to try to seize Mandrake!"

"What!" Dagon yelled jumping to his feet and going to the man.

"Yes my Lord. Before I was sent, there were over three thousand gathered, and the tribes just seem to keep swelling their ranks," he bleated, accepting Dagon's help to a chair.

"They cannot truly think they can take Mandrake, do they?" Lord Andras asked with a laugh. No one else joined him - the uncomfortable silence spilled into the room and chilled everything.

"I must get back to Mandrake!" Lord Dagon announced - his tone was grave.

"You do not honestly believe these savages could achieve this?" Dante asked.

The room was silent, as Dagon seemed to be fighting some inner turmoil with himself. "Mandrake is weak right now," he admitted, though everyone could tell it pained him to do so. "The moat is dried up, the lack of rainfall this year forced us to re-route the irrigation to aid our crops. The Northern wall is under repairs after a catapult malfunction collapsed a large section of it."

"That is troubling news," King Dante said.

"Take fifteen hundred mounted soldiers back with you along with the men you came with," Tundal told him.

"Only fifteen hundred?" Dagon asked, bewildered at his friend.

Tundal sighed, knowing his friend would act this way, but had hoped he would not. "I must think of the rest of the kingdom my friend. I want nothing more than to send the whole of Draco's army with you, and ride by your side, but I cannot. I am needed here…As is the bulk of Draco's army. If the barbarians are massing together and their Gifted have joined them, then I must have an army to defend the seat of power. If you ride swiftly, you may arrive before the attack arises. Once those behind the walls see their Lord riding into the enemy - and that army is flanking the barbarians with fifteen hundred mounted men, they will throw open the gates and Mandrake's army will charge out to meet you on the battlefield, where you will easily crush the enemy regardless of their numbers!"

Dagon's eyes flickered momentary confusion and anger, but just as fast, it subsided to reason. "I understand. I must leave at once. I trust my family can stay here until Mandrake is safe?" he asked, though he knew the answer.

"Of course they can, my friend. They shall remain here until you have cleared Mandrake of these cowsons." Tundal clasped his hand firmly. "May your horses travel as swiftly as the wind."

"Lord Dagon," Prince Berrit called before he had taken more than a few steps. "I will send with you half of my personal escort. They are fierce warriors and battle would do them good. Now go save your people, and be sure to send us swift word of your victory."

"I thank you Prince Berrit." Then Dagon was gone.

"May the Creator grant him a thousand kills," Andras said, grabbing an apple from the bowl of fruit on the table, polishing it on his shirt.

The sight of carnage still loomed in Rift's mind as he and Shahariel rode down the road toward Dragon's Cove. They had lost the Princess' tracks at the encampment and had crossed the river, hoping to pick them up again. There was not a single doubt in Rift's mind that the Princess had been in that supply wagon when it had arrived at the encampment. They had not found her body or the bodies of Ursa and his apprentice…which meant they were still alive. The supply wagon had not been touched, which meant it had arrived after the battle was over. That meant they were out there somewhere.

Rift's men that had left Draco Castle with him had caught up by the time he was done overseeing the body checks. He had ordered them to stay behind and help fortify the encampment in case the savages came back for another assault. They were of little use to him anyway.

Rift's mind had raced since the night he had left Draco Castle on why Ursa might have done what he did. But he could not come to any realistic conclusions. A large part of him hoped he would not have to kill the Wizard. Ursa had been a decent friend throughout the years. Ursa had healed him several times on the battlefield - saving his life more than once.

Ursa had also been a close, dear friend to King Borrack and the Queen for many years. King Borrack had put more trust into Ursa than anyone else that Rift had ever seen. That had to count for something. But Rift would kill him and Meath, just the same…if he had to.

Rift knew it would take everything he had to take the two Wizards down if it came to that. They were Gifted and he was not, which gave them the upper hand. But he had taken out the Gifted before. A handful of Shyroni lay dead by his quick hand and quicker instinct.

"You sure seem to be stuck in your thoughts today," The tracker said riding closer.

"I cannot get my mind around why they would have taken her. It just does not make any sense to me at all."

"I wish I had an answer for you, but I do not. Perhaps if I knew them better I might, but I have only heard stories about Ursa," Shahariel told him honestly. "Are you sure none of their bodies were back at that camp?"

"I checked every one - none were them," Rift grunted. He did not want to think of what had happened back there. He had seen worse, but still the sight of a brutal slaughter such as this did not please him. He had never liked killing and had only done it because he was good at it.

"Maybe there is more to this than you know," the tracker said. "Maybe Ursa did not kill the king and kidnap the Princess. Maybe he was saving her from whoever did kill the King. Something did not seem right about that Zandorian Prince - maybe he had more to do with what happened than it appeared."

Rift glanced over to the tracker with a half-hearted smirk and a shrug.

"Are you sure Dragon's Cove is where they would be headed?" the tracker asked.

Rift truly had no idea where they were headed. Dragon's Cove would seem to be a likely choice, no one there yet knew of the King's death and the Princess' kidnapping. He was sure the news would reach there before he did, but not by more than a day or so. "It is the only place that I can think of. The Lord and Lady of Dragon's Cove hold Ursa in the highest regards. He has done much for them. Maybe he believes they will trust his word and hide him."

"Seems a risky chance," Shahariel sidestepped his horse around a fallen tree.

"My senses tell me to go to Dragon's Cove and they have never steered me wrong." This was all Rift could say - he just hoped he was right. It had been tearing him up inside that he had not yet been able to save the Princess. If she were hurt, he would never be able to forgive himself. He whispered a silent prayer to Queen Lavira - asking for her forgiveness and that he would bring Nicolette home safe.

"Hopefully, we will not run into any savages out here." Shahariel eyes scanned the shadows. "I would hate to run into the tribes that overtook that encampment. There are dozens of tracks around these parts - it is going to be hard for me to determine which ones are the ones we are looking for. So what makes you the man for this job, Rift?" Shahariel asked, swatting several horseflies off his steed. Shahariel was in it for the money and he was being paid very handsomely for his services.

"I am oath bound to her. I am her Champion as I was her late mother… Queen Lavira's Champion." Rift replied softly.

The tracker nodded his respect. Unlike himself and the many others who had been paid, Rift's honor was on the line and for a man of his caliber that was the highest price.

"We will find the Princess." The tracker yawned. "I have always been able to find my charge."

They had been traveling with little to no sleep for days now, and it was beginning to take its toll on them. The clouds were beginning to turn dark purples and bright pinks as the sun slowly ascended from the clear sky. A thick crimson line rimmed the mountaintops. It would be dark soon and they did need sleep. He would need all his strength and wits about him when they found her. "We will make camp once we get to that rocky slope up the road."

The land had already begun to flatten out since they had crossed the Sheeva River. The high peaking mountains dipped down into rolling knolls. The trees thinned substantially - the dense thicket of different palms and opaque vegetation slowly transformed into large powerful evergreens and deciduous trees. Ferns and vines were replaced by long, rich green and golden grasses, thorny bushes and boulders.

They made camp just as the first stars began to shimmer in the darkening sky. They made a small fire and cooked a plump hare that Shahariel had caught earlier that evening. Rift had not allowed a fire before - as a fire would give away their camp at night. But tonight, high rocky slopes secluded their camp on three of the four sides and a decent growth of trees and foliage veiled the fourth. The fire would not be seen easily and Rift wanted a hot meal for a change to help lift his spirits.

"Well, with this terrain I should be able to pick up their trail again. They are not going to be foolish enough to travel on any of the roads openly. But I would bet my bottom silver they will not be far off." Shahariel turned the chubby hare over and juices dripped onto the hot coals with steamy hisses.

Rift inhaled the aroma of cooking meat, his mouth already watering with anticipation. "It will be easier for them to travel at night, not as many dangers here as in the jungle. But it will be harder for them to hide during the day. We will find them."

"They might already be in Dagon's Cove."

"It is possible," Rift replied. He hoped they were - it would make things easier - but he doubted it. He had to believe most of their traveling would be on foot and off the roads. Though knowing they had already made it across the river meant anything was possible. Ursa was never one to underestimate.

Rift got up to check the horses and make sure they could graze. While he was there, he patted his horse's neck and whispered, "We will get her back."

"If you do not get back over here soon, I am going to eat all of this without you," Shahariel called to Rift with a chuckle.

Rift gave his horse one last pat on the neck before he went back to the fire. "Give me a piece of that and I will tell you how bad a cook you are," Rift joked. It had been the first time he had laughed in a while.

"So the man does know how to laugh - who would have thought." Shahariel smiled handing a wooden plate with half the hare on it.

Rift examined it mockingly, "Well, it looks like you cooked it right, but looks can be deceiving."

"Well, if you are gonna be like that, give it back I will eat your share too," the tracker joked back, his lips and chin already slick with grease.

Both men ate greedily until there was no meat left. Shahariel broke a small loaf of bread and handed Rift half.

"We will take shorter turns on watch tonight. After what happened back there at the river camp, we should not let our guard down," Rift said, wiping his mouth free of the meats' juices and breadcrumbs.

"I was thinking the same thing. I guess I will go first. I am not overly tired," Shahariel replied.

"Good, 'cause I am," Rift chuckled, getting under his blanket and resting his head on his pack.

"You need as much beauty rest as yo…" Then all went silent.

"Forget how to talk?" Rift joked turning around just in time to see the tracker fall into the fire face first, a crudely made spear sticking in his back.

Within a heartbeat, Rift was out of his bedroll and had his sword in his hand. He scanned the dark growth, slowly making his way closer to a pile of rocks so he would have cover from the attack and could see where it was coming from. He heard the sound of something slipping off a rock and looked up just in time to see a dark figure dive at him from above. Rift was slammed hard into the ground as the man hit him. He pushed the body off himself - the man had been impaled right onto his awaiting sword. But Rift did not have the time to be thankful for his good fortune; another spear hit the rock he was standing beside, with a spark. Rift sidestepped the next one and threw his dagger blindly into the darkness in the direction the spear came from. When he heard the scream, he knew it had found its target, though doubted it had been a fatal hit.

Rift bolted to his horse and cut it free. He leapt onto its back while another dark figure ran at him from the side and jabbed a spear up at him. Rift parried the attack and was quick to reverse, slashing the man across the chest. He kicked his horse hard in the ribs and it sprang off at full gallop. Two figures stood in their path, but the horse did not falter and crashed hard into both men, as it shot off into the night. Rift held on tight - he could not see more than a few feet in front of him. With no saddle or reigns, he prayed the horse could find its way along the road without his help.

"Meath, you cannot stop fate!" The man in black taunted, his teeth showing through his wide grin. The rest of his face was obscured by the gloomy hood of his cloak.

Meath stood there in a void of darkness. All he could see was the man who had been haunting his dreams. His arrogant, egotistical grin boiled Meath's blood. The man's eyes pierced out from the gloom of his cowl - they were cold, dark green and bore deep into Meath's very soul. The worst part was they seemed so familiar.

They stood only an arm span away from one another, but there was no ground - nothing - just empty obscurity. Meath wanted to reach out and attack the taunting man, but knew it would do no good. This was just another vivid dream.

"I know who you are! You will be stopped!" Meath yelled, but his voice did not carry any further than the man in front of him.

The man laughed. "You really are a fool you know. You have no idea what is or is not. You do not really know who I am Meath, but I know who you are."

Meath fought to say something. The muscles in his face twitched as he tried to speak, but in truth, the man was right. They did not really know who he was. They knew he had The Gift and was pretending to be the Prince of Zandor, but his true identity was still unknown.

"See, you know nothing." His head titling back as he issued a mocking laugh, "and yet I know everything about you Meath. I know your strengths, your weaknesses, your fears, and doubts."

"Why are you doing this?" Meath interrupted through gritted teeth.

"Why? Why you ask? Because it is destiny - it is why I was created."

"I will stop you!" Meath barked, trying to take a swing at him, but his arms just hung by his side limply.

The man smiled back at him. "The question is, when the time comes, will you really want to?"

The question threw Meath off, "Show me your face! Stop hiding behind your hood you coward!"

The tooth-filled grin showed through the darkness of his hood again. "Run along now, I am done playing with you..." He lifted his hand out, the tips of his fingers pushed deep into Meath's chest, "for now..." Immense pain flashed through Meath's entire body causing him to spasm uncontrollably and collapse into the empty void.

Meath struggled for breath - as he came around, his eyes were blurred by tears and grit. His body was covered in a thick, greasy sweat, but he did not even notice. Pain pulsed and flared through his entire body with each gasp of air and was accompanied by a whimper of pain. He tried to move his hands up to his face to rub the grit from his eyes, but he could not seem to find the strength.

Why am I is so much pain, he wondered. *What had happened to me, why can I not remember?* He forced his eyes open and fought past the prickling sting that assaulted them. He blinked several times, clearing the grimy haze enough to make out a thick green canopy of trees and growth above him. Several scattered beams of light cut through the awning of growth, allowing enough light to see. *Did I fall?* he wondered. *Was this where I landed? Have I broken anything? I am in so much pain!*

"Meath, can you hear me?" An angelic voice said from somewhere.

Yes, Meath, that is my name - the voice was talking to him. He tried to answer back but all that escaped his dry lips was a mumbled moan of anguish.

He felt movement on his left and then a figure appeared above him. He blinked again several times and his eyes locked with the golden brown eyes gazing down at him. He knew those eyes, and that voice. He blinked again, his eyes sweeping over the whole figure that leaned over him.

Then it all flooded back to him. Vivid flashes assaulted his mind - Zehava and his capture at the Sheeva River encampment, their futile attempt at escape from the slave barn. The insane Shaman who had consumed an old Wizard's Gift in front of his eyes. Then his own savage torture as the Shaman prepared him for the same fate.

"What...what happened?" Meath laboured out, finally finding his voice. His throat was hoarse and dry.

The Princess's eyes welled up with tears - she lifted a water skin to his lips. "You are safe now. Everything is going to be all right," she cooed, her tears finding their way down her cheeks to roll off her slender chin.

Meath drank greedily for several long moments, ignoring the agony that went along with the movement. "How...did you..." Meath stopped himself. "Zehava, did you find him? Did he make it out too?" Meath stammered, trying to sit up in his panicked state, but the pain that followed stole his strength and he slumped back down.

"I am right here," Zehava coughed weakly several paces away, "though I did not fare well either."

Meath turned his head, ignoring the burning protest of his muscles to look at his friend, a small smile of relief creasing his lips. They had both made it out alive.

"How did you get us out?"

"Very quickly, and with more good fortune than the Creator normally bestows upon an army of men," Ursa replied. He handed the Princess a wooden cup filled with a runny yellow paste that he had just mixed.

Nicolette raised the cup to Meath's lips and he drank without argument. The potion was thick and grainy and tasted of mouldy yeast as it slid down his throat. He knew it would help dull the intense pulsating pain that engulfed his body, and right now taste was the last thing on his mind.

"I am sorry, Meath. I could not get to you." Zehava sat up, wincing from the pain of the forced healed whip wounds.

"There is no need for apologies," Ursa snorted in amusement. "You were both in dire peril. Though Zehava has the sense of one whom was moon-touched." Meath looked at the Great Wizard, confused.

"Your friend here could barely stand - the weight of his own sword was more than enough to off balance him. Yet he decides that he is able to fight his way through an entire encampment of enemy warriors in hopes of finding you," Ursa muttered, shaking his head. "Had he been delirious, it would be understandable, but instead it was just a senseless act of suicide." Ursa folded his arms and shook his head at the soldier. "I will give you this Zehava - you are a brave and loyal half-witted fool."

Zehava chuckled softly. "Well, if I would have known you were going to show up I would have stayed where I was."

"I am just so glad you are still alive!" Nicolette squeezed Meath's hand. "I thought you were already dead when I saw you. What were they doing to you back there?"

Meath turned his eyes on Ursa, "the Shaman was going to take my Gift." Ursa's expression turned grave.

"That is impossible!" Nicolette cried out, looking to the powerful Wizard.

"No, it is possible," Meath replied dryly. "I watched him do it to another."

"Why did you not just kill him with your powers?" Zehava asked, craning his head stiffly over to look at him.

"I tried." Meath explained. "I do not understand it but there was this white powder in a circle around me - it prevented me from using my Gift. I could still feel the power inside of me, but when I tried to use it…" Meath paused for a moment, remembering the immense physical and mental pain he had suffered when he had tried to call upon his Gift. He had tried to use that to his advantage, in a final effort to end his own life before the Shaman could finish his ceremony and absorb his innate powers, but he decided that he had better not mention that. "It shot pain through my entire body and mind like fire in my veins. There was nothing I could do."

"The white powder that you are speaking of goes by many names, the most common is Everto Sal - it means *Demon's Saline* in the old tongue. It just may very well be the rarest thing in existence. And it is the greatest weapon, and vilest curse of those with The Gift. It is said that it can render even the greatest Wizards useless," Ursa finally spoke. "I have only ever seen it a handful of times in my life and never in that quantity. A mere pouch-full is worth a King's ransom."

"What is it?" Zehava asked. "How is it made?"

"There are several legends - ranging from myths to the paranormal," Ursa replied, running his fingers through his long white beard, deep in thought. Had the sand not been useless after such a ring of power was created, he would have filled a leather pouch-full before their escape.

Meath cautiously shifted his body up and leaned against a log that lay beside him. He was finally feeling the numbing effects of the vulgar potion he had consumed - though the pain was still tremendous, it was bearable now. He had so many questions to ask Ursa - about the white powder and about why he had been unaware that one could have their Gift taken from them. However, he knew this was not the time for such questions - there would be time later. "What happened to you after we tried to escape?"

Zehava chuckled in a jaded tone that pealed like a tired bell. "Well, after we tried to escape - and failed bitterly I might add - I woke up next to our cell where a very strange half-breed girl showed up to feed me." He paused for a moment, recalling the memory. "I got her talking, and found out she was just as much a prisoner as we were. I do not really know how but I finally convinced her to free me - I would have gotten away then but her father arrived, just as she unlocked my cell." Zehava recalled the rest of the story aloud - up until his foolish but definite stand. He rubbed his right hand over his still tingling flesh where the devilish tip of the whip had tasted his body. Though the wounds had been healed, they felt like they were still there and throbbed painfully. Ursa had told him it would be like that for a handful of days. The flesh had mended, but the muscles and nerves still had a brand of damage.

"She did come to see me, but there was nothing she could do for me. Dawn was already fast approaching and I was far too weak - we would never have gotten out of there alive," Meath told him. "She made the only rational choice."

"There is no way I would ever leave you behind... if there was a chance you were still alive."

"I know." Meath assured him, not blaming Zehava for anything. "Though next time, given the same odds - save yourself."

"If the roles were reversed, would you?" he asked.

Meath smirked. "No, I would be just as foolish."

"Enough of this talk," Nicolette cried out, tears welling in her eyes. "You are safe now and that is all that matters. Soon we all will be on our way again to Dragon's Cove, where we will be safe from all this."

"Speaking of all of us, where is Dahak?" Meath asked, wincing from the pain that rippled through his body as he tried to make himself more comfortable on the hard ground.

"Dahak and that savage girl - Shania - went out scouting our trail." Nicolette said, happy for the conversation change.

Both Meath's and Zehava's eyes widened in surprise. "She is here with us?".

Nicolette nodded. "She helped us escape once we had found you. We still had no idea where Zehava was. If it was not for her we might never have gotten out of there alive."

"She did a very brave and desperate thing," Ursa added. "Thankfully it worked in everyone's favor."

Everyone tensed when they heard the rustling from behind them. Ursa was quick to summon a molten sphere of Wizard's fire - not willing to take any chances.

"It is just us!" Dahak called, before pushing through the thick foliage and into their small campsite. "Hey! You guys are awake." Shania was soon to follow, apprehension moulding her features, as all eyes fell on her.

"Are you guys all right?" Dahak asked, concerned for his two comrades.

"We will live to fight another day," Zehava replied with a weary grin.

"And we will have food for at least a few more of those days." Dahak pulled his pack off and pulled out several pieces of fresh fruit. "I would never have been able to climb up and get them myself - Shania here can climb like a monkey." She smiled awkwardly, fidgeting with her own pack before placing it beside Dahak's.

Shania stood there uncomfortably, not entirely sure what she should be doing. She looked up and noticed everyone was looking strangely at her - even the old Wizard seemed to be casting suspicious glances her way. Anxiety crept up into her, gripping her chest tightly and tantalizing her mind with apprehensive thoughts. She was the odd one out, again.As she had been her entire life. What had she been thinking? Now she was more an outcast than ever. At least among the barbarians, she had a place. Where was her place here among these strangers? Her breathing quickened - she could feel the color drain from her face.

"It is all right my child," the old Wizard gently said, obviously realizing her inner struggle. "You are safe here - we mean you no harm."

Shania licked her dry lips nervously and her eyes met the deep, grey eyes of the Wizard. They were soft and genuine - her tension eased a little and she found herself nodding to him.

"Thank, you," Meath said to the savage girl, "for helping us escape," Meath continued, seeing her confusion.

"You...welcome..." she replied nervously, still unsure of the circumstances in which she found herself. Her eyes met Zehava's and again she found a comfort in them. "You okay?" she asked quickly going to his side.

"I guess I am, alive anyways." In the daylight, he could see her perfectly. She was very beautiful, even more than he had first thought. She was dressed in a single strap, deer hide top that showed off her well-toned stomach and figure, and a short deer hide skirt with a high slit up one side, which made for easy movement and flexibility.

"I am glad," she replied handing him a fresh water skin.

Zehava took a deep drink of the fresh water, he had already drank plenty of water since being awake but did not want to risk offending her. He could tell she wanted to say something as she nibbled on her lower lip timidly. "What is it?"

"What happen now?" she asked him, her eyes glistening ... fear and tiredness spilling out with tears.

Zehava was caught off guard by the question and had no idea how to answer it. He truly had not thought about it, it had seemed impossible that he would have gotten out of enemy hands.

"What do you mean?" Nicolette butted in.

"With me..." Shania asked hesitantly almost afraid of the answer. "What happen now?"

"We are in the middle of something of dire importance," Zehava replied.

"You lied to me," Shania shot back, tears welling up in her eyes and her lips quivered involuntary as she shot to her feet defensively.

"What? No, no I did not," Zehava stammered out. Impulsively, he tried to stand, but agony and exhaustion prevented him and he groaned out loud falling back.

Shania flinched as if she wanted to go to him and help, but stood her ground. "You said if me help you, you take me with you. You said things be better! You...you...used me!" Anger flashed in her eyes and her hands instinctively touched the hilts of her weapons.

"What matter of foolishness is going on?" Ursa's voice boomed from behind them, causing their attention to turn to the powerful Wizard. "Our lives are hanging in a balance of something so much more and here you are bickering about something foolish! We are being hunted by more enemies than we could handle if they were to come upon us and yet your voices echo loud and clear." The old Wizard took a deep breath calming himself, lest he make himself look like a hypocrite. "What seems to be so important as to risk our lives over?" His eyes were hard as he glanced at each one, stopping on the young barbarian girl. "What is it my child, that has angered you so?"

"I got nothing, no one, I am a stray. My people hunt me. Your people hunt my kind." She paused, forcing the tears back before continuing, "I thought helping would change something. I thought..."

"You thought in your act of benevolence that some life-changing reward would befall upon you?" the Wizard asked sternly.

"No... that not it at all..." she cried out, but was cut off.

"There is no reward here for you my child," Ursa told her.

Shania could no longer hold back the tears and several escaped and cascaded down her dirty cheeks. She turned her back and began walking away, back into the jungle.

"Ursa no!" Nicolette cried out, running to him.

"This is not what was meant to happen!" Zehava barked out, shame and guilt sweeping over him.

Ursa's look silenced them. "All we have to offer here is companionship and respect," Ursa called out to the fading barbarian girl.

Shania stopped in her tracks hearing the words, her heart nearly leaping from her chest with elation. She turned around and walked back into the small camp, her steps wobbly. "You mean it?" she asked the great Wizard.

"I would have let you keep walking if I did not," Ursa told her. "Now after we eat we must get moving. We still have a few days of hard travel before we get to Dragon's Cove and the journey is going to be slow and even more dangerous with these two hurt as badly as they are."

Shania walked over to the old Wizard as Dahak handed out several pieces of fruit. They exchanged a few words, and then Shania ran off into the jungle without glancing back.

Ursa crouched down beside Meath. "Rest your head back."

Meath complied, "what is the matter?"

Ursa pulled Meath's shirt up and saw the burn mark had not faded at all. He placed his hand over the wound and let his healing abilities flow from his hand into the wound. Reluctantly, the wound began healing, but a fresh scar remained and would not fade.

"What is the matter?" Meath asked again, seeing the concerned look on Ursa's face.

Ursa shook his head to clear his thoughts. "Nothing, but I can waste no more effort right now on this, until we are safe behind the walls of Dragon's Cove."

"Wait! What do you mean?" Meath protested as Ursa stood up to walk away. "What happened?" He looked down and examined the scar that remained. "Why will it not heal?"

"He will be all right, right?" Nicolette asked, looking from Meath to Ursa.

"He will be fine - of that I am positive," Ursa replied, his gaze still on Meath's chest. "As for why it will not heal, I do not know that answer, but once we are safe..." he trailed off hearing footsteps from behind him.

Moments later Shania was back, several different lengths of poles dragging behind her. Ursa threw her a coil of hemp rope from the saddlebag and she went to work immediately, lashing the poles together constructing two litters for the injured party members to be dragged behind the horses.

With guidance from Shania, they found their way back to a barely used trail, heading west. Though travel through the woods would have been safer, with Meath and Zehava unable to walk, travel would be tremendously slow, and they needed to make some distance from their newest enemy.

Once on the road, Meath and Zehava did their best to rest, though every bump and jolt reminded them of their aches and pains. The litters were made very quickly by Shania and could be attached and detached quickly in case they needed to find cover in a hurry. Ursa rode the third horse, knowing it would add to the ruse that they were refugees.

Ursa knew if they ran across anyone, they could pass as town folk from the army encampment. They were a larger group now so he did not think they would have any trouble with the ruse. The only thing that vexed him was Shania - even though she was covered with a heavy cloak, if anyone paid close attention it would not be hard to figure out her heritage.

Shania ran up to Ursa and walked beside his horse. "Thank you," she told him, true gratitude showing in her eyes.

"You are more than welcome my child, but know that the road we travel will be long and full of life-threatening peril," Ursa told her. If it had fazed her, he could not see it.

"I used to danger," she replied. "I will not hinder you, you have my word. I be helpful. You will see."

Nicolette decided to walk beside Meath and not ride the horse, while Dahak rode the horse dragging Zehava and guided her horse that dragged Meath. She was so glad he was back with her - she had never felt so alone without him. She had not slept well the night before, and kept having nightmares of what had been done to him. She could not believe he was still alive after everything he had been through. He looked a lot better than he had when she found him hanging from the beam. She only wished she could have killed that Shaman for what he had done to Meath.

She could feel the anger flaring up in her at the thought of the Shaman - the rage knowing that if she had another chance, she would put a dagger deep in his chest. The thought of killing him filled her with delight - the fact that she would actually be happy she had killed someone, frightened her.

A large rut in the road jolted Meath's litter hard, causing him to groan loudly and open his eyes and see Nicolette staring down at him.

"I could get used to waking up and seeing you," he blurted out before thinking. "I mean.... I...just meant..." he stammered out.

Nicolette blushed at his admission. "I understand Meath." She went silent, her eyes wandering to the ground that passed by her feet.

"What is the matter?" Meath asked her, trying to block out the pain from the vibrations.

"I was so scared I would never see you again," she whispered.

"I thought I was going to die. All I could think about was you and how I would never see your smile again." She blushed again.

"What is that up ahead?" Dahak pointed straight ahead, "soldiers?"

"No, it looks like refugees." Ursa strained to see. "Princess, pull up your hood - we do not need anyone recognizing you. You two, be ready." Ursa glanced back at Meath and Zehava to make sure they were paying attention. They both moved their hands to their swords, concealed under the blankets.

Ursa rode up to Shania. "Stay close to me - keep your hood up, head down, and go along with anything I say."

"What do you mean?" she asked, a puzzled look, pulling the hood of her cloak down further.

"These people may not take kindly to you if they recognized your heritage, for your kind have killed their families and destroyed their homes," Ursa replied, keeping his focus on the group ahead as they came closer into view.

Anger glazed her eyes momentarily, "they are not my people!"

"I know - I did not mean it like that. But it will make no difference to them. They will still hate you and wish you harm."

"Then I will kill them!" she stated, her hands moving to her hilts under her heavy brown cloak.

"You will do no such thing!" Ursa told her sternly. "That would only make them right. You will not make any move for those blades unless I tell you to. Do you understand?"

Shania looked back at the Wizard, wanting to argue, wanting to tell him no one controlled her, but could not. He had been kind to her - these people had accepted her, and there was truth in the old Wizard's words. "I understand," she nodded begrudgingly.

They neared the large, gaunt group that appeared to have survived the attack at the encampment or possibly a nearby town. Most had nothing but the clothes on their backs - others carried precious belongings they had grabbed as they fled, things they did not want to leave for the savages to take…or destroy. Some walked beside horses or mules, while their wives or children rode on the animals' backs. Others walked beside friends or loved ones, helping them struggle along the road, too tired or wounded to do it alone. A few lay on litters like the ones Meath and Zehava were on, being dragged by horses or people.

The battered, defeated group eyed the newcomers suspiciously as they rode closer, wondering if they were friend or foe. One could never be sure if highwaymen or bandits would come around and prey upon the already helpless. But soon, they realized the newcomers were just other refugees and most attention went back to the wounded or the sad conversations of those they lost and lives destroyed.

Ursa led his group through the large crowd as fast as he dared - not wanting to cause too much discomfort to Meath and Zehava nor did he want to look overly apprehensive.

Several of the refugees shifted closer to the newcomers, in hopes to strike up a conversation and hear their stories. A middle-aged woman wobbled up near Shania. She was missing several teeth and had a fresh gash across her forehead.

"Morning dear, where do you folks come from?" the lady asked, tilting her head trying to get a look under Shania's hood.

Shania lowered her head even more and altering her direction away from the woman and closer to Ursa and the others.

"What is the matter?" the lady asked. Sour at being ignored, she reached out to grab at Shania's arm. "I just want to talk a moment, is that so wrong?"

Shania jerked her arm away from the lady's advance but the woman's grip was surprisingly solid. Instinctively Shania's other hand shot out to pull her arm free, exposing her darker skin.

"What foul trickery is this?" the woman hissed loudly, stepping back.

Ursa rode closer to Shania and motioned her to follow him as he picked up the pace- he ignored the curses and groans from Meath and Zehava. He knew they had to get through this crowd before too much attention was drawn to them.

"Savage! Savage!" The old lady cried loudly, drawing more than one set of alarmed eyes her way at the proclamation.

"What are you talking about?" a dark haired man asked.

"That one, right there," she pointed, "the one in the heavy cloak is a savage! I am sure of it."

Ursa knew they had better pass these people quickly before someone got the courage to confront the situation, or recognized them for who they really were.

Dahak instinctively rode his horse up to flank the other side of Shania, cutting off the people's view. His heart started to beat faster as the rumor spread like wildfire through the refugees. He licked his lips nervously, feeling a hundred sets of eyes upon them. It took all the will that he had to keep his eyes straight ahead and his hand off the hilt of his short sword.

They had almost made it past the group when Ursa noticed a mother and father crying over their young boy, on a poorly constructed litter - the sad pile that he was lying in was bloodstained and he was missing one arm. Even from this distance, Ursa could tell the wound was beginning to fester badly. He knew the boy would not make it more than a few more days if he was not helped. Ursa cursed himself stopping his horse. He knew they should just keep riding through, but an inner turmoil prevented him.

"What is the matter?" Dahak asked nervously, his hand touching the hilt of his sword while he turned his horse around to survey the scene.

"Why did we stop?" Nicolette asked. Ursa was already off his horse and was rummaging through his things in his saddlebags.

Shania was beside him - worry, and confusion shadowing her half-hidden face. She watched the crowd slow and glare - their curses and muttering growing louder with each passing moment.

Once Ursa found what he was looking for, he turned to explain. "That boy will not live for more than two nights if he does not receive help - I can help him. I cannot bring myself to just leave him to die," Ursa said, words thickened with emotion.

Dahak looked around at the gathering mob that held in white-knuckled fists. Makeshift weapons - mostly sharpened farming tools but a few short swords and spears sprouted like weeds. "Ah, Ursa, are you sure this is such a good idea?"

"I will only be a few moments. This is something I must do. I do not know why, but I must!" Ursa replied, ignoring the angry crowd as he went over to the family.

"What are you doing?" the mother asked, as Ursa neared them.

"I am going to help your son. That wound is infected and he will die if it does not get treatment soon," Ursa told her, beginning to mix several herbs and colored liquids together from his pouches.

The father looked down at him, then up at Shania who was walking closer, not wanting to be far from Ursa. "What the hell are you doing with one of them?" the man yelled, pushing Ursa aside, he stood in front of his son and wife with a rusted old broad sword in his hand. "We do not need your help! This is some kind of savage trick - you are going to poison him!" the man roared, lifting the blade aggressively.

"I would do no such thing," Ursa barked back. "As for her, she is my slave and will do no harm, you have my word." Shania looked at Ursa in shock - hurt stark on her face. She was about to protest, but Ursa stopped her before she could. "Now slave, go and get me some clean rags from my horse and bring them to me before I lash you for dawdling and for forgetting them in the first place."

Shania's eyes glistened with wetness- she bit her bottom lip, turned and went to the horses without a word. She knew his words were a ruse, but they sounded so real and his tone had almost matched that of her father's.

The man stared down at Ursa for a moment longer, still not sure whether to believe him. Instinct told him not too, but his heart cried a different tune. His wife took hold of his arm and whispered to him. "Please let him help our son. He is right - he will not last more than a few days, and I cannot bear to lose another child, husband. Please!" she said, tears streaming freely down her dirt-stained face.

The father swallowed hard, fighting to control his emotions as his blade tip sank toward the earth. Tears welled up in his own eyes as he nodded to his wife and then he stood aside. "Do what you can for him, but I will be watching your every move and if I see anything that shows foul intent, I will kill you," he growled, though his anger had subsided almost entirely.

"Please save him," the mother begged, wiping the tears that streamed down her chubby cheek with a fold in her ratty dress.

"They cannot be trusted!" several people cried out as they gathered round, gripping their pathetic weapons.

"They keep company with demons!" another screamed raising his knobby club in the air high.

"I mean your son no harm." Ursa stared the man hard in the eyes seeing the man was beginning to be lured by the crowd's chants.

"Shut up all of you!" the father screamed to his fellow refugees slowing their jeers and taunts. "Do what you can for him, stranger."

"I need you to hold him down - I have to get the pus out of the wound and it is going to hurt for a moment." Ursa took the boys severed limb and squeezed it hard, pushing the secretion out. The child screamed in pain, kicked wildly, and tried to pull away, but Ursa did not stop. He knew it was the only way to save his life.

"Where are my rags, you filthy little wretch?" Ursa yelled over his shoulder at Shania, hoping the poor girl knew he did not mean any of it.

Shania ran to his side, handed him the rags without pause, and then took a step back, wanting nothing more than to run away from the hurtful words and vicious stares.

Ursa took the rags and used one of them to soak up the blood and yellow discharge, which now dripped from the boy's infected stump. He flattened another rag on his knee and dumped half the mixture he had made onto it, smearing it around. He placed it onto the raw stump of the boy's arm and tied it on tightly with a piece of hemp twine. The child moaned a little at the sting it caused, but then was still and silent.

"This will keep it from getting worse. By dusk, clean the wound and use the rest of this mixture, and repeat what you saw me do," Ursa told the couple as he stood up. "He will need as much water and food as you can give him to rebuild his strength."

"Thank you! Thank you! By the Creator's will...bless you!" the woman cried, cuddling her boy.

The father stared down at his son for a while before walking over to Ursa, who was now at his horse packing his things. "I am sorry for the way I reacted before. I was just..."

Ursa growled, cutting him off, "I understand - trust is a hard thing to give in times such as these. I am just glad I could help." Then the man held out his hand and shook Ursa's firmly.

"I will not forget this. If ,one day you need anything, search me out, I will do what I can," the man told him. "We will be at Dragon's Cove. We are moving there, where it is safer behind massive walls and an army. If you need me, that is where I can be found," he said sincerely.

"Let go of me!" Shania screamed, trying to pull her arms free of the two men who now held of her and were pushing her to her knees.

"What is the meaning of this?" Ursa demanded, striding over to them. Dahak was right behind him, while Nicolette stayed with Meath and Zehava, who were trying to see what was happening, their swords gripped tightly in their hands.

"It is savages like this one that destroyed our homes and killed our friends and families," one of them barked, wrenching on Shania's arm causing her to cry out in anguish.

"You will let go of her at once!" Ursa commanded in a deep, voice, "or you will suffer far worse than anything you have thus far!"

"Not until we have our vengeance on this little bitch!" the other yelled. By now, the group of refugees was gathered around and cheering their agreement with weapons held high, their demeanor fierce.

"Leave her alone damn you!" the father of the boy Ursa had just helped yelled at them. "This man just saved my son life; he means us no harm. What is the matter with you all?"

"A man who keeps company with the likes of these demons is no good!" one woman yelled from the crowd.

"This savage girl had nothing to do with your tragedy. She has been my slave since she was but a baby," Ursa beckoned, his conduct growing more threatening. "If you do not unhand her, I will have my man remove you from her very unpleasantly." Ursa gave Dahak a look that said he should step in.

Dahak drew his sword and held it tightly, trying not to show he was terrified about the situation.He held firm knowing the Wizard must have a plan if things went wrong.

Both men stopped pulling and just held her, turning their attention to Ursa and Dahak.

"You would attack your own kind to save a savage?" one of them asked, with a menacing stare of disbelief.

"To protect my property that I paid for? Yes I would. Now unhand her, unless you want to join your dead comrades back in your burned out towns. I will not say it again!" Ursa warned and Dahak took a step forward, his stance offensive.

"Just let her go you fools!" the father yelled at them.

Both men released Shania and took a step back. She ran and hid behind Ursa, not knowing what else to do.

The crowd was disgruntled and started yelling taunts and curses toward them. Some began to throw rocks and dirt in disgust, while waving their weapons and poles in the air, slowly gaining courage.

"Get on your horses, now!" Ursa yelled, mounting up as fast as he could. He yelled back to Nicolette to jump on one of the litters, they kicked their horses and bolted out of the mob of people as fast as they could.

They rode hard only until they had made it around the next bend in the road - more than a mile away and until they knew the mob was not following them. Zehava and Meath lay in absolute agony, holding on for dear life, while Nicolette hung on tightly to the sides of the litter, trying not to put all her weight on Meath's already sore body.

"I am sorry about that," Ursa said back to them when the horses had slowed down to their regular pace.

Meath and Zehava both moaned their disapproval, but knew it might have been the only way they could have gotten out of there with their lives. He paused for a minute, to look at the two boys.

"I am sorry for that back there," Ursa told Shania. He could tell she was rattled by the experience and the words that he had used had cut deep. "But it was necessary."

Shania nodded her head in understanding, but did not speak.

"I really thought we were in for it back there." Dahak looked back down the road to make sure no one was coming after them. After several long moments, he was satisfied that they were safe, for the time being.

"How could people be like that, after we helped one of them?" Nicolette asked in disbelief.

"They were scared and defeated, their morale all but destroyed at the loss they have suffered. We cannot blame them," Ursa explained.

"What is that over there?" Shania asked pointing toward a large pile of rocks where flocks of scavenger birds were gathered.

"Some dead animal that was moved off the road I bet," Dahak answered.

"No, I think it is something else. It does not look right," Shania said, dismounting from her horse.

"We do not have time for this - we must keep traveling," Ursa called to her.

"There are bodies!" Shania called to them.

"What should we do?" Dahak asked the great Wizard.

"We had better go check," Ursa said with a renounced sigh. "But we must hurry - we have not the time for this."

"Oh no!" Nicolette cried, running over to the half-charred body that lay face down in the dirt. "That is Rift's saddle bag and things!"

At the mention of the champion, Ursa was alert and off his horse.

Shania flipped over the body to get a look at the man's face. "Is that your friend?" she asked Nicolette, but the Princess turned away, not able to stand the sight or smell.

"No, it is not. It is someone else. But why would he have Rift's things?" Ursa asked aloud.

"This man killed your friend then stole his stuff? It happens all the time," Shania said, walking back to her horse. "Then a tribe found him, and killed him too."

"I do not think that is how it was," Ursa said. He looked at Nicolette, who was looking back at him holding back her tears. "I believe this man may have been traveling with Rift. There are the other man's things over there. It looks like they were ambushed and Rift may have gotten away. But we should not stay here for long. That mob will see us again soon and may not let us leave so easily next time." Ursa led his horse back to the road as gently as he could, trying not to hit the litter against the large rocks that were scattered everywhere. He was hoping the Princess would trust his words and not think about what might have happened to Rift, although it seemed more likely she would go with the latter.

"How do you know he got away?" Nicolette cried, following in behind them.

"Because his body is not here, Highness," Ursa replied, hoping he was right. "Besides, you and I both know Rift - he would not be taken down so easily."

"Who is this Rift guy anyways?" Zehava asked her, once they had started down the road again.

Nicolette stared down at the ground as she walked. "He is my Champion."

"Oh…what would he be doing out here?" Zehava questioned, as he tried to move into a more comfortable position to absorb the bumps a little less painfully.

"He must be looking for me…but how he knew where to look I do not know." She looked down at the ground again and prayed to the Creator that he was okay.

"I have known Captain Rift for a long time your Highness. He is a smart and cunning man and it is his job to know how to find you. He looks to be going to Dragon's Cove, so maybe we will see him there."

9

Dagon and his Champion Jarroth - along with the fifteen hundred men Tundal allowed him to take, his original three hundred and the hundred and fifty Zandorian personal guard Prince Berrit had given - traveled hard down the dusty road to Mandrake Castle.

Dagon had several officers stop and question every traveler on the road to find out what they knew. Each person they stopped received two copper pieces for any information regarding the barbarians and their movements. Dagon wanted to know everything - fact or rumor.

They only stopped at night when the first stars were visible, then were back moving at sunrise. During the day when the sun was at its highest peak, they stopped long enough to eat and tend the horses. It was a bitter, tough journey but the soldiers were trained for it and not a man complained.

Dagon had sent men to travel ahead of them to each of the small towns they would pass by… or through. He had given those men plenty of coin to buy whatever food supplies the locals were willing to part with - for both the men and the horses. Several new wagons and horses were purchased to haul the cargo and they fell in behind the passing army with the other supply wagons.

Dagon knew not the situation they would encounter when he arrived at Mandrake. Whether the defenders could hold the walls and keep the savage horde out or if he would have to take back his castle from the horde. Regardless, he was not about to be unprepared and under-supplied - his men and their beasts would be well fed and alert when they charged into battle against their outnumbering foe. Dagon knew well from his own younger days in the army that hungry, thirsty men soon became demoralized and sloppy.

They travelled for a half a week and still had another two, maybe three days of hard travel to go until they reached Mandrake Castle. Dagon prayed he would not be too late. Along the way, Dagon had conscripted a handful of townsfolk who had wanted to help defend their country. He had accepted them in proudly.

"My Lord, there seems to be an abandoned wagon up ahead with a lot of rubbish around it," a brawny, blond soldier reported riding from the front to give him the news.

"Well, get it out of the way. We do not have time to slow down!" Dagon exclaimed, already angry that they were not making better time.

"There is no one around the wagon - no bodies or anything -, it is just sitting there," the soldier replied, a little nervous that he might make his Lord even angrier with the details.

"Get it out of the way! We do not have time for delays!" Dagon growled at the man. "They must have just left it behind and ran for their lives."

"Yes sir, right away, sorry my Lord." The soldier quickly rode off to deliver the orders.

A group of soldiers were pushing the wagon off the road as ordered - while others were clearing the debris, when a sharp blast of a horn sounded off in the trees not far from where they stood.

The sound of that horn sent a dreadful chill through Dagon's body. "It is a trap! Everyone! Arm yourselves!" Dagon screamed, drawing his sword, unstrapping his thick iron shield from his saddle and searching the tree line with his eyes, wondering where the attack would come from.

Arrows flashed from the undergrowth as three scores of barbarian archers came out of nowhere, throwing camouflaged blankets aside - bows notched, and ready to fire a second assault into Dagon's army. No one was prepared for the attack. Men fell off their horses like dead wood from the volley of arrows that sliced across the road from either side. Others were thrown off their startled and wounded mounts, crashing hard into the ground, and trampled into the mud by the terrified horses.

"Make two lines on either side of the road! Shield wall!" Dagon screamed to his men running from his horse with his shield and sword in hand to stand in the lines that were quickly forming.

"What are we going to do my Lord?" Jarroth yelled over the clamor.

"We attack them before we lose any more men," Dagon said, ducking his head behind his shield from the assault of arrows. "When I give the order, everyone with a spear or javelin throw, then charge them as one!" The command was passed down the lines. Within moments, both defense lines had their orders.

"Wait for it!" Dagon called loud. He listened for the last arrow to thud home in a shield.

"NOW!" He cried out as loud as he could, shields shifted and bladed shafts sliced through the jungle's growth, impaling their targets.

"ATTACK!" Dagon cried, charging into the trees, praying to get to the attackers before they notched another deadly volley of arrows.

Dagon and his men met the savages head on. The archers were not armored for defense and were cut down quickly as the defenders ravaged through the tree line hungry for revenge. The battle did not take more than a few brief moments- soon the enemy was dead or fleeing.

"Captain, bring me a report of the dead and wounded." Dagon ordered him, as he finished off the last wounded barbarian who was holding in his innards with his hands.

The rest of the men helped their wounded comrades and started to collect the run-away horses. In the few moments the attack had lasted - so many lives had been taken.

"Sir, it was not your fault we were ambushed," Jarroth said to Dagon, seeing his Lord's inner struggle as they walked back down from the trees to the road.

"I should have seen it sooner. We have not passed any travelers in days, wildlife is more scarce than normal, or when that soldier told me there was a wagon," Dagon barked loudly to his lone friend. "I should have made the connections that it was a trap!" Dagon cursed himself.

"There was no way of knowing sir. Not even you could have known what was about to happen," Jarroth assured him.

"Maybe you're right, old friend - we cannot let this slow us down. We must get to Mandrake. This was just as attempt by those heathen bastards to delay us. I will not rest until I kill them all!" Dagon growled when he had reached his trusted mount. The horse had been to war many times before and did not scare easily.

"My Lord, there are eighty-four dead, a hundred and nine wounded - forty-three will not fight again anytime soon." The CaptainCaptain reported to him when he returned.

"Put the dead in a pile and burn them - collect their armor and weapons and give them to the men who need them. We cannot spare the time to return them to their homes. As for the wounded, the ones who can still fight, stitch them up, and put them on horses. The ones who cannot, send them back to Draco with a small escort of conscripted men," Dagon replied. He could not believe they had lost that many men in such a short time. "Send written word with them to Tundal, so they will be paid what was promised to them for their service."

"Yes, my Lord," the Captain replied.

"Not in a score of years have I seen an ambush do so much damage so quickly," Jarroth muttered to Dagon who was wiping his sword clean of blood on his horse blanket.

"Neither have I. Normally it would be our side achieving such a feat." Dagon put in grimly. "We need to get to Mandrake. We will take those who have horses and ride south. When the others are done here, they can catch up." Dagon mounted his horse and yelled orders to the men he passed. They were all busy pulling the bodies of men and horses to the pile that was already set ablaze, and was now sending the smell of seared human flesh into the air around them.

"The barbarians are marching toward the castle, Sir," a guard announced, running into the hall where Furlac - the advisor of Mandrake - and Lazay - Mandrake's Wizard - had joined with the castle's Generals and Captains. They were all busy strategizing their defenses. The barbarian army had come out of nowhere in the last week, and every day it swelled even larger as more tribes joined the masses. When they had first noticed the banding of savages, two-hundred cavalry had ridden out to dispatch them. Only half the cavalry had returned, blood-soaked and defeated. It had been a trap. The savages had let a small portion of their gathered army be seen, knowing full well the defenders would ride out a small force to butcher them.

Furlac and the Generals had been furious at being fooled, and began to mass the whole of Mandrake's army to charge out and slaughter the wretches. Before they had, organized reports of how many enemies there truly were outside their gates began flooding in from scouts.

"How soon will they be upon us?" Furlac asked, frustrated and sure he did not really want to know the answer.

"Before the sun has set, I am afraid," the man stammered, not hiding his fear well. "They are massing together and establishing crude battle formations."

"What was the last count?" Lazay asked, also not wanting to hear the answer.

"Over twenty thousand," he replied, the number nearly catching in his throat.

"May the Creator have mercy on our souls," Kenden, the General of Mandrake's army mumbled.

"We are all going to be slaughtered!" one of the Captains barked, as he began to pace nervously.

Furlac stood by his seat, a look of worry creasing his face. He knew he had to lift their spirits or there was no way they could win. "We have held this castle for over a hundred years from these bastards and we will do it for another hundred! We must not lose heart before the battle has even begun, damn it! Now we all know what we must do, so let us get to it so we can send these bastards to the Keeper below! Let us make our Lord Dagon proud in his stead. We will not lose his castle!" he yelled triumphantly, stirring everyone's inner strength and pride as they all cheered with him, though some less enthusiastically than others.

"Furlac is right!" Kenden said, knowing what Furlac was trying to achieve. "We have killed thousands of these heathen mongrels, and now there are thousands more right outside our very gates waiting for the sting of our blades!" he roared vigorously. "Let us not keep these cowsons waiting!"

Archers and fiercely armed soldiers lined the battlements and watched the approach of the overwhelming enemy. No one had ever seen an army of savages this large before, not even when the majority of the barbarian tribes had come together under Azazel's bitter conquest had such a force been gathered for a single attack. Nor had Mandrake ever had to defend their castle under such weak circumstance. Their Lord was away with his fierce battle-hardened escort of three-hundred who were among the greatest warriors in

Mandrake. The northern wall was still under repairs from a catapult malfunction, though over the last days every stonemason in the castle had done their very best day and night to repair it as high and as solidly as possible. Though even with their best efforts, the wall was still the weakest point in their defenses and would need twice the men to defend it. The irrigation had been re-routed again and now the moat was well on its way to being full.

Though best efforts had been taken, Furlac still feared the battle to come. Of course, the enemy had to begin their attack at dusk, knowing their numbers were superior to the defenders. They could filter fresh warriors continuously into the attack all night and into the day that followed, wearing the defenders down until they were overrun.

"I wish Lord Dagon was here right now. He would know what to do better than I," Furlac muttered, staring at his withered old hands. He knew he was not the young, strong soldier he had been so many years before. Age had caught up with him many winters ago and he had all but given up the sword more than a score of years before that. He had given up the fight, for politics and to advise Lord Dagon in daily affairs of his lands. "Thirty winters ago I would gladly have stood here, blade and shield in hand awaiting the first poor cowson to leap over the wall. But now..." he trailed off.

"As you said, my friend! Do not lose heart before the battle has even begun. We will not lose our castle this night, nor the next! We can hold." Lazay said looking up toward the heavens. "We have to," he whispered to the light northern breeze.

Soldiers found their positions on the battlements and readied themselves for the oncoming attack. Some honed their blades with a whetstone, making sure every inch of their weapons was sharp. Others practiced with their weapons, testing the weight and preparing their muscles for the long night ahead. Many simply talked with nearby comrades about whatever came to mind, or stared off into the night at the incoming enemy hordes.

Furlac and Lazay walked along the wall, among the men, talking with them and giving words of encouragement. When they came to the western gate, they could not help but stop and stare out into the eerie sight before them. Through the darkening sky, they could see the torches of those who marched toward them - thousands of small lights making their way across the ground. As the enemy neared, the ground shook and the stone in which the defenders stood vibrated lightly but noticeably.

"There are so many of them," a young archer said aloud, as he stared unblinking.

"They are so big!" Another commented, wiping his sweaty hands on his pants.

"Makes them easier to hit," one of their comrades laughed to the side. "We do not even have to aim, just shoot."

"How can you laugh at a time like this Tyron?" The first archer said grimly, his face sickly pale.

"Why not Dreg? Their down there and we are up here." Tyron laughed again. "You do not really think we will lose to the likes of these cowsons do you? Most of them do not even have decent armor, just leather and bone breast plates and wooden bucklers."

"Yeah Tyron, you're right," Dreg replied, a little of his color coming back into his lips.

"They are just so huge!" the soldier to their right moaned again.

"That is why we are going to keep them down there," Lazay told the group of young soldiers as he and Furlac passed by.

The three young men looked up at the middle-aged Wizard, grins forming on their faces at his presences. He was not surprised by their fear - he doubted either one of the three had ever killed a man before, or been in true combat. Even several of the veterans he had passed, wore fear behind their words and demeanor, like garments that were barely visible.

"Tonight is going to be a very long night." Furlac sighed, adjusting the sword on his belt.

"Your brain and strategies are worth more to us than your sword arm is, Sir." The Captain of the western archer unit saluted.

"I will do my part, if they come over the wall, Captain." Furlac replied with a grin as he tapped his hilt.

"I shall see to it that does not happen," the Captain smiled and patted Furlac on the back, not mockingly, but with admiration.

Furlac was well into his sixtieth winter and had not fought in battle for a score of years, though he had turned the tide of many with his quick, strategic thinking. Though back in his youth, he had a well-respected sword arm, and even though by all accounts he was classed as an old man, he knew he could still fight a good fight.

"I pray my powers can hold out through this night. It will be easier for the men to hold them off tomorrow in the light, while I rest and regain my strength." Lazay truly wondered if he would be able to make it through the night. He had never used his Gift to the point of collapsing, but he knew he would tonight. He wished he had kept his apprentice for another year of final training, before sending him off on his own. Even a new apprentice would have been helpful now, but he had wanted to have some time to himself to hone his own Gift, before taking in another. Now that thought of solitude seemed selfish and ignorant.

"As do I, my friend - as do I," Furlac told him and turned to leave. "Watch yourself tonight my friend." With that, Furlac walked off, down into the courtyard.

Lazay stood watching the massive enemy march on the castle. Could they truly hold against such numbers, he wondered. The five catapults were placed by the walls, aimed in the direction of the on-coming masses. It was a shame they had not been able to collect more boulders, but with the barbarian army out there, they had not had much luck in finding more, without losing men. The boulders they did have were now being smothered with tar and flammable oils, to be set ablaze, before they were launched off at the enemy. *We will hold*, he told himself.

The people of the city who had not fled had been moved within the castle walls days before, and now every man willing to fight had a weapon and what armor could be had. The city was now an empty place, inhabited by the stray animals and scavenging rats. Everyone had only been allowed to bring into the castle what they could carry and no more. The city would likely be looted clean within a few days.

Half the women and all children were put into large guest rooms on the top floors of the castle where the cities' entertainers did their best to help them forget what was happening outside. The other half of the women were set up on the main floor of the castle in the massive dining hall with Mandrake's physicians - this would serve as their infirmary.

The blacksmith, bowmen and fletchers of the city had been working day and night - making spears, arrows, and swords. They had little or no sleep, but now resources were running low and they used what little metal and wood they had left to make arrows.

Mandrake had six hundred trained archers and twice that number of city folk standing beside them armed with bows. All of them were on that wall ready for the oncoming battle. Every bow in the castle and city had been gathered and was now being manned. With an army of almost four thousand trained soldiers and seven thousand farmers, merchants, and men from the city, they could hold the castle. At least Lazay hoped they could. He wished more of the city people would have stayed, as they could have tripled their army, but he did not blame them.

"Master Lazay! The enemy has reached the western city gates," a fierce looking warrior said, pointing off into the distance.

"Then it will not be long now," Lazay whispered.

"Loose!" General Kenden barked loudly. Eight hundred razor-tipped shafts exploded from their wielders long bows on cue, slicing devastatingly through the front ranks of barbarians who charged forward, grappling hooks and coils of rope in hand. "Nock, pull, loose!" Kenden yelled again. Again, the volley of arrows laid the charging force down in bristling heaps.

The defenders had stopped all attempts of the grapplers even getting close enough to the wall to throw their iron hooks. But the first of the enemy to arrive had been unprepared and unorganized, their battle frenzy had overwhelmed them and they charged foolishly toward the defenders in hopes to be the first to scale the walls and enter the fortress. But now they realized their folly and were now strategizing their efforts. Two tight rows of warriors marched forward, large wooden shields locked together, forming a wall in front. The row in the back held their shields high and angled upward, shielding the grapplers behind them from the vicious archers on the wall. Not far behind them were two other such walls of shields, behind the second were men carrying long wooden planks to place over the moat. The third shield wall protected enemy archers.

"Sir, we cannot get a shot," several of the archers yelled. "They are completely guarded!"

Kenden looked over the wall and saw the defense. "Here I was hoping they would let us kill them easily all day," he muttered to the nearest men. "Hold your shots! We do not need to be feeding their shields and wasting our arrows."

Kenden ran to the edge of the inner wall. "I need two units up here now!" he called down to the infantry below.

Enemy grapples were thrown high and locked tightly on the stone, enemies swung across the moat to the ten-foot landing in front of the wall. Some began to scramble up the branded hemp rope, while others waited behind to grab and secure the coming planks and throw the ends of the rope to their comrades on the other side of the moat, holding their shields over the top of their heads.

"Cut the ropes!" Kenden bellowed, slashing his own sword down, dropping the poor climber to his death below. Many of the enemy missed the hard earth and splashed harmlessly into the water. "Fire you fools!" Kenden barked at the archers who were just watching the display. "Get them while they're defenseless!" A dozen shafts embedded into the backs of the swimming warriors and they bobbed motionless in the moat.

"Incoming!" a call from the crowed bellowed out as a return volley of arrows cut through the sky. But the enemy's sense of distance had been off, and the arrows skipped and cracked harmlessly off the front of the stone wall, killing many of their own warriors.

The next assault of enemy shafts made the height and forced the defenders to duck and cover while those in the courtyard below held their shields high. Several cries and screams followed. Two more assaults followed, keeping the defenders pinned while the enemy worked fast in placing the long planks across the moat.

"General, we need to act and soon!" a soldier called over to him, seeing the trouble below.

General Kenden cursed to himself as another volley of enemy arrows rained down upon them, and again screams could be heard. The General counted the seconds that passed until the next attack, eight seconds between. He heard the last of the arrows crack into the stone and shields. "Ready yourselves!" He called out. "Let fly!" He roared after his count of six and the defenders let fly into the enemy archers just as their shield bearers dropped their guard to allow the archers a clear shot. The vicious tipped shafts found their targets and cut down the enemy line of archers, leaving only a handful alive.

"Light them up boys!" Kenden called to his men. Each man dipped the tip of their next arrow in thick oil and ignited them. "Aim for the planks!"

Hundreds of flaming arrows thudded into the thick, solid planks that made up the makeshift bridge. But most of the flames did not take and burned out within a few heartbeats - the barbarians had anticipated the move and the timber had been soaked with water.

"Bastards!" Kenden barked down to the enemy. "Again!" he ordered his men. Hundreds of more fiery shafts pounded on the soaked planks, this time more stayed burning, but still the majority sizzled out before long.

"They are charging!" a shout came from somewhere.

Kenden glanced over the wall to witness the flood of enemy warriors charging ferociously toward them. There were thousands of them, many carried grappling hooks while others groups carried long ladders.

"Fire at will boys!" Kenden commanded. The archers took aim time and again, showering down a deadly rain into the hordes that charged the wall. "Where is that bloody Wizard?" Kenden grumbled. "I need more men up here now!" He called down to the courtyard below and without hesitation, men began charging up the stairs to the battlements, weapons in hand.

"General, maybe it is time?" The fair-haired Captain asked him, a look of worry creasing his face.

"Not yet, we will save that surprise until we truly need it." Kenden told him. "Do not let a single one of those goat shaggers over this wall you hear me!" He ordered the soldiers on the wall and they all roared their response. He grabbed a passing soldier by the shoulder. "Go and find that blasted Wizard Lazay and tell him to get his arse up here!"

The archers pulled back to the rear of the wall conserving their ammunition. The eager infantry took their places awaiting the first of the enemy to scale the walls. Those first souls were met with fresh, shiny blade thrusts to their throats or vicious swings leaving them headless, their bodies crumbling down dislodging several of their companions as they fell. But that did not slow the ascending savages and within a heartbeat another was there reaching over the edge.

Two enormous warriors parried past the defenders and leaped onto battlements. With a hearty swing of their double bladed battle-axes, they cleaved through armor and bellies of the three defenders who had tried to press them back before more could scale the wall behind them.

Kenden charged in, his broadsword low. With a powerful upward arc, he hit the nearest barbarian slicing clean through his left thigh to his right shoulder - severing through his innards, ribs, and lungs. The brute stumbled back, already dead and fell from the battlements knocking the newest savage to reach the top down with him.

The second warrior brought his axe down hard, hoping to cut the General in two. Kenden sidestepped the deadly attack and drove his blade forward, aiming for the barbarian's chest. The barbarian was faster than Kenden expected and rolled his body around the attack. Using the momentum of the turn, the brute kept going and brought his huge blade around with him in a tremendous swing. Kenden did not have time to think and instinct alone saved him as he dropped like the stone, barely avoiding the attack. The barbarian's axe head smashed through several inches of stone behind the defenders and off balanced him as the blade kept going. The General took the luck and thrust his sword up into his enemy's chest and through his back - he pushed up as he went, opening the enemy's chest and spilling his insides. Kenden pulled his sword free and pushed the toppling corpse over the battlements into the frenzy below. "Where in the Keeper's arse is that damned Wizard?" the General growled, thrusting his sword tip into the face of the newcomer up the ladder.

They were holding, but Kenden could see the tiring in the farmers and city folk already. Their swings and thrusts were slowing and awkward, more and more ladders were being placed against the wall - more and more enemies were climbing up.

"Master Lazay, Master Lazay!" The young soldier called running up the stairs to the eastern battlements, where battle too had begun, though the thick of the enemy was attacking from the west.

"What is it?" Lazay asked, well he pulsed his Gift into a wounded soldier, who had been struck by an arrow. Within moments the blood slowed, then stopped and the hole closed up, leaving only a small scar. Lazay could have healed it to the point that the scar would have been gone, but he would not waste his powers at such a time.

"General Kenden needs you at the western battlements!" the man huffed loudly stopping in front of the Wizard.

Lazay helped the healed archer to his feet and sent him off to his post. "How bad is it?"

"Bad, I am afraid, they have covered the moat with water-soaked planks and ladders were already being raised when I was sent to find you," the soldier reported. "But I fear soon they will start ramming the gates.... If they break down one of the gates, we are..."

Lazay silenced the man with a nod of understanding. "You stay here and help fend off the enemy. I will go and see to it that they do not breach the western gate."

"But Master Lazay, I think I would be better served where the brunt of the attacks are," the soldier exclaimed.

"If the thousand savages down here take this wall, are we no less dead?" Lazay asked the soldier, who let the truth of the words sink in. "The main part of our own force is at the western and northern gates, I fear not that we will be overtaken there. It is the eastern and southern gates that have only a small handful of men - mostly farmers that I fear for. I would fear a lot less if I knew a soldier such as yourself was here in my place." The words struck pride in the man and he stood straighter.

"I cannot leave you to watch one meager wall!" Mandrake's Wizard asked Kenden as he ran up the stairs to the western battlements. However, the General was preoccupied with a massive brute that wielded a huge, metal, double-headed lance.

Kenden parried and strafed the wild jabs and thrusts of the brute unable to counter or advance. The metal seven-foot lance was brandished effortlessly by the towering barbarian and with a speed and agility that was deceptive for a man his size. Kenden could not break through the enemy's guard and was fast tiring from the endless dance. Kenden deflected the lance high, opening his enemy's guard and hoping to score a killing blow when a sizzling arc of power erupted from behind Kenden, bursting through the large savage's leather armor and chest, clean through to the other side, throwing the barbarian dead to the slick stone.

"You could have aided me sooner!" Kenden growled, between labored breaths.

"It looked like you had the situation under control," Lazay replied sarcastically, drawing a dangerous glare from the General - but only for a moment as he was quickly needed again as another section of wall was being pushed back by the enemy. Lazay grabbed a soldier by the arm and motioned to the courtyard and the man nodded his understanding and was off.

"Stand back!" Lazay commanded a group of soldiers who were desperately fighting several brutes who had almost made it over the wall. Knowing better than to question the mighty Wizard, the group quickly fell back. Thinking they had the advantage, the enemy quickly took the battlements in a frenzy, but before they had their bearings a relentless torrent of air smashed into them throwing them back over the battlements.

Lazay bounded up on top of the battlement walls, several bolts of energy raining down from his fingertips into the climbing hordes, shredding through limbs, torsos, and ladders alike. The bloody wreckage collapsed to the planked ground below, killing or injuring more than a few on impact.

Wasting no time, Lazay unleashed his fiery bolts and lighting arcs cascaded down from his perch into the swarms below. The water-soaked planks were no match for the intensity of his Wizard's fire and soon the makeshift bridges over the moat were aflame. engulfing and devouring all who stood upon them. The hungry flames consumed their way through the long wooden ladders with haste, toppling even more of the enemy into the bitter inferno.

With Mandrake's Wizard turning the tide, the defenders quickly regained the wall and with no more enemies scaling up, the archers moved back into place and once again began launching their deadly volleys into the scrambling hordes below.

Having no more comrades scaling the wall, enemy archers began their assault back, all taking aim on the valuable Wizard who still stood atop the battlements finishing off the remanding plank bridges underneath.

Seeing the raising volley of enemy shafts, Lazay's palms stretched out - a great pulse erupted from his hands violently disrupting the very atmosphere in front of him, sending the enemy arrows back at them with such force that some cut clean through warriors before they were stopped by the hard earth behind them.

"Now!" Lazay cried as loud as he could.

"Fire!" The engineer commanding the catapults yelled upon hearing his queue, and five flaming boulders sailed up through the air, high over the defenders, lighting up the night sky brilliantly. Defenders and attackers alike stopped to regard the fiery boulders in speculative amazement, but for the attackers that speculation was short lived as the giant flaming stones began their descent and crashed amongst the barbarian masses. The four hundred pound boulders bounced erratically through the enemy hordes, leaving crushed and dying warriors in their wake. By the time the boulders had ceased their rampage though the enemy ranks another flaming hail was cresting over the battlements and into the enemy.

Two more such attacks from the catapults rained down on the enemy along with scores of vicious arrows before finally, the enemies retreat horn was sounded and they ran back into the city and out of range of the defenders devastating defense.

"The dawn is fast approaching and we have finally pushed back the last of the enemies from all four sides of the battlements." One of Mandrake's Captains announced to the room.

"Thank you Captain - now go eat and rest with your men," Furlac told him.

"We held strong through the night." Lazay commented, weary relief in his tone. He had expelled the majority of his Gift in the defense of Mandrake and in the healing of many of the injured soldiers. Yet when he had left the infirmary there had still been many more. But he knew he needed to conserve his Gift - they had forced the enemy back this night, but the enemy was still far from defeated and would attack again before too long.

"What were the numbers?" Furlac asked Lazay, knowing the Wizard had come from there.

"Better than expected, but still disheartening." Lazay sighed as he rubbed his temples. "Close to four hundred dead, almost twice that number injured two hundred and thirty seven which can no longer fight…if they make it through the day that is."

"That is disheartening," Furlac muttered, his face deep set with worry and fatigue.

"I have always said farmers make horrible soldiers," General Kenden muttered. "Though I have to give it to them, they held their courage."

"If it was not for those farmers we would all be corpses," the young Captain Kermont said. "We have used up near a third of our arrows already. The fletchers, carpenters, and blacksmiths are working furiously to make more, but it will not be enough, there are not enough of them to keep up."

Furlac dropped his head into his hands, his fingers tightening around his hair, hoping the painful sensation would spark something, and it did. "The wounded!" Furlac stammered out as the idea came to him. "The ones that can no longer fight, we will put the ones who can to work helping making arrows and repairing weapons."

"We cannot ask that of them," Captain Kermont stammered out in shock. "These men are wounded and all but defeated - they need to rest and recover. We cannot ask them..."

"Cannot ask them what?" General Kenden intervened sharply. "Cannot ask them to fight on but in another way, to continue in our... no...their cause? If we cannot hold the enemy on the other side of those walls, we all die."

The young Captain opened his mouth to protest, but had no argument. The General was right, if they could not fend off the enemy, what would it matter? "I will go see to it," Kermont said and left the room.

"How long do you think it will be before they attack again?" Lazay asked.

"They will not let us rest for long; they have the advantage of numbers and strength. The harder they press, the less we sleep, the weaker we get," Furlac answered.

"They made a lot of mistakes last night - they were eager, too sure of themselves and their numbers. We routed them a little, and thinned out their numbers. They will not be so foolish next time," Kenden said. "The moat is thick with bodies and wreckage, the water in it is now tainted and undrinkable, we have but three wells inside the castle walls. Water will be scarce on the morrow."

"We have all the barrels and pails full of water... we can use them if needed," Lazay added.

"Maybe, that is if we are lucky enough and they are foolish enough to not rain down fire upon us," Furlac replied.

"That is doubtful." Kenden said.

"We will have to ration water then," Furlac said bitterly, the first day into the siege and they already had to ration supplies to their soldiers. That was never good for morale.

"Sir Furlac?" A soldier called, as he entered the room and found Mandrake's advisor. "Sir I... I..."

"Well out with it man; we do not have all day," Kenden growled.

"You need to come to the battlements," the man sputtered .

"Damn it man, just tell us already!" Kenden barked, as they crested the stairs of the battlements.

"Look," the man pointed west toward the city and enemy army - half Mandrake's army was on the battlements looking out at the sight.

"May the Creator have mercy on our souls," Furlac whispered, but all those around him heard it.

"How...how can there be more of them?" Lazay asked bewildered. "We killed thousands of them last night, and it does not look like we did a damn thing to their ranks!"

"How many do you figure are out there?" Furlac asked the General.

"I would say everyone we killed last night was replaced, maybe more," Kenden replied, his eyes cold and his demeanor grim. "Their ranks will swell day after day as more tribes and savages come forth. If they believe they will conquer and overtake us..." he trailed off. He did not have to finish; - the others knew what he would have said. Barbarians were like wolves, as soon as they smelt blood and an easy kill, the whole pack would emerge.

"How long do you think we have until they..." Lazay began to say, but stopped when the low blow of a horn was heard.

"Get them catapults armed and fast," Kenden said to Furlac, who nodded and left to arouse the engineers. "I will need you up here with me this morning Wizard."

Lazay looked into the General's eyes; a hard, bitter set determination was engraved there. "Do you think we can hold them back?"

"We will today."

"Fire!" the engineer manning the five catapults bellowed. All five great arms lurched forward with tremendous speed and power, hurling the giant blazing boulders up over Mandrake's battlements into the scores of enemies below. The fuel-smothered rocks laid waste to all in their rampaging course.

Already, fifteen such devastating assaults had been released from the five mechanical weapons of warfare. More than their fair share of enemies that now littered the killing field had been humbled beneath the earthy ammunition. Though the terrifying catapult attacks slowed the enemy's charge, it did not stop them.

The barbarians' strategy had altered greatly this time, truly bitter by the defeat they suffered before. Their archers were first to charge in - thousands of them, not slowing for anything. If they feared the giant stones falling from the sky, they did not show it as they negotiated the gore-littered field to Mandrake's impressive wall. Once inside the range of the lethal catapults, they attacked in full.

Thousands of powerful wooden long bows were pulled back and released in no timed fashion. This time, each enemy archer had been instructed to nock his bow at will rather than on command. The effect of which was a constant barrage of arrows raining down on the defending archers, giving them no hope of striking back.

The first volleys of enemy arrows were so thick they dimmed the very sun, causing the defenders to look up in petrifying surprise. Many in the courtyard were caught off guard by the sudden attack and had no defense against the raining death that fell upon them. Many of Mandrake's defenders were cut down in those first few moments, some being impaled by more than a score of the wicked barbed shafts. Many more were injured beyond fighting again. Men scrambled this way and that trying to find cover anywhere they could from the deadly bombardment. Those with shields held them high and ducked tightly to the ground, blocking hundreds of crude shafts.

The raining death was continuous - the defenders did not receive a single moment of reprieve. Several engineers were killed in the first moments, the remaining found cover near the wall - it forced the catapults to cease their devastating attack, which meant the enemy army was nearly unopposed.

Atop the battlements, the archers were forced to stay hidden behind the wall, as thousands of arrows skipped and cracked off the stone all around them. Every now and again an archer got brave and took a shot down into the advancing enemy, but more often than not their efforts were in vain and they were struck down dead or wounded.

"General what do we do?" Several soldiers cried out to Kenden, who was hiding behind a large metal shield, Lazay ducking behind the wall several paces away.

Kenden knew the enemy was building their planked bridges again unobstructed, and that soon ladders would be placed on the wall and enemy warriors would flow up like ants and storm over the wall. But there was nothing they could do well under this volley of arrows and once the volley stopped it may be too late.

"Wizard I need you!" Kenden barked and Lazay turned to regard him.

"What is it?" the Wizard yelled back as several arrows skipped by his tightly curled up legs.

"I need you to do something about this!" the General yelled back watching several more of his archers taken down. "Before it is too late and we are all dead.

"Like what?" Lazay bellowed back.

"Damn it Wizard! Do something!" Kenden growled.

Lazay rolled his eyes - he had been trying to think of something he could do to turn the attack around or at least buy them some reprieve so they could defend themselves. There was only one thing he could think of, and it was risky. But war was full of risks.

Lazay grabbed a large body shield from the nearest soldier, ducking behind the wall beside him and stood facing the barrage. Dozens of barbed shafts slammed into the metal plated shield, several with enough force to puncture through the coating of metal and into the wood, the tips just visible on the other side.

Lazay blocked out the eerie sound of snapping arrows from his mind as he called upon his Gift. The air all around Lazay began to stir, slowly picking up swiftness as it whipped his long blond hair all around. All the broken shards and shafts around him began to roll away and were pushed to the front of the wall, creating a pile of kindling. Within heartbeats, the air around the Wizard was so forceful that hundreds of arrows that fell around him were blown out wildly as if striking an invisible wall. Lazay released the shield and it flew over the wall into the enemy, as did hundreds of the deadly shafts they were firing. Soon, the air torrent's momentum was overpowering, scattering all debris from the stone wall and causing all the soldiers on the wall to tuck down close to the stone or for some, to grab hold of something solid for fear of being tossed over the battlements.

The sky-darkening volley of arrows met the tremendous potency of Lazay's Gift and was hurled back into the hordes of enemy below with divine swiftness and force, mincing through armor and flesh like it was tearing through parchment.

Scores of enemy fell dead or dying within heartbeats of Lazay's summoning. Many others had dropped their bows and found cover, knowing the more they fired the more of their own would die.

"Get those catapults loaded!" Kenden yelled down to the hiding engineers. Soon, impending stones were again launched over the battlements into the overwhelming hordes below.

As fast as it began, it ended - as Lazay slumped to the cold stone, ceasing the dominant current of wind. The execution of such a summon took much out of him and he needed a moment to gather himself.

"Good job Wizard, next time, do not wait so damn long," Kenden said rushing by Lazay to the front of the wall. "Get up you cowsons! You have had enough rest, we have blood to shed!" he barked out in encouragement not a moment too soon either, for the first of the enemy warriors began to crest the battlements, only to be met by the defenders' cold steel.

For more than half the day, not a single savage gained a foothold on Mandrake's battlements, but soon the defenders began to tire, their blades dull from the scores of fallen, their muscles burning and their reactions slowing. In several places along the wall, enemies were able to push back the defenders and gain ground on the battlements. Most were short-lived, but a few held solid.

Kenden wrenched his blood-drenched blade out of an attacker's neck, spilling his lifeblood over the already slick crimson stone. Without slowing, he charged another that cleared the battlements, carving through the brute's midsection and spilling his entrails before he could even stand straight.

Kenden's muscles ached unbearably with every swing, thrust and parry. Sweat drenched every part of his body and dripped into his eyes, stinging them bitterly, but he had not the time to wipe them away. One false move or drop in defense and he would be as dead as the hundred enemies that had fallen by his blade that day. With every passing minute that he fought, he tired a little more. A score of wounds riddled his body, several were deep enough to be serious, but he had no time to think of that.

Kenden could see the defenders were losing ground, as they were forced back near the other side of the wall and now nearly as many enemies lined the wall as defenders. If they could not turn the tides soon, Mandrake would be lost.

"Sir, sir!" a blood-soaked soldier cried out as he ran across the northern battlements to Furlac. The fighting was much less over here and the enemy had not come close to gaining a foothold against the defenders.

Furlac slashed his sword down, cleaving an enemy warrior's skull near in half as his head came over the battlements. "What is it?"

"We are losing the western wall Sir; we will not be able to hold them back much longer."

Furlac stepped back from his crimson-soaked area on the northern wall and wiped the thick grimy sweat from his brow. He looked down both lengths of the wall, fighting was thick the entire length down, no fighters here could be spared to help reinforce the west side. He cursed. He knew once they had run out of boulders to fire into the enemy that this would happen.

"Soldier!" Furlac bellowed to the messenger. The soldier slashed his sword down twice dispatching a duo of enemy warriors breeching the wall before he turned to regard Mandrake's advisor.

"Yes sir?"

"Do you know where Lazay is?" Furlac asked.

"I believe he went to the infirmary to rest and regain his strength."

"Good, I need you to go to the engineers manning the catapults, tell them to load them up with whatever they can find that will kill, anything! We need that reprieve at least!" Furlac ordered.

"Lazay! Where is he?" Furlac barked bursting through the makeshift hospital doors and grabbed the nearest man. "Where is Lazay!"

"Over there!" The surgeon pointed off to the far corner where sheets had been hung up to add some form of privacy.

Furlac released the bloodstained man and ran across the room to where the man had pointed. The stone floor had sand all over it, to help soak up the blood and allow walking without slipping.

"Lazay, Lazay!" Furlac hollered, pulling the sheet aside.

The Wizard lay on a small wooden cot. He looked weak and weary; his once thin age lines were now deep and gloomy turning his once soft and bright demeanor, ominous. He looked as if he has doubled in age since last Furlac had seen him.

Lazay's eyes pulled open. "What? What is it?"

"We need you old friend and whatever powers you can possibly muster. We are losing the western wall. It is only a matter of time; it may already be too late," Furlac explained, regret starting to pain him at the sight of his friend.

Lazay pulled himself upright, his feet planted uneasily on the gritty floor. He took a large swallow of lukewarm water from the mug by his bed. "I will do what I can," he said as he stood, his knees almost buckled under his skinny frame, but Furlac was there to support him. "I just fear it will not be enough."

"Are ye sure lad?" the engineer replied, his right eyebrow cocked high in wonder.

"Furlac said anything that could be loaded into the catapults that would inflict casualties upon the enemy!" The soldier repeated loudly over the sound of battle above. "We need to slow the enemy down however we can; every moment that passes is another inch on that wall we lose."

The Captain understood that reasoning with firm determination. "Every one of ya's get going and grab anything you can, anything that can kill, anything that has a good weight to it!" he barked out to his score of men. "Now get moving ya sheep shaggers!"

Within moments, several men had already returned with ammunition for the large weapons. Blacksmith's anvils, sledgehammer heads, heavy chairs, and many other random finds were loaded into the catapults large buckets.

The sound of the catapults firing and the speedy shadows that flew overhead again gave the defenders on the wall renewed strength and they began to fight with a bitter vigor. Slowly, they pushed the enemy back, gaining a solid defensive line again.

Furlac half-carried half-dragged Lazay up the stairs to the battlements, the sight of the catapults firing again speeding his steps. He did not know how long they would be active, but he knew they would slow the enemy down a little, hopefully long enough for Lazay to give them the upper hand again.

"I need to be at the edge of the wall," Lazay muttered weakly.

Furlac knew better than to question the Wizard. "Clear a path to the wall!" he bellowed loudly and the soldiers on the wall picked up their pace seeing Lazay on the wall again. The men pushed forward and made short work of the enemy intruders.

Furlac led the Wizard to the wall, "now what?"

Lazay swayed slightly gripping the stone wall. "Stand back." He closed his eyes and deepened his breathing, forcing out the violent sounds of steal on steal, and the grunts, curses, and screams of the wounded and dying. His focus and concentration made him nearly forget his body and its weakened state. His breathing slowed and his entire body began tingling, as he tapped into the deepest part of him, his innate given Gift. He pulled on his inner essence, his very internal fibers summoning every ounce of potency he could. He could feel his body begin to quake as he forced all his efforts out, he pictured the moat below, covered with wooden planks, ladders, wreckage and bodies. Sensing his will, vicious flames sprung forth all along the moat of the western wall, quickly consuming the timber planks, wooden ladders, and bodies, dead and alive alike.

"He is doing it!" Several cheers went up around the battlements as the hordes of enemy that cascaded over the wall slowed and the defenders quickly dispatched the enemies who were left.

"Lazay you did it man!" Furlac cried out, relief washing over him, but was short-lived when he heard several thuds and knew the sound to be arrows puncturing through exposed flesh. He looked around to the men near him, looking for the victim of the assault, but saw none. Fear stole his breath and his eyes shot back to Lazay, - several shafts were embedded in his chest and he slumped over the wall and fell.

Lazay knew his Gift was nearly exhausted and yet somehow he continued to release, seemingly calling upon some unknown inner quintessence. He could no longer feel his body nor could he sense the world around him any longer. All he knew was his Gift as it overwhelmed him.

"NO!" Furlac screamed, charging forward trying to catch his friend, but it was too late. Lazay's body plummeted to the chaos below. The corpse of Mandrake's Wizard crashed hard into the flaming wreckage in the moat below, a blistering detonation of inconceivable power erupted. The defenders were thrown back and forced to hide behind the stone wall to avoid injury from the sudden magical epidemic that raged and consumed all around Mandrake's moat, flaring up as if the water was tainted lantern oil.

"What is the update?" Furlac asked the weary man who entered the room, his voice hoarse with grief and exhaustion.

The soldier looked just as somnolent. "The flames still burn fiercely around Mandrake Sir, holding the enemy at bay."

"Good," Furlac replied, his voice almost cracking from emotions. The fire burned because of some abnormal phenomenon that had taken place with the death of Lazay.

"Yes Sir," the man said, licking his cracked lips before continuing hesitantly, "but we do have a problem because of it. The gates are burning on all sides, another few hours and there will be nothing left. Also, the intense temperature has heated the stone of the battlements and now it is near impossible to set foot on it. It is only a matter of time before the stone begins to crack."

"Thank you," Furlac said, letting the solider take his leave. "What are we to do now?" Furlac muttered, fear gripping his words.

"We fight, and we win," Kenden replied, as if it was as simple as that.

Furlac looked at his friend dumbfounded for but a second. "I respect your enthusiasm Kenden but I fear it is not so easy."

"But it is, that easy," Kenden replied matter of fact.

"In less than two days the enemy has destroyed near two thirds of our army, exhausted the catapults to the point we are using furniture as ammunition! Not to mention we are collecting enemy arrows to fire back at them because our own are depleted, and some of those arrows we have gathered are the very arrows that have killed our own soldiers!" Furlac cried out bitterly, as frustration consumed him. "So where is the easy part?"

Kenden stared hard at Mandrake's advisor, a harsh tint glazing his eyes as he considered the man before he spoke. "We have near four thousand fighting men, pride of family, friends, and home in their hearts. We have breath in our lungs, blood in our veins, and steel in our hands and an enemy at our gates. We cannot run - we cannot hide - all we can do is fight." Kenden replied. "So as I said, we fight, and we win, it is that easy."

The wild Wizard's fire had ignited all around Mandrake, following the path of the moat. The flames had leapt high in the air, thrice as high as any man standing and as hot as the flames of the Keeper's domain. Half a day it had burned wrathfully, fuelled by some unyielding essence of Mandrake's noble Wizard after he had perished. Now the flames were subsiding, and smoldering on the last remains of wreckage around the moat. Over half the water in the moat had evaporated, but the water that was left was degrees below boiling.

The battlements were too hot to man, so they were now barren. Three out of four of Mandrake's thick, solid gates had burned through, leaving large, charred gaping holes and diminishing their defenses severely. Only the south gate still stood, though it was damaged greatly and would not hold for long against any attack. It would not be long before the enemy attacked in full and then they would be overwhelmed.

"They are breaking through!" An archer shouted as he aimed for a barbarian who had moved his shield and now taunted those inside by pissing toward the castle. Six arrows found the man's chest as he died in his own waste.

The defenders had squandered no time with the final reprieve they were given by Lazay and blocked up the massive gateways with wagons, and debris to buy them as much time as possible.

The enemy archers fired at will over the walls or through the holes in the crudely fashioned barriers into the men who stood inside waiting for them. Wave after wave rained down upon them, as men fell dead or wounded everywhere. They had not been expecting this now, and had little time to react. The barbarians climbed out of the warm moat and through the gateway doors and hacked their way through the blockade. The archers on the still hot walls fired at will, doing their best to kill as many of the swimming savages as they could while their backs were exposed. Soon, the moat ran crimson again and the bloating bodies of the enemy made it hard for the living to swim over.

"Stop their archers, damn it!" a Captain screamed, as he let loose an arrow into the enemy archers who were persistently unleashing arrows over the walls and into Mandrake's weakening army.

"But Captain, what of the moat?" the soldier beside him bellowed.

The Captain spun on the soldier and grabbed him angrily. "It will not aid us if we are all cut down by arrows, boy! Now kill their archers!"

"Yes Sir!" The man cried out as the Captain released his grip.

The next arrows launched from the walls hit home in the lines of enemy archers, forcing them back beyond the defenders' range and stopping their own volleys on the battered castle. But that did not stop them from the action - bows were thrown aside and devilish blades were drawn as they sprung forward to swell the charging ranks.

With the ceasing of enemy arrows raining down on them, Mandrake's defenders soon realized how few of them still stood. The enemy had broken through the barriers blocking the gateways.

"We cannot hold them off, Sir!" a young soldier screamed, fighting furiously at the oncoming onslaught of barbarians.

"Yes we can, damn it! We have no other choice!" the General yelled back, as he charged forward swinging madly, cutting through sinew and bone as he went. But within his rage-filled assault, he dropped his defenses and a searing pain shot through his side. His sword fell out of his hands as his strength failed him - he tried for one final roar of defiance before death took him.

Furlac heard the cries and roars from the courtyard below and his heart sank as all hope faded. He had failed to hold his Lord's castle- he had failed to keep those inside the walls safe from the enemy. He had simply, failed. A sudden flash of metal and a searing pain erupted in his left shoulder as an enemy blade scored a hit through his meager parry. Sudden rage exploded through him and he plunged his long sword into his attacker's belly and tore it free. He may have failed, but he was determined to make the attackers bleed every inch they took. "Retreat to the castle!" He bellowed.

The last few soldiers limped through the thick, oak castle doors to join the remaining few who had managed to escape. Furlac watched as the last few men, who sacrificed their lives were cut down as the castle doors were shut and barred.

A heavy guilt lingered in the air. An unspoken shame glistened in the eyes of every man in the room at the final screams of their fathers, brothers, and friends from outside.

Furlac slumped against the doors, his mind blank, and his heart heavy with humiliation. He looked up at the survivors, so few in number - most suffering from injuries, many who would die because of them before the enemy could finish them.

General Kenden knew the mood had to change if they were to make a worthy final stand. "Get up now!" he hissed to Furlac, who looked up at him as a child would an angry father.

"It is done - we have lost," Furlac muttered, only loud enough for Kenden to hear. "It is over."

"Get up!" Kenden ordered firmly, offering his hand, "and lead us to an honorable death," he added, words softening.

Furlac looked hard into the General's eyes, not a hint of blame could be found there. He took the General's arm and was pulled to his feet. "Thank you my friend, I do not know what overcame me," Furlac whispered.

Furlac's eyes washed over what was left of Mandrake's defeated army. Many of these men, he knew their names, their families, their hopes and ambitions. Others, he merely recognized and those are the ones who pained him the most - he would never know more of them.

Less than a thousand fighting men were left - all were exhausted and bloody. Behind them was the infirmary, where a several scores or more dead, dying or wounded men laid moaning in agony.

The sound of an axe cracking into the thick doors behind him stirred Furlac from his thoughts and he realized all eyes were on him, waiting for his command. Waiting for him to lead them - to their death.

"These doors will not hold them out forever - chances are they are already finding other ways in. Our best choice is to make our final stand in the upper hallways where the woman and children are being kept. The hallways are narrow and they can only attack from two sides, we should be able to hold them,..." his voice cracked, "for a while."

Several axes hacked into the doors with angry crunches, starting several long cracks and splitters in the thick wood. "We must hurry - we will not have long!" Furlac called, making his way for the staircase.

"Furlac!" General Kenden called out. Furlac stopped in mid-step up the staircase and turned to regard the General.

"The badly wounded will be of no use to you and will just slow you down. I will stay here with them. We will buy you as much time as we can."

Furlac's voice caught in his throat and before he could say anything, the tip of an axe pierced through the wooden doors of the hall.

"Now go!" Kenden barked at him.

Kenden looked over the remaining men. Many of the severely wounded filtered into the group from the makeshift infirmary behind them. Grief stabbed his heart, as he knew all these men would be butchered corpses in but moments.

"Sir, I just want you to know that it was an honor to serve under your command," one of the men said as he limped over to him and saluted as best he could. Half the man's hand had been chopped off and thick blood oozed through the bandages.

The General could not help but be overcome with pride. They were all great men and had fought better than anyone could have ever asked for. Even in their last moments, they stood tall and if any of them feared what was to come, it did not show.

"Never in the history of this world has there been a group of braver men, and never could a General be more proud of the men who served under him," the General roared with respect, tears stinging his eyes.

The doors groaned in protest as the enemy hammered into them with all their weight. Large gaps in the doors had been hacked through and the sound of the hungry enemy was deafening.

"I never could have hand-picked a better group to die by my side!" the General yelled to them over the screams of savages at the doors. "I am proud to die by alongside you. I will see you all in the afterlife as we dine in the great halls of the Creator," he cried out, drawing his sword and turning to face the breaching doors.

Furlac ordered his men to grab anything, from chairs to tables, in the hallways and rooms that they passed by on their way to where the women and children were being kept. Fear coursed through his veins like never before. He knew they would not be able to hold off the enemy for long, and so did every man who was with him.

"Block both sides of the hallway with whatever you find," he ordered once they had reached their destination. He had just over six-hundred men left with him now. The rest had stayed with General Kenden. He ordered men into the rooms with the women and children and rallied whoever was willing to fight.

"Sir, what are we to do once the barbarians come?" A man asked nervously, as he had helped to finish blocking up one side of the hall.

"We kill all of them," Furlac said coolly. The soldier grinned proudly and nodded before grabbing another chair to strengthen the barrier.

Furlac could not believe this was how it was all going to end. They had tried everything they could and still failed, and had nothing left to do but wait for the enemy to cut them down. He racked his mind for anything he could have done differently - he knew it did not matter now, but he wanted that assurance, to ease his failure and the guilt. As if sensing his inner turmoil, one of Furlac's soldiers confronted him.

"We did all we could Sir - there is no shame in that," the man told him. "Besides, it is not over yet," he finished with a wink.

"Sir, some of the women will stand and fight with us," another man said coming out of one of the rooms.

"Good, make sure everyone has a weapon and anyone who does not know how to use it, show them the basics," Furlac ordered, even though he knew they did not have enough to arm everyone.

"Yes Sir."

Furlac walked over to a group of soldiers that he knew personally and ones he knew would carry out the task he was about to ask of them. "I need two of you in each room with the remaining women and children."

They looked at him with confusion as to why they were being sent into the rooms, when they should be out here fighting with the others.

"When the time comes, do not let..." Furlac choked as he finished. "Do not let them take the children and women. Spare them the fate that awaits them when we fall."

The men knew what he meant for them to do. He did not want the women and children to have to suffer the barbarian's wrath of rape, torture, and slavery.

"If you do not have the stomach or heart, I will find others who do," Furlac told them. None of the men said no as they made their way to the rooms, not looking back at the others.

Those in the hallway had not heard what was said to the group that now entered the rooms, but they knew by the look on Furlac's face, what he had asked them to do and all understood it was for the best.

Now, in the hallway, stood a weak army of six-hundred battered men and roughly two thousand terrified women, with less than half of them armed. The ones who were lucky held bloody swords, daggers or broken arrow shafts, while others had taken some of the fireplace instruments that were in the rooms or anything else that could be used as a club or would do damage.

Furlac turned to them as he stood in the front of the hallway awaiting certain death. He could not help but shed tears over all those who had died, or were about to die. He could hear the whimpers and cries of those who stood ready to fight with him, as they prayed to the Creator for strength and courage. He wished he had some momentuous, uplifting words to say to them - something that would make it all easier - but he did not. All eyes upon him seemed to understand and accept that.

A mighty roar of laugher burst from the mouths of the barbarians, when they reached the defenders and their pathetic furniture-built walls. One of the defenders hurled his spear through the debris and into the chest of an enemy. The laughter stopped and the enemy roared angrily as they began ripping and chopping their way through the tables, chairs and bookshelves that blocked their path.

Pathetic it was, the barrier served its purpose in slowing the enemies' assault. The defenders wasted no time in taking full advantage of the hindered savages as they stabbed their weapons through the holes in the makeshift walls into unprotected flesh.

A score of savages died within minutes, and now their bodies added to the defenders' barrier, as the enemy had to climb over their fallen. An ear-splitting blow from a horn ended the attack and they pulled back to the ends of the hallway to regroup.

The meek walls of furniture and the desperation of Mandrake's survivors proved more perilous than either side would have guessed. Only three defenders had died and several more wounded, but they had held.

"Quickly repair what we can!" Furlac cried out as he and several others took advantage of the moment's reprieve.

"What do you think they're doing?" One of the men asked Furlac.

"I do not know," Furlac answered, "but it cannot be good."

"FIRE!" A scream from behind them erupted and they turned to see a dozen torches thrown onto their wooden barrier.

The flames took easily with all the wooden and cloth debris. Both sides of the hallway were now ablaze and the smoke began thickening.

"Those bastards!" one man bellowed holding a torn piece of his shirt over his mouth and nose. "They are going to smoke us to death!"

"Let us make them think we are all dead!" Furlac replied as a final plan sparked in his head.

The intense firestorm that blackened the stone walls did not take long to devour the fuel that blocked the hallway. Not long afterward, the smoke bellowed out to a tolerable level from the open windows. All was silent - the bodies of the defenders littered the floor, many on top of each other.

The enemy slowly marched in, their cruel blood-caked blades held ready as they carefully picked their way through the bodies and debris until both ends met near the middle. Their eyes shifted all around, taking in everything, expecting something. Several words were passed from both groups before several sheathed their weapons or relaxed them as laugher and cheers were voiced at their apparent easy victory. But soon those cheers were silenced as their eyes rested on the locked chamber doors that held the woman and children, and devilish grins spread through the enemy ranks like wildfire.

"Now!" Furlac screamed, rolling over and stabbing his sword through the belly of an unaware savage. Before the barbarian had even realized he was dead, Furlac was on his feet, his bloodied sword cutting through the flesh and sinew of another.

All around, the defenders' piled bodies became animated with life. Swords slashed, daggers plunged and clubs crushed and the naive enemy died all around them - few had time to lift their weapons to defend. Within heartbeats, scores of savages laid dead, but now more poured down the hallway, roaring angrily at the trickery that had befallen their brethren.

Furlac's blade hissed through the air as he swung it madly into the horde. He had taken more than a handful of serious wounds and could feel the strength dwindle from him. Still he fought on, for there was nothing left, the only way to preserve life longer was to take another's life away. Every horrifying second was bittersweet bliss.

Furlac's sword lanced through the chest of a huge barbarian, the brute twisted with the hit, and pulled Furlac's blade from his hands as he fell. Before he could react, a powerful blow to the side of his head lifted him from his feet and into the sidewall. Everything seemed to slow down as he slumped to the floor. All around him, men and woman were being cut down with ease now as exhaustion and panic dissolved all resistance. They had fought valiantly and to the end, no one could have asked for more. Furlac focused on the brute who had taken him down, a massive axe cutting through the space between them. Furlac closed his eyes - the sound of metal on stone was absolute.

The barbarians toyed with the last surviving women in the hallway, taunting and jeering, but refusing to kill them. Soon the women realized what fate awaited them and without hesitation turned their weapons on themselves, robbing the enemy of that sadistic pleasure.

The once grey stone floors were now thick with gore. The vibrant tapestries and paintings now splattered with drying blood and black soot. Bodies of both sides littered the hallways.

The doors to the chambers were kicked in, eager enemies awaiting unwilling flesh, but once again, their grotesque desires were robbed from them, as the bloody sight of mercy lay all around. The saviors awaited death on their knees, sobbing and shaken by their dark, compassionate deed.

10

The six had no difficulty getting into the city of Dragon's Cove. They had trailed in with other townsfolk and refugees. They had disguised Shania days before, so her heritage would not be noted easily. She had not fought the idea for long, before understanding the need for it. Now she passed as a poor farmer's daughter.

The mood in Dragon Cove City was gloomy and depressing as the streets and avenues were littered with refugees and their ratted belongings. Sorrowful cries of mourning and anguish moans of pain echoed throughout the large city as the group shuffled through the milling crowds.

They did not wander far before settling on a well-worn tavern called The Nails Edge. The tavern was not as packed as the group has first expected it to be, but soon understood why as they were promptly greeted by a large bearded brute, who's left eye showed signs of a fresh bruise.

"If ya'll got no coin, then ya'll not welcome here and best be moving on," the brute told them.

"We are looking for a room for a few nights," Ursa replied.

"All rooms are full - all we are offering now is drinks," the brute grumbled back.

Ursa smiled up at the man as he pulled out a silver coin and handed it to the man. "But we have coin." He finished with a wink.

The brute nodded his understanding. "Follow me - I will take ya to the boss." The bouncer led them through the crowd to the counter, where a large brawny armed man was pouring tankards of ale for one of the tavern's wenches.

"What do you want Bull?" The bartender barked.

"These folk got some good coin they wanna give ya." Bull told the owner and then walked off back to his post by the door before anyone tried to sneak in.

The bartender eyed the group from under his bushy brows for a long moment. "Well, what do ya want?"

"We need a room for a few nights," Ursa told him.

"Out of luck strangers - rooms are all full," the man replied, turning his attention back to pouring more drinks.

Ursa slid a gold coin across the counter. "We need a room," Ursa said again, his voice firm.

The owner looked down at the gold, his brows rising just slightly at the sight of the money. He took a deep controlled breath as he pocketed the gold. "Give me a moment then; I will see what I can free up."

Moments later, the tavern owner led a half-naked man and one of the cities lesser whores down the stairs and ordered them away, fully ignoring their curses and complaints and the eyes of other curious patrons.

"Come on then, this way."

Meath and Zehava did their best to climb the uneven wooden steps without help, and without giving away their condition. Injured persons made easy prey for thieves and cutthroats. Still, to a trained eye, it was noticeable.

They were led down the dusty hallway to the furthest room to the back. The tavern keeper unlocked the door and ushered them in as he handed Ursa the brass key.

"I will have a meal brought up to ya'll in a few moments. If you need anything else just let me know, and I will see what I can do for ya'll." The owner said turning and going back down stairs.

The group entered the dimly lit room and was assaulted by the musty smell of cheap love and even cheaper ale. The room had two windows, one on either side of the far corner overlooking the city street in front and the tavern's ally on the side.

There were two beds set side-by-side along the left wall, with only a small night table separating them. Both looked to have seen far better days.

"Well, I have slept in better." Dahak chuckled, as he unloaded his pack on one of the beds.

"We have slept in worse too." Zehava chuckled back as he and Meath sat down on the beds, which shifted and groaned loudly under their weight.

"It will do for the time being," Ursa replied, crossing the room to look out both the grimy windows.

"So what do we do now?" Meath asked. "It is gonna take a miracle to get into the castle unseen."

"That or a well calculated plan," Ursa casually replied. "Dahak, I need you to wander the city, find out what is going on around here. What events are taking place, what relief effort is being used to make room for all of the refugees. Anything that might aid us in getting into the Castle without involving scaling the walls in the dead of night."

"What? Why me?"

Ursa turned a stern eye on him and silenced him before he muttered anything else.

"Fine, I will go. How long do I have to be out there for?" he asked, grabbing the doorknob, clearly unimpressed.

"Until you hear something that will be useful," Ursa countered.

"I shall go with him," Shania piped in. "Two sets of ears better than one."

Ursa was about to refuse, but then decided she may be right. "Just do not take your hood off girl, lest you want to wind up dead in an ally somewhere."

"I will keep safe," she replied as she and Dahak left the room.

"You think that was wise?" Zehava asked several moments after the door had closed.

"Wise, most likely not, but sometimes necessity overrules reason." Ursa replied, "our saving grace is the city is packed with new faces. Unless they do something to single themselves out, no one should pay them any heed."

Almost every street and ally was littered with refugees and the meager belongings they had carried with them. Most of them were huddled in small groups around small pit fires for warmth, cooking what food they had or could afford. Those without fire lay up against building walls absorbing the heat that came from the inside. For nights in Dragon's Cove grew chilly with the western wind blowing in off the Serpent Sea.

Anytime someone neared the groups, distrusting eyes and glares shifted at the newcomers, several times verbal and physical fights broke out and the city guards had to break them up. At the beginning, many of the offenders had been courted away to the citizen jails, but now those were full and could hold no more, so now lashings were given depending on the severity of the offense. The only street ways not overflowing with people were at the higher ends of the city, where gates had been erected, and paid guards posted by nobles and wealthy merchants.

Dahak and Shania slowly moved in and out of the crowded streets and alleyways, ears perked to hear whatever conversations they could. But after a good part of the night they had heard nothing of any value. Just bitter heartbreaking stories, rumors and prayers.

"You hear anything worthwhile?" Dahak asked Shania as they met up at an arranged placed.

"Nothing," she replied. "What we do now?"

"Well I do not know about you but I am starving!" He exclaimed as his hand rubbed his belly to ease up the grumbling. "Let us go find somewhere to eat and get a drink, and then we will think of what to do next."

They entered a small tavern on the eastern side of the city called The Crooked Stool, by now most of the patrons had gone home or been thrown out for lack of coin.

Not many eyes lifted their way as they found a table off to the side where the least amount of activity was. The table was sticky with spilt ale and wine and several flies partook in sampling each spill.

The bar itself was just as grimy - the floors were tracked with mud and slick with several pools of vomit that had yet to be tended to or simply had sawdust thrown over them. The walls and hangings had a thick layer of dust, dulling their true colors and details.

"I figuring you have coin to spend or you would not be here," a tired, less than impressed barmaid grumbled. "All we got left for dinner is lamb and leek stew, but as far as drinks go we still got plenty of everything."

"Well I guess we will each have a bowl of stew and a mug of your coldest ale," Dahak replied cheerfully.

"That will be four coppers," the wench said flat toned, not at all fazed by Dahak's friendly smile.

He reached into his coin pouch, pulled out his last silver, and handed it to the server. "Keep the change." He said, his smile not wavering.

The wench looked hard at him. "What is the catch stranger?"

Dahak laughed, "well, none really, I was hoping when you return with our food and drinks that this might have put you in a far better mood for the night." Dahak had just caught a glimpse of her smile before she walked away.

"What all that?" Shania asked. "Why would you give her extra coin?"

Dahak chuckled, "because it is a kind thing to do, we will get better service now, better quality and it made her obvious bad night just a little better."

Shania cocked an eye at him from beneath her hood as if he had been struck by madness. "You strange, but have good heart, me guess. Good quality for husband, bad quality for warrior."

"Yes, well I guess that is why I'm not a very good soldier," Dahak replied, his tone turning slightly solemn.

"I seen worse," Shania said flatly. "You not so bad - back at camp you fought proudly."

"I was scared out of my bloody wits."

"Fear was there, but did not stop you from fighting," she replied without pause. "Man who fights with no fear, foolish. Little fear reminds warrior of what he has to lose."

The bar wench set two steaming bowls of stew down in front of them with a small basket of fresh flatbread. "I will have your ale for you in a moment," her tone and expression far more pleasant.

"Thank you kindly." Dahak dipped his wooden spoon into the thick stew.

They both ate greedily and nearly licked the bowls clean and washed it all down with a tankard of dark honey mead. That was only slightly cooler than room temperature.

Shania's eyes swung over to the doorway as three well-adorned soldiers walked in and surveyed the crowd with interest. They stood tall and with purpose, their sharp eyes took in all the aspects of the tavern and its inhabitants.

"I would have all your attention for but a few moments!" the one in the middle called out, silencing everyone in the tavern.

Murmurs and curses were whispered, as eyes turned to see why they were being disrupted.

"My name is Captain Dugger - Lord Marcus and Lady Jewel of Dragon's Cove are offering one gold piece to every man who joins the army and starts training immediately," the man explained. "Those with families, your families will be giving temporary lodgings and three meals a day, until said time, when it is safe enough for you to return to your own towns and homes."

Several heads perked up and whispers rippled through the tavern as several men walked over and accepted the deal that solved the problem many of them were trying to drink away.

"Being a soldier of Dragon's Cove, you will also receive recruits' pay on the day of every full moon."

Three more men stood and wandered over to the small group of recruited men who now stood in the doorway.

The Captain went on for several more minutes adding more and more positive information about joining, yet none of the negative was even hinted at. His voice echoed with pride, yet his eyes showed necessity.

"If any of you change your mind, come to the eastern barracks and ask for me." The Captain and the dozen patrons that had joined walked out of the Crooked Stool.

"Well that might be helpful," Dahak said, finishing off his ale in a fast gulp.

"What you mean?" Shania asked. "You are already soldiers."

"They do not know that," he replied with a boyish grin. "Go back to The Nail's Edge and tell the other what we heard here."

"What?" Shania blurted out, but it was too late, Dahak had already gotten up and ran to the doors.

"Wait! Wait!" Dahak shouted nearly slipped in the mud.

Captain Dugger and the others turned to regard him.

"What is it?" The Captain asked.

"I wish to join you," Dahak replied, as he skidded to a stop a few paces away from the group. "For the sake of my family," he added, seeing a raised brow from the Captain.

The Captain eyed him for a moment suspiciously. "Where did you come from?" the Captain asked.

"The Sheeva River encampment sir," Dahak blurted out, as it was the first name that came to mind.

"And what did you do there?"

Dahak began to wonder if the Captain somehow knew who he was and what he was about. He began to get nervous and his palms began to sweat. "I was a butcher." He could think of nothing else.

The Captain eyed him harder, looking him up and down. "Interesting attire for a butcher, would you not say? Military boots and a standard issue claymore. Might you add how it is you came to own such attire?"

Dahak's heart thumped hard in his chest - he knew his breathing was quickening, no matter how hard he tried to keep it steady. "I...I... they were my brother's sir - he was a soldier at the encampment. But, the first volley of arrows that assaulted the encampment caught him off guard and he was one of the first to die. So I took his boots and sword and swore vengeance."

"And did you stay and fight?" Dugger asked, though knowing the answer.

"No sir, I...I fled like a coward with the rest of the townsfolk," Dahak replied, the stuttering in his voice from being nervous only added to his story as a show of emotion.

"Hard to get revenge when you run away with your tail between your legs boy," one of the tavern's drunker patrons barked out, drawing a laugh from several others.

"Silence!" the Captain snapped, turning a sharp eye on the man.

"I am no soldier sir, but I want revenge!" Dahak growled. "Only way to get it is to become a soldier!"

The Captain's eyes softened at that. "I thought you said you were doing it for your family?"

"Just 'cause my brother's dead sir, does not make him any less family in my eyes!" Dahak barked back. "Plus the rest of my family has nothing now; my brother was always the protector. With him dead, I fear it falls on me to help out more."

"What your name?" Dugger asked.

"Dahak."

"Well Dahak, I promise you here and now, I will help you get your revenge!" the Captain replied. "As for your family, I will send someone to gather them and their things on the morrow."

"Thank you sir."

Shania sat at the table, suddenly feeling very alone and even more vulnerable. She peered under her deep hood and scanned the small crowed that still inhabited the tavern. Her heart began to pound hard in her chest; she could hear it beating in her ears and was sure everyone else could too. She could not help but feel like all eyes were on her now. Each glance thrown her way was like an arrow slamming into her chest. Every creak in the floorboards caused her to flinch and look behind her. Every whisper was regarding her, every grin full of malice.

Shania's breathing quickened, small beads of sweat slid down her neck. Both hands clenched the handles of her twin blades hidden beneath her cloak. It took every bit of her self-control not to draw them.

"You look like you have seen a ghost Hun," the tavern wench said looking down at her with concern.

Shania's eyes shot up and met the woman's with both fear and rage at being startled. "I fine! I fine!" she stuttered out.

The woman continued to look down at her. "Are you sure Hun? Where'd that man you were with go off too?"

"None of your business!" Shania snapped back. She jumped to her feet and bolted for the door, drawing more than one pair of eyes her way at the sporadic scene.

Shania jumped off the wooden steps leading up to the Crooked Stool, hit the muddy earth below and slipped, landing hard in the mud. Quickly regaining her feet, she looked around and saw several people walking over to her.

"You all right Miss?" one stranger asked.

Shania pushed him hard out of the way and ran, her eyes scanning everything around her, trying to take in any abnormal shadows or movement that might be danger.

"What was that all about?" one man asked another.

"Have not the foggiest of ideas," the other replied as he stepped aside giving room for the three men leaving the Crooked Stool.

Shania skidded around a corner into a narrow ally and slumped behind an old wooden crate. Her breathing was hard, her heart hammered in her chest as she tried to fight away the anxiety. How could he just abandon her like that? Just leave her alone in this strange place. He must have known she would not remember the way back to the inn. How could he not? Now here she was hiding in an alleyway, lost, alone and scared.

Shania wiped the tears that streaked her cheeks and took several deep breaths, calming herself a bit. "Calm down Shania, you are stronger than this," she whispered to herself, the sound of her own voice soothing her more. "This is nothing - you been through worse!" she reminded herself.

"Who you talking to?" A female voice said from the shadows several feet away to her left.

Shania's heart nearly stopped and her face paled as she swallowed back bile. The stranger must have noticed her unease.

"I am not gonna hurt you, I promise," the young girl said as she crawled out of the gloom so Shania could see her. "You ain't gonna need them, I swear it," the girl said, looking down at the curved blades in Shania's white knuckled hands.

Shania turned her head to look at the girl and was surprised to see the girl could not have been more than ten or eleven winters old. Her mind eased a bit and she loosened her grip on her curved blades.

"Those are mean looking weapons you got. What are they?" the girl asked, moving off to the other side of the ally wall to sit in front of Shania.

Shania looked down at her curved blades then back up at the girl. "I was told they are called scythes."

"You are not from around here, are you?" the girl asked.

Shania's eyes shifted uneasily, remembering her heritage was not accepted among these people. "No."

"What brings ya to Dragon's Cove?" she asked, reaching in her tattered dark green cloak and pulling out a small hunk of bread.

"Came with friends," Shania said bluntly, not wanting to say too much.

"Would you like some?" the girl asked, lifting up the food.

Shania shook her head. "I do not take things from strangers."

The girl laughed aloud but stopped herself quickly, a look of worry crossed her face momentarily as she looked up and down the alley. "I almost forgot, my name's Keisha. What's yours?"

"Shania," she replied nervously, not sure why she was answering at all.

"Where are your friends?" Keisha asked, biting into the bread hungrily.

Before Shania could answer, two shadows loomed towards the alley's entranceway and the voices of two men could be heard.

"I know she came this way," one of the voices said.

"How can you be so sure?" The other asked.

"I can tell by the tracks she left in the mud," the first voice answered.

"There are a hundred footprints; how can you be so sure you are following the right ones?"

"Because you cowson, she was running and frightened by something and you can see these footprints are longer in stride and her footing was uneven and unbalanced each time her feet touched the mud as they are not clear footprints, more like foot smudges."

"And where do they lead then, oh great tracker?" the second man replied sarcastically.

"Into that alley," the first man said again, drawing a dagger from his belt.

"Friends of yours?" Keisha whispered to Shania.

Shania shook her head, her knuckles tightening on her weapons once more.

"Follow me!" Keisha got up and waved Shania to follow.

Shania sprang to her feet and sprinted after Keisha, nearly tripping several times over discarded garbage and ruble.

"There she is!" The two men yelled and began to chase.

Shania skidded out of the alleyway and searched frantically for where Keisha had gone. She looked down the alley; the two men were nearing the end, their curses, and grunts leading the way through the darkness.

"Over here!" Keisha waved from a broken window frame to a large worn down building.

Shania bolted over and Keisha helped pull her through into the dark warehouse.

"They went in there!" one of the men yelled.

"Come on, we got to keep moving. Here, take my hand - I know where to go." Keisha grabbed Shania's hand and took off through the dark at a steady pace, weaving through dark unknown silhouettes.

Shania's eyes soon adjusted to the near absolute darkness. The small amount of moonlight shining through various cracks and holes allowed her to see her surroundings within arm's length.

A loud crashing sound behind them alerted them that their pursuers had found another way into the building.

"We are almost there!" Keisha called back, as they began climbing a long set of stairs, taking them two at a time.

"Over there, their going up the stairs!" a voice yelled from the dark.

"We got them now!" the second man called out.

The stairs ended and they found themselves on a rope-suspended walkway. The swaying plank way ran parallel along the back wall; boarded windows lined the length of the building emanating dusty beams of moonlight through their fissures.

Their sudden weight rocked the suspended bridge, making balancing difficult with every quickened step. The aged, decaying wood beneath their feet groaned in protest at the newly given weight of each awkward footstep.

Keisha stopped and pointed to a beam of wood tied down to the walkway and leading to a large hole in one of the windows. "Quickly, get across!"

Shania looked back at their pursuers. The two men were half way up the stairs.

"Come on! We are almost out!" Keisha cried to her.

Shania placed a foot on the beam and then the next, collecting her balance from the swaying before starting forward to the window. Within seconds, Shania was across; she looked back to see Keisha already making her way across.

"I do not think so, you little bitch!" one of the men screamed cutting one of the rope handrails, causing the whole walkway to shift violently.

The beam beneath Keisha jerked suddenly, her footing faltered and she fell forward. Her arms frantically searching for the beam as she fell, she grabbed hold of it in a death grip.

Shania looked down at Keisha dangling from the wooden beam, and looked back over to the men, who were moments away now.

"Just go!" Keisha yelled. "There's nothing you can do for me!"

The first pursuer had reached the beam and began cutting away at the rope holding it in place.

Shania snarled and sprinted across the beam, her blades flashing into her hands. The man looked up just in time to see a curved blade sink deep into his shoulder and neck. The man lurched backward with a scream, pulling Shania's right-hand blade out of her hand and with him as he disappeared over the side.

The other man was clinging to the rope suspended pathway, not being able to get his balance now that one of the ropes was cut. Shania was about to pursue him when she remembered Keisha and turned back to see the street girl had inched her way to the window ledge and was climbing up.

"Come on," Keisha waved her back over.

Outside the window was a thick rope that lead to the ground; they slid down and were happy to be on solid ground once more with a sigh of relief.

Keisha looked up at Shania, shock and awe in her eyes. "You risked your life back there to save mine, why?"

"You helped me get away and had no reason to."

"Ya, but I was just helping you so I could steal those wicked blades of yours," Keisha confessed with a look of shame. "You, you helped me like... like a friend would help another friend."

"You were going to steal from me?" Shania snarled, tightening her grip on the one blade she had left.

"Was, yes, I am a thief - it is what I do, but now..." Keisha stopped to think for a moment. "No way could I rob someone who saved my life, out of simple good will."

"Hey! What is going on down there?" someone yelled out from down the alleyway.

"Come on, let us get out of here," Keisha said, and they melted off into the shadows of the night.

Ursa stood motionless looking out the tavern room's window. Dawn was just beginning its assault on the darkness of night. Pushing eerie shadows back to the gloomy corners and hiding places they had emerged from many hours earlier. A light, morning mist drifted calmly from the cool earth, dissipating into nothingness before it had even reached the lowest of rooftops.

No more than a small handful of people were about this early; most were wandering homeless, using the vacant streets and alleyways to search for fallen coin, or discarded scrapes of food.

"I am beginning to get worried," Zehava said, walking over to stand by Ursa.

Ursa turned to regard him for a moment doing well to hide the fact that he had not heard the man get up from the bed, where the others were still sleeping. "I too, am starting to worry." He went back to looking out the window.

"Do not get me wrong, Dahak is extremely trustworthy and loyal, and will do whatever you tell him to do if it is important," Zehava said, sitting down on the chair by the window. "Now whether or not he can achieve what is asked of him..." Zehava paused briefly, "that is a different story. What do we do if they do not show up?" But Ursa was not listening, his attention focusing fully on something going on outside.

"What is it?" Zehava asked, looking out to see a military standard wagon pulling up to the tavern with several armed soldiers.

"We have a very serious problem," Ursa snapped around, "everyone up!"

"Wha... what is it?" Meath mumbled, as he rolled onto his side to look at them.

"Get ready to move!" Ursa barked at him as he began gathering their things.

Meath was about to ask why, but stopped himself, he knew better than to interrogate the Wizard on something such as this, and was on his feet in a flash, momentarily forgetting the stiffness and soreness of his present state.

"Meath what is going on?" Nicolette asked her eyes wide and brimming with concern.

"It will be ok - just grab your things. We may have to go soon," Meath told her, strapping on his sword belt.

"What are we going to do?" Nicolette asked.

"Depends on what happens," Ursa replied, still watching out the dirty window. Three of the armed guards had stayed with the wagon, while the other six had made their way into the tavern. "For now, we wait. But be ready to do exactly what I say."

Time seemed to slow painfully. Every heartbeat felt like forever. Finally, footsteps could be heard coming down the hallway to their door. Meath and Zehava gripped their swords tightly, expecting the worst.

There was a light knock at the door. Ursa grabbed the doorknob and took a few deep breaths, being ready to summon his Gift in an instant if need be. He opened the door slowly and peered out into the hallway, to see the young servant girl standing there.

"There are some soldiers downstairs looking for you," she told him.

"Soldiers?" Ursa asked. "Do you know what they want?"

"They said you are to go with them to new housing within the training encampment as part of a deal made with Dahak."

Ursa cocked an eyebrow at the mention of that and smiled to her. "Tell them we will gather our things and be down shortly." She smiled upward and then turned and ran back down to the tavern.

"What happened?" They all asked in union as soon as Ursa closed the door.

"That crafty halfwit did it!" Ursa muttered, shaking his head in utter enlightenment.

"Who did what?" Zehava asked, looking to Meath and Nicolette confused.

Ursa turned to them and smiled, "gather your things. You two hide your weapons and act like poor farmers. Princess, rough up your looks and keep your hood up, and eyes down and stay by me at all times."

"Okay what is happening?" Meath blurted out, still confused.

"Dahak and Shania found us a way in," Ursa grinned.

The process was less stressful than any of them anticipated. The Captain and his men had spent most of the evening and morning collecting the families of the new recruits and had grown tired and complacent and paid little mind to those whom they gathered now. Even the Captain merely greeted them - he made sure their things made it into a wagon, and then sent them on their way to the castle with two soldiers to accompany them.

Within an hour, they were set up in a large canvas tent in the midst of hundreds of others. The only furniture in the tent was four cots, a wooden table and chairs, and an ironwood stove for cooking simple meals. They were simple accommodations but it was far better than what most of the refugees had in the city.

"I cannot believe he got us inside the castle walls," Zehava said softly. They were only feet away from other tents on all sides of them and privacy was unlikely.

"This is the southern military training grounds," Nicolette said, finally pulling back her dark hood. "After Lord Marcus built the improved Northern training grounds, this one was almost never used."

"Well, it appears they have found a use for it now, and it just so happens to work perfectly for us," Zehava added, checking his bedroll to ensure his sword was still easily accessible. Not that he would dare draw blade inside the castle compound even if they were caught for that would ensure certain death, but it was just a soldier habit.

"Anyone else wondering where Dahak and Shania are?" Meath asked, the question had been playing on his mind since they arrived.

"Dahak will be busy with his training duties until late in the day," Ursa replied, still pacing. "But I myself was wondering just the same thing about Shania. I had hoped she would be here waiting for us, but as that was not the case, I am beginning to worry. From a distance and for short periods of time, she would have been fine and her heritage would most likely have gone unnoticed. But to the trained eye after any extended length of time she would run the risk of being discovered even more so now that it is light out."

"You think they were found out?" Nicolette gasped.

"No, if they were found out we would not be here, we would have been fighting our way out of that tavern. No, Dahak must have set this up without Shania - or with her out of sight."

"But then where is she?" Zehava asked concerned.

"That answer we will only know when we can talk to Dahak. We will have to wait here until this evening when he has done his training and is allowed to visit us," Ursa said sitting down on the stiff cot.

Meath walked over to the opening wincing slightly with each step - the aches in his body were fading faster each day. He hoped by the next day they would be gone. "What are we to do in the meantime?"

"We wait," Ursa replied back, his eyes already closed as he lay on the cot.

"Lovely, my favorite," Meath muttered.

Zehava moved off to one of the cots, "as good a time as any to catch up on some sleep, since who knows what is going to happen and when we might get this opportunity again."

Meath walked over to the entranceway and peered out at the canvas city that surrounded them on all sides. People milled about here and there, in small groups of two or three talking among themselves, paying little heed to anyone else around them.

So much had changed so quickly, it seemed like only yesterday Meath had awoken in his room in Draco Castle to begin his normal everyday planned events and training and now...

"You okay?" The Princess's soft voice said behind him and Meath turned to regard her, not even aware he was smiling now.

"I am fine, just thinking of everything that has happened that had led us to this point. Everything has changed so drastically, so quickly it is hard to think of how we will put everything right again."

"I think the same thing." Nicolette replied. "Hopefully it will not be long before things begin to turn back to normal once we find a way to get into the castle and talk to my Aunt and Uncle."

They had wandered down a score of filthy alleyways, gone through a dozen dank abandoned buildings, and had to hide several times from passing guardsmen or other shady wonderers that had a vile cutthroat look to them. The dawn finally was cresting the horizon when they climbed through the rotting boards of a fence, entering a large cluttered, filthy courtyard. Several groups of people stood around, almost all of them looking haggard and seedy. In the middle of the courtyard stood a crumbling, rotting three-story mansion, the siding was rotted and hanging loosely, windows were all but boarded up. Yet the place radiated a certain level of dominance and power even in its decaying state.

"You stay with me, right at my side," Keisha told her sternly. "Do not speak, or touch anything until I tell you too, and keep your head up high - do not show fear. My people do not like outsiders, but it will be okay - we just need to see my brother."

Shania nodded in understanding, stepping closer to Keisha as she noted more eyes shifting their way to rest upon her.

"Come on let us get this over with." Keisha straightened herself up and walked forward, Shania was quick to follow, doing her best to hold back her anxiety. They walked straight toward the entrance of the mansion covering the dusty ground as quickly as possible without looking like they were anxious.

"Hey there Keisha," a scrawny, toothless rat of a man said, stepping in front of their path. His tattered, filthy clothes hung off his wiry frame and the smell of urine and feces drifted off him once he was close. "Where ya been? I've been looking for you," He grinned nastily, showing the handful of rotten teeth his mouth still held onto. "Who is your friend?"

"I do not have time for you right now Malaki," Keisha growled, trying to push by him, but he grabbed her arm firmly and spun her around.

"Do not try to ignore me Keisha!" He hissed. "You know our deal - where is my money?"

Keisha swallowed hard, trying not to look into his filmy grey eyes. "I do not have it yet - last night did not go as planned. You'll get your money, just give me another night." She tried to pull her arm free, but his grip only tightened and she winced.

He grinned wider. "That was not part of the deal. A full silver coin by this morning to settle our debt, or..." His grin deepened, "a full day of your flesh at my disposal. I see no silver, so your body is mine!"

By now, several other had gathered closer to hear what was going on between the two thieves and the stranger.

"I know our deal Malaki," Keisha replied, her voice thick with regret. "Let me take the newcomer to Burnaby, and I will come find you right after, for... payment."

Malaki burst out laughing, his grip still not relenting. "You think I am daft Keisha? I let you go and I will never see you again! I know well of your disappearing acts."

"If you were as good as a thief and spy as you say you are, then you should know where I am and how to find me anytime you want," she snapped back, several in the crowd of thieves chuckled.

Malaki's lips quivered in rage. "Enough of this horse shit - we had a deal! You have a debt to pay, and I mean to take it if I have too! Though fighting me will not benefit you in the deed that will be done." He pulled her arm hard, dragging her with him several feet as she tried to pry her arm free of his grasp.

"Stop!" Shania yelled, her voice showing only a little fear in it.

Malaki turned to regard her. "What do you want outsider? You have no voice here! The fact that we have let you live this long is a wonder."

"I will pay her debt." Shania responded, tossing a silver coin in the air for Malaki to snatch with his free arm. Ursa had given her two silver coins and six copper several days before, in case they were separated for any length of time. He had told her it was enough to keep her fed for several days if need be or buy her way out of trouble if she was cornered.

Malaki examined the silver piece, and then looked up at her, a perplexed look on his face. "Why would you do that?"

"She is...friend."

That drew a hardy chuckle from Malaki and several others. "Your friend, do you truly believe that? We have no friends - do not fool yourself. She brought you here to be robbed and killed," a handful of the crowd around her chuckled maliciously agreeing with his testament.

"Her debt is paid, let her go!" Shania growled, doing her best to sound intimidating, ignoring his statement and the cold stares around her.

"Who are you anyway?" Malaki asked, clearly irritated.

"She helped me out there, saved me from falling to my death," Keisha stammered out. "She just came in with a group of refugees, got lost."

Malaki shook her hard, silencing her. "Shut up, I did not ask you!"

"Her debt is paid - let her go!" Shania hissed again, keeping her face shrouded mostly by her cloak, so her lineage was not noticed.

Grinning toothlessly, Malaki pocketed the silver. "You can toss all the coin you want, but her debt is her own! And I will get payment from flesh!" He turned and began pulling Keisha with him again.

The sound of steel rang out as Shania pulled her curved blade free. "Let her go!"

Several others pulled blades at the challenge, muttering and growling at the newcomer's foolishness in drawing a weapon in their compound. Shania's heart thundered hard in her chest now, coming here was a mistake, she had been foolish to follow Keisha blindly, but she had not known what else to do, and now she was most likely going to die. She gritted her teeth - if she was going to die here, she would leave several bodies in her wake.

"You dare draw a blade on me?" Malaki laughed. "You are dumber than I thought. Look around you - there are forty of us, and one young, foolish you. What are you going to do?"

"What is the meaning of all this!" a stern voice said from behind the gathered crowd, and everyone stepped aside allowing the finely dressed man a clear view and path. Everyone was silent and still. "I asked what is going on here?" the man barked, his temper flaring slightly.

"Malaki was claiming a debt Keisha owes him. But Keisha brought this outsider into our compound and the outsider tried to pay Keisha's debt. Malaki took the outsiders silver, but claims Keisha is still in debt since the outsider has no rights here," a fat greasy man replied quickly looking to gain favor.

The man stepped forward, getting a closer look at the situation. He eyed the outsider closely, though she was hidden mostly behind her cloak. His eyes flashed toward Malaki and Keisha. "Is this true Malaki?"

Malaki licked his lips nervously, releasing Keisha from his grip. "Aye it is, Barnaby."

"So this outsider paid Keisha's debt?" Barnaby asked, pulling a slender dagger from his belt as he cleaned underneath his fingernails casually.

"The outsider gave me a silver coin in hopes I would release Keisha from her debt, yes. But an outsider has no right inside this compound - therefore, I feel no need to oblige her."

Barnaby nodded slightly. "Outsider, what is your name?"

Shania turned to the well-defined man, and knew he was the leader of this band of cutthroats. "My name, Shania," she answered nervously, her knuckles going white on her blade handle, her eyes trying to take in all the movement around her, expecting an attack at any moment.

Barnaby took several casual steps to the side, his eyes still on the task of cleaning some dirt from beneath his nails. "Well, Shania, why would you, an outsider to our," he paused for a few seconds while thinking of a word he wished to use, "let's say, 'organization' try and pay Keisha's debt so freely?"

Shania shifted her footing to square up with Barnaby, not liking his tone or casual demeanor - she expected that dagger to snap her way at any moment. "She helped me, and saved my life."

Barnaby took several steps closer to the side, inspecting his job on his hand. "So you owe Keisha a debt of life is it then." He mused a moment, his eyes looking up at the hooded outsider. "I see only one way to settle this, appropriately." He smiled mischievously, "Malaki your claim of debt over Keisha is true, so is your claim that the outsider has no rights here for paying off Keisha's coin debt." Malaki grinned widely as his grip found Keisha's wrist again. "But a debt of life has no rules, and listens to no rules, accept to be paid back." He turned to Shania. "Outsider, if you want to pay your debt back, you must fight Malaki for Keisha. You win, your debt of life will be fulfilled and her debt will be cleared, you lose and, everything stays the same, aside from you will be dead." He spread his hands out to the sides, emphasizing his conclusion.

Malaki grinned and released Keisha as he drew his chipped short sword and dagger. "This shall be quick Keisha, so do not go anywhere. My lust for flesh is always heightened after I have taken a life." The crowd of bandits and thieves moved in closer, cutting off any openings for running. Their jeers and cheers were absolute - no single curse or hate-filled words could be discerned.

Shania squared up with Malaki, her fingers tightening harder on her one curved blade, her other hand feeling naked without its twin. She looked over to Keisha who was looking at her with dread, her eyes moistened with fear, be it for herself or Shania she did not know. Shania had to wonder even if she won this fight if they would let her live. Her eyes shifted to the man called Burnaby, his arms were crossed and his stance was relaxed still, almost as if bored by it all, yet his eyes twinkled with anticipation. Shania took a deep breath; chances are she was going to die anyway, if that was the case, this Malaki would die before her.

Malaki shifted quickly to the left, then to the right, altering his weight on the balls of his feet, working his body's momentum up with far more grace then Shania would have expected from the scrawny thief. His blades twitched in his hands and moved fluently. Shania could tell he was a skilled fighter despite his weak stature.

He jumped to the left, faked to the right, and exploded forward, his sword arm raised across his chest for a forward slice, his dagger posed below for a deadly thrust in case his sword did not find its mark. Shania folded her knees and dropped back into a roll, Malaki's sword blade cutting nothing but empty air. He adjusted his dagger's downward and thrust, hoping to sink his blade into her chest when she rose. But she had anticipated the move and instead of coming up onto her feet she let the momentum take her back once more onto her hands and kicked her foot up hard catching Malaki's outstretched hand at the wrist jarring the blade from his hand. His face betrayed his shock at the flawless counterattack and loss of one of his weapons. He retreated several steps - murmurs and curses sounded from the crowd of thieves around them.

Shania wasted no time and snapped to her feet, her free hand retrieving the fallen dagger in the same movement. She bolted forward, not wanting to give him any time to recover. She brought her blade down hard, meeting his blade as he snapped it up to block, with a quick twist of her wrist, her curved blade trapped his short sword, and she forced his arm out wide. She thrust the dagger for his chest but he shifted in time to avoid the killing blow and the blade bit deeply into the meat of his shoulder.

Malaki hissed in pain and kicked up - his thick leather boot punching hard into Shania's mid-section, doubling her over.

Shania fell to her knees gasping for air, knowing her time was running out. She looked down at her hands, both were empty, she cursed to herself.

"Stupid bitch," Malaki barked, pulling his dagger from his shoulder. "Now let us get a look at that face before I cut it up!" He stepped forward and reached for the hood of her cloak.

Shania punched forward as hard as she could, throwing all the strength and momentum she could fathom into her last chance attack. She doubted he would be brash enough not to anticipate the desperate attack and was surprised when her knuckles connected between his legs. His groan and laughs from the crowd confirmed her mark had been hit. She looked up at Malaki as he slowly sank down to the muddy ground, both his weapons dropped to the earth beside him, as his hands clutched at his manhood. His face twisted in pain and anguish.

Shania threw another punch, landing it square in his jaw, dropping him backward to the ground. She retrieved her curved blade and stood above the fallen cutthroat - she raised the blade high in the air ready to plunge it down.

"Wait!" Barnaby's voice boomed loudly, stopping her a heartbeat before. The crowd hushed down and waited for Barnaby to speak.

Barnaby walked forward and stopped steps away from the fallen Malaki and the outsider. He looked down at the groaning pathetic form of Malaki, then up at Shania. He cocked his head slightly, trying to catch a glimpse of her face from under her hood. "Normally I would have let you kill the fool, but living with this lesson and defeat, will serve as greater punishment than the easy death you would have provided him."

"What if I decide to end him anyway?" Shania hissed, not looking up at him, knowing if her bloodline was discovered, she would be killed.

Barnaby chuckled heartily. "Bold question, very bold. If you were to insist upon it and kill him, then I would be forced to have you killed. Not because you killed the halfwit, no never that - he would have brought that fate upon himself. No, I would have to order your death for the denial of my simple request. After all, I could have ordered my men to kill you outright just for entering our compound, but I did not." He smiled arrogantly. "Not to say that I will not order that later. However, through my generosity I allowed you to conclude your debt of life while also freeing Keisha from her debt to Malaki. So your denial of my request would wound me and so your death I would demand." He finished, his voice taking on a very serious tone. "But at the moment I am intrigued by all that this is, and for that I shall give no such order... yet. That is, of course, if you are willing to spare Malaki's sad little life." Humor found his voice again at the last.

Shania snapped her blade around and sheathed it with ease. As callous and arrogant as this man was, he also did not seem vicious and evil like many of the others around her. She found it even odder that she felt like she could trust him and his judgment, he did not seem to want ill to fall upon her. She took several steps away from the fallen cutthroat and stood next to Keisha.

"You did not have to do that," Keisha stuttered out, but her eyes never left Barnaby's.

Barnaby sheathed his dagger and eyed the crowd curiously, gauging their expressions and stances. "Anyone have anything to add to this?" When no one spoke up, he continued. "Good, then it is resolved and I will hear no more of it. Now stop standing about and get out into the city and do your jobs!" His voice rang with authority. "Keisha, I would like to see you and your friend inside, now!" Barnaby turned away from the slow dispersing crowd of cutthroats and walked back into the rotting mansion.

"Come on, let us get this over with." Keisha began toward the mansion, as she passed Malaki she spat down at him.

"This is not over Keisha..." he groaned, slowly climbing to his hands and knees.

Shania followed Keisha quickly, ignoring the bitter grunts and curses as she passed several of the by standers. Her heart thumped hard in her chest as she neared the house. She did not know what to expect; she truly was surprised even to still be alive. She knew once she was inside those doors that her fate would be sealed to whatever this man wished and yet she kept walking forward.

They followed Barnaby through the rotting double doors to the mansion, and Shania gasped when they were inside and the doors closed behind her. The interior of the mansion was nothing like the exterior - the outside was a ruse. Inside the walls were flawless brown painted wood, no cracks, no rot, no aged twists, or bends. The floor, solid wooden planks with, dark but colorful carpeting placed with purpose throughout the rooms to accent the surrounding elegant furniture and wall hangings. Nothing about the inside indicated anything less than what you would expect the riches of a merchant's house to look like. Even the handful of the house's inhabitants that were about were far better dressed than the ruffians outside.

"I can see by the look on your face that you are surprised by the difference of the house's structure on the inside." Barnaby said, hardly giving her a second glance.

"Yes," Shania mumbled out, still not sure about the situation in which she had found herself.

"Well, if the outside looked anywhere near like the inside, the cities governing officials would take less kindly to us 'common thieves' than they already do. But we are anything but common, as you can see. We are… quite established," Barnaby explained with a wink stopping in front of a large solid set of double doors. He grabbed both long, polished doorknobs and opened the grand doors into an exquisite sitting area. Marble tables and plush ivory chairs and chesterfields awaited them. "Please sit." He gestured to Shania to sit in one of the chairs as he closed the doors tightly.

"By the Keeper's third testicle, Keisha, what are you thinking?" He barked out, throwing his arms up in the air and turning a glare on the young thief, who just rolled her eyes. "Do not take me lightly! No, no you do not dare roll your eyes at me! Are you trying to get us caught? Do you know what will happen to us if we are discovered?"

"What was I to do?" Keisha replied, trying to keep her calm, "she saved my life and needed help."

Barnaby stared hard at the young thief, his expression of utter disbelief. "And bringing her here was helping her? Has a crane beetle crawled into your ear and made a lunch of the grey matter in there?" Again, he threw his arms up in the air in frustration, turning around and pacing the room overly animated. "Oh yes, let us bring an outsider into a thief glides compound to help her out. Yes, 'cause that sounds like a sound idea to me. Not to mention adding that much more stress and attention on our own problem here!" He rolled out dramatically. "Damn it Keisha!"

Shania sat in the plush chair staring hard at the two thieves in complete disbelief. The firm, controlled Barnaby who she had met outside in her fight for Keisha's debt was not the Barnaby who paced around in front of her wildly now. She was truly lost now and had no idea what was going on, and that made her nervous. "What is this?"

she stuttered out, slowly rising to her feet, her right hand slipping beneath her grubby cloak to find the hilt of her weapon.

Barnaby and Keisha stopped arguing and looked over to Shania. Barnaby's face twisted up in aggravated perplexity, again throwing his arms high in the air out of the simple need to do something physical. "Damn it all! I forgot about you for a moment." He ran his hands through his long obsidian hair. "Can she be trusted Keisha?"

"Of course she can, I would not have brought her here if she could not be."

"No, you brought her here knowing she could be trusted to believe and keep the secret of a guild of thieves that would help her find her friends," he corrected. "This, well this goes a little further beyond that little secret do you not think!"

Keisha turned to Shania, who had pulled her blade part way out of its sheath already. "Well, can you be trusted?"

Shania licked her lips nervously, her eyes darting from one to the other. "I do not know what you mean - I do not know what going on here. You lied to me Keisha!"

"No," she stepped forward. "I did not lie - we will help you find your friends. I mean it. I just did not know all this was gonna come out."

Barnaby sighed and stepped in front of Keisha. "As much as I would rather not get involved in anything else that is going to take up my time and require me to stretch my neck any further out there then I already have it. We will help you, but I require two small things from you, sort of a quid pro quo. First, I need your word you will speak not a word of what you have heard in this room." He looked at Shania and she nodded hesitantly. "Second, it is plain to see by the way you have been hiding your face since you entered this compound that your identity is of some pressing concern to stay concealed. If I am to involve myself in your venture of finding your friends then I require knowledge of who you are and why you feel the need to hide yourself so."

Shania's heart jumped a beat. If the others saw her face then would have seen the blood drain from it. "I...I cannot - you would not understand. I am different.... You would not accept.... I cannot!"

"We are all different - at this point I highly doubt your secret of identity outclasses mine being the head of a highly organized thief guild. Whatever you identity hides, it is safe within these walls," Barnaby told her. "Let us face it, you're among a colony of cutthroats and thieves. We all have wished to hide our identities outside this compound, lest we find ourselves with our necks on the block or in a rope. Not to mention what you know of Keisha and I already is more than enough to jeopardize our plans severely ..." Barnaby stopped; a pained look came across his face. "Why am I still telling you things, when I just need to keep my mouth shut?" He rubbed his eyes with his hands. "I do not want to sound cruel, but I need to know who you are and what you're about, and if you refuse...I would have to do something most unfortunate, and I really do not want to have to do that."

Shania fought with her inner self, knowing she should just run away. Just try to find Ursa and the others on her own. She was crafty and smart, she could do it. No, she knew she would not be able to find them by herself, she would not even know where to begin, and even if she did, it would not take long for someone to glimpse her heritage. She found her hands on the edges of her hood slowly pulling it back until it fell from her head. She kept her eyes closed tightly, not sure of what she should be expecting.

"Well, you are not disfigured or hideous to look at - actually you are quite beautiful really. The state of your hair and skin shows you are not from money or power," Barnaby said, his fingers rubbing his smooth chin. "I have not the slightest idea as to why you were so worried about your identity."

Shania's eyes were wide, "I... I am a savage..." she mumbled.

"A half breed at best, but I already knew that," he replied, "I could tell your heritage when first I saw you by the skin tone of your hands dear girl. Is that the big secret?" he laughed. "Here I was thinking... well I do not even know what I was thinking. Rest assured if that is the biggest secret you were hiding you have no fear of that here."

"You do not care?"

"Of course not, why would I?" Barnaby replied. "You have not done any harm to me, and you have saved my sister's life. Just because you have the misfortune of being born a half-breed, really does not seem like a good enough reason to hate you. I was born a peasant and a con artist - we all have to play with the cards we are dealt."

Shania sank back into the plush chair, finally feeling more relaxed than she had in the last several hours. "Thank you."

Barnaby held up his hand, "do not thank me yet, I have not done anything. Now, tell me about your friends."

Dahak walked through the rows of tents, his eyes staying in one spot only long enough to read the painted numbers on the outside of each tent. The sun was already fading in the sky and within the hour, all would be dark, aside from the main cooking fires littering the refugee grounds. The first day of training had been how he had remembered from several years before. Hard physical drills repeatedly until you could not do them any more and then short breaks to drink and eat, well being questioned on offence and defensive strategies. He had stood out from the others, almost too well - he had to remind himself on several occasions to slow down and to answer wrong, lest his commander would begin to get suspicious of him. Still, he had shone out, and had gotten several words of praise from his superiors, words he had wished he would have heard the first time round.

Finally, he came to the number he had been looking for; he pulled the door flap aside and walked in.

"Dahak!" Nicolette cried out being the first to see him.

He smiled wide, glad to see his friends again. "Are you guys a sight for sore eyes."

"By the Creator's grace lad, you got us in!" Ursa greeted him with an unusually wide smile.

"Well, you know you told me to find a way in, so I did." He boosted proudly, "nothing to it ya know, just had to find a feel for what was going on and the rest just fell into place."

"Where is Shania?" Zehava asked, his tone boarding fearful.

The blood in Dahak's face drained, his boyish grin of pride was replaced with fear and guilt. "She should be with you... I told her to come back to the... I left her at the..." He sank down into one of the wooden chairs. "I am an idiot..." he muttered to himself."I left her all alone at the tavern, and expected her to find her way back on her own..."

Ursa cleared the room and lifted his face up. "Tell us what happened from the beginning."

Dahak quickly told them everything that happened from the time they left the others to the time he was drafted himself into Dragon's Cove's refugee army. "I am a damn fool - I should have known better than to leave her on her own."

"She is a smart girl and crafty enough to manage the streets of Dragon's Cove for a while; I have no doubt of that," Ursa stated, hoping to ease his guilt a little. "But there is nothing we can do about that right now - she will have to hold on out there a little longer. Right now we need to get into the castle and find Lord Marcus and Lady Jewel."

"We...we cannot just leave her out there!" Dahak bellowed. "We have to go and find her."

"It is unfortunate but we have not the time for that now." Ursa snapped back, his tone firm and unyielding. "We have a more dire matter at hand to deal with."

"But we just..." Dahak started, but a sharp look from Ursa silenced him before he went any further.

"How are we going to get into the castle?" Zehava asked, patting Dahak on the back in reassurance.

Ursa grinned slightly. "I am not the one who knows how to best answer that." He looked to the Princess and Dahak.

11

As the moon reached its apex in the clear, star-littered night sky, five forms darted from shadow to shadow, slowly nearing the back courtyard near the stables. Nicolette had spent the better half of her life in Dragon's Cove and knew the castle grounds well - she also knew the guards changed shifts shortly after the moon had risen to the highest point in the night sky, meaning the guards would be tired and unfocused.

The group moved as fast as they dared through the wagons and supply crates riddling the courtyard. Normally, the grounds around the castle were never this crowded or disorganized, but this was an unusual circumstance and time. It served the group well, - there would have been no way to get this far had it been under normal circumstances. They were careful to watch the guards on the wall and only moved when they knew their attention was elsewhere.

Three armed soldiers stood around a side entrance near the stable yard talking about something that had their interest peeked and so they paid little heed to anything else.

"We will need a distraction to get them away from the door and closer to us," Ursa whispered, looking up to see the guard on the wall walk from view and he knew they would only have a few moments for this to work. "Meath, Dahak stumble out past the wagon and pretend to be drunk and fighting."

"Are you serious?" Dahak demanded, but the stern look from Ursa answered the question.

Ursa glanced up at the wall again, making sure the guard had not returned early. "Quickly now - get them as close to the wagons as you can!"

Meath grabbed Dahak and pushed him out into open view of the guards. "You… you… cheating bastard!" he slurred out, as he wobbled into view, pushing Dahak sluggishly again.

"I did… did not cheat you… you just… do not know how to throw the die," Dahak stammered back, pretending that he could barely hold himself up.

"Hey what are you to doing around here? This area is restricted!" one of the soldiers barked out and the three turned their attentions to the two drunks.

Meath ignored the soldiers and stumbled forward swinging a sloppy punch at Dahak, who easily sidestepped the feeble attack and tripped Meath to the ground, slurring something incoherent down at him. As Meath slowly pulled himself to his feet, he noticed that none of the three guards that walked toward them had their hands near their weapons, meaning they had fallen for the ruse and believed there to be no threat at all with the two drunks.

"Yous… yous guys should help me," Meath bellowed out to the approaching soldiers. "This guy… no…this… this cheat stole my coin!"

"How did you two get in here?" one of the soldiers asked, his voice showed he was annoyed at being disrupted so close to the end of his shift.

Dahak charged Meath and tackled him through the soldiers and to the ground.

"You dirty whoresons! Stop your damn fighting!"

All three of the soldiers reached down to pull the two drunks apart, cursing as they did. "You know, if the jails were not already filled you two would be spending a few days in there for…" The soldier in the middle started to say, but he voice stopped short as he fell over Meath and Dahak face first into the ground, not moving.

"What the?" both soldiers blurted out in union at seeing their comrade fall to the ground limp.

The soldier on the right turned to look behind him just in time to see Zehava's sword pommel crack into the side of his head, dropping him next to the other fallen soldier.

The last standing soldier took a step back getting his attackers into view, his hand dropping to his sword hilt and he tried to pull it free. Meath's hand shot up and gripped the soldier's wrist, halting the blades release before it had gotten more than a handspan from its sheath.

The soldier turned to look down at what had stopped him. "What are you doing?" he bellowed in terror, but said nothing else as a solid sphere of ice connected with his skull. He wavered on his feet for several heartbeats before his eyes rolled into the back of his head and he joined the others on the ground.

"Quickly, we do not have much time!" Ursa urged running over the soldiers towards the door.

"What about them?" Meath asked.

"We do not have time for that," Ursa replied, his eyes darting up to the wall to where he knew the guard would be coming back shortly. "Come now!" He waved them to the doorway.

They entered the stable's large equipment room. It smelled heavily of raw leather, lard and metal. The worktables were covered with thick elk hides that were being cut and shaped into saddles, bridles and other riding equipment. The craftsmen had long retired for the night and now the room was still.

They moved through the rows of worktables and stacks of finished and unfinished gear to the rear of the room, where the only other door was. This would lead them into the castle's servant hallways that rimmed the whole castle- these made it easier for the servants to go about their chores without disturbing the nobles and their guests.

Ursa put his ear to the wooden door and listened intently for any sounds coming from the other side that would alert them of people in the hallway. After several long moments, he decided it was safe and hoped that at this late hour no one would be about. He pushed the door open slowly and peered out the crack, again listening for any indication of movement.

"I think someone found the soldiers outside!" Zehava stammered, looking back the way they had come and hearing shouts from beyond the doorway.

"Princess, you know the castle far better than I," Ursa whispered. "What is the quickest way to Lord Marcus' and Lady Jewel's chambers?"

"I have never been in the servant's hallway before," Nicolette replied, anxiety creeping into her words. She watched Ursa's eyes glance at the back door where the shouts were getting louder and saw the worry in his eyes. "But… but I think if we go left that will lead us in the right direction."

"Good enough!" Ursa pushed the door open fully and began a fast-paced jog down the hallway.

The thick candles were burning low in the iron wall brackets. Many had already burned out, leaving dark sections down the long, empty, stone hallway. Ursa stopped them when they reached the first junction and looked down the dimly lit hallway. He saw movement near the far end and decided against going down this one. Before moving along, he glanced back the way they had come and knew guards would be filling the hallway any moment now.

The next junction was better lit with newer candles, and no movement could be seen down its length. Behind them, much noise could be heard, as the several guards began their search of the hallways.

"This one should lead to the western wing's main staircase of the castle to my aunt and uncle's room," Nicolette said, panic rising in her chest, "at least I think it does... I do not know for sure," she cried out.

They quickly went down the hallways not having any choice in the matter now.

"Stop where you are!" two soldiers yelled out stepping in front of the opening.

Ursa cursed, but did not slow his pace. He lifted his hands and called on his Gift - a forceful current of air pulsed down the hallway and slammed into the soldiers, knocking the wind from their lungs and hurling them to the ground.

Ursa stopped just before the hallway opening and peered out to make sure all was clear. The two guards on the floor were curled up in a fetal position still trying to draw breath. He looked back at the others. "Whatever happens, do not draw your weapons! We are not assassins, the enemy, nor should we give them any reason to believe that we are."

"We got trouble coming up our flank!" Meath called ahead, fighting all urges to draw his sword at the sound of armed men coming toward them.

"Princess, which way once we get up the stairs?" Ursa asked urgently.

"Their rooms are to the right, at the end of the hallway!" Nicolette stated, glad she knew where they were again.

Ursa took the stairs as fast as a man half his age, making it to the stairway's middle landing. He turned to make sure the others were close behind him. "Hurr..." he started to say but his voice stopped in his throat as he watched a half score of men file into the room below in defensive formation. All armed with either loaded crossbows or notched long bows. "They knew we were coming," he mumbled out as the group stopped on the landing beside him.

"Of course they did." A deep, powerful voice said from above them. They all turned to see Rift standing at the top of the stairs, sword in hand and another half score of archers rimming the stairwell behind him.

"Rift, what are you doing?" Nicolette cried out in both joy and confusion.

"It is all right your Highness - I will have you safe and away from these vile creatures shortly," he called down to her taking a step further down the stairs, his broad sword pointing straight at Ursa. "Ursa, if you value your worthless hide you will let the Princess go right this instance. I know your tricks, and you know there are more than enough men here to stop you! Just surrender!"

"No Rift you do not understand!" Nicolette exclaimed stepping forward. "They saved my life from Prince Berrit, he is…"

"No Princess - Ursa has you fooled with some mind trick!" Rift barked down. "You leave her mind alone, demon!"

"That is not even possible!" Meath barked back - it took all his strength not to draw his sword.

Rift's eyes glared at Meath. "You would do best to not talk boy, lest my anger turns on you for past transgressions!"

"Please Rift, stop it!" Nicolette pleaded. "You are wrong - all of this is wrong!"

"Let her go Wizard or I will have no choice." Rift raised his hand and the sound of bow strings going taunt filled the stairway.

"Your Highness, go up to him," Ursa said, his tone defeated.

"What?" Meath, Zehava and Dahak stammered out at once, but Ursa held up his hand and silenced them.

"Are you sure?" Nicolette asked.

"Yes your Highness, go. It will be all right - you are safe now."

Nicolette took two steps up the stairs toward her champion and his outstretched hand, and then stopped and looked back at Ursa, Meath and the others. Fear and bewilderment showed plainly on her face, as she seemed to fight the urge to go back down the stairs. Her eyes locked with Meath's and she could see the turmoil on his face as he fought back his emotions and his urge to grab the hilt of his sword. This was not how it was supposed to work out. They were supposed to be safe here[to tell the full story of what truly happened that night in King Borrack's chamber, and then find a way to stop whoever was posing as Prince Berrit.

Rift took another step down the stairs, his sword still pointed at Ursa as he reached his free hand toward the Princess. "Quickly your Highness, give me your hand, you are safe now."

Nicolette turned back to Rift, her demeanor changing from meek to determined.

"Quickly your Highness, what are you waiting for?" Rift called down to her confused.

"NO Rift, no!" she said with as much authority as she could garner and loud enough for everyone in the stairwell to hear. Confused looks and mumbles filled the room. "Ursa is not some vile creature - he did not murder my father or kidnapped me. Ursa tried to warn my father and save his life that night from the real villain and murderer."

"Your Highness, just give me your hand and come up here!" Rift urged her. "We can talk in length of what happened once you are safe from harm."

Anger flared across the Princess's face. "I am safe!" she cried out. "These men," she pointed down to Ursa and the others. "Ursa, Meath, Zehava and Dahak have kept me safe all this time, against countless misfortunes that could have befallen me and themselves. They risked their reputations and their very lives to bring me here securely so that the truth could be heard. I will not stand by and have my saviors treated like vile murderers and cutthroats simply because you are too thick-headed to listen to reason!"

Rift's face twisted in puzzlement at the Princess's outburst. "But I… I just…" he started to say when his eyes looked down at Ursa and anger clouded his features once more. "I said get out of her mind Wizard or I will kill you!" He raised his hand to signal his men again when a powerful voice boomed out and trumped his command instantly.

"Stand down!" The voice commanded, "I have given no such orders." Hesitantly, all the soldiers relaxed their bowstrings, but kept them notched.

Lady Jewel walked out onto the landing to stand near Rift - her presence commanded authority and all the soldiers parted way, careful not to hinder their Lady's path. "I am the Lady of the House and only I shall determine such fates inside these walls."

"But, Lady!" Rift began to say. Lady Jewel raised her hand to silence him and he halted his protest begrudgingly.

"I have been listening from above and I am conflicted by the evidence brought to me not long ago, and the evidence before me now, not to mention my own contradictory emotions with the accused. Since Rift has brought me the news of what has happen back at Draco City early this morning, I have been fighting with every emotion the human mind possesses in trying to sort and make sense of all that has come to my attention." She stopped for a moment, drawing a firm, deep breath to help calm herself from the rising emotions her voice betrayed. She looked down hard at Ursa, her demeanor strong and controlled once more. "Master Ursa, you and I have been friends for more seasons than I could count. My husband and I have trusted in your council countless times. King Borrack and many of the other Lords of Draco Kingdom have trusted in your council and friendship for just as many seasons if not more. You have aided this Kingdom undisputedly with not only your knowledge and wisdom, but your Gifted powers and devotion since the time the King and yourself erected the truce for the Gifted. Yet here you stand accused of the foulest, most treacherous crimes one could be condemned of, which defies all realms of reason and purpose." She stopped again and took a step down the marble stairs, her eyes not wavering from Ursa's. Hervoice powerful and controlled, yet on the verge of breakdown. "I ask you this, Master Ursa, this and simply this - are you guilty of such crimes?"

Ursa looked up at his old friend, his face calm and serious, his eyes securely set on hers. "No my Lady, I did not commit the transgression that have been placed upon me."

The stairway was eerily still, even more so silent as a score of armed men awaited orders to the bizarre situation. Lady Jewel stared hard into Ursa's eyes as if searching for any possible hint of deceit in his conviction.

"Lower your weapons," she said, an audible sigh escaping her as her hand grabbed the nearest banister to steady her.

"Your pardon my Lady?" the commander on her right asked confused by her sudden order.

"I said have your men stand down, Commander," she replied calmly, taking several more steps down closer to Ursa. "I believe him."

Rift took another step down closer following her, his sword still pointed directly at Ursa. "Lady, I do not think you should jump to such simple conclusions!" he protested sternly.

"Yet you would have me jump to the latter more complex, yet dubious conclusion instead?"

"But the facts my Lady point to…"

"What facts Rift?" Lady Jewel questioned plainly, cutting him off. "The facts are; the King was murdered, and only three lived to witness it. Two in which stand before us now, two of our own, who travelled here of their own free will. One being the very Princess of the murdered King - the other one of Draco's most trusted subjects and dearest friends to the King himself. The other is a pompous, vile Zandorian Prince, of whom we know very little. So think me not a fool Rift and believe me when I tell you I have made no such simple or hasty conclusions."

Rift was about to come back with a retort but was held speechless for a moment as her words and logic cut through him like a knife. He looked from Lady Jewel down to Ursa and the others. They did not stand before him like men guilty of such horrendous crimes of treason, but rather men desperate for friends, refuge and a chance to tell their side. Why else would they have come this far? Why else would they be standing in the stairwell of Dragon's Cove Castle, surrounded by a score of armed soldiers, and not have lifted a finger in retaliation to save their own lives when death was near certain not moments ago. Guilt and dishonor washed over him in a flood of emotions. "You… you are right my Lady," he stammered out, his rigid demeanor crumbling almost instantly. He looked back up to Ursa and the others. "I am sorry… I must go now… I am sorry…" With that, Rift walked back up the stairwell and through the rank of soldiers and disappeared down the hallway.

"I am sure you are all very weary, so let us go sit and eat and you may shed some clarity onto this tragic tale." She turned and went up their stairs beckoning them to follow, "Commander."

"Yes my Lady." The commander straightened and awaited his orders.

"Give your men the rest of the night off and I would like this information to go no further than this room at this present time, am I understood?"

The commander saluted, "Yes my Lady, you are understood."

Lady Jewel sat and listened to Ursa, Princess Nicolette and others recount their tale, from the moment when Ursa had found the Princess in the Royal gardens and they had overheard the treacherous plot against the royal family, to the present. Jewel sat and listened to every detail not saying a word until the story was finished. She sat back in her cushioned oak chair, near the low burning hearth, mulling over all she had just been told.

While the tale was recounted, they ate much of the smoked venison and fish that had been brought out for them by a servant, along with a full tray of flat breads, cheese and fresh fruits. Now while they digested the heavy meal they sipped on a sweet honey wine or fresh cool water and awaited Lady Jewel's comments.

"That is quite a tale," she started, "and as hard to consider as it is, it makes far more sense than the latter." She stood from her seat and went and sat next to Princess Nicolette , pulling her into a deep embrace. "My poor dear child, I am so sorry for everything that has befallen you these last days. You are safe now, and I assure you we will right these inexcusable wrongs."

Nicolette did not even try to fight back the tears thatflowed as she hugged her beloved Aunt.

Finally, after several long moments Jewel pulled away and wiped numerous tears from Nicolette's rosy cheeks. "You have all been through so much, and it is getting very late. I propose we all retire for the night and continue in the morning - a rested clear mind will be far more calculated in dealing with this grievous matter." She stood and rang the small bell on the table of near empty food trays. Within moments several servants appeared around the corner - some went straight to work cleaning up the dishes, while one awaited commands. "I took the liberty of having baths prepared for you all. Nicolette my child, your room has yet to change and is as you left it. The rest of you, if you would follow Vivienne, she will show you to your quarters for the night."

Once everyone had left, it was just Lady Jewel and Ursa left standing alone in the quaint discussion room. Lady Jewel nearly threw herself into a tight embrace with the tall, slender Wizard.

"Oh Ursa, when I heard the rumors I knew they could not be true! I beg it all to be a lie and that something was amiss." She hugged him tightly.

Ursa gently wrapped his arms around her to comfort his dear friend. "I tried to get here before the word spread, knowing you and

Marcus would be our only hope to clear this ill charge on our heads. I did not know where else to go, or what else to do." Tears began rolling down the old Wizard's creased cheeks. He had been so concentrated on getting to Dragon's Cove with the Princess alive that he had not yet had time to grieve his dear friend Borrack's death, or Saktas'.

Jewel pulled herself away at arm's length and stared up at the Wizard. "I am glad you came and straightened the truth out, I will do everything in my power to correct this and bring the perpetrators to justice!"

Her words were not lost on Ursa, for he remembered what the Princess had said when she had arrived at Draco Castle. "Is Marcus still with us?"

Thicker tears welled up in Jewels eyes. "Yes, but I fear not for much longer. I have had the best healers and physicians visit him and try their remedies." She had to stop fighting back a complete breakdown. "Nothing has done more than ease his pain for a while. He has not awoken in several days now."

"Take me to him - I will see what I can do, even if it is just easing his pain."

Ursa stood beside Lord Marcus' bed, one hand on the ailing man's damp chest, the other gripping his frail hand. Ursa's eyes were closed as he focused his healing energies into the dying man's fragile body. He knew this would not save his dear friend, for The Gift could only heal the physical wounds on one's body, not the internal ones such as the fever. The only good this would do for Marcus was to take away the aches and soreness his body was enduring through its battle against the illness.

Finally, Ursa stopped, knowing there was nothing more he could do for the man that night. He looked down at his dear friend - his eyes were sunken deep into their sockets now causing dark circles around his eyes. His thick hair was noticeably thinning; his hairline had receded significantly and bald patches were now visible. His skin was no longer taut over his once powerfully built frame, but was now sagged loosely over his deteriorating body. Even his color was fading from the tanned bronze he once had. Now, it was an ashen color.

"I have done all I can for him this night," Ursa said softly, looking across the bed to where Lady Jewel sat staring down at her bed-ridden husband, distraught.

"I thank you Ursa from the bottom of my heart."

"You know there is no need for that my Lady." Ursa handed her a piece of paper with several herbs and ingredients written on it. "Have someone find these for me, and on the morrow I will make an elixir that will lessen his pain for longer periods of time."

"You shall have them as soon as it is possible," Jewel replied, glancing at the list only briefly. "Vivienne will be waiting outside the door for you - she will take you to your quarters so you may rest."

Ursa nodded his thanks and turned to the door and opened it ajar, then turned to Jewel. "Be sure you find sleep this night."

Jewel smiled at him, "I will, I just will be a moment longer with him."

Meath looked down at the now grey, filmy water in the bronze tub as he dried himself off with the fresh linen towel that had been left for him. It always amazed him how a good bath could rejuvenate someone, even after all they had been through. It was almost like he had washed clean the last several days and it was finally almost over. Now that they had made it to Dragon's Cove and cleared their names, they could finally relax. Now all that needed to be done was to a plan to stop the false Prince and bring him to justice. Meath was happy to know that he most likely would not have any part in that process.

He threw on the grey cotton nightclothes that had been left on his bed for him, as a servant had taken his clothes to have them cleaned so they would be fresh come morning. Once he was dressed, he walked out onto the rooms' small, private balcony that overlooked the western grounds of the castle and in the background the Serpent Sea.

The cool night air was moist and salty to the taste - not like Meath was use to in the jungles of Draco, where the air was humid and the senses could easily be overwhelmed with the many scents.

His began to wonder a dozen things all at once. Now that the truth would be uncovered and the false prince would be dealt with, what would happen? With the King dead, who would rule the kingdom - surely the Princess was not ready to take up that mantle just yet. Not to mention now that there would be no wedding and marriage between countries, what would happen with the treaty?

Who would she marry now? Each thought assaulted him with a hundred different possibilities, all foolishly leading him to the same thought.

He shook his head as if trying to shake loose the unconceivable thoughts that would only hurt him more in the end. "That is none of your business Meath and you know it," he told himself aloud as he went to his bed.

Morning came early for those who now sat in the private study of Dragon's Coves Castle. The topic of discussion was far too sensitive not to take such precautions. They could not risk word spreading of their planning in any way, for no one knew what ears could be about or what price someone was willing to betray their kingdom for. They knew little of their enemy, and needed all the advantage they could.

Nicolette sat nearest to one of the private study's open windows, the light breeze off the sea, reminding her of her many years spent here. It had been several hours and already the sun was high in the sky threatening to become early afternoon, and still nothing had been decided upon.

She looked out the window at the activity around the castle and wished she was anywhere but here. But she had been summoned to be here, as she would with all the meetings now that had anything to do with the Kingdom. Her Kingdom - for she was Queen of Draco Kingdom now, no longer just a Princess. Now she had more responsibility than ever before. How she hated that word.

"I still say we march in there and take the bastard out, by any means necessary!" Lepha- Dragons Cove's oldest Wizard -grumbled again.

"We have been over that," Antiel - Dragons Cove's other Wizard - replied with a deep sigh of frustration running a hand through her short blonde spiky hair.

"Yes, but I still do not see why not." Lepha replied leaning back in his chair. "The longer we wait to act the longer he has to do whatever it is he is planning, which already has been catastrophic."

"I have to agree with Lepha." Uveal, Dragons Cove's advisor said. "Our King is dead, how much more damage needs to be done?"

"The problem with that plan is he has at least one other working with him, in whatever his plot is," Lady Jewel interjected, knowing if she did not the two Wizards would be at it again. "Without knowing who that other is, or what their mission is, we are going in blindly and may do more damage than good."

Lepha threw his arms up in the air in frustration as he stood from his chair. "More damage is being done every day that we do not act. Who knows what this Wizard is doing right now - he could be killing others as we speak. I say we go there and we kill him."

"How will you find him?" Ursa replied casually.

The question seemed to throw everyone in the room off.

"What do you mean, how will I find him?" Lepha asked. "Look for the man who looks like Prince Berrit."

"He has mastered a form of the Gift that has allowed him to alter his appearance. What makes you believe he cannot change himself into someone else? You would never know who it is," Ursa reminded them.

Lepha sat back in his seat, the look of respect and contemplation on his face. "I had not thought of that Ursa, that statement holds much truth."

"Then, what are we supposed to do?" Barkel, Dragon's Coves Champion asked. "If he can change his appearance we may never be able to track him down."

"We will send assassins," Uveal cut in. "Several of them so they have a better chance. We will inform them of what to be aware of and what the situation is, that is what they are trained for."

"Assassins?" Antiel laughed aloud.

"I do not hear you offering a better plan," Uveal shot back.

"Yes well, assassins are outlaws and to be arrested if their identities are confirmed," she replied. "I do not see reason using one evil to help take care of another."

"Desperate times call for desperate measures," said Uveal, his tone not hinting any disapproval. "This is a unique circumstance, and our options are few."

"As much as it pains me to do so, I must agree with Uveal," Lady Jewel said, her eyes glistening with inner conflict.

Antiel nearly fell backward from her chair. "You cannot be serious?" she stammered out, forgetting to address Jewel by her rank.

Jewel sighed, "Desperate times call for desperate measures," she echoed with a shake of her head, then looked directly at Uveal, "I do not like it any more than you, but if it is necessary. Then I will permit it."

"I may have a solution to this problem," Ursa announced. "I have been thinking this over for many days now, wondering about this very problem." Everyone stopped and waited for him to explain. "I remember a story my old mentor Solmis told to me of a rare, enchanted relic he had acquired after saving a strange man's life. It was a very old, simple dagger - I recall seeing it but once. The quality was poor and it looked to be of little worth, yet when held you could feel the power within the blade. The man claimed the blade, could filter through the falsehoods of deception and see what was hidden behind. I believe this relic may be the instrument we need."

"Can you be sure it will work?" Lepha asked, hope hanging in his every word.

Ursa's grim expression was more than enough to answer. "I cannot be certain, all I know for sure is when I held the blade I could feel its power. I cannot even be certain Solmis still has the relic. But if he does, it may be our best chance at ensuring we find our enemy and his accomplice."

"That does not give us much to go with, now does it?" Barkel grumbled. "A magical dagger, that may or may not even work for what we need it to. Not to mention, we do not even know if the dagger exists, or if it has been lost to time. I do not like it."

"It is not much to go with, but I suppose it is better than what we have come up with so far." Antiel shrugged her shoulders in defeat.

"Where does Solmis live?" Lady Jewel asked.

"Apologies my Lady, but I cannot tell you his whereabouts," Ursa replied, his hands held out in apology. "Solmis is a very private man, and does not like strangers knowing how to find him."

"This is absurd!" roared Barkel. "This is Lord Marcus' lands and he has the right to know who lives upon it!"

Lady Jewel held up her hand and silenced the Dragon's Cove Champion. "Take what you need. How long will you be gone?"

"I shall return within the week," Ursa replied, standing from his seat. "I shall leave immediately."

"I shall have an escort waiting by the gate, to take you out of the city so you are not delayed or recognized," Jewel said.

"What if you do not return in time?" Uveal asked.

"Then do as you must," replied Ursa.

"I shall pray each night that it does not come to that Ursa," Lady Jewel replied. "But if it does, we will send the assassins." Ursa nodded his understanding.

Ursa turned to leave but stopped and faced the group again. "I would ask a small favor of Antiel and Lepha, if I may." Jewel nodded. "While I am away, will you see to my apprentice Meath, and continue with his training. It would serve him well to be occupied while I am gone." Ursa glanced at the Princess for but a moment, but no one noticed. Both Wizards nodded their agreement and Ursa thanked them before leaving the room.

"This meeting is adjourned, we shall resume our normal tasks until the time given for us to make a decision," Lady Jewel said, standing from her seat as the others nodded their respects and left, until only Nicolette was left. "I am sorry for this my child, but you are needed for these proceedings now. You are the Queen of Draco Kingdom now, and you need to bear witness to all the events which take place within it."

Nicolette smiled up at her aunt, "I know Aunt, I am just overwhelmed and not prepared for all this.

"I know my dear girl, I know. How could you be? It will be all right - we are all here to help you, until you are ready to take full control of the kingdom. Then the process of finding a suitable suitor will come next, someone who has nobility to become a king."

The last words out of her aunt's mouth turned Nicolette's stomach and her aunt must have noticed.

"That is a long way off my child. I am sorry for bringing it up - that was foolish of me. I was not thinking clearly."

"It is all right - it is something that will have to come to pass sooner or later," Nicolette replied, fighting the sick feeling inside her. "It is just all so much, with father's murder, our mad flight here and the false Prince pretending to be Berrit, the man whom I was meant to wed. I just… I just am so… so very lost." Nicolette looked up at her aunt, who was returned her gaze with compassion. "I do not believe I am ready to be the Queen of Draco Kingdom - I do not know if I ever was."

"Hush child, do not say such things." Jewel embraced her tightly. "You are just under a lot of strain and your world has changed so drastically… so quickly. It is to be expected that you feel such things, but do not allow it to take firm hold. You are the Queen of Draco, and you will be a magnificent Queen. One who will be loved and remembered forever, like your father is and will always be." Jewel pulled away to look at Nicolette. "Relax my child, Lord Tundal and Lord Dagon and I, along with Ursa will see to the running of Draco Kingdom until things have settled down and you feel you are ready to take your rightful place on the throne. Until then, grieve and mourn and find yourself again."

Nicolette embraced her aunt tightly. "Thank you, I am sure after sometime I will be able to clear my thoughts and know what I need to do."

A ruckus outside drew both their attentions to the window. "What is going on out there?" Lady Jewel asked, looking out the open window by which Nicolette had been sitting.

"We were told to stay within the castle's walls Dahak!" Zehava argued sternly.

"So what, we are just to leave her out there, alone and helpless on her own, in a strange new place full of folks that hate her kind?" Dahak shot back, his temper flaring at his friends.

"We understand the situation Dahak - we do not like it any more than you do, but our situation is still in peril outside these walls for the moment." Meath interjected.

"No, your situation is in peril outside these walls," Dahak barked back. "No one knows me; no one cares about who I am. I am not the one who has a bounty on his head!"

"Dahak listen…" Zehava tried to say.

"No, you listen. I left her out there - it is my fault she is not here with us now. It is my fault she might already be dead out there!" Dahak eyes brimmed with tears of guilt.

"I am sure she is fine for now," Meath replied, finally seeing what was really bothering his friend. "She is a smart girl…she has survived in more hostile environments most her life."

Dahak looked both his friends hard in their eyes. "Would it be different if it were me? If I was the one lost out there, would you just

wares, but with little interest for the cheaply crafted bronze blades, kataras and other concealable hand weapons.

"Ah, welcome," the rat-faced vendor said, a wide rotten toothy grin on his face. "You like what you see, yes?" He spread his hands over his shameful wares.

Barnaby picked up a small bronze dagger and frowned at the vendor disappointedly. "I see nothing of worth, which makes me believe my sources were wrong in telling me you had quality wares." He tossed the dagger down on the bench with a sigh. "Unless you have something of value to show me I shall take my silver elsewhere." Barnaby pulled out the purse he has stolen earlier and jingled it to make his point.

The vendor's eyes widened at seeing the bulging purse. "I may have something more to your, standards." He turned and opened a large wooden chest behind him and pulled out a fold of leather. "I just got this piece this morning and was told to hold it for a few days," he placed the leather fold on the table and opened it, "since it still had blood on it."

Shania gasped as the vendor revealed the twin blade she had lost, when she had saved Keisha's life.

"Ah, I see by your acquaintance's reaction that she is indeed interested in this piece." The vendor rubbed his hands together eagerly, anticipating a high sale.

"That is my weapon!" Shania demanded, reaching for the lost blade.

The vendor pulled the weapon away from her grasp quickly, "it can be, for a price."

"How much do you want for it?" Barnaby asked.

The Vendor smiled wide, "Well it is a splendid weapon, finely crafted, and appears well tested in battle."

"I will not buy my weapon back!" Shania demanded. "Give it to me!"

"I give nothing away!" the vendor snapped, "besides there is no way a street urchin like you owned a blade this fine."

Shania snapped the other blade out in her hand and leaned forward.

The vendors eyes widened in shock and fear. "Your weapon? The previous owner to this blade is wanted for the death of the man it was found in." The vendor grinned. "You sure you want to make that claim so eagerly The city guard is just over there, I am sure they would be interested in your story of why your blade was found buried in some poor sap's chest." The vendor's grin was abhorrent.

"You are not the one buying the weapon, I am." Barnaby cut in, looking at Shania, seeing this was not going to go well if he did not. "Now, I know it is a fine weapon - I have had the pleasure of seeing its twin in use just the other day. I am not here to barter for it, what is your price?"

The vendor's eyes glistened with greedy anticipation. "Fifteen silver should do it."

"Fifteen silver!" Barnaby barked loudly, completely taken back by the outrageous number. "I expected to be taken for a few extra coin, but not robbed flat out... not even by a crooked wretch like you. I will give you nine silver and you will be grateful for it."

"I will have fifteen silvers for this weapon and you will pay it or I will be calling over the market guards and informing them to whom this blade belongs. I am sure they would reward me well for such information." He smiled maliciously, holding his hand out, awaiting payment.

"You have no idea whom you just offended, you crust-bellied worm!" Barnaby snarled, reaching for several more coins.

"I offend many in my line of work." The vendor held out his hand even further.

The quick ring of steel being freed of its sheath sounded in the air, a flicker of light flashed and the thud of a blade embedding in wood was absolute over the noises of the crowded market.

The vendor stumbled back, staring down in shock at his severed hand, left on the table. "You... you... cut off my hand!" He cried out, his other hand clamping over the stump trying to stem the flow of blood.

Barnaby stared wide-eyed at Shania as she pulled her blade free of the table and leaped over retrieving its twin. "You cut off his hand!" He stammered out in disbelief. "I would have paid..."

"I know his kind," Shania replied, leaping back over the table. "He would have betrayed us anyway."

"Help me!" The vendor cried out, drawing the attention of all those around. "They are trying to kill me! Guards!"

"We need to leave right now," Barnaby said, seeing the market guards drawing their swords and rushing over. "This way!" He grabbed Shania's arm and turned to flee but halted as the tip of a guard's short sword pressed into his chest. "This is what I was referring to about not needing any more complications in my life."

Meath's ironwood practice sword crashed hard into the wooden cross post from a downward chop, chipping off several more flakes. He pulled the sword back and lunged forward, spearing the tip into what would be the wooden dummies abdomen. Again, he pulled his ironwood sword back and went into a defensive stance before launching into another barrage of attacks.

Meath had ignored Master Lepha and Master Antiel's summons - they each had sent one to him by way of servant. He had sent the servants away with return word that he was occupied and would continue to be occupied until he saw fit. He had expected the Wizards to come and find him and scold him profoundly. Half the day had passed and still they had not, nor had further word found him. Instead, he had spent his day training alone in a small corner of the northern courtyard, hidden away from view by unused supply wagons and an assortment of building materials.

Meath had borrowed an ironwood training sword and had set himself up several wooden targets. He had spent most the day destroying them with hand numbing attacks that rendered the targets into kindling.

Sweat dripped into his eye and he squinted against the stinging of salt, eyeing up the last of his wooden dummies that had not been defeated. He rushed forward imagining his target doing the same. He fainted left with his footing as he neared his target then changed his charge back to the right as if the target had fallen for the ruse. He hacked hard with all his strength for a low strike across the target's legs. The wooden pole holding the cross beam upright snapped in two sweeping the target up flat like a man who had just been bowled over. Meath carried through with his momentum, his sword arcing up high as he spun a full circle and brought the wooden blade down hard across the chest of the falling target slamming it into the dusty earth in defeat.

"It would appear you have defeated all your enemies," a voice said from behind him.

Meath turned around to see Nicolette standing there in a dark blue silken dress. He stood up and finally wiped the sweat from his eyes. "That is what one hopes to be able to do." He walked over to her, resting the practice sword against an old barrel. "Yet there always will be one enemy who will forever be above me and undefeatable." He turned his eyes away from hers. "What brings you out here?"

"Your return word to Master Lepha and Antiel has them in quite a profound conundrum. They are not sure if they should storm down here and punish you for your disobedience or just leave you be for the day. My Aunt made the decision for them - you are free for the day, but she will expect you with them on the morrow."

"If I decide to join them on the morrow I will," Meath replied casually.

"Ever defiant," she smiled at him, but her smile did not last long. "What is this undefeatable enemy of which you spoke?"

Meath's casual smile turned into a grimace, "you know the one, for it plagues you as well. Status."

There was a long awkward silence, both pained by the truth of the word, yet fixed on different ends.

"I do not think I can do this Meath. I do not think I can be a Queen, rule a Kingdom, and marry without love. It just does not feel right; I feel trapped, lost, confused and alone." This all blurted out in a rush, her eyes moist with tears.

"I know, but we will have to, we will have to learn to live the life we were given," Meath told her, hating every word that came out of his mouth. "We cannot run away from our lives."

Nicolette's eyes brightened, "why not?"

"What do you mean why not?" Meath stammered out, confusion plain on his face.

"Why not run away from it all Meath? We always talked about it, so why not?" She took a step towards him, her eyes alive with wonder.

"Do you even hear yourself? We cannot, we have… we have…" His voice trailed off. "You are serious?"

She nodded, "more than I think I have ever been in my life."

"What about the Kingdom, family, friends, duty?" Meath questioned.

"I do not care anymore Meath, I do not care, I just want away from it all, to be with you," she confessed.

Meath stared hard into her golden brown eyes, which danced with possibility. "When?"

Nicolette's eyes lit up more than he had seen in a long time. "We will leave before first light and be far away before anyone notices we are gone. We can do this Meath… we can."

"We will." Meath told her, hugging her deeply against him. "We will."

The two cloaked figures rode hard from the small band that had left Dragons Cove before dawn. They rode northeast with no discernible destination in mind, just glad to have made it out without incident. Meath had noticed the group of people preparing to leave the city as he and Nicolette had been working up the courage to storm past the gate guards. They had decided to see if they could join up with the small group so they would be less noticeable. It had worked - the group was more than willing to take on two more. Once they had travelled far enough from the city they had abandoned, the group quickly and rode off without a word.

The sun had just pulled itself out in full from behind the eastern horizon when they slowed their horses to a walk, so the beasts could rest. They wanted to put as much distance behind them as possible but they needed the horses and could not afford to ruin them. Though Meath had slipped into Ursa's room and taken a nearly full coin purse, which was more than enough to buy several new horses, that coin needed to last as long as possible. Meath had also left Ursa a letter explaining what they had decided to do and why they ran off. Meath would miss Ursa, but deep down he knew he would see him again, one day.

"We need to stop for a moment," Nicolette told him.

"What is it?" Meath asked, watching Nicolette dismount her brown mare with ease.

Nicolette smiled at him as he dismounted. "There is something we need to do before we go any further." She pulled her dagger from its sheath.

"What are you doing?" he asked, the confusion plain in his voice.

"If we are to start fresh and stay hidden I will need a new look…a more permanent look." She handed him the dagger and turned around. "Cut my hair."

"What?" Meath stammered. "No we can keep it hidden until we are far enough away and have started a new life."

"We cannot take that risk Meath - no one will look twice at us if my hair is short. Now do it."

Meath collected her hair into one hand and held the dagger at shoulder length down it. "You ready?"

"Do it." She replied, holding her breath.

Meath ran the blade through her hair, cutting it as clean through and as straight as he could manage. "Done," he turned her around and held the clump of hair in his hand.

Nicolette stared at her severed hair, mixed emotions rolling through. "How do I look?"

"As beautiful as ever," Meath replied, with a grin, "though it will take some getting used to."

"We should get moving again." Nicolette turned to mount her horse, but Meath grabbed her hand and turned her to face him.

"I love you." He pulled her in and kissed her deeply. "We can do this."

"I cannot take much more of this." A voice came from behind the trees and someone stepped out onto the road. "You are a hard man to find, you know that Meath."

Meath spun around to face the voice, his sword ringing free of its sheath. "Who are you? And how do you know my name?" Meath asked the man, hoping they had not been followed and caught by spies of the castle.

"Calm down, there is no need for weapons. My name is Daden," the man said coolly, as if his name was important. His voice was sturdy and firm, "and I have been looking for you for quite a while now, but you have been all over the land."

"Why have you been looking for me? What do you want?" Meath asked, his voice hard and untrusting.

Daden stepped toward them, but stopped when the tip of Meath's sword rose up. "I was sent to find you, because we need your help with something." Daden laughed, "I know you are confused, I understand that, but it will all be explained later."

"I do not know what you are about, Daden, but I have no intention of helping you, so you best be on your way." Meath ushered Nicolette toward the horses.

Daden took another step forward. "Come now Meath - do not be like that. I have travelled a long way to retrieve you and I would really rather not have to do it the hard way."

Meath stepped toward Daden, his sword poised for a fight. "Do not threaten me or I will kill you." Meath spat.

"Meath, let us just leave," Nicolette urged him, handing him the reins of his horse, before mounting her own.

"If I catch you following us, I will kill you," Meath said sternly. He sheathed his sword and quickly mounted his horse, not taking his eyes off of Daden.

"Do not do this Meath," Daden warned.

"You have been warned," Meath replied, turning his mount to ride off.

"So have you," Daden whispered. He stomped his foot into the earth, a ripple like a stone hitting water ruptured from where his foot connected and quickly spread underneath the horses, causing the beasts to spook. Meath was thrown from his horse and hit the churned earth beneath him, while Nicolette barely managed to get her horse under control. "I warned you Meath - we do not have to do it this way."

Meath got to his feet, Wizards fire already forming in one hand. "You just killed yourself," he growled, throwing the crimson sphere at Daden. Before the flaming ball had cleared half its distance, a torrent of air collided with it, displacing it from its course and into the hillside - the side of the road ramped.

"That was a little uncalled for do you not think?" a female voice said, emerging from the other side of the roadway.

"Leave us alone!" Nicolette cried out, dismounting her skittish horse before is threw her.

Meath drew his sword again, and began backing away from the two strangers and toward Nicolette. Fear gripped him, as he knew these two strangers were more powerful than he was.

"Just come with us peacefully and everything will be fine, I promise," Daden said, as he walked closer to them.

"What do you want with me?" Meath ordered, making sure to watch both strangers and their hands.

"That is not to be discussed here. You will not be hurt, I promise you that," the girl replied coming to stand by Daden.

"I want nothing to do with you, I do not care what you think you need me for, and I will not help you." Meath knew their only chance of escape was if he surprised them and acted fast. He grabbed for his dagger and ran toward the man with his sword ready. Meath got two steps before the ground beneath him turned to a thick mud and he sank down to his hips, stopping all forward progress.

"No!" Nicolette cried out. She started for Meath.

"Stay where you are Princess!" Daden warned, his hand pointed in her direction, flames licking from his fingers.

"Leave her alone!" Meath begged. "Do not hurt her, please!"

"Will you stop trying to fight us?" the girl asked.

Meath knew he had no choice. "Yes." He tossed his sword and dagger off to the side.

"Good," the flames dispersed from Daden's hand. "It really did not need to go like this," Daden crouched down near where Meath was. "You know I still do not trust you." Daden stabbed a small dart into Meath's neck and within moments Meath's eyes rolled into the back of his head and he slumped into drying mud.

"Why?" Nicolette cried. "Why are you doing this? Just leave us alone!"

"What do we do with her?" the girl asked, helping Daden pull Meath's limp form from the thick mud.

"Nothing - we were sent to get him," Daden replied. He lifted Meath up. "I suggest you go back, Princess. There is nothing you can do for him. He is coming with us."

"Please do not take him from me!" Nicolette pleaded, falling to her knees in defeat. "We finally found a way…"

"I assure you, our need for him trumps your own." The girl replied. "Now go back home Princess - it is not safe out here."

"Grab his things Kara," Daden called back to her as he began climbing the embankment to the tree line.

Nicolette watched Kara turn her back and walk over to where Meath had thrown his dagger and sword and a surge of anger erupted through her. She scrambled to her feet and charged the girl, slamming into her hard with her shoulder knocking her over. Nicolette scooped up Meath's fallen sword and swung around to face Kara, who was already back on her feet. "Let him go or I swear to you I will kill you," Nicolette hissed, the sword shaking in her hands as she pointed it at Kara's chest.

Kara burst out laughing, "What do you think you are going to do with that?"

Nicolette took a step forward, thrusting the blade threateningly. "I will do it, do not test me! Now let him go!"

"What is going on here?" Daden asked, turning around to look at the heroic display the Princess was putting on.

"Nothing I cannot handle Daden." Kara replied. "I am going to give you one more chance to put that sword down Princess."

Nicolette lunged forward, hoping to stab Kara through the chest, but Kara had been expecting the attack. She easily stepped aside and countered, her fist connected hard with Nicolette's abdomen, knocking the wind from her lungs. The sword dropped from Nicolette's hands and she crumpled to the earth gasping for air.

"What did I say? Now be a good little Princess and stay put now. We are not going to hurt him, I promise you that."

"Stop playing around Kara and let us be off," Daden yelled back to her.

"Do not try to follow us - we will be long gone before you can get help." Kara told her then ran up the roadside and disappeared into the woods.

"You do not have to come with me," Dahak said, his dturning toward the castle gates.

"Why would I not?" Zehava asked. "Two sets of eyes will be better than one."

"Thanks Zehava," Dahak replied. "I wonder where Meath is - I have not seen him since midday yesterday."

"I do not know- I am sure he is busy with his Wizard's training or something." Zehava's attention turned to the gateway. "What is going on over there?"

"That is her!" Dahak cried, seeing a duo of guards bringing in two shackled prisoners. "Hey stop!"

The guards stopped to regard the two strangers jogging toward them, their hands instinctively going to their sword hilts. "What do ye want?" One man grumbled as they got near.

"Dahak! Zehava!" Shania cried out, relieved to see faces she knew.

"That girl there, she is with us - she is our friend," Zehava explained to the guard, who blocked their path of getting any closer.

"I do not care who she is to you," the guard replied. "We caught these two attacking a vendor, trying to rob him, even cut off his hand, they did. I was gonna hang them when I found out she was a half-breed savage filth. But then found out she matched the description of someone Lady Jewel was offering a reward for. Hence why we are here, now get out of my way."

Dahak stalked up to the guard not caring at all that his hand rested on his hilt. "Watch your mouth on who you are calling filth you whoreson!"

"I should cut your tongue out!" the guard growled back angrily, his partner coming up beside him.

"Your friends are quite defensive," Barnaby whispered to Shania as he watched the men argue.

Shania smiled wide, "they good friends."

"What is the meaning of this!" Lady Jewel barked out above the shouts of Dahak and the guards.

"My Lady," the guard bowed. "My apologies for my outburst, but I bring you the half-breed you were looking for."

Lady Jewel looked toward Dahak and Zehava. "Is this your friend, the one who helped save you and the Princess?"

"Yes, this is her," Zehava answered, letting go of Dahak's arm, now that he was no longer trying to attack the guards.

"Release her." Lady Jewel ordered.

"My Lady?" The guard asked in surprise. "I caught these two robbing a vendor..."

"I said release her." Jewel said again, her voice stern as she cut his off.

"Yes my Lady, sorry for my impudence." The guard quickly unlocked Shania's shackles, "and him?"

"Do you know this man?" Jewel asked Dahak and Zehava. They both answered no. "Then show him to a cell and we will deal with him when we have time."

"Yes My Lady."

"What?" Barnaby bellowed out. "But I helped your friend!"

"I am sure you did, for some price or another, or you were going to rob her..." Lady Jewel started but her sentence stopped short, her eyes no longer on Barnaby. "Child, what happened?" Jewel pushed past the group to where the Princess now stood in the entranceway of the gate.

"They took him... they took Meath!" she cried as she collapsed to her knees.

12

Meath woke to the sway of a horse - he opened his eyes to see his hands were bound by a hemp rope tied to the saddle. His head shot up and if not for being tied to the horse, he would have fallen backward. He felt like he was drunk, everything was disoriented and blurred. He tried to focus on the people in front of him but could not make them out - his horse was tethered to the horse in front of him. He wondered where he was being taken and who these people were. Meath closed his eyes hard trying to clear his mind and vision, when the last thoughts he could remember came back to him. Anger raged and he yanked on the ropes to slow the horse but the beast did not pay him any heed.

The horses stopped and the figure in front of him turned to look back. "He is awake now. We should stop and rest the horses now anyway," Kara called forward to Daden.

"You are right, but do not let him out of your sight," Daden grumbled sounding clearly unhappy.

"I do not think he is going anywhere anytime soon - the drugs we gave him will keep him tame for a few more hours at least," Kara replied with no concern in her voice at all.

Daden dropped down from his horse and helped Kara from hers. "If we let you down, will you be good?" Daden asked Meath mockingly.

Meath tried to talk, but no tangible words came out, so he nodded his head in agreement. The two Gifted strangers helped him down from his horse, his legs felt like jelly and the world spun around him. They walked him over to a tree and rested him against it. Meath knew even if he wanted to there was no way he could escape these people in the state he was in, he would have to wait this out.

"You stay here and watch him. I remember a creek being around here somewhere. I will fetch some water for the horses," Daden told her, grabbing a large water skin from his horse.

Kara quickly went to her horse and grabbed something from her saddlebag then returned to Meath. "Here, drink this. It will help counter the effects of the drug," she whispered to him, making sure her companion was nowhere around.

Meath was not sure he should trust her, but realized if they wanted to hurt him, they could easily do so at any time. She pressed the small vial of topaz liquid to his lips and he drank it in a few small sips.

"There…In a few moments things will start to clear up and you will be able to talk and maybe even walk again," she told him, sitting down on a nearby rock.

Kara sat there watching him; slowly things started to resolve a little and Meath's vision began to clear. By the time things had cleared enough for him to realize he might be able to attempt escape, Daden had returned and was letting the horses drink from the skin.

"Why are you doing this to me?" Meath finally managed to ask bitterly. "What do you want with me?"

"I know you do not know it yet but we are helping you and a lot of other people too," Kara replied, a hint of compassion behind her words.

"What do you mean? Where is Nicolette?" he barked, trying to stand.

"She is safe - we did not harm her," Kara said, pushing Meath easily back to the ground.

"Enough questions - let us get moving, and we were told not to tell him anything Kara."

"I know I was just…" Kara started to say before he cut her off.

"Yes I know you were just trying to ease his mind, but you know our orders."

"I remember them clearly Daden," Kara snipped back.

Soon they were moving down the path again, faster than before, now that Meath was coherent enough to stay in the saddle without falling off.

Meath thought about escaping, but he doubted he would be able to do so with both of them so close in his still disadvantaged state. It did not appear as if they had any plans to harm him, so he could bide his time.

"What were you doing out there Nicolette?" Lady Jewel questioned sternly, her voice on the edge of rage, "and do not dare lie to me!"

Nicolette stood there looking into her Aunt's unyielding golden-brown eyes; she could tell by her Aunt's demeanor that she already had figured out the truth. It would have been nearly impossible to hide with all the facts pointing to it. The well supplied horses, the travelling clothes, the secrecy of sneaking out, the distances they had travelled and then her hair. "You already know the truth, so why ask?" she replied, trying hard to look into her Aunt's eyes without guilt.

"Why would you do something so imprudent? What were you thinking?" Jewel scolded angrily. "You are to be a Queen - to rule this Kingdom in the name of your father. Does that mean so little to you? What if they had taken you, or worse?"

"I do not care, I love him!" Nicolette cried in frustration, tears falling freely now. "I never wanted all this. I never asked for this birthright!"

"You had better start caring!" Lady Jewel exploded furiously, stepping forward and gripping Nicolette's shoulders roughly. "No love is worth further ruining a Kingdom that is already falling in turmoil! More lives than just your own hang in the balance of the decisions you make now." Jewel released Nicolette and stepped back, composing herself. "I know you love him - I have known it since you were a child. I know it hurts, but you were born into obligations; to your family, to your people, to your Kingdom. You must put this to rest, accept it, and move forward for the betterment of your Kingdom. You are no longer a child Nicolette, but a Queen - you need to learn to act like one." Jewel turned away, went to the windowsill, and stared out into her city.

Nicolette stood there feeling more alone than she ever had before. Her Aunt had always been there for her, had always been kind, compassionate and understanding of her needs. She had hoped out of all people, Jewel would have understood what she had tried to do. "What about Meath?" Nicolette asked, stifling her tears.

"I have sent out several search parties, along with Master Lepha," Jewel replied, not taking her gaze from outside. "They will find Meath and bring him back to us, where he will follow instruction from Master Lepha and Master Antiel until Ursa has returned. We will solve our problem in Draco and put your father's killers to justice - then you will be ordained Queen. You will learn to rule as your father ruled." Jewel turned back to Nicolette. "Then when the time is right you will find a suitor and marry."

"That is it then," Nicolette said, not in question but in statement. "My life has already been mapped out, detail by detail of how I am meant to act, who I am meant to be, whom I shall marry!" she barked out bitterly, her anger flaring through her meek demeanor. "Yet no one ever asked me what I want."

"I know you are confused child, and hurt. Your world has taken a horrible plunge with the recent events and your emotions are in turmoil." Jewel stood in front of Nicolette again, her façade softened. "You were born to be Queen; that is your destiny. You need to embrace it, not fight it."

A soft knock at the door turned their attentions to a servant.

"Yes, what is it?" Jewel asked, annoyed at being interrupted.

"Sorry to disrupt you my Lady," the man bowed his head, "but Lord Marcus is having another coughing fit, and Master Antiel told me to find you."

Concern flashed in Lady Jewel's eyes. "Yes, thank you. I will be there shortly."

"Yes my Lady." The man bowed and left.

"You have had a long trying morning - go get some rest. I will inform you as soon as I know anything more on Meath," Jewel told her with a compassionate smile.

"Thank you Aunt," Nicolette replied, her tone indifferent.

Nicolette paced her room. Angry curses erupting forth one moment, tears of sorrow the next. She prayed Meath was all right and that they would find him and the bastards who had taken him. She cursed herself - if only she would have been stronger, faster, and less afraid, she might have been able to stop them from taking him and they would have been able to run away together as planned and none of this would be happening.

She fell to her knees in defeat - she just wanted to close her eyes and sleep until Meath was found. She looked over to see her refection in her mirror. *How pathetic*, she thought. The person looking back at her was weak and frightened. Tears stained her face - her eyes were clouded with fear and limitations. *They wanted her to be Queen? How can I be a Queen, responsible for an entire Kingdom when I cannot even keep herself together?*

Anger flared through her and she threw the mirror to the floor, shattering it into pieces. "I will not be her any longer!" she yelled to herself determinedly.

There was a light knock at the door. She wanted not to answer, but knew she had too. She opened her door to Zehava, Dahak and Shania.

"Are you all right?" Zehava asked true concern in his voice.

Nicolette just stared at the trio overwhelmed with emotion. These were Meath's friends - dare she say, her friends - and they had been through so much together already. She went forward and hugged Zehava tightly, silent tears falling onto his shoulder.

"We will get him back! Do not worry we have been through worse." Dahak lied.

"I just cannot believe he was taken." Nicolette whimpered, they came in and she shut the door, not caring if anyone saw. "Why would they take him? How did they know where to find him?" The last question brought an awkward silence and Nicolette could sense what they were thinking. "Yes, we were running away together," she said bluntly, her eyes not leaving theirs. "The only way for us to be together was to leave everything behind. So we did, or tried to."

"I am sorry it did not work out as you two had planned it," Zehava replied remorsefully. "You were nearly all Meath talked about when we were in the army, you know."

"Leave again, once they find him and bring him back, leave again." Shania said straightforwardly.

"It would not work - they will watch us and never allow something like that to happen again. My Aunt has already made that more than clear. We were foolish to attempt to disrupt our true destinies."

"We will help you if you would like," Zehava told her, his tone serious.

Nicolette chuckled softly. "You really are the truest of friends to him." She smiled deeply.

"Not just him, but you as well." Dahak smiled softly.

Nicolette's smile almost overwhelmed her tear-streaked face, "thank you."

"Does he always get into trouble like this?" Shania asked, trying to change the mood a little.

"As much as I hate to say it…yes," Zehava chuckled.

Meath has a way of attracting trouble," Dahak added with a smile.

Nicolette watched the trio talking, making jokes, she knew they were trying to lighten the mood and she thanked them for it, but still guilt gripped her heart. "Teach me to fight." They stopped in mid-sentence.

"Pardon?" Dahak asked, thinking he has misheard her.

"I want you to teach me to fight; to use a sword, to throw a knife, shoot a bow, to be strong, to fight and kill if necessary!" she begged them.

"Why would you want to learn to fight?" Zehava asked, thought he knew the answer.

"If I had known how to fight, he might not have been taken, had he not had to worry about me…"

"You cannot blame yourself for that…" Zehava started to say.

"Yes! I can." Nicolette countered. "Every time something bad happens in my life everyone tells me it is not my fault, that I cannot blame myself. Well I do and I am. If I had known how to fight and defend myself, I might have been able to help save my father and none of this would be happening. Had I been able to fight, Meath might not be gone now!" She roared out. "If, if, IF! No longer will it be if. My Aunt told me I am Queen, and that it is time I start to act like one if I am to rule this Kingdom as my father ruled it. My father was a warrior - he knew how to fight, and he rode into battle with his men. He fought fearlessly and held the respect of everyone in the kingdom because of his deeds. If I am to rule this Kingdom, then I need to know how to defend it! How will I be able to defend a Kingdom if I cannot even defend myself?"

The room was silent as everyone digested what Nicolette had just said.

"I will not stand by helplessly again and watch those I love fall victim to danger because of me," Nicolette cried out in frustration.

"I help you - I teach you to fight - everything I know," Shania said,high respect for the Princess and her reasons unfolding from her every word.

Zehava ran his hand through his thick brown hair in contemplation. "All right, we will help you when we can, but Dahak and I have been consigned back to full service here until we can go back to our regular posts."

"I will deal with that -it is time I start being a Queen and having my voice and wishes heard and followed." Nicolette smiled boldly.

"If you deal with that, we will deal with the rest." Zehava reached for the door handle.

"We will get you first thing in the morning, I guess," Dahak added following Zehava.

"I want to start right now," Nicolette told them. "The day is not yet half done."

Meath woke again from the rocking of the horse. He did not know when he had passed out - he only remembered vague parts of when he was awake last. His vision had cleared totally and his mind was no longer scattered. He looked around and could tell it would be getting dark soon. He looked up and saw Daden and Kara riding in front of him. He summoned his Gift to burn the hemp rope binding his hands. Pain shot through his body like when he had been held prisoner at the barbarian camp. He tried to fight back the scream of agony, but could not.

"We will stop." Daden looked back to see Meath barely on his horse now.

Kara turned her mount around and rode to Meath's side. "I would not try to use your Gift again."

"Why are you doing this to me?" Meath demanded, trying to sound threatening.

"Calm down - you will find out when we get there. Until then, do not try anything stupid and everything will be fine," Daden said, unhooking Meath from the horse so he could get down and stretch his legs. "Now come on down and walk a little. I do not want you to get blood clots in your legs."

Meath climbed down from his mount and as soon as his legs hit the ground, he drove his shoulder forward, knocking Daden to the ground. Wasting no time, he bolted into the lightly wooded forest as fast as his stiff legs would carry him. Meath had no idea where he was running to or where he even was - he did not care. Right now, he had to get as far away from his captors as possible.

He was only a few hundred steps into the woods when several thick tree roots shifted upward catching Meath's foot causing him to trip. With his hands tied, he could not break his fall and he crashed hard into the earth with his left shoulder.

Meath groaned, rolling over onto his back. He knew his chance of escape had just ended. He looked over to see the roots slowly return to their rightful places under the ground. "What the..."

"I really did not want to have to do that," Kara said looking down at him. "Now, are you going to behave or am I going to have to ready another spell?" Kara held her palm down toward the earth and Meath could see black markings on the inside of her hand.

"You are a Druid?" Meath muttered in shock forgetting all about the pain in his shoulder.

Kara smiled down at him. "Answer the question please."

"You bastard - if you ever do that again I will..." Daden yelled catching up to them rubbing the back of his head from where it had hit the ground.

"It is okay Daden. I have him under control now. He is not going anywhere," Kara called back. "Are you?" She smirked back at Meath.

"Are you part of the Shyroni?" Meath hissed out, fear gripping him at the thought.

Daden laughed, "Why does everyone always assume that?" He reached down and pulled Meath to his feet roughly. "You hit me again and next time I will hit back," Daden threatened, raising his meaty fist and giving Meath a shove back to the horses.

"When I hit you again I will make sure you do not get back up," Meath muttered.

"What was that?" Daden growled.

"Meath, look out!" Kara screamed.

Meath turned around as a torrent of air collided with him and threw him a dozen paces, slamming him into a thick cedar tree.

"Daden!" Kara snapped, running to Meath's aid. "What are you doing? We are not to hurt him! He is the key to so much! What is the matter with you?"

"He is fine. If he is so tough than that will not bother him...much," Daden replied acidly. "Besides, he threatened me. I am just letting him know he does not stand a chance."

Kara pulled Meath to his feet slowly. "Are you okay? You are not hurt are you?"

Meath grimaced slightly, but otherwise showed no thought to the pain at all. "I am fine -it will take more than a coward's backstab to hurt me."

"Move," Daden ordered, pointing back toward the path and their horses. "As you know, your Gift is useless to you. That hemp rope that binds you has been coated with a rare substance that ensures it so. To save you the trouble of finding out later, if you try to cut through it, you will find the pain might just kill you - so I would not suggest it."

Meath did not say anything just kept walking to the horses with an angry glare on his face. He hated this feeling of helplessness.

"We should make camp here, it will be dark soon. And there has been much barbarian activity around here, it would be best not to risk it." Kara pulled her saddlebag from her mount.

The trio sat around a small cooking fire. Daden had caught two fat hares before the sun had set and they now roasted on the low flames. The smell made Meath's stomach rumble madly - the last thing he remembered eating was a small meal before he and Nicolette had secretly left the castle.

He still had not said a word to either of them. He did not know what to say. They did not seem to want to answer his questions. He just observed them, their movements, possible weaknesses anything that might help him succeed in escaping next time.

Kara took the two rabbits from the spit, laid them on a flat rock and began cutting thick, juicy chunks off of them.

Daden grabbed a piece and plopped it into his mouth, but quickly spat it out. "Damn that is hot!"

"Well of course it's hot - it just came off the fire." Kara laughed at him playfully.

Daden glared over at Meath, "should we feed him too?"

"Of course we feed him too, do not be an idiot!" Kara snapped, taking a few meaty pieces and putting them in a small turtle shell bowl. "I will bring it to him. I do not need you two at each other's throats again."

"Be careful. I do not trust him. I can tell he is a lot like..." Daden quickly stopped in midsentence.

Kara ignored her companion and walked over to where they had tethered Meath. She had used her powers to displace a large root to anchor the rope to then the root had sunk back into the earth. "I know you do not understand all of this, but you will soon enough, I promise," she said, handing him the shell bowl with a sympathetic look. "And when you do, you will know why we had to do this and chances are, you will be grateful."

Meath cursed himself for being so hungry and took the bowl and she left. He ate the meat slowly, not wanting them to see he was as hungry as he was - he watched them while he ate and listened to their small talk.

"We have to make better time than this - tomorrow we only make two stops to rest," Daden said, wiping the grease from his mouth with the back of his dirty hand.

"The horses will hate us, but I agree we still have a long way ahead of us," Kara replied, packing the dishes they had used back into the saddlebag.

"Travel will slow once we pass the river. We are going to need to change our route home. Since he does not want to cooperate, I do not want to be seen by others. They will not understand and might try to stop us to help him and we do not need that hassle."

"Good idea - it will take a few days longer, but will most likely save us much grief," Kara agreed, looking back to Meath who hid the fact that he was listening. "I do not think we will have many problems with him now, he has to know now that he cannot escape us. I just wish we could tell him why he has to come with us."

"That is not our place. We have our orders."

"I know, it just seems really cruel," Kara said compassionately, "to take someone from their life like this with no knowledge of why."

"We had best get some sleep. I will take first watch." Daden got up and stretched getting the blood flowing in his body again to help keep him alert.

"You sure? Kara asked, "I know you have not been sleeping well... I could take first watch."

"I will watch him first, besides I am not tired. I have a lot on my mind."

"Wake me when it is my time," Kara told him, crawling into her bedroll. "Night Daden - night Meath."

Meath rolled over, facing away from the camp and covered himself with the wool blanket he had been given. He had no plans for making another attempt at escape tonight; he was exhausted and knew he would need all his wits to escape when the time presented itself. It bothered him that they knew so much about him. What bothered him more was how they had known where to find him - it seemed impossible, yet they had. So many questions taunted him, yet he knew they would not be answered anytime soon. Finally weariness overpowered his thoughts and he drifted off....

"Wake up Meath. It is time to get moving," Kara nudged Meath's foot with her own.

Meath rolled over and glared at her. Her eyes recoiled down to where the rope was submerged into the ground. Her palm pointed toward the earth and once again Meath saw the strange black markings on the inside of her palm. A strange aura of energy filtered up from the earth to her outstretched palm causing the black markings on her palm to brighten a collage of colors until she closed her hand and cut off the energy flow. She focused her other hand where the root was and as she lifted her hand, the root lifted from the earth as if she was pulling it up with some unseen rope.

"You have never seen a Druid before have you?" Kara asked, seeing the intrigue in his eyes while she untied the hemp rope that bound him.

"No," he muttered, standing up. Ursa had only vaguely talked about other aspects of magic such as druids, mages and sorcery. It was a topic Meath had been eager to learn more about, but other studies had been more pressing.

Meath rode silently the whole morning, just listening and taking in his surroundings, being sure to make note of important landmarks. He had discovered they were traveling to the northeast, back toward the jungle and around the north side of Sheeva Lake. He wondered how they planned to cross the lake, or even the northern side river. They would have to use one of the boatmen or pulley riggers to cross, and they had to know Meath would not keep silent. He hoped it was something they were overlooking. If he could not escape before then, that was his sure thing.

Nicolette woke late the next morning - every muscle in her body screamed at her from the training her friends had put her through the day before.

"They told me this would happen," she groaned, slowly pulling herself out of bed. Zehava had told her they would come for her as soon as the sun came up, but from the looks of the sun it was well past morning.

Nicolette got dressed as fast as she could manage and made her way through the hallways trying not to look like she was in as much pain as she was. She used that pain to fuel her every step, storming past everyone who tried to make small talk, not caring at all if they thought her rude. She was in no mood for pleasantries.

"Where are Zehava and the others?" she demanded to one of the servants in the hallway as she passed by.

The servant girl was caught completely off guard by Nicolette's wrath, "I…I… I am not sure Highness. I am sorry." The girl kept her eyes to the floor.

"I saw them Highness, they were in the stable yard!" a young noble boy told her as he passed by her.

Nicolette did not even thank him. She just stormed off to the stable yard - she did not even notice that her body was screaming in agony.

"Why did you not wake me this morning?" Nicolette demanded angrily, coming up behind the trio sitting on a fence overlooking the horse pen.

"We thought is best that you get more rest today," Dahak stuttered out, seeing anger radiating from her.

"Do not say that. I said we should wake her," Shania put in, not wanting to take the blame for them.

"You said you would get me as soon as the sun was up!" Nicolette barked back.

"You cannot overdo it - you will not become a fighter in a few days." Zehava hopped off the fence to stand in front of her, feeling slightly guilty.

"I will tell you when I feel I have overdone it! That is not up to you to decide," she pressed, her icy glare cutting into him. "I will not become any kind of a fighter if you keep treating me like a Princess!" She pushed him back hard, surprising them all. "When you were sore from training did they let you sleep in?"

"Well no, but…" Zehava started, completely taken back by Nicolette's aggression.

She stepped mere inches from his face, "then what makes you think I should be sleeping in when I am in training? Is it because you do not think I have what it takes?"

Zehava stood there dumbfounded, unsure of what to say next.

"You have what it takes," Shania cut in, stepping between the two. "Prove it right now, you have the spark in eyes, you are ready."

Nicolette took a deep breath. "Promise me you will not belittle me like this again."

"Promise," Zehava and Dahak both said together.

"We have wasted too much time already today. What are we doing?" she asked, the adrenaline still pumping through her body. But before they could answer they were interrupted.

"There you are!" Lady Jewel bellowed hurrying across the courtyard to where the group stood, Rift following quickly in tow. "What is this lunacy I hear that you are doing?"

"It is far from lunacy my dear Aunt, and yes it is true," Nicolette answered sternly catching Jewel and Rift off guard.

"That is absurd! Why would you do such a thing?" Jewel replied in utter shock. "You are to be a Queen. This is no duty you need."

Nicolette smiled snidely at her Aunt. "On the contrary, if I am to be Queen I shall rule as my father ruled and my father was a warrior when needed, as will I."

Rift stepped forward, "I will not let you continue this nonsense! You have had a trying time of late and are simply confused in the right ways to deal with it."

"How dare you Rift!" Nicolette growled back, all the while Zehava, Dahak and Shania stood behind her wishing they were somewhere else. "You out of all people should be supporting such an act, since it is more than apparent that you are not always around when I need you." She knew her words cut him deeply and he quickly recoiled back and lowered his eyes.

"Yes, Highness, I am sorry, I was merely looking out for your wellbeing, but I see now that so are you."

"A Warrior Queen?" Jewel scoffed. "Do not be ridiculous my child."

"I am woman and I am warrior!" Shania cut in, taking offence to Lady Jewel's remark, but Zehava quickly pulled her back not wanting her to be in the middle of such a conversation.

Nicolette's jaw firmed. "If you are going to continue to call me child and belittle my efforts to become the Queen my Kingdom needs, then I will have to insist that you call me by my title and remember your place underneath it!" Nicolette's tone was sharp and unwavering, as she stood her ground against her Aunt.

Lady Jewel was astonished by Nicolette - her face paling as if Nicolette had slapped her. "I…" she paused, clearly unable to determine what she wanted to say. "I guess we will leave you to your training then, Highness." Jewel turned without another word and walked away, clearly hurt and in dismayed.

"You are also dismissed Rift," Nicolette said, turning back to her friends. "What are we doing today?"

13

Meath had been traveling with his captors for near half a fortnight and now they were deep in the heart of the jungle. They had crossed the Sheeva River three days prior by means Meath had never imagined possible until he had witnessed it. Kara had spent several long moments drawing on the life force of the vast vegetation around them so much so that much of the foliage began darkening in color as it began to wilt. She had then used that bulk of energy to manipulate the very earth and rock beneath them, forming a crude earthly bridge that spanned the river. He could tell the effort had drained her significantly, as she paled and her eyes grew clouded and her face taut. Holding the bridge up was still drawing strength from her and they crossed quickly.

Meath had thought to try to make a run for it, but Daden had taken no chances prior to the spell and tethered them together with a short rope. Once they crossed, it crumbled away into the fast flowing river leaving no trace of it ever existing, aside from some turned up earth on the far side.

Considering the terrain had become very difficult for the horses to move through they were making descent time. Yet Meath had still not been able to discover where they might be headed. He knew they continued to travel northeast, but aside from that, he knew nothing. He had hoped his capturers would slip up and mention a name or something that might give him a clue, but they had not.

Night had fallen upon them and again the two sat talking around a small cook fire while Meath listened and ate quietly away from them, tethered to a root.

"I will go gather some water from the creek and scout around us." Daden got up and grabbed the empty water skins. "Do not get close to him - I do not trust him. He has been too quiet - I think he is planning something."

"I will be fine Daden." Kara watched Daden vanish into the darkness and knew he would be gone for a while. She looked back to Meath, who was showing her no mind at all. "I know you think we are your enemies Meath, but we are not. You will see that soon enough, I promise." She walked over to him and crouched down just out of his reach, just in case Daden was right. "It is not healthy for someone to be so quiet." Several long moments passed and still Meath said nothing. "I am not like Daden - I do feel horrible for what is happening to you. I hate that we are not allowed to tell you why we have taken you from your life. I cannot change that - I have my orders. But that does not mean it has to be like this." Kara explained to him, truly concerned for him. "Like it or not, we are stuck together for a while - we can make it less traumatic by at least being civil to one another. I will not press you, but know I am here if you want to talk. I am the closest thing to a friend you have right now Meath... just remember that." Kara whispered to him getting up and going to the horses just as Daden emerged from the trees with water.

Meath could tell by Daden's scowl and demeanor that he was annoyed that Kara had been trying to talk to him again, he smiled at that. He watched and learned, and was beginning to see by the way Daden talked to and looked at Kara that he liked her more than just a work companion did, but he also noticed that she did not seem to have those feelings for him. That was the only reason she was out here with him, because she was ordered to be by whoever had sent them out to collect him. This he could use to his advantage he hoped. Meath laid down on his bedroll.

The next day things were much the same, slow and silent travel. Meath was becoming increasingly frustrated - he had hoped he would have had another opportunity to escape by now. But nothing had presented itself, and Daden was being overly watchful of him, allowing him no chances to seize any small opportunities that might have occurred.

Meath could smell smoke in the distance as they were nearing a small town. Though he was not too familiar with all the towns and villages out this far north, he did know that most likely there was a road that would take him to somewhere he would know.

"Tomorrow we will sell the horses back to the man we bought them from in Tigris," Daden said to Kara as they set up camp a few short miles from the town.

"I thought we would make it before it got dark," Kara moaned wanting to sleep in an inn or even a barn.

"I know - me too. Normally I would say let us keep going until we were there, but the path is too dangerous and I do not want risk breaking one of the horses' legs. Not to mention with all the barbarian attacks of late, I do not want to draw any extra attention to ourselves by coming in the night, especially with him," Daden replied, eyeing Meath suspiciously. "I am sensing he is about due to try something stupid."

"Leave him alone Daden," Kara snipped. "I sure am going to miss the horses - it is so much easier traveling with them.

Daden chuckled. "Oh come on, you love it out here, back home that is all you do is complain on how you wish you were out here on adventures running through the land. Now that you are, all you do is complain and wish you were home."

"I am not complaining, I am just saying we have been gone a very long time and been doing nothing but traveling hard for what seems like forever," she said, trying to redeem herself a little, knowing he was right.

"We will pick up supplies tomorrow in town so we do not have to hunt anymore; it is only slowing us down," Daden told Kara, wanting to be through with this mission already and back home as well.

"What are we going to do with him tomorrow?" Kara asked, glancing over to Meath. "You know as well as I do, we cannot just walk in there with him tied up without drawing curious stares."

Daden nodded his agreement. "I am sure our 'friend' here will not exactly keep silent either. Is that not right Meath? Would not want to make it easy for us would you?"

Meath just sat there staring hard at him, wondering what they were going to do with him after all. If they left him alone that might be his only chance to run, if they brought him into the town he might be able to get help from the locals.

"Well we cannot just leave him alone; he is devious like we were told he would be," Daden mumbled, clearly annoyed.

"Well you go into the town and I will stay with him, you trade the horses back for what money you can get for them and buy the supplies and I will watch over him," Kara replied, even though she had wanted to go into the town and have a warm bath and maybe buy something to bring back with her.

"Are you sure Kara? Daden asked, not liking the fact that she had taken such an interest in Meath. "Maybe I should watch over him."

Kara sighed and shook her head. "You know as well as I Daden that you will be far better off selling the horses and buying supplies for a better price than I would be - a lone girl walking around in town may attract trouble we do not need."

"True enough I guess. I will go first thing in the morning, as soon as the shops are open. I will be as quick as possible." Daden looked over at Meath trying to determine what he was thinking. "You know him being so quiet all the time is really starting to irk me."

Kara turned and regarded Meath with a shrug. "I do not blame him; I cannot say I would not be doing the same thing if I were in his position."

"You take first watch tonight." Daden grumbled while he unrolled his bedroll and crawled into it.

Meath woke to a sharp sting in his shoulder and his eyes opened wide to see Daden standing over him with a dart and a self-satisfying grin. "There, now I will know for sure you will not be causing any trouble while I am away." He winked.

"Damn it, Daden I told you that would not be necessary," Kara barked angrily rolling out of her bedroll.

Daden turned around and walked past her toward the town. "I will be back shortly. Keep alert." He walked to the road that led into the town with the horses in tow.

Meath fought hard against the drug that was dragging him down and making him want to slip into unconsciousness. He could see Kara standing in front of him and her mouth was moving but he could not hear anything. He watched her retrieve something from one of the packs and rush back over to him. He vaguely felt something bitter and warm roll down his throat before the drug won.

Meath woke to the feeling of cold water hitting his face. He jumped forward startled, not sure of where he was or why water was hitting him. Something hit his shoulders and pushed him back to the ground, causing waves of nausea to assault him.

"There, he is awake, now let us get going - we still have a long trip ahead of us." Daden said, though it sounded more like an order.

Kara bit back a retort and helped Meath to his feet. The drug's effects had been diluted by her elixir - she knew Meath would still be greatly disoriented for a while longer. "We should let him have some time to rest Daden. If he trips and breaks something it will greatly hinder you!"

"He will be fine. This way he will not even think to try and escape." Daden replied harshly picking up the end of the rope that was attached to Meath's wrists and pulled him along.

Meath wavered on his feet, barely able to keep upright. He knew he did not have it in him to try to fight now so he started off behind Daden. He tried as hard as he could to remember the landmarks and direction they were going but it all just blurred in his mind as he tried to focus on walking.

They traveled for nearly half the day without a word. Kara walked behind Meath a short distance and Daden lead the way through the dense growth. By now, the drug had worn off thanks to Kara's help and Meath was fully aware of everything, yet he continued to stagger as if the effects still lingered.

"We will stop and rest," Daden told them when they reached a small familiar clearing. "We should be able to make it to that cave we camped in if we do not waste too much time."

"Good, it looks like it is going to rain tonight," Kara replied bitterly, taking a gulp of water from her skin and handing it to Meath.

Daden looked back at her and shook his head in frustration. "You know Kara, I do not understand what your problem seems to be - you should have thanked me for drugging him when I went into the town. He might have tried something. You know, you could have gotten hurt or worse," he told her through gritted teeth trying to justify his actions.

"Let us go, I am done with my rest!" Kara called back to them storming off to the east, resolutely taking the lead.

They made it to the cave just as the last few rays of sun dropped behind the mountains. They ate in awkward silence near a warm fire a dozen paces into the cave. Meath could tell the cave was manmade - the sides were rough and jagged from pick axes and hammers. The cave entrance was not very high or wide but as you made your way inside, it expanded into a fairly large chamber. He guessed it must have been made by bandits as a hideout and a place to stash their goods, which meant roads could not be that far away.

"Look Kara, I am sorry about what I did back there, I...I just thought it was best," Daden pleaded, trying to end this feud growing between them before it got any worse.

Kara stared hard at him for a while. "It is not me you should be saying you are sorry to, now is it?"

"You have got to be joking? You cannot be serious?" Daden moaned knowing full well she meant it. "You know what, fine, Meath I am sorry I drugged you because I figured you would try to escape, which would cause us much grief in having to find you again! There, are you happy?"

Kara started laughing lightly. "Okay fine, I forgive you, but I am not a little girl anymore. I can take care of myself. Not to mention Meath is not some kind of monster."

"I know, I just worry is all. I do not want to see you get hurt again," Daden remarked.

"It is late and we all need our sleep. We should be safe enough in here tonight not to need to keep watch," Kara said, making sure to end the topic of discussion.

Kara tied the free end of the hemp rope around her ankle. "I really wish I did not have to do this Meath - it really is undignified to you and really hurts my integrity. But it needs to be done."

"She is a very light sleeper, you even try to remove that rope from her leg and you will regret it," Daden laughed, putting a few more small branches onto their small fire before crawling into his bedroll.

Soon Daden and Kara were fast asleep, and Meath watched the embers of the fire glow in the otherwise pitch-black cave. Frustration began welling inside him - he was beginning to wonder if he was ever going to be able to get free. He still did not know what these people wanted him for or where they were taking him. He wondered what was going on back in Dragon's Cove, and what his friends were doing, if they were looking for him or assumed him dead after so long. Ursa would be back and have a plan to stop the evil Wizard in Draco, which would be more important than coming after him. His trail would be near impossible to follow now - much time had passed.

"Wake up you two, now!" Daden screamed, rushing back into the cave going straight for his things. Dawn was just breaking over the mountains.

Kara and Meath both were on their feet quickly. "What is it Daden?" Kara asked, her adrenaline was already pumping hard.

"We need to get away from here now!" Daden bellowed out in fear, throwing his pack over his shoulders after retrieving a dagger. "We are being surrounded by a small party of barbarians, they have seen me!"

Kara paled, "not what we needed! How many are there?"

"I do not know Kara - I did not stop to count!" Daden barked back. "The size is not what we need to worry about…"

"What is it Daden?"

Daden swallowed hard. "They have Priestesses with them." He replied gravely.

The blood from both Kara's and Meath's face drained - barbarian shaman were minor tricksters and illusionists for the most part, but priests and priestesses were deadly with their Gift of tainted magic. It was a whole different kind of Gift, not like that of a Wizards, druid or mage. It was something straight from the Keeper's pit itself.

"Untie me! I can help! I am a Wizard and a soldier. I know how to fight!" Meath begged, knowing the trouble they were now in. "Three have a better chance than two!"

"Like we could trust you! You would just run! Now let us get out of here." Daden ran for the entrance and Meath and Kara followed.

They ran out of the cave just in time to see a quad of barbarian warriors and three priestesses come into view from the tree line.

"So much for a clean get away!" Kara groaned wasting no time drawing the mystical life energy from the plant life around her. Within moments, she had enough for her spell. She scooped up a handful of the shale rock around the mouth of the cave and threw it at the emerging barbarians at the same time releasing the energy she had just absorbed. The jagged shale burst through the air toward the enemy. The razor sharp pieces sliced viciously into two barbarians, cutting jaggedly into their flesh and embedding deeply into their chests. They continued their charge valiantly for several more steps before death made itself apparent and they crashed into the cold earth.

"Run!" Daden urged them, releasing a bolt of power scoring a hit on a savage, spinning him around wildly nearly tearing his arm and shoulder clean off.

They ran quickly, hoping to lose the barbarians in the dense jungle before they were surrounded. When they reached the trees, the ground shifted violently causing Meath and Kara to stumbled and trip. Daden threw himself into a forward roll avoiding the fall and came up paces away from a massive barbarian whose bone war club arced down and smashed into his side, cracking ribs and dropping him to the earth gasping for air.

Kara watched in horror as Daden was hit across the back with a sickening crack. She pushed herself up with both hands, drawing energy from around her. When she had drawn enough energy she slapped her hands together, a bolt of raw jade energy crackled through the air exploding through Daden's attacker's abdomen sending him sprawling to the dirt in a blackened gory mess.

"Cut me free! I can help!" Meath pleaded knowing their chances of escape were fading quickly. Kara pulled her boot knife out and slashed through the hemp rope binding Meath's hands and Gift without need of more incentive.

Meath wasted no time and rushed two enemies who were coming in from behind them. He called forth his innate power and fire leapt from his hands engulfing the two savages in a wild eager hunger. The two dropped to the ground in agony trying hopelessly to extinguish the Wizards' fire that consumed and blistered their flesh mercilessly.

Meath snatched up one of their large rusted swords, the weight of the blade almost made Meath want to leave it; he knew he would never be able to fight well with it, but instinct would not let him drop it. He needed to know he had something other than his Gift to rely on.

Three more barbarians emerged from the growth, leading them was a ragged, deranged looking Priestess. Knowing full well he would not be able to fend them off, he turned to run. A sharp pain erupted from his ankle before he could take more than a step. He looked down to see a thorny vine slithering up his leg from the earth. He slashed the blade through the vine and ran to where Kara was now standing drawing more energy for another spell.

"We cannot win this - we have got to run!" Meath told her trying to pull her along.

"I will not leave without Daden!" Kara cried out dropping down digging both hands into the earth. The ground trembled and a crack formed in front of her and rapidly cut forward widening as it went. By the time it reached Daden the fissure was the length of a tall man and caught a handful of barbarians who were charging Daden off guard, swallowing them into its depths.

Meath watched the attacking barbarians disappear into the fissure Kara had made, buying Daden precious time and already she was drawing energy for another attack. Meath knew Daden could not last much longer as more enemies advanced on him. Already the ground around him was littered with bodies.

Meath heard a strained war cry and pulled Kara to the ground with him on instinct - a large war axe flew by where they had been standing. They clamored to their feet and turned to see three Priestesses standing a dozen strides away, the fighting had stopped and the enemy was eerily still, awaiting what their spiritual leaders would do to punish their enemies.

"This might be our only chance." Meath whispered to Kara nervously.

"What are you talking about? We are dead now," she whispered back in defeat.

Meath turned to her with a look of sheer desperation. "Then we have nothing to lose. Be ready." As he finished the words, he charged into a dead run toward them with sword held high.

One of the Priestesses howled in cackling laughter, she swung her arm out releasing an arc of ebon energy hitting Meath's shoulder throwing him to the ground shuddering, but not before he had released his own Gift, sending a torrent of air at the Priestesses along with the heavy sword he had been holding. The rusty blade impaled through the cackling hag's belly, sending her to the dirt, screaming madly in a dying fit. Another was caught unprepared by the torrent and was thrown back to the ground winded momentarily.

Kara watched Meath's bold move in utter amazement almost too stunned to proceed. She watched Meath try to scramble to his feet desperately and knew the final Priestess would release her spell before he could get away. "Get down!" Kara screamed, a spiraling flame released from her outstretched palm nearly engulfing Meath's head as it passed. A warrior pushed the Priestess out of harm's way and was overwhelmed by the Druids bitter fire. The warrior threw himself to the damp earth and rolled, unlike Wizards' fire, Druids' fire could be put out and the enemy knew this.

Daden had made it to his feet and slammed his dagger into the stomach of the barbarian closest to him, then reversed back the other way driving it into the heart of another who had just noticed the fighting had continued.

Seeing the opening Daden had made, Meath staggered to his feet and sprang into a limping run, grabbing Kara's hand as he went. They reached Daden and ran into the thick overgrowth nearly being impaled by several hastily thrown spears.

"I thought we were gonna die back there." Daden coughed, holding his side, grimacing in pain.

Kara had finally forced a stop to rest, knowing Daden and Meath's wounds were serious and needed attending too. Escaping death at the hands of the enemy would mean little only to die of the wounds inflicted.

"We would have, if I had not cut Meath's bonds!" Kara wheezed, trying to catch her breath. "You saved all our lives back there you know." She smiled at him.

Meath wished he had a bit longer to catch his breath and let his wounded leg rest, but knew the longer he waited the less likely he would be able to escape. Before anyone could react, Meath sprinted into the jungle as fast as his exhausted legs would carry him not caring about the burning pain through his body or lungs.

"Damn it, stop!" Daden yelled getting up to give chase but pain erupted through him and he collapsed in a coughing fit, holding his side wincing.

"Meath come back - you cannot do this, not now!" Kara cried out in frustration.

"Go after him! Do not let him get away!"

"What about you? I cannot just leave you here, what if the barbarians find you? They will kill you!" she said, helping Daden back into a sitting position.

"We need him, now go!" he ordered her. "I will be fine." He assured her. "Now go!" Kara took one last look at her injured friend before running off into the jungle after Meath.

Meath knew he was leaving an easy trail to follow, but he had to get far enough away before he could tend to his wounds. His left shoulder and arm that had been hit by the Priestess burned and pulsed horribly, and his leg had gone fearfully numb. He knew he would have to stop soon or he would risk bleeding out and infection.

Finally, exhaustion dropped him near a small murky pool of water. Small pools of water in the jungle were a dangerous thing - they could be full of sickness. Meath searched quickly and was content that the pool looked to be filling up from a small rocky fissure. He did not even cup the water in his hands but plunged his face into the cool water and drank until his stomach was bloated.

Feeling slightly revitalized, he ripped away his buck-skinned pants up to his knee on his wounded leg, and soaked it in the water, washing away the dried blood and dirt. He slowly and painfully began pulling out the razor sharp thorns that were embedded into his ankle. The cuts and tears were turning a charcoal black, which seemed to be slowly spreading throughout his leg in vein-like streaks. He tied a strip of leather around his calf to stop the oozing blood and hoped it would slow or prevent the black infection from going any further up his leg. He pulled off his shirt and looked at his burnt, torn shoulder. The wound was bad and he feared without proper healing or tending he would lose his arm.

"What I would not give to have my potions with me," Meath moaned. He wished he had learned how to heal with his Gift, but it was one of the hardest things to learn and he doubted he had enough strength left in him to do so anyway or even attempt it like he had so long ago with Stewart.

He stood up and was glad to find his leg was still fairly numb and that he could still put weight on it. He found a thick stick to help support his weight, and then used the sun to turn west hoping to find a road. If he did not he would have to find shelter before nightfall. Other than his Gift, which he did not think he could concentrate enough to use, he was weaponless, which made him easy prey to anything that could be about.

Meath walked until it got dark. The only shelter he found before total darkness was a small overhang in a rock wall. He took it without complaint knowing it was better than nothing.

The night seemed colder than normal - he did not know if that was from loss of blood or the fact he had not eaten all day. He wanted to light a fire to help warm him, but knew better than to risk such a thing.

Hunger began to grip his thoughts and Meath started searching under rocks and digging around his shelter, eating the insects that hid under them. He thought back to when he was training in Drandor with Zehava and Dahak and the first time they had to eat grubs to pass the survival test. Dahak had vomited before he had even swallowed.

After eating the few he could find and catch his stomach stopped aching as much and he drifted off into a fitful sleep wondering if he would ever see Nicolette or his friends again, or if he would even wake up.

Kara sat in a large dead rotted-out stump she had stumbled upon just before nightfall and decided she would stay for the night, not wanting to be stuck out in the jungle with no shelter. She had gathered some large flat leafs and built a temporary roof in case of rain and to help keep her hidden; she had almost been sighted several times by barbarians and did not want to be caught while she slept.

Not knowing how much longer she might be out here looking for Meath and then getting back to Daden, she rationed her small supply of food wisely.

She had followed Meath's trail and had found the small pool where he had stopped to clean his wounds and was sure he could not be too far ahead of her now. His wounds were bad and that would mean he was traveling slow. She hoped she could get to him in time; she knew his wounds were worse than he might think. Priestess magic was an evil thing indeed, his wounds would already have started rotting and decaying and if it spread long enough it would kill him. If she did not find him within the next day, she was not sure if she would be able to save him.

14

Ursa dismounted as he neared his destination, he walked the beast the rest of the way - thoughts flooded back into his mind of his time spent here long ago as a young man. He picked an apple from a nearby tree in the grove and gave it to his horse, which ate it greedily, and then looked for another. He scratched behind the beast's ears, letting it know it had done a great job getting him here swiftly, and then fed it another of the crisp apples.

Ursa could feel the raw energy all around him - it made the hairs on his arms and neck tingle. It had been so long since he had last been to Solmis' Haven, but he still remembered it - down to the last blade of grass. He had spent the better part of his youth here - learning, training and practicing in the arts of his Gift. It felt like yesterday since he had been in the same spot he walked now, casting his first spell - a bolt of energy that he did not release in time and had left him very sore and humbled.

He chuckled at the memory - it reminded him of Meath's first attempt at the same spell. Ursa smiled widely and shook his head; in his youth he had been so much like Meath. The questions, the eagerness, the stubbornness and even the attitude, yes how they all seemed to fit, more than one would have thought, since Ursa was not his blood father.

He came to a well-worn path that led to a thickly wooded area - beyond those trees was the man he had come all this way to see. The man who in so many ways was the closest thing to a father he had ever truly known and respected. A man who had changed his life and gave him an opportunity to be something more than what he was becoming.

Ursa released the reins so his horse could graze freely on the sweet, grasses and cloves of Solmis' Haven. Then he began down the path into the woods towards the large stone and log cabin that waited. It was not a long walk but each step brought back many memories - all of them made Ursa smile wider. Before he knew it, he was standing in front of the same cabin that he had lived in for so many years. A place he would always call home. Excitement welled up inside of him like a child about to receive a Gift - he could not wait to see Solmis again, though he knew he could not stay long to reminisce with his old mentor, he would be sure to come and visit again as soon as possible. He had promised Meath once everything was put right that they would travel - this would be among one of the places they would visit.

Ursa knocked firmly on the door and waited. Several long moments passed and still nothing inside the cabin stirred. Ursa knocked again, then slowly pushed the door open, almost expecting a word to be expelled to detour him any further. Familiar smells assaulted his nose, from the mint and pine leaves Solmis used for his tea, to the smell of oak and cedar that the cabin was built from - it even smelled the same.

Ursa looked over to the low burning hearth. It was emanating just enough light in the dark corner to show Solmis form sitting in his cushioned chair, where he spent many hours in meditation or just relaxing watching the flames of the undying fire. It had been over thirty years since Ursa had seen his mentor, and from what Ursa could see, he had barely aged at all. Solmis had been somewhere in his sixties when Ursa had first arrived more than a half-century ago. Ursa was not surprised that the man was still alive. He had heard stories about Solmis' Haven being enchanted and those who stayed there would live long past their expected years.

Ursa waited, not sure how to approach his old Master and friend - he was beginning to wonder if the old hermit even realized anyone was in the house with him. The man in the chair did not stir an inch or voice any words. Maybe time had finally gotten to the old Wizard - the thought almost brought a tear to Ursa's eyes. No, it was a test, he was sure of it.

"After all these years you still feel the need to test me?" Ursa asked about to take a step towards him when he was assaulted with an uneasy feeling.

"Another step and you will find yourself to be a dead man," a woman's voice said coolly from behind him. "Who are you and what do you want?"

Ursa fought the urge to spin around and attack, "my name is Ursa and I came here to see my old friend and mentor about some deeply urgent matters," he replied calmly, listening intently for any movements to indicate exactly where she was.

"You make it a habit of just letting yourself into other people's homes without being invited," the woman's scowl deepened, stern lines edging her face.

"I knocked, and when there was no response I began to fear the worst for my dear friend and thought it acceptable to let myself in to check on him. But it seems I was not cautious enough," Ursa replied, his voice hinting dangerous intent. "What have you done with Solmis?" he questioned.

"I have done nothing with Solmis," the woman shot back. "Now turn around slowly," she ordered. "And do not think to try anything foolish or I will kill you."

Ursa gritted his teeth, resisted the temptation to attack, put his hands out to the side, and slowly turned to face the fiery red haired woman who held a finely crafted staff pointing straight at his chest. He could tell she meant what she said, for the staff's head was fitted with a perfectly round obsidian gem that swirled and sparked with raw power ready to be expelled at either a thought or command word.

"What would you like now?" Ursa asked politely. He could tell she was nervous - her blue eyes radiated uncertainty and her slender frame was fidgeting with insecurity.

She licked her lips nervously. "If you are who you say you are then you will not mind answering a question."

"I will answer to the best of my ability," Ursa replied with a slight bow of his head.

"What was Master Solmis' favorite spell?" she asked, shifting her weight slightly onto her back leg, preparing to defend herself if Ursa attacked.

"He always favored ice, believing it was more natural and powerful to fire," Ursa answered.

Talena eyed him for a long moment before lowering the staff - the obsidian orb blackened and the unnatural light faded from the sphere as she relaxed. "My name is Talena and I am sorry, but I had to be sure it was you, I was told to take no chances."

"I understand - I would have done the same if I were you." Ursa relaxed his posture. "Now it is imperative that I speak with Solmis!"

Talena flinched at the name. "I am afraid that is impossible."

"What do you mean?" Ursa questioned, looking back to where he had seen Solmis in his chair but now there was nothing - then it dawned on him that Talena had questioned him in past tense.

"He passed last winter," Talena said, knowing that is what he was wondering.

Again, grief struck him - another of the people he loved was gone. "And you?" Ursa asked. "Who are you and where do you fit in?"

"I will tell you all you need to know on the way. We must not waste any time - we need to get going," Talena pressed, reaching for a pre-packed bag near the door.

"What do you mean we need to depart? I am here for reasons of great import and I cannot leave until I find what I am looking for," Ursa countered, searching the room with his eyes for any sign of the dagger.

"You are looking for the dagger of Tabal. You need it so you will be able to identify the false prince no matter what form he is hiding behind. I have the dagger with me."

Ursa stopped in his tracks and turned back to her, his mouth slightly agape. "How did you know that?"

"I will explain everything on the way I promise, but we must hurry. We are wasting valuable time," she urged him.

Ursa followed her out onto the cabin's cedar deck and stopped. "Where are we going and why such a hurry?" he question, still not sure of the situation that was occurring.

Talena stopped and sighed in frustration. "We need to reach Dragon's Cove quickly. An army of barbarians - the size of which has not been seen in a score of decades - is marching there as we speak. If we are not within the castle walls before they arrive, everyone within the walls will die."

Ursa's face went ashen. "How do you know this to be true?"

Talena walked up to Ursa and stood face-to-face with him, her blue eyes glistening with urgency. "I promise you, I will explain everything on the way. But I need you to trust me right now, and Solmis, for he is the one who has prepared me to help you. If we do not leave right now, everyone you know will die."

They rode hard through the day and stopped for the night only when the final rays of sun faded from sight. Ursa had wanted to keep going, but knew the horses were exhausted and the terrain was hazardous even in the light. They could not afford to risk injury to their mounts.

Ursa tendered to the horses while Talena gathered wood for a small fire and began mixing several leather wrapped ingredients that she had packed into a small tin pot to make soup.

Ursa finally sat down on the opposite side of the fire and inhaled the flavorful aroma that steamed from the pot.

"I was Solmis' last apprentice for the last half score of years," Talena said, stirring the continence of the pot. "He never intended on taking in another apprentice for his final years, but quickly dismissed the idea after he had a very disturbing vision of the future to come. At first, he decided not to concern himself with the outcome, for it would be after his time on this earth, but then he came to reason that he was granted the vision from the Creator in hopes he could change its outcome. He knew he would pass before the vision would begin to take place. Therefore, he knew he would need someone to carry out his will after he had left this world. That is where I come in." She paused and tested the soup. Satisfied with its taste, she poured the broth into two tin mugs and handed one to Ursa along with a small loaf of flavored flat bread. "Solmis left his dwellings and went to the city of Kaltra near Ceta Lake in search of an untrained Gifted. It was truly happenstance that we came upon one another. I was one of the city whores. My parents both died when I was young and I had no other family to take me in. I did what I had to, to survive. I saw Solmis in the market, noticed his bulging coin purse and approached him. My thought was even if he did not want my flesh - I could easily overpower him and take his coins regardless. I knew I had the Gift. My parents had told me, though they told me never to tell a soul. On two occasions when I found myself in a very precarious situation, I had summoned my Gift by chance, but I was confident that I could do it when needed. I approached him and tried to sell my wares, but as expected, he refused. So, I followed him and when the time was ripe, I tried to rob him. To my surprise, I soon discovered he was Gifted too. I was sure he was going to kill me so I unleashed my Gift and tried to save myself." Talena paused and smiled, remembering the memory fondly. "He tossed me his whole coin purse and told me that if that is all I wanted out of life then there it was, but if I wanted to change my life forever to meet him at the northern gates at sunrise. All night I fought with the idea, I had more than enough coin in the purse to live like a Lord for a very long time, yet his words burned into my soul and would not allow me to sleep. On the journey to Solmis' Haven, he explained to me what it was he needed and expected of me. He did not try to lie or hide any of the truths behind it. Once we reached Solmis' Haven, every waking moment was dedicated to training me for this single purpose of ensuring his dark vision did not play out as it had in his mind."

"Did he tell you his vision?" Ursa asked, finishing off his soup.

Talena nodded. "Yes, but I cannot tell you yet - please do not ask. If you were to know the details, things may not work out as they must and then this all would be for naught."

Ursa had expected as much and so he did not press the subject. "May I see the dagger of Tabal?"

Talena smiled and pulled her staff to rest across her legs. "It is in here now."

Ursa gazed at her, perplexed. "I am not sure I follow you." When he had first seen the magical weapon pointed at him it had appeared to be no different from many other enchanted staves he had seen in his time. Its gnarled appearance resembled some long ago petrified oak, or other powerful tree. Now that he looked closely, he could see that was not the case at all. Yes, there was indeed a base of a wooden staff among the construct but most of what he could see along the length was not wood at all instead it was different shades and colors of melded metals and stones.

"No, of course not, I shall explain. Near all Solmis' enchanted items are now infused within this staff. After Solmis' vision, he knew you would come to seek his guidance. He also feared he would be long dead before you ever got here. Yet knew he could not search you out and disrupt the flow of events that would lead up to now. He trained me to the best of his abilities with the short amount of time that he had, but that would never be enough. He needed me to have the ability to call upon an immense amount of power far exceeding my short years of training."

"So he found a way to fuse together all his enchanted items into one?" Ursa asked, truly confounded by the idea.

"Even more than that," her eyes flickered off his.

"What do you mean, more than that?"

"His research led him to a Shyroni Warlock of unfathomable power and knowledge. Solmis bargained a deal with the Warlock for his help and knowledge in this area."

Ursa's eyebrow rose. "Solmis bargained a deal with the Shyroni for their help?"

"Not the Shyroni - one of their powerful Warlocks. He is doing so behind the backs of the other members, for if they knew of it they would likely kill him," Talena explained.

"What deal was made? And why would this Warlock risk such a deal?"

Talena sighed. "When I am done fulfilling what Solmis has prepared me for, then I am to seek the Warlock out and give him the staff."

Ursa nodded his understanding. The staff was clearly a powerful weapon and one that likely could never be replicated. Once the staff was in the Warlock's hands he would likely be the most powerful among the Shyroni and therefore, their leader. "So Solmis told you how we will defeat the false prince?"

Talena smiled at him. "As long as he is in the presence of this staff, it will show his true form."

Ursa nodded. "So what will happen when we reach Dragon's Cove?"

"I do not know details - all I know is as long as we make it before the enemy does, many lives will be spared."

Ursa pondered what she had said as he watched her pack away the dishes. He wished he had more to work with on a matter such as this - his mind reeled with defense strategies and scenarios. "So how powerful is that staff?"

Talena smiled widely, "very powerful. It is connected to me, to my Gift, except amplified. The elemental summons are stronger, the mind abilities are enhanced and the flow of energy that is uses in me lasts far longer. Alas, the staff's potential far exceeds my abilities to wield it. If I was stronger with my Gift and more experienced, I am sure I would be able to do far more with it than I can. I just pray that when the time comes I will be strong enough to do what is needed of me."

"Do not take so much of the pressure on yourself, you will do fine. I will be with you when we confront the false prince, you need just ensure he cannot hide behind some deceitful identity and I shall see to the rest," Ursa assured her with a gentle smile.

"Yes, you are right." She smiled back at him anxiously.

"That could be a very dangerous weapon in the wrong hands." Ursa replied, concern etched in his tone. "We must ensure that it stays safe until it is needed."

"Yes, it could be," Talena nodded. "But it would do little good to anyone else." Ursa cocked an eyebrow and she continued. "The staff was created for me and during the melding ritual a sample of my blood was required, I am melded with the staff in a sense. It will only work for me, so there is no need to worry."

"It is getting late - we should get some sleep. We have a long way to go yet and will need all our wits about us," Ursa said, rolling out his bedroll. "We should be safe within the valley tonight - I see no need for us to stand watch. Though we will be leaving the valley tomorrow, so enjoy tonight for tomorrow night we might not have that comfort."

The weather was dreary and wet and they were soaked with thick summer rain for most of the day. They talked little as they rode as hard as they dared through the sodden day. The rain finally stopped not long before dusk and they were lucky enough to make refuge under a thick wayward tree. Ursa allowed a small fire only long enough for them to heat a small pot of tea to help warm them so they did not fall ill.

The next day the sun was hot and dried their damp clothes and warmed their chilled bodies. When the sun reached its zenith, they stopped to rest.

"How did he die?" Ursa asked. It had been a question on his mind since he had first found out, yet other matters had quickly forced his attention away. Now though, he had time to ask.

Talena's face went ashen at the question - her eyes darted away from Ursa's. "I am not sure you would want to know." She had hoped to avoid this conversation, but Ursa's eyes pressed the question and she finally relented. "After much study, preparation and guidance from the Shyroni Warlock, Solmis had everything he needed to meld his enchantments into the staff. The only problem was the spell's ritual needed the lifeblood of a Wizard, the more powerful, the better. I begged him to find someone, anyone, but he would not...." Tears began streaming down her smooth cheeks. "The ritual required his death to be completed."

Ursa nearly slumped to the ground at the news, but held his legs under him. He knew it should not come as a surprise to him - he knew most rituals Warlocks undertook involved blood sacrifices.

"Are you all right?" she asked, truly concerned for the older Wizard.

Ursa was about to reply when an arrow cut through the air and grazed Ursa's side, tearing a deep wound through his flesh spinning him around and toppling him to the earth. Before he could gather his wits, a dozen armed men rushed through the tree line.

"It is him!" one man cried over his shoulder to the others. "I knew it was."

"We have you now, Ursa you traitorous bastard!" another barked angrily, gripping his sword, eagerly awaiting a fight.

"What is going on?" Talena asked Ursa, gripping her staff hard, expecting to be attacked, as several bows were pulled taunt.

"Do not move a hair's breadth or you will feel the sting of a dozen barbed shafts!" the man who looked to be in charge hissed out.

Ursa sighed and pushed himself up to his knees grimacing from the sting of the arrow wound that he had already begun to heal. He eyed the men around him, he had almost forgotten about the soldiers who would still be looking for Meath, the Princess and himself. These men had probably been out here searching since the first day.

"Stay down filth, lest you want to find your guts spilt on the ground! I will not tell you again!" the commander barked. "Now where is the Princess you faithless pig?"

"I do not have time for this now," Ursa muttered under his breath.

"What did you say?" the man barked angrily, taking a threatening step closer.

Ursa was about to act when a movement behind Talena caught his eye. Before he could warn her, the pommel of a sword cracked hard into the back of her skull. Her eyes rolled back and she crumpled to the earth releasing her obsidian staff.

Ursa lurched toward her but stopped quickly when the edge of a blade touched his neck.

"I know your kind," the commander hissed down to him, his blade pressed hard enough to draw a thin trickle of blood. "I also know you Ursa." He kicked Ursa hard in the ribs dropping the old Wizard to the earth wheezing for air and pushing his blade hard into his back so he would not move. "Do not take your bows off of him for a second. Tie them up tightly. We will take her back to camp. Markect, I want you and your men to do what you do best with him."

A massive Zandorian stepped between Ursa and the commander with a twisted grin. "Aye Jarrel, we will." He stepped down on Ursa's face with so much force Ursa was sure his jaw and cheekbones would break.

"Markect, try not to kill it, until you have found out where the Princess is." Jarrel turned and left with Talena and his small group of men.

"You made it a long ways from Draco Castle you traitorous cur," Markect said bitterly, lifting Ursa's limp form to his feet while one man bound his hands tightly and another held fast with a bow taunt on Ursa's chest. "But we knew we would find you - we always find our prey." He landed a hard blow into Ursa's guts nearly causing him to vomit. "I am going to offer this once - so listen well and think good on it. Tell me where the Princess is and I promise you I will kill you quickly and painlessly."

Ursa looked hard at Markect as he fought back the pain of the last blow he had suffered. He cursed himself for not acting sooner but he had hoped to spare some lives. But he knew now, that would not happen and the longer he waited the less likely Talena would still be alive and if she died, they may never be able to stop the false prince. "She is safe - you need not worry."

Markect chuckled. "Well I am glad you cleared that up for me. You hear that boys?" He turned around to look at the three armed soldiers behind him. "He says that Princess Nicolette is safe, and here we were all worried she was in danger." They all shared in on the hearty laugh and Markect turned back to Ursa. "You wasted your chance Wizard, but I want you to know I am really going to enjoy this!"

"As am I," Ursa replied, his hands flashed in front of him ice blades leaving both his hands and finding their way deep into Markect's abdomen.

"You bastard!" Ursa heard from behind him and he twisted his body just in time to avoid the arrow that streaked by him and into the chest of one of the armed soldiers standing behind Markect.

The soldier who had tied Ursa's hands charged forward - his blade leading the way, but was met with a blast of air from Ursa's outstretched hand that sent him sprawling back hard into a solid pine.

The sickening crack of his head that resounded ensured Ursa he would not be returning to the fight.

Ursa turned quickly to see the two bowmen behind Markect release their strings, at the same instant a stream of Wizard's fire ruptured from Ursa's other hand. So intense were the flames that the arrows entered but did not emerge from the other side. The two bowmen threw themselves to the ground barely avoiding the blistering fire that reached for them.

The first bowman fumbled with an arrow trying desperately to notch it in time before the angry Wizard remembered him. A loud crackle and bright flash alerted him that he had been too late. His eyes quickly cleared and he saw that he held the splintered remains of his recursive bow. His eyes continued down to where he felt a warm, wet sensation trickling down his legs. His eyes widened at the sight of his entrails seeping from the gaping hole in his abdomen. He tried to cry out in agony but death stole his voice before it could escape.

Ursa turned his attention back to Markect who was struggling to stay on his knees as he tried in vain to pull the two icicles from his midsection. "Where is your camp?" Ursa asked coldly.

Markect tried to hold his composure as he looked up at the deadly Wizard. "You are wasting your time - I will not tell you a thing," he coughed out and thick blood oozed from the corners of his mouth.

"Tell me and I will kill you quickly." Ursa kicked him in the chest and toppled him over, causing Markect to cry out in agony.

"I would rather suffer the wrath of a thousand slow deaths than ever help you!" He tried to push himself upright, but his arms no longer had the strength.

"Have it your way," Ursa replied, walking past him and over to the two archers would were slowly recovering from the Wizard's attack. "Which one of you wants to live?" Ursa asked his tone deadly.

"I would rather die!" the first spat.

Ursa's hand ignited into flames and he grabbed the archer around the throat. The Wizard's fire took to the man's flesh like dried tinder and his wild screams of suffering were short lived. Ursa turned to the other archer who had turned pale at the sight of his friend's gruesome death.

"To the East, it is not far I swear to you! Please do not kill me!" the man pleaded like a child.

"If you are lying, I will find you, you do not want that." Ursa retrieved Talena's staff, secured it to her horse, and took off to the East in pursuit of Talena and her captors.

"Wake up filth!"

Talena woke to her head snapping to the side and a burning sensation pulsing through the side of her face. She blinked back the tears that threatened to escape and turned her head back to face her attacker.

"Where is the Princess?" Jarrel asked, wiping her blood from his hand with a rag.

"I…I do not know what you are talking about," Talena muttered, trying to move her arms, but finding they were tied behind her back to a post.

"Wrong answer," he slapped her hard again causing her nose to bleed even more. "Just tell me what I want to know, and this will all stop." He took a step back. "Now let us try again, where is the Princess? Where did Ursa put her?"

Talena spat out the blood that was filling her mouth and glared hard at the brute who had hit her. "I told you I know nothing."

Jarrel's face exploded with rage. "Where is she?" he screamed, now a mere finger-span away from her face, showering her with spittle. "Tell me you little wench or so help me I will make you regret every breath you have ever taken in this life!"

Talena tried to fight back the tears, but no longer could and they streamed freely down her face. The thick, rancid smell of stale liquor assaulted her nose and eyes in ragged breaths from the Zandorian leaning over her. She cursed herself for not being better linked with her Gift, had she been she would have burned this man alive in an instant.

"She is not going to talk Captain - let the boys have some fun with her," one of the big brutes in the tent said. "Maybe after that she will feel like talking." He finished with a wicked grin.

"You hear that? Is that what you want? Jarrel taunted. "Do you know what they will do to you if I let them? Tell me what I want to know and I promise you no one will touch you. If not, then I will let me men ravish your flesh until it peels from your bones!"

Ursa stalked into the small, temporary encampment. He wasted no time being stealthy or trying to survey the camp before he entered it. He knew there would not be more than a handful of men left. Every moment was precious and could be Talena's last - if she died all was lost.

The first Zandorian Ursa saw was readying a cooking fire and had not even known the Wizard was there before a vicious sphere of Wizards' fire engulfed him. His death screams alerted the others, but Ursa did not slow his pace.

Two more armed Zandorians climbed out of their canvas tent only to be met by arcs of raw power that lacerated through their chests and threw them back into their tents, smoldering in death.

An arrow streaked by Ursa's face nearly stopping the Wizards' assault on the camp. He turned angrily to the man who had already notched another arrow, and was drawing the string back. Flames licked the bowstring - rendering the weapon useless. The Zandorian threw the bow to the ground and charged, pulling a dagger from behind him. Several steps into his charge he threw the blade hoping to score an easy hit. A fierce surge of wind met the whirling blade and hurled it back into the throat of its owner, dropping the man to the earth gurgling on his own lifeblood.

Ursa stopped a dozen paces from the largest tent - there stood a large Zandorian soldier and Jarrel. Talena was held firmly in front of him and kept in place by a blade to her throat.

"One more step and I swear I will cut her throat," Jarrel told him, a hint of fear in his tone.

"I am going to give you one chance to live." Ursa called to him, his demeanor deadly. "Let her go."

Jarrel laughed. "And give up my only leverage? I highly doubt that."

Ursa's arm flashed forward and the Zandorian soldier standing beside Jarrel pitched backwards - a large ice shard protruding from his torso. "You had your chance." Ursa stalked forward, fire dancing in his hand.

Jarrel slashed his blade across Talena's throat, threw her to the side, and ran forward to meet the Wizard.

15

"Come on - faster!" Zehava urged as he and Nicolette sparred on the grass with ironwood practice swords. "You need to be faster than that or you are as good as dead."

Nicolette parried Zehava's low thrust and swung it up high, but was not nearly fast enough to get her own blade down to block his slash across her midsection. He let her know it by slapping his blade across her hard leather stomach guard.

They had spent the last few days building up her endurance and strengthening her muscles. It was slow going, but after only a few days one could not expect much - she had done better than any of them could have expected.

"Every move has a counter move either to better your advantage over your enemy or to put you both back on even terms." Zehava explained to her, again wiping sweat from his brow. "Now attack me!"

Nicolette gritted her teeth and lunged forward, hoping to spear Zehava. As she expected, he easily parried the attack and brought his sword around for an overhead chop, which she barely managed to block in time to avoid a blow to her shoulder. She stepped back, putting distance between her and Zehava - as he had shown her to do -n to give herself time to recover. He stepped forward closing the distance quickly and she slashed her sword for his abdomen, but again he easily parried the attack wide, leaving her open for him to score a hit.

"Better, but still dead." He chuckled, though he was truly impressed with her increasing skill over such a short time.

"I know, it is just this sword is too heavy. I cannot move it fast enough and control it because the weight throws me off balance," Nicolette complained again, growing a little frustrated.

"I have to say, you are getting a lot better than before," Dahak replied hoping to encourage her.

"Well that is enough sword practice for the day, now we jog with loaded pack and then we will see how well you can shoot a bow," Zehava said, packing up their equipment.

"Where is Shania today, Zehava?" Nicolette asked, pouring herself a mug of cool water from the clay jug.

"She said she was going to go visit that Barnaby fellow she came in with," Zehava replied. "She wants to see if she can convince Lady Jewel to have him released since he helped keep her safe in the city."

"He did not seem to be a bad guy," Dahak added. "Though from what the guards told me, he is a leader of a thieves' guild."

"Barnaby?" Shania called into the gloominess at the figure on the other side of the iron bars.

"Well look who finally decided to come visit," Barnaby replied drearily, turning around to face her. His normally spotless clothes were now stained with grime - the look on his face and way he moved toward her showed his disapproval.

"They not let me see you until Lady Jewel permitted it," Shania told him, her voice full of remorse. "I sorry you are here for helping me."

"Always a curse for my ever-giving generosity," he replied with a small smirk. "So aside from coming to apologize to me for having me arrested and forced to spend the last few days in this filth-infested cell, what brings you here?"

Shania smiled, glad to know he had not lost his kind, forthcoming demeanor. "I am going to try and help get you out of here."

Barnaby nearly leapt towards the bars, gripping them in obvious excitement. "Really, you are going to get me out of here? How? When?"

"I am going to try," Shania repeated.

"How?" he asked eagerly. "I really do not like being caged up you know - I get very anxious in small spaces."

Soft echoing footsteps turned their attention to Lady Jewel who had finally arrived, though the look on her face was obvious that she had no wish to be here.

"My extended greetings, my Lady," Barnaby bowed courteously.

If Jewel was at all impressed, it did not show. "So this is the great Barnaby, who I have heard so much about."

"I am sure my reputation has been exceedingly exaggerated through its travels to your beautiful ears." He grinned.

"I am sure it has," Jewel replied callousness and indifference edging her voice. "Let us cut the witty banter and get to the heart of the matter. Shania has asked that I release you since you so graciously helped her when she was lost and alone in the city. Though these last several days, events have proven miraculous - marvels can and do occur. I have a difficult time believing that your assistance did not encompass some underhanded motive."

"I assure you my Lady - my assistance in aiding Shania was a selfless act of repayment of the purest intentions."

"Yes - she told me about saving your sister. But I have little faith in 'honor among thieves'."

"No, he means what he says - he is not a bad person," Shania cut in. "He has much honor and…"

"Shania my dear, I have dealt with his kind a hundred times before," Jewel stopped her. "He will talk the talk and present all the right signs for the naïve to take his bait. Then, once he gets whatever it is he wants you will likely end up dead with a dagger in your back."

"What!" Barnaby gasped in utter dismay. "I am truly insulted and hurt by such prejudiced slander against me!"

"You are nothing more than a common thief and cutthroat and your kind has never done more than pray on the naïve and innocent, plaguing this fair city with your criminal ways!" Jewel barked back. "I am sorry Shania - I truly would like to believe him, but I have been around far too long to fall for such deception. He shall remain here until I believe he has paid for his crimes."

"You cannot be serious!" Barnaby exclaimed with a groan of bitterness.

"You are wrong! He is a good man!" Shania begged, but to no avail.

"I am sorry. I have made my decision." Jewel turned and began walking back to the stairs. "Come, Shania."

Shania stood there in complete shock that Jewel did not set him free. Yet somehow, she had known it would be this way.

"Thank you for trying at least." Barnaby sighed. "If you could go and check in on Keisha and make sure she is all right, that would mean a lot to me. She has more enemies than I do and not the means to defend herself against them without me."

"Come now Shania - this is no place for us ladies," Jewel called to her from near the stairs.

"Check on her yourself," Shania whispered through gritted teeth. She reached down her top, drawing a gasp from Barnaby and pulled out two thin metal picks and quickly tossed them into Barnaby's cell before she followed Jewel without looking back at him.

Barnaby picked the metal picks up, his eyes dancing with excitement and possibility. "I will remember this."

"Ursa should have been back by now my Lady - we must act now before it is too late," Uvael, Dragon's Cove's advisor told her.

Jewel paced the room where her sick husband lay, too weak to speak. "Maybe we should give him one more day - I am sure he just fell a little behind. He might have the answers we seek," Jewel replied, trying to convince herself more than her advisor. They had had this conversation the day before when Ursa's deadline had ended - she had already given him the extra day.

"My Lady - with all due respect - you have a duty to your people - this evil Wizard who has found a way to fool so many is not only a threat to Draco but Dragon's Cove and the whole Kingdom. We may have a plan of action that might solve the whole ordeal without war or having the whole kingdom in an uproar," Uvael pleaded. "You must think of the big picture here my Lady, a lot is at risk."

Jewel went to her husband's side and looked down to him, how weak and defeated he looked. "What I would not give for you to be well my love." She looked hard into his closed sunken eyes, knowing he could hear her, for his eyes had tears in them. "I do not know the best course of action my husband - I was never trained in the arts of war and battle and how to rule in such a manner, but I shall do the best that I can my love," she whispered kissing his forehead. "Send the assassins to Draco Castle, their payment of a thousand gold coins will be waiting here for the one that brings me this bastard's head," Jewel ordered, her voice again stern.

Uvael bowed his head and backed out of the room. "Yes my Lady, I believe you have made the right choice."

"I pray that I have..." Jewel whispered once the door had closed.

"You are all clear on what needs to be done?" Uvael asked one more time to the five assassins Dragon's Cove had hired days ago, in case Ursa did not make it back in time with a plan.

"Of course's we do - you nag worse than a woman." One of the assassins laughed in a deep, thick accent. He was the only one of the group from the desert kingdom far to the east.

"I am just trying to make sure there are no mishaps, no one may know who you are and what you are doing there. This has to be clean and flawless," Uvael told them firmly.

"We heard ya the first time," another one barked back. "We are assassins. We have trained our entire lives to do this very thing - we understand the stakes better than you do."

"Yes, I guess you are right," Uvael muttered, trying to hide his nervousness. "Well then, you are all clear on payment then? Whichever one or ones make it back here with the target's head gets a thousand gold. If you work together then you will have to split the reward any way you like - that is not Dragon Cove's problem." The mention of the large reward had the men's eyes glistening with anticipation and greed.

"All right men, go do your job and may the Creator grant you much fortune," Uvael ordered, giving them a bow of his head.

"Ahh, luck is for women," one of them muttered on his way out.

"Wait Pavilion, I need to speak with you," Uvael called to the last assassin about to exit the room, who stopped to regard him.

"What is it now, old man?" Pavilion asked with more than a hint of annoyance.

Uvael looked around and out the door to make sure the others had left before answering. "You know you have a great advantage over these men. You know your part in this, Pavilion. You are the only one who stands a chance - you let the other four do their thing and when this evil Wizard is distracted, you finish him."

"I know what I am to do, I fully understand the plan," Pavilion replied callously.

"Good, we cannot afford any mistakes. If you have to kill the others, then so be it. They are nothing but vial criminals anyway," Uvael whispered to him. "This false Prince must be killed at all costs. If the only chance you get will blow your cover, do it and get out of there as fast as you can. If you are captured, make sure you give them this ring," Uvael told him, handing him a small crafted ring with Uvael's own personal symbol. "This ring should buy your freedom or in the least will send word to me so that I may explain your actions."

"And what if it does not?" Pavilion asked, not caring either way.

"Then know you died for a great cause and I will be sure your name goes down in history as a hero, not a villain," Uvael assured him.

"It now matters not anyway," the assassin replied, walking out the door.

"You will have a thousand gold coins, more than enough to start a new life Pavilion - do not give up yet," Uvael called to him but he was already gone.

Nicolette's shoulder flexed with the strain of pulling back on the bow. Her fingers brushed the corner of her mouth and she halted her draw. She adjusted her aim to the left a finger's span to counter the light breeze coming off the Serpent Sea. She exhaled slowly and before she drew another breath, released the barbed shaft. Within a moment, she heard the familiar thud of her arrow hitting the straw target.

"Another great shot," Zehava gasped in awe. "That makes four out of five so far."

Nicolette quickly notched her next arrow, repeating the sequence, but this time she did not hear the rewarding sound of her arrow striking the target.

"Too high," Zehava told her. "Seventy yards is a hard shot for anyone."

Nicolette snatched another arrow from her quiver and let fly. The arrow cut through the air effortlessly and embedded itself into the straw target just outside of the bull's eye. "Last time I released while I was exhaling - threw off my shot."

Zehava looked from the target back to Nicolette several times. "You are a natural Highness. Where did you learn to shoot like that?"

Nicolette gave a small bow, in jest. "I used to hunt with Rift and my uncle Marcus often. They refused to take me with them until I could shoot near as well as them. So I practiced as often as I could, until I could hold my own with them."

"Well hold your own you do," Zehava chuckled.

"I think she is a better shot than you Zehava." Dahak laughed.

Zehava held his arms out in defeat. "I cannot argue that fact - I know I could not have hit that last target in two shots."

"What is it?" Dahak asked, seeing Nicolette's anxious expression ... as if waiting to speak.

"You do not need to call me by my title. We are friends, and I would not want friends to place me higher than they are."

"Well you are, the Queen," Dahak replied earnestly. "We swore an oath of…"

"I know of the oath soldiers take!" she snapped back, and then quickly softened her voice. "I do not want our friendship and time spent together to be based upon oaths and titles."

"I understand what you are saying," Zehava said. "We will try our best to remember."

"Thank you."

"Think you can hit those targets a score more times?" Zehava winked, handing her another quiver of arrows.

By the end of the afternoon Nicolette's arm was so sore she could hardly hold the bow upright, let alone pull the string back. As with most of the evenings recently, Nicolette made her way to her chambers early, where a warm bath and a fresh bed awaited her and her tender body.

A tear rolled down her cheek at the thought of Meath - how she missed him. She prayed he was all right and safe. She could hardly believe any of the trackers who sought him, had found him. The trail had gone cold several miles from the Sheeva River, in the northeast.

As soon as Ursa returned and explained his plan, they would leave to go find Meath. She knew her aunt and Rift would try to stop her - she was determined to go along for the search no matter what. Ursa would be back on the morrow she prayed, he was already two days late, and that was not like the great Wizard. She hoped he fared well and had not encountered trouble. He was their only hope in finding Meath and saving her kingdom. Although she knew it was wrong of her, she feared more for Meath than her kingdom and her people. She knew Ursa would not stop until he found him, not like everyone else who had given up the search and presumed him long gone or dead. No, she would not believe any of it. He was still alive - she could feel it.

"My goodness, you are filthy," Jewel gasped. "I do not know why you feel you need to do this my dear, but if it is what you need to do then I hope you achieve your desired results."

"Thank you - now what is it that you wanted Aunt? Is Uncle all right?' Nicolette asked fearing the worst, for her aunt was clearly a mess and would not bother her during her training otherwise.

Lady Jewel sighed. "No, it is not your uncle. He has gotten worse, but he has not passed over. That is not why I have called you here. I believed since you are now Queen of Draco Kingdom, I should inform you that due to Ursa being overdue, we had to take action. We have sent assassins to Draco Castle to remove this false prince," Lady Jewel said, pacing the room, looking up at Nicolette every once in a while to gauge her reaction.

"But what about Ursa - what about when he does get here if he has a plan and sending these assassins ruins it?" Nicolette questioned.

"Well dear, then we will have to figure something out when the time comes, but we could not stand by and do nothing any longer. Ursa himself said if he was not back that we should do what we deemed best," Jewel answered, stopping to stand right in front of her niece.

"And how do you know this was best?" Nicolette asked bluntly.

"I do not." Jewel sighed deeply, doubt lining her face. "But I have to believe it is. With your uncle on the verge of death, and Mathu still too young to rule Dragon's Cove, I must make these choices. As hard as they are, they need to be made. You will find out in time with the choices you will be required to make as Queen. Sometimes you will make the right ones, other times you will not." Jewel finished and Nicolette could tell her aunt was having a hard time with all of this, as anyone in her shoes would.

"I am sorry for arguing with you - I too am at a loss about all this." Nicolette replied giving her aunt a reassuring embrace. "I am sure the plan will work."

"All we can do is pray, my child," Jewel said. "You really should go and talk to Rift. He is deeply wounded - both in spirit and in honor. He could use uplifting words from you to set him back in the right mindset. He is your Champion and he needs to be reminded from you."

"I know, I was thinking much the same thing," Nicolette sighed. She had known that she should seek him out and talk to him, but she had just been so preoccupied of late, that it was always forgotten.

"I also want you to know I am deeply sorry about Meath," Jewel continued.

"Then why is there no one out there looking for him?" Nicolette questioned, her anger flaring again at the topic.

"I told you - the trail died and they could not pick it up again. I am sorry there is nothing further we can do. He is in all our prayers - I am sure he will find his way back to us," Jewel said sympathetically, wishing there was something more she could say to ease her niece's mind.

"Of course there was nothing more that could have been done," Nicolette replied, her voice tipped with rage. "They must have just disappeared." She turned and walked out of the room.

Dahak rounded the corner to the royal garden and was not surprised to see everyone waiting for him already. "What is it? What happened?" he asked clearly seeing something was wrong by the solemn look on everyone's face.

"They have completely given up the search for Meath," Zehava answered bitterly.

"What?" Dahak gasped out. "Why? It has not even been that long - how could they give up so quickly?"

"I know why," Nicolette said, drawing everyone's eyes towards her. "My Aunt knew I was willing to give up everything, leave everything and everyone behind to be with Meath. But if he is gone, and never comes back, then she does not have to worry about me making such bold moves again."

"That is horse dung!" Zehava barked out angrily.

"What are we going to do?" Dahak asked. "We cannot just let this happen!"

"There is only one thing to do," Shania exclaimed. "We go find him."

"We go find him," Nicolette repeated, her gaze steel as she looked over her companions. "If you want no part in this, I will understand. Just walk away now."

"I am in," Dahak answered instantly, no hesitation in his tone.

"As am I," Zehava added. "When do you want to leave?"

"Right now." Nicolette reached behind the smooth marble bench and retrieved two packs of supplies. "We just need a way past the castle gate guards." They all paused and looked at one another, until Dahak began to laugh.

"I have an idea," Dahak said eagerly.

"Where do you boys think you are going this evening?" One of the three guards at the gate asked the small departing group.

"We all have tomorrow off duty, so we thought we might sneak into the city for a few pints and maybe a whore or two," a young, new recruit replied and his group of friends behind him agreed with various hoots and cheers.

"We were ordered not to allow anyone out at night until everything has settled down," the guard replied.

"Really? Come on, give us a break," the young recruit bellowed out.

"Ya, we have been busting our balls for nearly two fortnights now and this is our first reprieve," another added.

"We have our orders," the guard said grimed faced.

"Come on Randal," another one of the gate guards cut in. "You remember what the first two fortnights were like as a new recruit."

The first guard laughed aloud. "That I do, that I do."

"Remember how pissed you were when we tried to sneak out for a few drinks and maybe a taste of flesh?"

The first guard's jaw firmed as he fought some inner moral battle. "All right, all right, I will let you all into the city." The small group cheered. "BUT! You all need to be back within these walls before sunrise, before my shift ends, or it will be my ass on the line."

"You got yourself a deal Randal," the young recruit said, clasping the guard's hand in thanks and they quickly filtered out of the castle gates and onto the road into the city.

"And for the love of the Creator do not cause any trouble!" Randal called to them, but was sure they did not hear him. "Why do I get the feeling I am going to regret this later."

"Do not trouble yourself about it." His comrade patted him on the back. "You did the right thing."

Ursa sat stirring the small cook fire under the wayward tree he had been lucky enough to spot from the road before nightfall. He was glad to have found it for the ground beneath it was relatively dry. It had rained on and off for the last two days and nights and even though it did not look like it would rain this night, it was just comforting to know they would be dry if it did.

Talena lay beside him, the light of the fire glistening in her eyes. Ursa had been lucky to be able to force-heal her fatal wound before she choked to death on her blood or bled out. The only negative side effect so far was her voice had not returned. Ursa prayed that it would come back in time. But she seemed to accept the issue without complaint.

"We will reach Dragon's Cove tomorrow," he told her, handing her the water skin hoping it would help sooth her throat. "And it would appear we will make it before the enemy. Though I feel the stirring of energy in the air, something drastic is coming, more so than we already know." Talena nodded in agreement to his feelings. "How are you fairing?"

Talena smiled and shrugged, letting him know she was managing as well as one could expect.

Ursa's chuckle was heartfelt. "It was a dim-witted question, I know - I am sorry. Tomorrow will be a busy day. We should sleep."

Talena curled up into her bedroll and watched the remaining flames of their small fire burn out, her hand gripped her magical staff tightly as she drifted off to sleep.

"Lady Jewel, Ursa is back!" a servant shouted as he ran into the room where Lord Marcus rested and Lady Jewel spent most of her days.

"Thank the Creator," she whispered to herself, getting up from her husband's side.

"Ursa, thank the heavens you are all right - we were getting worried," Jewel proclaimed, glad to see her friend well. "What impeded your hastily return?" She embraced him tightly.

"Nothing worth discussing, I am afraid. What of the coming army?" Ursa asked bluntly, truly doubting they had any idea of the coming danger.

"What army?" Jewel asked, confusion apparent.

"We need to ready the army!"

The castle and city were alive with activity as Dragon's Cove whole army was assembled and prepared for the coming of an army they had not even seen yet. Scouts had been sent out in every possible direction an oncoming army could march from.

"I am to assume since I was late in returning that you have acted as was discussed?" Ursa asked once they were in private.

Jewel glanced over and regarded Talena then back to Ursa.

"Talena is trustworthy, and possible the final piece to solving our problem."

"We hope to have the problem resolved shortly. We sent five assassins to Draco Castle to dispose of the false prince - one of the assassins is Pavilion," Jewel explained.

"When did you send them?" Ursa asked, wishing he had made it back in time.

"Yesterday morning, we are confident in their ability to get this job done without much concern," Jewel said.

"I pray they are." Ursa told her, recalling the only time he had ever met the Gifted assassin, Pavilion.

"Who is the girl you have returned with?"

"Talena was Master Solmis' final apprentice." Ursa explained everything he had learned on his trip and Jewel listened eagerly to every detail.

"That is quite the destiny she has put on her shoulders," Jewel remarked. "Will her voice ever come back?"

"I cannot be sure, but I hope," Ursa started to say.

"Y..esss." Talena managed to say. "It… will."

"Thank the Creator!" Ursa beamed with relief then turned back to Jewel. "I must speak with Antiel, Lepha and even Meath so we may strategize our defense if there proves to be an army marching toward us." Jewel's face went ashen at the mention of Meath's name. "What is it? What happened?"

"Meath was taken not long after you left," Jewel explained, guilt in her tone for not telling him sooner.

"What?" Ursa bellowed, jumping from his seat. "What do you mean he was taken? By whom?"

"Two Wizards, several miles northeast of the castle."

Ursa shook his head in disbelief. "Two Wizards - but why? And what do you mean several miles outside the castle? What were they doing outside the walls?"

Jewel's demeanor changed, her back stiffening. "They were running away together," she answered bluntly. "They were going to leave it all behind and just escape together."

The words hit Ursa hard and he slumped back into his chair. He had not truly considered the thought that Meath would actually go as far as to try to run away with Nicolette. Nor the possibility that she would agree to such an act.

"We acted as quickly as we could, and sent out the best we had to track them down. Their trail went dead after they crossed the Sheeva River on the northern side of Sheeva Lake. I am sorry Ursa," Jewel told him regretfully. "At some point I would suggest talking with Queen Nicolette, for further details since she was there to witness it."

Ursa rose from his seat again and motioned for Talena to do the same. "Yes, send word to her that I have returned and would have word with her. I shall be in my room." Ursa turned to leave, Talena in tow. "When the scouts return with news, send for me." Jewel nodded.

Ursa collapsed at his desk, no longer able to hold back his emotions. Tears began to cascade down his weathered cheeks. He noticed a folded piece of parchment on his desk and reached for it. It was from Meath.

I am sorry father, but I had to follow my heart. I hope you will understand and forgive me with time. We will see one another again someday, of that I promise,
Meath.

Ursa crumpled the parchment and threw it against the wall. "You half-witted love-drunk fool!" He bellowed and in a fit of rage swept his arms across his desk hurling the contents across the floor. He looked up to see Talena still standing there looking at him with remorseful eyes. "You knew?" he asked resentfully. "You knew he had been taken and yet you did not tell me."

Talena's eyes went to the floor. She could not bear to look into his eyes. "C...ould not... tell you."

"WHY!" Ursa screamed, rushing over to her and pulling her head up forcing her to look him in the eyes. "Why? Why could you not tell me?" he begged. "He is my son!"

Talena's eyes softened with tears. "I... am... sorry," she choked out.

Ursa released her and slumped back into his chair when a knock at his door drew his attention. "What do you want?"

The door creaked open and a servant entered nervously at seeing the room in such a fray. "There is word of the barbarian army Master Ursa - Lady Jewel wishes you to meet her in the counsel room."

"How did we not know of this earlier?" Jewel barked to her Generals. "How does an army of this magnitude just cross our land without our knowledge?"

"We do not know, my Lady," one of the Generals replied nervously.

"That explanation is not good enough General Miles!" Jewel hissed back. "Is this not your duty to ensure the safety of our lands from our enemies?"

"Well we have known that there has been a larger amount of barbarian activity lately, but that is normal for this time of year - nothing seemed out of the norm. A few small towns were sacked and robbed, a few dozen caravans and supply wagons, but nothing unusual," Miles tried to counter.

"Why have I not been informed of such issues?"

"In all due respect my Lady, we know you have been busy and seeing to Lord Marcus - we did not think to bother you with such trivial reports," Miles explained to her.

Jewel's eyes went wide with astonishment. "Am I not the Lady of this land?

"Yes my Lady," General Miles replied nervously.

"Then I will be damn well treated as such!" she raged. "Do not ever presume to spare me the details of the goings on of my lands!"

"My apologies," Miles replied with a bow of his head.

"Uveal, what can you tell me about our enemy?" Jewel asked, calming herself.

"It looks like they have been traveling in small groups, which would explain why we did not notice any large armies. The sighting of so many small groups would bed thought that one group was moving often rather than being different groups entirely," Uveal explained. "But now as they near, the tribes are merging together. It would appear Master Ursa was correct when he informed you that they would try to take the castle. Their numbers are staggering."

"That is ridiculous!" Barkel blurted out.

"What do you suggest General?" Jewel asked stone-faced.

"We prepare for a siege my Lady," General Miles told her, "and quickly."

"Make it so General," Jewel ordered and everyone got up to leave. "Ursa, Barkel, and Rift I would have you stay for a moment." Once the room had emptied, Jewel spoke. "I have gotten word the Queen Nicolette is nowhere to be found."

"What!" Rift cried out.

"Furthermore, Zehava, Dahak and Shania are also missing from the castle." Jewel told them.

"Where could they have gone?" Barkel asked, truly overwhelmed.

Ursa sighed loudly. "They went to find him."

16

Pavilion watched the other four assassins make their way through the city toward Draco Castle. He had to admire them - they were by far, the best assassins he had ever seen. They had arrived in Draco late in the evening of the third night. They had made incredible time, though men fueled by the promise of riches normally did.

The four assassins had traveled together to Draco, Pavilion wondered if they did so for the company or to brag about how many men they had each killed, to try to intimidate each other. Pavilion doubted any of them would be so easily intimidated - they were the finest at their trade. Once they had reached the city, they all went their separate ways - for that was the way of the assassin...and of greed.

Pavilion had not traveled with them, but instead, had kept a distance. He could have easily passed by them and made it to Draco before them, but instead he stayed behind watching them - learning from them, who they were by their movements and their skills. Pavilion was a loner now, and preferred the company of silence rather than men. However, these men could well become his enemies and he wanted all the advantage he could gain.

He watched the four men swiftly maneuver through the streets and allies and finally he lost sight of them. He knew he could easily find any one of them again, but decided he too had better get to work. For if what he had been told was true, this would be his greatest target. For most men, that thought alone was enough to bring some form of emotion - be it happiness, excitement or even fear - but it stirred nothing in him but indifference.

Tundal sat at the large oak desk within Borrack's grand study, a mountain of parchments surrounding him. There were so many delicate affairs to stay on top of, to keep the prosperous Kingdom running smoothly in such drier times, and Tundal refused to let any of it slip. Borrack had slaved away for too many years to build the Kingdom's wealth, for him to allow it to falter now.

Tundal drained his wine cup in a single gulp, his head already dulled by the effects of wine he indulged in earlier. He had received word that afternoon that Mandrake had fallen and now was in the clutches of the enemy. Dagon had asked for more men so he could take back his castle and lands.

Tundal poured himself another cup of wine, knowing he did not need it, but he required it. To help him make the hardest decision he had ever had to make before - one he wished was not his to make. He swirled the wine in his cup, its ruby tones and hues reminding him of the color of blood. The analogy was not lost on him, nor did it make his decision any easier. So much blood already spilt and yet so much more would be before anything could be resolved.

Tundal went to the doorway and called over the first servant he saw. "Find Lord Dagon's messenger and bring him to me at once, I have made my decision."

Tundal returned to his seat and waited, knowing it would not be long - he drained the remains of his wine. Liquid courage, as if he was telling his friend his decision in the flesh. *"I am sorry my friend,"* he whispered to himself.

"You sent for me my Lord?" The messenger asked, entering the study with a hesitant step.

Tundal stood and gestured the man over. "My apologies for making you wait so long..." His voice trailed off as he noticed Prince Berrit follow the messenger in. "Prince Berrit, is there something I can do for you?"

"I was merely keeping our guest entertained, when you summoned him. I would be lying if I did not say my curiosity is piqued as to your decision," he replied with a smile. "Shall I leave?"

"You may stay - I need to speak with you afterward on other matters." Tundal told him. "Now where was I? Yes, right, my heart and soul burns with the desire of vengeance for the defeat Dagon and his people have suffered. And I share the same yearning to flood the enemy with cold steel and spill the lifeblood of every savage to set foot in our Kingdom. But I cannot grant Lord Dagon's request of a thousand soldiers."

"What?" Both the messenger and Berrit blurted out - surprised by Tundal's decision.

Tundal took a deep breath to steady his nerve. "Furthermore, I will require Lord Dagon and what men he has under his command to ride back to Draco Castle immediately, so that we may regroup."

"Are you mad?" Prince Berrit exclaimed.

The messenger stood there, his mouth agape. "My Lord, are you sure about this?"

"I am sure. I know Lord Dagon will not understand, but I need him to trust in me and my judgment. Once he has returned I will fully inform him of all my reasoning."

"Reasoning?" Berrit barked out. "I see no reasoning, only madness!"

Tundal did his best to ignore Berrit. "That will be all, gather whatever supplies you will need for the return trip and obtain a fresh horse from the stables and make haste."

"Yes My Lord," the messenger replied, clearly dumbfounded by the message he was to carry back to his Lord as he left the study.

"Have you been moonstruck?" Berrit bellowed out as soon as the messenger had left. "Why will you not grant Lord Dagon the men he requests?"

"I do not appreciate your tone," Tundal warned, "or your lack of formality in front of my men. Nor is my decision any of your business. But I will excuse your insolences, for I shall not have to suffer them again."

"What is that supposed to mean?" Berrit snapped back closing the study door.

"It means - my good Prince Berrit - that you have overstayed your welcome here and on the morrow you will be departing back to Zandor," Tundal replied sternly.

"Excuse me?" Berrit stammered as if he had been slapped.

"I believe you heard me well enough." Tundal leaned against the desk. "I will have your men gathered and ready with your carriage and belongings. With additional hundred and fifty men to make up for the men you leant to Lord Dagon to escort you to the borders of Zandor. When Dagon arrives, I shall have your men well supplied and sent with haste back to Zandor."

"Who do you think you are? Ordering me around like I am some sort of commoner!"

"I am the Lord of this Kingdom, until Queen Nicolette is returned, and if she is not and it comes to be that she is dead, then I am the new King of Draco. That is who I am. Who are you in this Kingdom? Now leave, I have more important matters to attend to." Tundal turned back to the parchments on the desk.

Berrit's face twisted in rage. "You... you impudent..." Berrit's demeanor calmed eerily. "No, no more of this pathetic charade."

"What are you talking about?" Tundal turned back to face Berrit, but a stranger stood in his place. "What foul deception is this?" Tundal bellowed stumbling back hitting the desk awkwardly.

The man grinned maliciously. "I am actually glad this happened now, I was getting so tired of dancing around you. Things will go so much smoother with you out of the way." The stranger pulled his dagger, intent imprinted on his face.

"You whoreson! I knew something about you was not right!" Tundal growled, his hand frantically pulling his own dagger as he lunged forward.

Astaroth easily sidestepped the sloppy assault and drove his dagger through Tundal's rib cage into his beating heart, and gave the dagger a twist.

"Foolish old man." He yanked his dagger out and let Tundal's body collapse to the carpeted floor.

"My love, your anger is making you careless." a voice purred behind him.

Astaroth turned to see Vashina - his partner and lover - standing a dozen paces away by the window with a dangerous looking man at knifepoint.

"Who is this?" Astaroth muttered clearly frustrated at the night's events and how they were unfolding.

"I am assuming he was working for Lord Tundal and was going to try to kill you - I saw him sneak into the library from the back, like only a highly skilled assassin could - so I followed and lo and behold, once you killed poor Lord Tundal, he went to make his move while your back was turned. You may thank me later," Vashina cooed seductively.

"Thank you, later I shall." He ran his blade over the assassin's face tauntingly. "Did our good Lord Tundal hire you?" The assassin spat in Astaroth's face, his features defiant and his eyes void of fear.

"Looks like we have our cover up," he snarled, thrusting his dagger deep into the man's chest several times.

Vashina pouted disappointedly letting the dead assassin crumple to the floor. "I was hoping you would let me play with him for a while."

"There will be time for play later," Astaroth smirked. "Now make yourself scarce - this mess may take a while to clean." His featured returned to those of Prince Berrit as he let out a terrified scream for help.

"Well my love, there is one more problem out of our way," Astaroth laughed, taking a large sip of wine while sinking into the huge tub, glad the long night was nearly over.

"I cannot believe that old man would act so boldly as to hire an assassin - the very nerve of some people," Vashina replied, watching him from the bed lustfully.

"No matter, I am just glad he is no more. It was convenient that our good Tundal would pick such a well-known assassin. The guards recognized him, making it all the easier to convince them that the assassin tried to kill us both." Astaroth grinned. "Lord Tundal - the hero - jumping in front of us to help me, but unfortunately took a very fatal blow for his efforts. Then I quickly dispatched the assassin in hopes to save us both." Astaroth laughed cruelly, recounting the story he had told everyone and had been thankful he had been easily believed. "Come, join me my pet," he beckoned to Vashina. "I am in need."

Vashina smirked playfully as she stalked over to the steaming tub, her flawlessly curved hips swaying seductively with every teasing step. Her slender, skillful hands quickly undid the several straps holding closed her dark crimson leather vest. Enticingly, she pulled open her vest revealing her toned, smooth stomach, knowing each exaggerated moment intensified his lust for her. Finally, she reached for the ample suppleness of her breasts and let the armored garment fall carelessly to the dark marble floor. His excitement was evident - his quickening breath and the animation dancing in his eyes. She ran her hand down between her breasts and continued until her fingers found the thick black belt holding up her unique, dark armored leggings.

Astaroth admired her sexually seductive show with a quickly growing desire. He watched her slip out of her leggings, leaving her completely naked with the exception an enchanted knife sheath, strapped to her right thigh. She almost never removed it. The enchanted sheath held an endless supply of throwing knifes, no matter how many she threw, there would always be eight more at the ready. She had acquired it many years before, at an extremely high price.

"Things are not going as smoothly as we had expected they would," Vashina reminded him as she slid into the steaming tub and caressed his cheek fondly.

Astaroth frowned at her for the reminder. "Yes, I am well aware of that, thank you. Ursa escaping with the Princess is definitely causing minor troubles, but other than that, everything is going as expected. Our barbarian comrades have taken out Mandrake and are preparing as we speak to march on Dragon's Cove. And now they believe enough in the cause that the high priests and priestesses are joining in the war," Astaroth cooed wickedly, a grin spread widely across his face.

"I would so have loved to get a taste of Ursa's Gift - his young apprentice too," Vashina commented, while pouring more scented oils into the steaming bath.

"We will have them soon enough my love, but for now we will have to settle for those Wizards who shall be here in a few days," Astaroth replied, his attention snapping to the other side of the room at the slight sound of footsteps.

"You just now realized, my darling? You are getting too comfortable in this castle life," Vashina teased, having sensed someone in the room moments before.

An arrow shot out toward Astaroth's back from the far side of the room, he summoned his innate ability and the arrow ignited into ravenous flames, incinerating the shaft before it had time to clear the distance.

"Come out and your life may be spared, fool!" Astaroth commanded angrily stepping out of the bath, another arrow sliced out from behind the large bookshelf. Again, the arrow ignited in flames, but as soon as it did so, the arrow exploded sending sparks and flames into Astaroth's face. He threw his arms up in defense of the flaming shards.

Another assassin took his cue, leaped out from behind the thick drapes with both short sword and dirk in hand, and sprinted toward Astaroth's unguarded back.

Vashina saw the second attacker from the corner of her eye, her hand flashed down and she let fly two of her deadly knifes in a single snap of her wrist. The assassin deflected both spinning blades with his own blades masterfully, without slowing or faltering his charge. His skills were impressive, his experience and abilities quickly apparent. He reached his target, his sword down and to the side he slashed upward, hoping to get a quick finish without his enemy ever seeing it.

Astaroth did see it - anger now burning in him. His arm came from across his face toward the attacker and with it; several small icicles formed in an instant at the ends of his fingertips and propelled forward embedding deeply into the assassin's chest, sending him staggering backward. The assassin dropped his weapons and tried to grab at the ice blades imbedded within his torso but he could not get a firm grip as his hands slipped on the fresh blood.

Another arrow sliced through the air toward Astaroth's unprotected side, but his now heightened senses alerted him and he spun around and snapped the arrow shaft out of midair before it could pierce his flesh.

Astaroth's fury was nearly uncontrollable and Wizard's fire flared to life across his body as he walked toward the hidden attacker at the other end of the room.

The assassin - knowing the plan had failed and his chances of survival were limited against such a foe came out from behind the bookshelf - dropped his bow and went to his knees, begging for his pathetic life.

Vashina was out of the tub and scanning the room for any other unknown invaders that might decide to show themselves. She turned her attention to the wounded assassin on the ground who was fumbling with a handheld crossbow trying to direct it at her. A wicked smile crossed her lips and a tiny flame licked the bowstring and snapped it before he could release the small but deadly bolt.

"Please do not kill me!" The assassin cried to Astaroth who now was standing before him in his flaming glory. "I was only doing as I was told!"

The flames dissipated and Astaroth's eyes bore into the assassin's soul. "Tell me why I should spare your life after you tried to kill me, assassin."

"I… I have four children your greatness - they need me. I only do this to feed them!" The assassin stuttered pathetically, his eyes shifting around the room not willing to meet Astaroth's.

"Well I guess they're going to be orphans now!" Astaroth hissed, kicking the man hard in the stomach and doubling him over. "Now enough of your lies assassin, tell me who sent you and I might actually spare your life … for your children's sake."

The assassin lied. "I do not know, your Greatness. He sent a street urchin with a letter to me and it said that if I killed you, I would be richer than I could imagine in my wildest dreams."

Astaroth turned his head to regard Vashina. The assassin saw the opening and took his final chance, lunging forward with a poison-tipped curved dagger. Astaroth was no fool and was well aware of assassins and their tricks. With reflexes defying the norm he grabbed the assassin's arm and twisted violently to the side, causing the man enough pain to drop the tainted blade. With a look of sheer evil, Astaroth grabbed the man's face with his free hand and began to summon his Gift. Fire wavered in his hand, slowly burning and blistering the assassin's face, head and neck. His screams were muffled but full of anguish - Astaroth did not relent. The assassin's flesh began to melt and peel away from his bones, he kicked and thrashed but it was soon too late and death consumed him. Astaroth released him and let him fall limp to the floor. All that remained of his face was a grotesque, blackened skull.

He turned his attention back to Vashina and the badly wounded assassin, who had both watched his display of power. Vashina was grinning in awe while the assassin's eyes glistened with unspoken dread.

"Now, maybe you will be of more use to me," Astaroth said, calmly walking over. "Who sent you?"

"It … it was Lady Jewel of Dragon's Cove," the assassin whimpered, truly afraid knowing his wounds most likely would not kill him, but these two surely would.

"What? How do they know?" Astaroth barked in confusion.

"It is rumored that the Wizard Ursa and Princess Nicolette made it to Dragon's Cove,cleared their names and told them the truth about you." The assassin answered without pause, praying if he told them everything he knew, they would grant him at least a quick death.

"So it was not Tundal after all," Vashina mused.

"How many assassins were sent for me?" Astaroth ordered his frustration clearly growing in his features.

"Just the two of us were sent."

"Why do I get the feeling you are lying to me!" Astaroth hissed stepping closer to glare at the bleeding assassin.

"I have no reason to lie now - I know I am as good as dead."

"One already tried to kill me today, before you two showed up." He backhanded the assassin across the face, leaving burnt blistering where his fingers had struck.

"Maybe Tundal did hire one on his own," Vashina said, quickly dressing herself and throwing Astaroth a robe to cover his nakedness.

"No I do not believe that - he had too much honor to do such a thing." Astaroth glared down at the assassin again. "Last chance - tell me the truth or suffer a fate far worse than your comrade did."

The assassin held his ground and did not reply until fire ignited in Astaroth's hand. "They sent five of us to kill you," he quickly blurted out. "They wanted to be sure it got done and smoothly," he cried out, backing his head away as the flames got closer.

"Let me have some fun with him," Vashina purred with a menacing smile and Astaroth nodded and stepped away to retrieve his clothing. "I will get all the information you want from him by the time I am done."

"I will tell you anything. I will help you! I know who the other assassins are - I can kill them for you," the assassin begged.

"Why would we need your help? We already stopped three." Astaroth mused. "Besides - you are wounded. You would hardly be of much help for much longer."

"No, no I am not hurt badly - please, I will help you for my life." He pleaded desperately seeing his chance at surviving dwindling.

"Funny thing about assassins, their loyalties always lay with the better offer," Vashina remarked.

"I would rather work for you, yes. You are far more powerful than everyone else - it would be an honor to serve you," he said, forcing himself to sit up this time and doing his best to wince away the pain from the wounds.

Astaroth paced in front of him, knowing he would not be as bold as the other to try to attack him. "Yes, we could use your help - then again, how can we trust that you will not betray us like your former employer?" Astaroth questioned, raising his dark eyebrow.

"You have my word, your Greatness!" the assassin replied, licking his lips nervously.

"The word of an assassin - the irony in such a statement." Astaroth gave Vashina a nod and before his head had even stopped moving, three knifes were embedded in the assassin's chest.

"What are you doing?" The assassin gurgled desperately, slumping back down to the floor.

"Never trust an assassin." Astaroth muttered, his lover continued to pump knife after knife into the man, her speed so deadly she had twelve blades in him before his final breath escaped his quivering lips.

"I was beginning to wonder what happened to my darling wife-to-be and her cursed Wizard guardian," Astaroth deliberated after Vashina had ceased her attack on the dead assassin.

"Well, they will not be alive for long," Vashina said, searching the assassin's bodies for anything she might want. "All within Dragon's Coves walls will be slaughtered soon enough."

"I want you to go to Dragon's Cove and see to its downfall Vashina. If Ursa and his apprentice are there, that means Dragon's Cove has four Wizards to defend it," Astaroth told her.

"Dragon's Cove will fall - they do not need me. I would be of more use to our cause here, by finding the last two assassins and making sure no one else tries to stand against you now that Tundal is gone," Vashina argued. "You will need me. I already saved you once tonight - next time you might not be so lucky."

"I need no luck," Astaroth replied, his tone firm. "I want you there to make sure nothing goes wrong. I have a feeling that Ursa could be more trouble than we truly would like to believe. He is wise and powerful - I will not take any more chances when regarding that one. Once we have total control over Draco Kingdom with the help of our barbarian 'friends,' we will be unstoppable Vashina - nothing will stand in our way. Then we can go take back what was taken from me!" Astaroth roared with enthusiasm. "Besides, I do not fully trust our counterparts in this - it would be wise to have a watchful eye on them."

"Fine, I will go help the savages," Vashina muttered, clearly displeased. "Though I do hope you have fun here. With Tundal dead, no Lords are left here to help see to the ruling. You have placed yourself in a very unstable position - I hope you have a plan." Vashina began to walk away.

B

"Vashina!" Astaroth said loudly and with full authority. She stopped to regard him.

"What is it?" she asked, indifferently clearing under a nail with one of her blades..

"If we are to make this work, we need to work together and not have any doubt in one another."

"Of course, I have no doubt we will succeed," she replied coolly.

"Good, you know we need each other in this - we cannot do it alone."

"I want what you want, Astaroth. I will stand by your side 'til the bitter end," Vashina answered back.

"Go now Vashina, to the meeting place. Stay hidden until I get there." Astaroth ordered, finally turning around to face her.

"Of course," she turned and seemed to melt into the shadows.

Astaroth walked over to the large full body mirror that was in his room. "Oh mother, how you should have believed in me," Astaroth growled to himself while transforming back into Prince Berrit. "How I do grow tired of being this pathetic form."

Pavilion watched from the shadowed corner of a window as Astaroth's features melted into those of Prince Berrit's, and he stalked out of the room. He had fully intended to complete his mission but had noticed the other two assassins in place and decided to give them the opportunity. He was glad he had now, he had not expected Vashina to have such skills and that would have likely gotten him killed. Not that dying bothered him - he was just an empty husk of the man he had once been - but he had an important job to fulfill, which meant death would have to wait a little while longer for him.

Pavilion scaled down the wall effortlessly, stopping only long enough to avoid the night guards who patrolled the grounds below. He melted through the many shadows of the courtyard as naturally as if he were a shadow wraith.

Pavilion's eyes caught sight of a guard making his way to the gates. Normally, a random guard would not have caught his attention, but this guard did not have the same rough posture or leisurely stride that was expected. He followed the guard beyond the gates and out of the city onto the eastern roadway, where finally the

C

guard's form wavered into his true design. Pavilion was truly intrigued by Astaroth's shape shifting abilities, never before had he encountered or even heard of such an ability existing.

Outside the city, Pavilion prepared himself to strike as he followed his target off the main road into the growth of the jungle. Several times, he thought to strike when he caught a glimpse of movement from the gloom that engulfed the jungle. Vashina was out here with them, watching Astaroth's back in case of such a bold move from the last two assassins.

Pavilion held off his attack and even fell back further making sure Vashina did not catch sight of him. He was sure he did not want to tangle with the both of them at once. He knew his mission was to kill this Wizard, but instinct was telling him to watch and learn what he could. Something more was afoot than what anyone expected - he was sure of it.

Pavilion knew they were nearing their destination when he noticed several barbarian sentries lying in wait. He altered his course around them, being sure to keep a mental tally of how many he saw in case events turned to a fight.

"Vashina, you can come out now," Astaroth called out, stopping in front of a group of large dangerous looking barbarians. Almost on cue, Vashina emerged from the gloomy foliage - she had been completely unseen. She smiled dangerously as she stopped at Astaroth's side, knowing the barbarians were taken aback by her stealth.

"There are nine," Vashina told Astaroth.

"Nine," Astaroth mused regarding her for a moment then back to the brutes in front of him. "It would almost seem like you did not trust me."

"Trust is earned," the largest of the savages muttered.

"Were you followed?" The leader of the group asked - his demeanor calm and sharp - his English only showing a hint of his true ancestral accent.

"I would not be standing before you had I been," Astaroth snapped in reply.

The leader snapped in reply. "Things are going well on our end. Mandrake fell just as we had planned, with fewer losses than we expected...with the knowledge you provided us."

"Good, now what of Dagon and his forces?" Astaroth questioned eagerly, hoping the Lord was lying dead somewhere. "Have they been dealt with yet?"

The leader cleared his throat awkwardly, clearly not wanting to address this question. "Their numbers have been nearly cut in half - Dagon and his band will be finished off shortly without much more hindrance to us."

"From my reports, Dagon has been a great hindrance to you and much to our entire plan," Astaroth countered.

"He knows the land better than we do and he uses that fact well to his advantage," Another one of the barbarians cut in, his features sharp and hawk like. "His numbers are fading - our warriors will crush them soon!"

"They had better. Now, how soon will Dragon's Cove fall?"

"Three more nights and the attack will start," the leader replied.

"Why three more nights?" Astaroth questioned, his tone displeased. "The attacks should have begun by now. Dragon's Cove should nearly be ours!"

"We know, but we do not have the men in place to attack, must wait for more," the leader replied firmly. "Dagon and his men have killed many warriors who were sent from Mandrake to join with tribes near Dragon's Cove."

"Thought he had not been that much of a hindrance?" Vashina added sarcastically drawing bitter glares from the savages that stood before them.

"The longer you wait, the more time Dragon's Cove has to set up their defense!" Astaroth raged. "Has the element of surprise never occurred to you?" He wondered if he should inform them of the other two Wizards who were now in Dragon's Cove, but quickly decided not to. They would discover it soon enough and a few more dead savages was not entirely a bad thing.

"Too many die, must wait for larger army before attacking. Winning back land no good if we all dead," a thick accented barbarian shot back.

"Dragon's Cove does not even have a moat or catapults! It should be easier to take down!" Astaroth hissed.

"They have two powerful Wizards and can only be attack at by the north and east side," the hawk-faced warrior barked back. "Steeper walls and harder terrain…!"

"Enough!" the barbarian leader growled before Astaroth could open his mouth to argue. "Valka also wants to wait for the Priests and Priestesses to arrive. With more of them joining the fight, our warriors will be inspired to fight harder to gain favor with Valka and the Goddess. Do not concern yourself with the fall of Dragon's Cove . Besides - we have heard you are having your own troubles within the castle walls."

Astaroth smiled snidely. "Yes there have been a few minor setbacks on my part within the castle. But my part is far more delicate and tedious and requires far more skill in the act than merely the siege of a castle." He did well to compose himself - he hated acting as if he were inferior to these pathetic creatures, but if he was to get what he wanted, he had to play his part. "On the morrow I shall send word to Drandor and tell them to send aid to Dragon's Cove. By the time they arrive, you should have Dragon's Cove and you should easily be able to defend against the reinforcements. Once Drandor's army arrives to aid Dragon's Cove, your army will march from Mandrake to overtake Drandor—if, of course, Lord Dagon and his boys are not still causing too much trouble for you," Astaroth said coldly. "Once you have those three castles secure, I shall order the surrender of Draco Kingdom to your leader. You will have your lands back and then Kinor will give me what I seek."

"I shall tell our leader everything is going as planned, and so it had better, Astaroth," The barbarian barked while he and his men walked back into the jungle.

Several minutes passed before Astaroth spoke. "Once I no longer need him, I am going to enjoy gutting him like a pig."

"Now, now my love, play nice with the pawns. We need them, remember," Vashina reminded him with her saccharine sweet tones dripping in her voice.

"Go now, to Dragon's Cove. See to it that it is ours as soon as possible. And keep an eye on Valka - I will never trust her." Astaroth told her as she melted into the darkness.

Pavilion could not believe what he had witnessed - this was so much more than Dragon's Cove believed it was. This was not just one man causing problems. This was what everyone had always feared - the barbarians finally had the edge they needed to take over Draco Kingdom, had someone powerful on the inside, and they were succeeding.

Pavilion knew what he was sent here to do, but now he knew killing Astaroth would not be enough - things were already set in motion. The information he knew was far more valuable. He had to get back to Dragon's Cove. He had to warn them of what was transpiring - he just prayed he could get there before it was too late.

Dagon watched the activity around his castle and city from the rocky crest of the hillside he and his men were camped by. There were so many of them now, they kept filtering out of the wastelands to the east. Dagon had at first been surprised that they had not burned down the city after they had overtaken it. However, realization soon came that the enemy had not intended ever to leave and now made full use of the city to house their growing army.

He and his men were doing the best they could winnowing that growing number, but it seemed for every enemy they killed two more replaced them. But that would not stop him - he would fight until he won back what was his, or until an enemy blow took the life from within him.

Dagon turned his horse around and headed back to one of the small camps he and his men had set up around the land. From his original eighteen hundred soldiers, only a thousand remained. But more and more refugees from all of the towns and small cities that had been sacked or threatened by the barbarian invasion were joining his army daily, in hopes of helping rid the land of these heathens. He had close to two thousand men now, most simple farmers or shopkeepers, but they all had one thing in common - they had lost their family, friends and homes to the same enemy, and a man who has lost everything fights hard to reclaim it.

Dagon had several small camps, a score of men in each set up all along the eastern river flowing out from Mandrake's lake. They kept the smaller tribes of barbarians from coming out of the wastelands and joining with the large army already residing in Mandrake castle.

The smaller armies made it easier to pack up and run when they needed to. Now, many of the tribes were sending their warriors across the lake in boats from Mandrakes harbor, avoiding Dagon's men entirely. Dagon had already run his lines thinner than he would have preferred, so there was no way they could guard the whole lake and stop the boats. The rest of his soldiers were in three larger groups of three hundred each. They were doing their best in stopping or hindering all the barbarian warriors from leaving Mandrake that were heading west or that went out to sack and pillaged the lands around them.

Lord Dagon knew the barbarians were up to something big. Every day, more and more bands left the castle and traveled to the northwest. Dagon and his men did their best to see to it most of them never made it far. In the beginning, the barbarians came out in small packs of a score or more, so it was easy for Dagon's men to overwhelm them. Now they were growing smarter and sending out several larger bands at a time of four or five scores, so Dagon would have to join his three groups into one instead just to take on one of the enemy armies. Too many were getting through to wreak havoc on Draco kingdom.

Dagon prayed that the messengers he had sent to Tundal at Draco Castle asking for the aid of more men would soon arrive with another army. He had also sent messengers into Zandor to Besha -where he also asked Lord Andras for the aid of his armies. He had doubts that any aid would come from Zandor, but his options were limited and his hopes high.

Dagon arrived back to his camp and watched his men prepare for the battle that would soon take place. The barbarians had sent out the largest army thus far the day before - fifteen hundred warriors. Along with them were several dozen heavily loaded wagons. He knew weapons and food supplies were in those wagons, but he had no idea where they were heading with them. They were up to no good and he was not about to let them get away with it if he could. Additionally, his men needed those supplies badly - their own stocks were dwindling down to nothing.

He had called in two scores of men from both of his other large groups patrolling the northwest. Along with his three hundred, he had a further army of seven hundred and they were about to break camp and begin the chase. They were outnumbered over two to one, but not a single man complained. Dagon knew a straight out attack would only get his men killed. He had something much different in mind.

"What are you thinking my friend?" Jarroth asked, riding his horse up to Dagon.

Dagon looked over to Mandrake's Champion. Jarroth was more than that - he was Dagon's best friend and comrade. They had grown up together - trained together, fought wars together and talked of things one would only talk about with someone you completely trust. "I am thinking tonight is going to be a bad night to be our enemy," Dagon smiled, the gleam in his eyes full of anticipation.

Jarroth patted Dagon's back. "That it will be, my friend, tonight we will all get our fill of enemy blood."

"It is almost dusk - tell the men to eat lightly tonight. Once it is dark, we ride out," Dagon told him, staring off into the distance eagerly awaiting the coming battle.

Seven hundred men marched through the night, using the moon and stars as their only source of light - torches would give their movement away. Traveling was easy - this part of the country was lightly wooded and mostly flat. They stopped a mile away from the enemy camp to prepare, sending out their most experienced scouts to spot and eliminate the barbarian sentries, so they had the full element of surprise.

Dagon split his men into three groups; two for the main assault, and one for the surprise distraction. He sent a score of men with bows and full quivers to the north side of the enemy - they were to be the diversion. Once they were in place, they would start to unleash their attack of arrows down on the enemy. Their orders were to fire until their quivers were spent, then to retreat and circle back southeast behind where Dagon and his men now waited.

Once the attack started, the bulk of Dagon's force would charge in from the south, catching their enemy from behind as they fended off the arrow assault. Dagon's men were to fight hard until the enemy got organized, and then they were to retreat to where a hundred more archers waited to cover them. Once their arrows were depleted or the enemy forces that followed were killed, they too were to draw back to the south and join with the whole force again.

"Fight well this night Jarroth, and may the Creator guide your blade through the soft flesh of ever enemy you meet," Dagon said to his friend, clasping his hand firmly as a gesture of luck.

"You as well my friend, I shall be watching your back," Jarroth replied.

Dagon watched a single flaming arrow streak through the night sky from the north, signaling Dagon and his men that the attack had begun. Dagon drew his sword and spurred his horse forward, leading his five hundred riders into a charge. They met the barbarian encampment in a frenzy - taking full advantage of the confused, half-asleep warriors who were scrambling about trying to make sense of what was happening.

Dagon's men cut through the encampment with force, littering the cold ground with the dead and dying. For several long moments it was a one-sided slaughter - most of the barbarians did not even notice they were being attacked from behind. Quickly they began to get organized and Dagon's men were forced to sound the retreat before they became trapped within the camp. They retreated slowly, making sure that the enemy was pursuing them. Not nearly as many of the enemy had followed as they had hoped for, but those who had were soon showered from the night sky by a silent death.

"Congratulate yourselves men - you all fought gloriously!" Dagon roared, receiving a cheer of enthusiasm. "But that was only the beginning. We have a lot of work to do this night if we are to crush our foe. We attack again at dawn and this time we kill them all!" An even loader cheer ensued.

"We only lost thirty four soldiers - eleven are wounded to the point that they can no longer fight," Jarroth reported to Dagon after his speech.

"I was hoping for less." Dagon replied, his thoughts elsewhere.

"What is it?" Jarroth asked, knowing full well something was playing on his friend's mind.

"I have a gut feeling something is amiss."

"We could call off the dawn attack."

Dagon grimaced. "No - we need this victory and more so, we need those supplies." He paused. "I just cannot shake this feeling."

"We have prepared and planned this attack nearly flawlessly. The terrain has been set to our full advantage - the enemy will be tired and unprepared for another assault so soon," Jarroth explained, knowing Dagon knew all this already.

Dagon sighed gravelly. "You are right, let us get to work my friend - there is much to be done."

Dawn came quickly and once again, Dagon and his men prepared to march on their enemies' camp. This time the strategy was different, Dagon knew his men were still tremendously outnumbered and would be overrun if they fought head to head. He was hoping to fool the enemy one last time and if all went as planned, they could end the battle this very morning.

Arrows were running thin even with the crude arrows they had taken from the enemy dead and their own arrows they were forced to reuse. Out of the two hundred archers, there were only enough arrows to fill a hundred of those quivers. The remaining archers joined in the infantry for the fight. The rest of Dagon's men - almost six hundred strong, would ride into the enemy camp again and wreak havoc among their foe until the retreat was sounded. Dagon knew the barbarians would chase in full this time around. It was light enough to see clearly - they would not take two insults such as this without demanding blood. They would chase.

A half-mile away from the enemy camp, his men had prepared for a standoff. The woods in this area were thicker and a little harder to maneuver in and there were steep hillsides on either side of where Dagon and his men had set up. They had spent all night gathering all the dry wood, leaves and burning material they could find in the area and piled it almost as high as a man in a semi-circle in-between the slopes, leaving a small gap in the middle where Dagon's men could run through when they retreated. The tinder wall was soaked with all the lamp oil they had, which Dagon hoped would be enough to get the dry timber burning hot and fast.

Behind the tinder wall awaited the two hundred archers with what arrows they had left. Once Dagon and his men were clear behind the flaming wall the archers were to fire at will until their arrows were spent. A tight knit group of men would hold the opening while the rest of the army would begin launching the assault of hundreds of crude wooden javelins they had made the night before into the throng of enemies.

Dagon glanced over at the men chopping and preparing the giant timbers, not with the purpose of falling them, at least not yet. The trees were massive and likely hundreds of years old - when they fell, they would crush and confuse a score of the enemy. After the trees were felled, there would be no more tricks. They would have to fight the hordes of barbarians that were left, which Dagon hoped would not be many.

Dagon could see that many of his men were weary from the long day and night of battle and labor. He knew most of them by name and had fought beside most of these men many times before - he prayed he would have the honor to do so a thousand more times after this day.

"We are ready my Lord," A young dark haired soldier informed him, a thick gash scabbing the side of his face.

Dagon nodded to the young man. "Hone your blade, and keep your senses sharp as well," he told the young man who was just a year or two older than his eldest son Ethan. "Be sure that after this fight you get that wound cleaned."

"I will my Lord. It is an honor to fight with you - we will get our homes back," the young man finished then walked away. The sentiment brought a hard smile to Dagon's face.

A tall muscular barbarian barked out orders to a group of warriors - they had been piling the bodies of their comrades all night so they could be burned. Many of the barbarians had gotten no sleep that night - they had been busy moving the dead, tending the many wounded and putting out the fires from the attack in the night. The last of the bodies were thrown onto the massive piles just as Dagon's men came into sight of the camp in a full charge, their blades and armor gleaming in the rising sunlight.

Dagon crashed hard into a group of confused savages, his horse trampling over them - crushing bones and life as it went. He swung his sword viciously left and right in an arc taking down warrior after warrior as they scrambled to find a weapon or get out of the way of the murderous warhorse. A tingling sensation overcame him - his eyes scanned quickly trying to see what the trouble could be. Then he heard the long dull sound of horns from the distance. His eyes spotted the trouble from the far end of the enemy camp, as hundreds upon hundreds of barbarians poured out of the forest to join their brethren in battle.

Dagon and his men cut forward, hacking their way deep into the enemy camp - soon for every one they felled, three more were there to replace them. The retreat was sounded and they made a hasty retreat out of the camp - being pursued by more than they were prepared to handle.

Dagon's mind raced as he kicked his horse's flanks, urging the beast to go faster. He could see the wall of timber flare to life as the archers set it ablaze. He raced through the opening - his horse had not even fully stopped before he was on the ground yelling orders and getting ready for the battle that was about to take place. He fought the urge to tell his men to retreat straight away - he knew the enemy was far larger now than he and his men could handle. Yet he could not bring himself to give the order. He knew they could hold the enemy for a while thinning their numbers and maybe, just maybe...win.

The archers took aim and let loose, taking down the first line of barbarians that charged toward them, while the rest of Dagon's men got through the opening and prepared for the raging onslaught.

"It was a trap, I cannot believe it." Dagon cursed to Jarroth who was now by his side.

"There was no way to know, so do not waste your time pondering it now," Jarroth yelled over to him, picking up one of the javelins.

"We cannot beat them - there is too many of them now," Dagon cried, launching a javelin into the throng of enemy warriors and striking one through the chest dropping him dead where his corpse was trampled.

"Maybe not, but we can hold them for now and wear down their numbers," Jarroth shouted, impaling a savage on the other side of the wall of fire.

Dagon stumbled back, watching in horror as the hordes of enemies churned toward them. The archers fired their last arrows and began hurling the wooden spears. Every fiber in his body told him to sound the retreat, but he refused his instinct and forced back the words.

Bodies piled high all around the opening and edge of the flaming wall, for every one of Dagon's men who fell, they took with them more than their fair share of the enemy. The order was given and the ropes holding the ancient timbers were cut - they fell over the burning wall into the cluster of savages, crushing handfuls of tightly packed enemies under each one.

Confusion sprang out through the masses of barbarians as the trees crashed down upon them. They pushed each other down and trampled one another to death, trying to avoid the falling pillars. It bought Dagon and his men precious time and they used it to their advantage charging into the crowd of barbarians from the small gap, hacking them apart. The javelins were running low, so each man picked his shots carefully - making sure each shot scored a mortal blow.

As soon as the last trees fell, the confusion stopped and the barbarians pressed their attack furiously, trying to overtake Dagon's men before any more deadly surprises occurred. But Dagon was out of tricks now - he had been counting the odds to be in their favor by now, but that was far from the case. Savages kept swarming in - he could tell they were outnumbered more than five to one and the odds were growing against them with each passing breath. The men holding back the opening were flagging fast, even though they were continually swapping out the front line. The only thing saving them from being completely overrun was the constant problem the enemy was having climbing and tripping over the dead that littered the front and sides of the opening. In some places, the bodies were four or five deep now.

"They are breaching the ends of the wall!" Several cried out in alarm and men rushed to both ends of the flaming wall to stop the enemy from getting through their only saving defense.

The javelins were depleted and the burning wall was dying down quickly. Enemies were beginning to dive through the flames to the other side where most met a quick end for their efforts, but some managed to hold their ground in defiance.

Jarroth grabbed Dagon and forced their eyes to meet. "It is over - we have to sound the retreat!"

Dagon nodded his head, not being able to form the words in his own mouth as he watched the battle collapsing around him.

"My Lord Andras - there is a messenger here to see you sir. He says he is one of Lord Dagon's men...from Mandrake," a servant told him, averting his eyes from his naked Lord and Lady who soaked in a large thermal spring, one of many found in this region of Zandor.

"What did you say?" Andras questioned, giving the man his full attention and pushing his wife to the side.

"Yes my Lord, a messenger from Mandrake." The servant repeated, trying desperately not to glance at Lady Seera's naked form.

"Well bring him here," Andras ordered, climbing out of the steaming pool, putting on his silk robe and throwing his wife a towel to cover herself.

Moments later, the servant returned with a haggard man held up by two other guards.

"My god, get this man some food and water!" Andras snapped, and the first servant ran off to do as commanded. "Why are you here, messenger?"

"Lord Dagon... begs for help... Mandrake..." the messenger started to say between deep labored breaths and violent coughs. Finally, the servant rushed back with a large skin full of cool water followed by another servant with a large tray of fresh fruits and cheese. The messenger refused the food but took the water skin and downed several large gulps, which helped clear his dry throat, and seemed to revitalize him a little. "Mandrake was overtaken... by savages.... The land is swarming with them... more and more each day, Lord Dagon asks... for your help to—"

"Yes I know Mandrake was taken over by those monsters, Andras cut the man off indignantly. Why are Prince Berrit and the Lords of Draco not doing anything about it?"

"We do not know... sent messengers there... no word back." The messenger coughed out, then drank deeply from the water skin.

"Take this man to a guest room and let him repose - bring him to me once he is rested and revived again," Andras order.

"You cannot seriously be thinking about this my Lord!" Meresin bellowed frantically.

"Meresin - I know you are my steward - which is why I asked for your opinion on the matter. But you do not seem to be looking at the bigger picture," Andras told the reedy man.

"I am my Lord. I see it as such - the barbarians are menacing enough to take a stronghold like Mandrake and that means they may be strong enough to take Besha Castle," Meresin explained.

Andras paced frantically around the room running his hands through his thick brown hair. "What do you think, Velkain?" Andras asked his champion.

"I will stand by you, no matter what your choice is my Lord," Velkain replied in a deep voice that had come to be expected with his massive frame of nearly seven feet and three hundred pounds. It was rumored that he had barbarian in his blood, which gave him his size and strength, but no one dared to question him.

"That is not what I asked."

"I care not for those of Draco Kingdom my Lord, but I would be lying if I said I would rather see it in the hands of filthy bastards," Velkain replied.

"Someone bring me the messenger and fetch my two sons," Andras commanded.

"Kain, we are to ride to battle - get your things ready son," Andras said with a smile to his oldest boy, who grinned eagerly back at him, excited to finally hear those words leave his father's lips.

"Yes father," Kain replied, running off to fetch his armor and sword.

"What of me, father? Am I to ride with you as well?" Andras' youngest son Jamus asked.

"No my boy, I need you to stay here to take care of your mother and our land, and to see to it that no savage steps foot in Besha's boarders." Andras knew his boy was hurt that he could not come along.

"But father, I can fight! I want to come," Jamus argued, thrusting his chest out trying to emphasize his point.

"Jamus, you have your place here. Do not argue with me," Andras said firmly and Jamus finally nodded his head knowing to obey his father.

"My Lord, this is madness, you truly should rethink this," Meresin pleaded.

"I have already made up my mind Meresin - Lord Dagon, I know, would help us if we were asking for this of him. We are allies now, if you do not remember," Andras said, annoyed with being questioned.

"But sir, the treaty was never properly signed and the Princess has not even been found. She is likely already dead. Prince Berrit will not be marrying her and will not be King, which means we are not allies," Meresin cried, running after Andras who was already on his way to his General's quarters.

"That is enough, Meresin! I will not have you second-guess me again! I am the Lord of these lands, not you. If I hear one more discouraging word from you, I will cut out your tongue and feed it to the buzzards!" Andras raged on the tiny man who shrank back in defeat.

"I... I am sorry my Lord, I meant no disrespect," Meresin whimpered.

Andras stormed away without another word to inform his Generals of the news and see to it that his men were ready.

Early the next morning, Lord Andras, his son Kain, the messenger who was almost fully recovered and six score of hardened soldier's road north to Lord Dagon's aid.

Prince Berrit stood by Lord Tundal's wife, Lady Tora and their children Thoron, Salvira, Calmela and Drandor's champion Raven, while watching the smoke rise into the sky from Tundal's pyre. Dagon's family, Lady Angelina and her two boys Ethan and Leonard were also present, along with many of the respected citizens of Draco who had come to pay their final respects.

Berrit did well to pretend to grieve. How he could not wait until all of these people were delivered the bloody truth, when they would all fall to their knees and beg for their pathetic lives. *Just a while longer*, he told himself, reminding himself not to grin.

In the morning a meeting was called, Lady Tora, Lady Angelina, Raven Drandor's Champion, General Morris and Prince Berrit were summoned to attend. The mood in the study was very solemn with the news of Lord Tundal's assassination still fresh in their minds.

"Thank you all for attending this morning." Lady Tora addressed the small group, her eyes still puffy from a night of mourning.

"What is this meeting about, my Lady?" General Morris asked, leaning back in his chair.

"With the unfortunate and untimely death of my husband," Tora paused to stifle the tears that threatened to escape, "Draco Kingdom is once again without a leader. No one present has the right or the mind to run the kingdom."

"Lord Dagon and Lord Marcus are the only two with the right, the blood line and the authority to," Raven commented.

"Agreed," Lady Angelina concurred. "The problem we face is by last report Lord Marcus has the fever and does not look as if he will recover and Dagon is in the field with his army fighting the barbarians to take back Mandrake."

"It would appear Lord Dagon is the only option we have then. We should send word to him immediately," Morris replied.

"Yes, the problem is we are not sure where to find him,' Tora admitted."He could be anywhere out there by now, if he is still alive. It may take a fortnight or longer just to send word to him."

"I know, but what choice do we have?" Morris commented. "I do not understand your haste."

"I think I know what the ladies are trying to make apparent," Berrit interjected and all eyes went to him. "While the search for Lord Dagon is underway, there is much that needs to be achieved and kept up in Draco."

Lady Tora nodded in agreement. "Thank you Prince Berrit. We cannot just let the Kingdom wane until Dagon is found and returns. Yet none of us are completely qualified to take rule into our own hands."

"So what are you suggesting we do?" Raven asked.

"A council." Lady Angelina began walking around the table. "We form a council until my husband returns to Draco and can take the reins so-to-speak."

"No single one of us - aside from Prince Berrit - truly has any understanding of the full scope of ruling a Kingdom," Tora began. "Prince Berrit, I hope you understand I mean no disrespect when I say this, but since you are Zandorian and have no true ties to us…we could not allow you to take control of our kingdom, but your knowledge is always appreciated."

"No disrespect at all my lady. I never expected anything else," Berrit replied, using all of his resolve to control his rage. This was not how he had hoped nor expected things to go after the death to Tundal. He had hoped they would be so grief stricken and unfocused that he would be able to pick up the reins of rule without much opposition.

"But together we all have the measures to see to the running of Draco. No it may not be a perfect solution but I believe it is better than our current circumstances," Tora finished.

"I agree completely," General Morris replied. "It seems to be our most logical standpoint at this time, until Lord Dagon returns."

"Good, we will all have our stations and tasks, which we are to oversee at our own accordance. Yet when situations arise that impact the whole, we will come together and hold a vote as to the best course of action with a wider outlook on things," Lady Angelina finished.

Standing off to one side, barely concealing his anger, *we shall see about your precious council*, Berrit thought to himself.

17

Meath woke to the sound of flowing water and a soft, soothing voice singing an old song that he had not heard since he was a boy. His head began spinning wildly when he tried to open his eyes. He fought to stay conscious. For a few minutes while he lay there, he almost forgot where he was and what had happened to him. He wondered if he was dead and the voice singing this alluring melody was a servant of the Creator coming to collect him. He rolled over to get a glimpse of what his collector looked like and agony assaulted his every sense.

"Are you okay Meath? You should not try to move," the voice informed him.

Meath opened his eyes and looked up to see whose voice had delivered the sound. Kneeling in front of him was a beautiful redheaded young woman that Meath was sure he had seen before. She was staring back at him with an extremely distressed looked upon her smooth face. She dampened a cloth in a cup of water and placed it on his head. Meath flinched when the cool water touched his skin, but quickly rejoiced in the soothing feeling that accompanied it.

"It is okay Meath - I am not going to hurt you," she whispered tenderly.

It all started flooding back into his mind. The memories came back so fast it disorientated him even more and he had to fight the urge to vomit. He tried to speak but no words escaped his dry lips before everything went dim and he slipped out of consciousness again.

"I promise it will all stop soon Meath - the poison is almost out of your system," Kara whispered to him, rolling him over on his side and remoistening the cloth on his head helping hold his fever at bay.

Kara had found Meath the morning after he escaped - he was unconscious when she had found him, and the poison in his wounds had spread further than she had expected. She did not know if she could save him. The last two days and nights she had been using every potion she could possibly think of and find ingredients to make . She had absorbed so much life force from the vegetation around them that for a dozen paces in each direction everything had wilted and died, even the dirt had lost its rich, moist texture and was now close to ash. She hated defiling the land like that, but knew it was necessary to save his life. She had been able to heal the physical wounds and stop the poison from spreading further, but he still had to fight what was already in his system. The battle seemed to be going nowhere, for over the last two days he did not seem to be getting better, but neither did he seem worse. Today was the first day he had come to - even if it were only for a moment, it was a positive sign.

Kara wondered how Daden had faired and hoped he found shelter and safety. She knew Daden could take care of himself, but he too had been wounded badly in the fight and if barbarians had discovered him, he might not have been able to fend them off. She sighed deeply. She could not let all these questions assault her mind - it was driving her to her mental limits. She hoped Daden was well and waiting for her and as soon as Meath was able, they would go find him and continue on their way.

Meath woke again, this time to the sound of birds chirping. He opened his eyes and saw Kara asleep a hand-span away from him with her back against the inside of the large hollowed out stump they were residing in. He peered out the leaf-covered opening and saw the faint light of dawn emerging through its cracks. Slowly, with gritted teeth, he rolled himself over onto his arms and knees and had to stifle a cry of agony as pain assaulted him from his mended shoulder and leg.

Meath glanced over at Kara to ensure she had not heard him move. His attention was captured for moment by Kara's sleeping form - her fiery red hair framed the soft angelic features of her face. Her lips were plump, alluring and a vivid scarlet. If she had not wronged him so profoundly, he may have found her attractive. Relieved to find she still slept, he crept out the opening into the fresh crisp morning air.

Meath gathered himself up and tested his weight on his injured leg and was disappointed to find it would not hold much weight before the pain was too much.

"Leaving without even saying thanks?" a very sarcastic Kara said from behind him. "Just like a man."

Meath did not even turn to look at her, he just ran, trying to forget the pain he was in. He did not make it more than three steps before he pitched forward from the pain erupting through his injured leg and body.

"Please Meath, do not make me be the bad guy and have to restrain you again," Kara pleaded with him. "Just cooperate with me, you are still weak and exhausted from your wounds and the poison that was in your system," Kara explained to him, putting her hands out to offer to help him off the ground. "We have enough enemies out here," she gestured to their present surroundings. "Neither one of us can afford more right now."

Meath knew she was right. He could not escape - he was far too weak and with the barbarians and Priestesses about, he would not last long in his present state. He started to move his hand up to reach for hers when he noticed he was not bound by the hemp rope they had used before to impede access to his Gift. He would ensure she would not get it around him again. He grabbed her hand and she helped him up.

"Let us sit outside and get some fresh air - I am sure it will do you good," Kara said, leading him over to a log she had moved over the day before to use as a seat.

Meath looked around and noticed all the dead foliage and the ash-covered ground then looked back to her, confused.

The weak smile she gave him was full of guilt. "It took a lot of life energy to heal you and I could not afford to move around and collect it - you needed it as quickly as I could draw it out."

"You have my thanks."

She smiled at him, "you are welcome." She made a small pile of branches and dried shrubbery and started a fire. "Hand me that pot, but be careful."

Meath picked up the small pot and was surprised it was partly full of water - he took the lid off and noticed several small crayfish swimming inside. His stomach promptly reminded him he had not eaten in days and he returned the lid and handed her the pot.

"I thought I found you too late. I was sure you were going to die on me," she admitted with true distress, placing the pot on the small fire to boil. "I will give you the rest of today and tonight to rest and build you strength, then we must find Daden and get to Salvas as soon as possible, this has taken far too long already," Kara explained to him, and then realized she had said something she should not have.

Meath's mind raced with questions that he so desperately wanted answers to. He watched her busy herself with the crayfish - he could tell she was hoping he did not catch what she had said. "Why are you taking me to this place, Salvas?" He asked bluntly, hoping since Daden was not around that Kara might indulge him some answers finally.

Kara bit her bottom lip and muffled a curse. "Meath, you know I cannot tell you. I just need you to trust me."

"How am I to trust you? You took me against my will, confined me like a prisoner, almost got me killed to take me to a place I know nothing about, for reasons you will not tell me! You talk of trust like you have earned it." Meath responded bitterly.

"I know I have no right to ask for your trust, but I am asking anyway. I am not asking as a friend, or as someone who has earned the privilege, I am asking as someone who has spent nearly a year of my life looking for you because I know how important you really are."

"I could have left you two to die back there," he muttered coldly trying to hide his shock that she had been looking for a year.

"Then why did you not, Meath? Why not take your chance and run when I cut you free and let them kill us? Do you know why? Because I know why."

"I am not a heartless bastard who just lets people die, unless I truly know they deserve it."

Kara smiled softly. "And that is why we need you, because you are not heartless, not like him. You are different, you are the better," she replied, again realizing she said more than she should have and turned back to the boiling pot. "I guess we are even. You saved my life and I saved yours," she quickly added, hoping to curve the conversation.

"Why am I needed? Who am I not like?" Meath asked and seeing her hesitation added, "give me something Kara, you owe me that much at least."

Kara stared silently at the small wavering flames before answering him, wondering how much she should tell him. "You are needed Meath, for something far greater than you could ever realize," she said with an unknown awe in her eyes.

"And what if you have the wrong guy?" Meath countered.

"No, it is you - I can tell by your eyes. They are the same as theirs." Kara answered. "I can tell you no more Meath. You will get all your answers when we reach Salvas - I promise you."

Meath sighed in near defeat. "I have never heard of this place before - it is on no map I have ever seen."

"That is because it is not on any map, only those who live there know of its existence." She removed the pot from the flames to let it cool.

"I am sure people have stumbled upon it by mistake, or have seen smoke from its fires."

Kara smiled, shaking her head softly, "no one can see the town - it is hidden by magic. The only way in and out is if you have a key." She was staring down at a finely crafted ring on her right hand. It was a solid black band but not of metal - it had the look of smooth stone from what Meath could see. "It is such a wonderful place Meath - you will like it there."

"That smells so good," Meath said, his stomach growling angrily at him.

"It is plain, but it will take that growl out of your gut," Kara laughed.

"I am sure it will be the best thing I have eaten in days," Meath joked.

"You are a lot more talkative now that Daden is not around," Kara smirked.

"The company does not seem as hostile." Meath laughed, taking the small wooden plate she handed him with two steaming crayfish on it.

"Are you going to come willingly now?" Kara asked bluntly and very seriously after they had finished inhaling the crayfish.

Meath put his plate down. "It does not seem like I have a choice either way, now does it?" Meath remarked a little bitterly.

"No you do not, but I would really rather not have to drag you there kicking and screaming the whole way," she said honestly with a hint of humor.

"The sooner we get there, the sooner I can leave," Meath lied.

She smiled at him. "I am glad to hear that. Now you need to do some walking to get your muscles working again, not to mention you need to bathe."

Meath turned his head down and sniffed himself and frowned at the horrendous smell rolling off him in waves..

"Yes, it is that bad," Kara teased.

She helped him down to the creek, not far from their camp and let him wash and clean himself up while she went upstream a ways to give him some privacy and to search for more crayfish.

Meath was surprised about the amount of space and freedom she was allowing him. He thought about running while he was down at the creek, but decided it was better if he waited - she could be testing him. He decided to earn her trust more - besides, he knew he was still too weak to make it far. Tonight he would make his escape and he would let nothing stop him this time.

They sat together later and ate dinner, a small trout Kara had trapped in a side pool of the creek and the last few dry pieces of cheese Kara had left in her pack. She took the dishes down to the creek to wash and left Meath poking at the small fire. As soon as Kara was out of sight, he grabbed her pack and began searching through it. Near the bottom, he found a length of the hemp rope they had used on him. He smiled widely as he stashed it in his blanket. He quickly put everything back the way he had seen it and put her pack back where she had left it.

He watched the last few pinks and purples in the sky fade to night through the thick canopy - he thought of his friends and how he could not wait to see them again. He thought of Nicolette and how he would take her in his arms and kiss her deeply when he saw her next - he did not care who was around.

"What are you thinking about?" Kara asked, catching him by surprise.

"Oh, nothing, nothing of importance," Meath stammered, his cheeks flushing slightly.

"Anything that makes someone look as happy as you just were would be of importance, I would think," Kara said, sitting down next to him.

"I was just thinking about my friends," Meath replied, staring into the embers of the dying fire.

"You will be with them again one day. Now let us get some sleep - we have an early start tomorrow."

Meath lay awake, knowing the sun would soon rise and he would finally be free. His hands played with the length of enchanted rope

James Fuller

underneath his blanket. The plan had seemed so simple at the time he had thought of it, but now he wondered if the enchanted rope would work the same on a druid. It did not matter now - he had to do something. He would do it before she woke up, it would give him that extra moment of surprise.

He rolled over to face Kara, who was only a short distance away from him. She was fast asleep on her side. He knew she was a light sleeper and he had to be fast and accurate. He made a loop in the rope at one end and gave it a good pull to make sure it would close fast and hold strong. Slowly, he inched his way over to her and began sliding the loop under her hand and to her wrist. She began to wake up and Meath pounced on her, rolling her on her stomach and holding her firmly to the ground, grappling with her hands behind her back as fast as he could before she realized what was happening.

"What are you doing Meath?" Kara screamed, trying to buck him off.

"Changing the plans just a little. I am not going with you Kara," Meath said, after making sure the enchanted rope was not coming off. "Do not bother trying to escape - it is the same rope you used on me," Meath said, getting off her and backing away.

"Meath, please do not do this!" Kara cried, rolling onto her back to face him.

"I am going back to my life, and if you or anyone else comes for me again, I will kill them. I swear to you I will," Meath replied coldly. He backed out of the shelter to the sight of a few rays of sun gracing the sky, making the beginning of a new day. He smiled widely - he was finally free again.

"You cannot just leave me here Meath! I will die without being able to use my powers and my hands bound behind my back," Kara yelled out to him. "How am I to defend myself when I am found by enemies?"

Meath's smile faded - he had not thought about that. He had only thought of escaping. He was, however, glad to see the rope would hold her too. He knew she was right - if he left her like this, she would surely get caught and killed. But if he released her, or left means for her to free herself, she would follow him.

Meath threw the large dried leaves Kara had used for a roof off the hollow stump. Kara sat in the middle staring at him with tears streaming down her cheeks, but with a hint of relief at seeing that he was still there.

"I am not a monster. I am not going to leave you to die. But I cannot let you go, now can I? So that leaves one option - you are coming with me until I can figure out what to do to be free of you," Meath said firmly. "Now get up - we are leaving."

"Meath please, you do not know what you are doing. We have to go to Salvas," Kara pleaded.

"I am going home - either you come with me or you stay here and accept whatever fate becomes you," Meath explained, picking up her pack and beginning to walk west. Kara cursed as she managed to get to her feet.

They traveled in silence for a long time and Meath had to chuckle at the role reversal as she walked in front of him. On several occasions, Meath had to stop and help her over fallen trees or other obstacles, but still, nothing was said between the two.

"Is it a lot different point of view being the captive and not the captor?" Meath said smugly.

"I know very well what being held captive is like!" Kara snapped at him in a tone that Meath would never have thought possible from her.

"Well believe me - I would rather not have you captive right now. I would much rather never have met you. All that has happened since you abducted me is your doing. So, I think you are pointing the blame at the wrong person," Meath hissed right back.

Kara pondered telling him everything she knew of why he had to go to Salvas, but she knew he would not believe her now. He was doing what anyone in his situation would - he was trying to get back to his life that she had taken him from. No, he was better than most, Kara reasoned. She was sure anyone else would have left her to die, or even worse, killed her themselves to get away. She slowly worked her wrists in the hemp rope, trying to loosen the knot, but Meath had done a great job securing it tightly, not giving her much room to work with.

They hiked through the jungle until dusk and made camp under the thick canopy of large branches that were bent downward almost to the ground, making a good, dry place to sleep.

"Finally, we made it," Dahak moaned as they rode around the last bend of the road leading them toward Caligo city, which was right on Sheeva Lake and their last stop before their search for Meath really began. The city lights emanated a soft welcoming glow in the darkening sky as they rode closer.

It was the fourth day they had been traveling; they had passed through several small towns and heard nothing but rumors of the barbarian activity heading toward Dragon's Cove. More than a few people were fleeing to walled cities or further north or south in hope of avoiding the inevitable encounter. Many of those people had fled to Caligo City because it was the closest walled city and was well defended.

They rode up to the guards at the gate and were halted. "What business do you have in Caligo City this late night?" a big burly, unshaven guard asked his tone irritable.

"We are looking for a place to rest for the night and fill our bellies." Zehava told him. "We will be on our way again in the morning once we restock a few supplies."

The other balding guard walked through the group, taking a measure of them. He stopped when he arrived at Shania. "Lift your hood girl."

"What is the meaning of this?" Zehava muttered out.

"Shut your mouth." The balding guard snapped back to him then turned back to Shania. "Lift it!" Very hesitantly, she pulled her hood back, revealing her half-breed heritage. "Keeper's balls!" the guard barked, taking a step back and drawing his sword aggressively.

"What is this then?" The first guard barked, drawing his own sword and looking at Zehava suspiciously.

"Calm your blades boys." Zehava motioned for the guards to lower their weapons. "She is a slave and will cause no harm." Zehava explained, not needing any serious attention attracted to them. As far as the country knew, the Princess was still missing and the reward was only growing.

"We do not allow any kind of savage within our walls - half-breed slave or not! Have you not heard of all the attacks of late? If she comes in here and is noticed, there will be uproar!" the first guard said.

"I can assure you fine gentlemen, she will not be noticed." Zehava leaned down from his horse, drawing both guards closer. "My partner has very exotic tastes in the flesh he enjoys between his

legs and the sadistic practices he partakes well enjoying those tastes."
All three of them looked over to Dahak who gave his best effort to
grin wickedly.

"I still do not think it wise to let you in," the balding guard
commented, though a spark of interest gleamed in his eyes.

"We have had a hard long day," Dahak cut in. "What will it take
to change your mind?"

"Two silvers for both of us," the balding guard answered quickly.

"What?" Zehava stammered out. "That is outrageous!"

"We could leave you out here for the night," the balding guard
replied smugly.

"Or arrest you for keeping company with savages," the other
guard added.

"Boys, boys, there is no need for things to get heated," Nicolette
cooed. "I will pay and we can be done with this nonsense." She
flicked both guards their silver.

Both guards cracked huge grins at the silver in their hands. "All
right, you can enter, but you had better keep a low profile."

"We always do." Dahak smiled eerily as they rode passed the
guards and into the Caligo City.

"I am sorry for that, Shania." Zehava said once they were far
enough away.

Shania pulled her hood back up and tightly around her face. "I am
getting used to being the savage slave," she said, almost laughing.

"We will get supplies in the morning, then leave to find where
Meath's trail ended by the river. I hope we can pick it up again,"
Zehava said, while riding off the main rode in search for a quieter
part of the city to find an inn.

"We will find him - I know we will," Nicolette told him, not a
hint of doubt in her words. "I feel it."

They found an inn that was fairly secluded from the main part of
the city. Zehava tossed the night stable-boy two copper coins, and
told him to take good care of their horses and he might see another
two. The boy smiled widely and assured him the beasts would be
treated like kings.

"It is not the castle, but it is a roof over our heads," Dahak sighed,
removing his pack and gear when they had gotten to their room.

"You have been living the high life for too long Dahak." Zehava
laughed, "you have forgotten your roots."

"They can stay forgotten," Dahak joked back.

"It is better than the castle - a lot better," Nicolette chimed in with an ample smile.

"What do you mean?" Zehava asked, truly bewildered by her attitude.

"No rules, no politics, no high stature to uphold. It is freedom."

"I would still rather be at a castle," Dahak mumbled half-jokingly, sitting down to rub his feet.

"Nothing better than this right here, friends and adventure," Shania piped in.

"I agree, we are only missing one thing," Zehava said solemnly.

"What is that?" Dahak asked, missing the tone in his friend's voice.

"Meath..." Nicolette whispered, loud enough for everyone to hear.

"What do you all say about going to the tavern across the street and getting a hot meal and a cold drink?" Zehava asked, wanting to keep morale high.

"I thought you would never ask," Dahak replied, his mood instantly changing at the prospect of food.

"That sounds good - I am starving now that I think about it." Nicolette dropped her gear on the floor by the bed.

The group sat in a corner of the bar where the lights were dimmer and the crowd thinner. Everyone was too busy drinking away their sorrows and telling their sob stories to notice them.

"What can I get you?" the short, busty barmaid asked.

"Four of whatever you have on special tonight and four mugs of your finest mead," Zehava told her.

She eyed him for a moment. "That will be a full silver for the lot of you."

Before Zehava could pay, Nicolette pulled out her coin pouch and tossed the barmaid a silver coin. The barmaid's eyes widened momentarily at the bulge of the purse before she strolled away to fetch their food.

"A hot meal, I cannot wait! I am wasting away here," Dahak joked, licking his lips in anticipation.

"Did you see her eyes?" Shania asked and everyone turned to regard her.

"Whose eyes?" Nicolette asked, bewildered.

"That woman's eyes when you pulled out your coin purse," Shania whispered, her hooded gaze never leaving the barmaid who now stood at the bar talking with the owner. "They went wide with greed."

Zehava glanced over to the bar suspiciously. "I doubt anything will come of it, but for now on Nicolette, it might be wise if you keep your coins hidden or let me pay."

Nicolette nodded. "From what I heard back at Dragon's Cove, we are about a day's ride from where they lost Meath's trail."

"Tomorrow we will follow the riverside 'til we find something that looks promising." Zehava said, moving back against his seat, so the barmaid could give them their food.

"Sorry about the wait," she said, making small talk. "So where you all from? Have not seen your faces around here before."

"We are traveling to the coast to visit family and friends," Zehava lied cautiously.

"Well you are gonna wanna be careful out there, a lot of barbarians about of late causing all sorts of troubles for folks like yourself. Even a lot of folk gone missing." She finished unloading her tray, smiled and left back to the bar.

"You guys have to try this stew," Dahak mumbled between each spoonful of his already half empty bowl.

"Have you even tasted it?" Nicolette joked.

"I do not think he has," Shania added, digging into the warm meal.

"Let us eat and get out of here - I am getting a troubling feeling," Zehava whispered, noticing the bartender was now talking to a table where four large brutes sat downing mug after mug of ale and glancing over at them.

They finished their meal quickly with little conversation, trying hard not to make eye contact with the group at the far table.

"Can I getcha all something else?" the barmaid asked, coming to collect their dishes as they were getting up to leave.

"No thanks, about time we call it a night, a long road ahead of us.' Zehava told her, pretending to stretch and yawn.

"All right then, you all have a great night and a safe trip - hope to see you again next time you pass through," she said as she left with their dishes.

"I think it best if we do not go straight to the inn," Shania whispered once they were outside the doors.

"Why not?" Nicolette asked, with apparent confusion.

"Shania is right - if those men do mean to cause trouble, it would be best if we lead them away from where we plan to sleep tonight and hope to lose them along the way," Zehava explained looking over his shoulder to the tavern doors almost expecting to see them.

Dahak shifted his sword belt and pulled the blade free a finger's span from the hilt, ensuring its quick release if he needed to draw it. "Just in case," he smiled half-heartedly.

They walked through the quiet city, taking lefts and rights through alleyways and on main roads, blending with the small crowds of refugees who were homeless. Before long they noted they had not seen anyone following them or looking suspicious so they reasoned it was safe to return to their room.

"Hey, there you are," a familiar husky voice said from behind them. They turned to regard them with hands on hilts, but saw that it was the two guards from the gates and a few other guards.

"Good evening gentlemen, what can we do for you?" Zehava asked calmly, hoping to be rid of them quickly.

"What do you think we want?" the shorter guard from the gates said, licking his lips and running his hand through his uncombed hair. "We want a taste of that savage whore." He finished with a smile, showing all his broken and rotten teeth. "Your friend is not the only one with different tastes in flesh."

"Aye, and we brought a few friends along who would not mind a little taste neither," the balding guard said looking back to his three large friends who all wore stupid lustful grins.

"No one is touching her - she is our property and we do not share," Zehava said, putting his hand on the hilt of his sword again.

"Oh come on now, I got me friends all worked up for some fun. Do not make me disappoint them," the balding guard replied, his voice going hard. "We might even be willing to give you back your coin from earlier."

"Sorry to disappoint, but you will have to look elsewhere you pigs." Nicolette burst out angrily, surprised by her own reaction.

"Looks like that one's got some spice to her too - maybe we should take her for a while too. What do you say boys?" one of the dirty guards from behind said, looking to his comrades to see their wide grins and nods of agreement.

"I think you are right Clyde - that is a mighty fine idea." Another of the brutes laughed, taking a step forward with his arm stretched out toward Nicolette.

The ring of steel echoed in the night air as Zehava's sword cleared its sheath. A glint of light flashed as he brought the blade down and he severed the man's hand off at the wrist. "You will lose a lot more than that if you do not walk away right now," Zehava explained through gritted teeth while the man howled in pain and backed away, cradling his bloody stump.

"You are going to pay for that you whoreson!" Clyde hissed, drawing his curved sword - his comrades following suit.

Dahak and Shania both had their blades out and were positioning themselves on either side of Zehava.

"We do not want any trouble!" Nicolette fumbled with the mini crossbow at her side that she had been given by Saktas.

"You should have thought about that before you cut my friend's hand off, wench," the balding man hissed back rocking his blade back and forth.

"You should have just let us enjoy that little exotic cunt there!" Clyde exclaimed angrily, pointing to Shania. "Nice little knives there girly. I will be sure to use them to mar your pretty little flesh up when you are begging for your life."

Shania stepped forward no fear in her stride or in her dangerous green eyes. "My blades will feast well on your life blood!" Zehava put out his hand stopping her from going forward further.

Zehava heard the soft click of a small bolt finally being loaded into Nicolette's crossbow. "I will give you one more chance to walk away with your lives."

Clyde laughed callously. "Should be your own hides you are worried about lad."

Zehava smiled vainly. "Let me break it down for you thick-headed mules. My friend here does not miss at this distance and will have one in your heart before you can take a step. Your buddy there is missing his sword hand and looking a little pale and needs to have that dealt with before he bleeds out. So he is already dead in this fight. You have offended my exotic friend here and her skills with those 'knives' are unmatched by the likes of any of you. You will all die and for nothing but the sake of your foolish pride and the blood in your loins." Zehava looked hard at each man, his demeanor sure of his every word. "Just walk away."

All five brutes stood there pondering his words and slowly one by one they realized the truth in them. "I want you out of the city by the time the sun is out from behind the mountains. If you are still here, I will rally every man in the city to hunt you down," the balding man hissed in bitter defeat, slowly backing away with the others.

"Can we please go back to our room now?" Dahak asked nervously after the men were out of sight.

Dawn came quickly and shortly after, they were out of the Caligo City and on their way down the bank of the Sheeva River. They followed a poorly traveled path, but soon realized their horses would be no good and would not last on the rocky uncertain trail. They took their things and released the beasts, continuing on foot.

They traveled all morning and into the afternoon without slowing, their adrenaline was high for the prospect of finding Meath's lost trail. Finally, Dahak could take no more and called for a much needed stop for all of them.

"This looks like as good a spot as any." Zehava dropped his pack and stretching his stiff limbs.

Nicolette stumbled over to the river's edge and splashed the cool water across her face - it refreshed her more than she had expected. She was so tired and her feet and legs burned with cramps. She had wanted to stop long before, but her thoughts of finding Meath fueled her to keep going and not to be the weak link.

"Try soaking your feet in the cool water, it will help soothe the soreness," Zehava said, coming up behind her with his empty water skin.

"What?" Nicolette asked wondering how he could have known about her sore feet.

"I noticed you were stumbling and limping a lot the last while. Soak your feet in the water it will help them," Zehava told her. "Just make sure you dry them off fully before putting them back in your boots."

"I was hoping no one noticed - I do not want to be the weakest link of the group." Nicolette sighed and ducking her head in shame.

"I did not just come down here to get more water - I came down here to soak my feet too," Zehava lied. "That was a hard hike - do not feel ashamed." Zehava encouraged her while taking off his boots and submerging his feet into the river with a groan of satisfaction.

"You read my mind." Dahak wadded down to where they sat and put his feet into the refreshing water.

They ate quickly, and then were back following the river's edge. Several times they spotted signs indicating barbarian activity but

Shania assured them the tracks and campsites were days old and they need not worry.

They traveled almost until dark, but stopped when they got to a large flat opening right by the river. It was smooth and almost perfectly flat with a soft layer of silt atop of it. They made camp and set up a canvass tarp they had gotten from Caligo City to help give them some protection from rain at night while they slept now that they were nearing the rainy season.

With the four of them, they decided that only two would take watch at night allowing the other two a full night's rest. Then the pairs would switch the following night, ensuring no one went without sleep for too long.

Nicolette sat up against a nearby tree where she was well hidden and could see the campsite in full. Since they did not have a fire going, all the light she had was from the bright moon and the radiate stars shining off the water and through the canopy of trees around them.

Normally, she would have been terrified, being alone in the dark like this, but now there was a certain calm about it. She almost felt at peace, like the darkness understood her feelings. She had changed so much - had become stronger, not only physically but mentally and spiritually as well.

"I know you are out there Meath, somewhere close," she whispered to the night. "I will find you, and it will be me who saves you this time, I promise."

Nicolette glanced up at the moon and noticed her time on watch was up. She gathered herself up; thankful she would soon be fast asleep listening to the sound of the flowing river, when movement caught her attention. She froze where she was and scanned the tree line for what had caught her attention - her heart nearly froze in her chest when she noticed several looming shadows creeping toward their camp from the north. At first, she thought to cry out a warning to the others, but stopped when doubt entered her mind. Maybe they were just lost travelers looking for help. She grabbed her bow, notched an arrow and waited to see. If they were barbarians, they would have charged in for the kill already.

The sound of a blade clearing its scabbard finally made up her mind. She pulled her arrow back and let loose, the darkness impeded her aim and her arrow sank deep into the front man's leg. He howled in unexpected pain and crashed to the ground.

Within moments, Zehava and Shania had climbed out of the makeshift tent, weapons drawn and senses alert. Two dark figures melted from the gloom and charged them - one wielded a single-bladed battle-axe and the other a short sword.

Zehava met the axe wielder knowing the best defense against an axe was not to let the opponent have the room to use it. Zehava had hoped for a quick end, but the man was a lot quicker than Zehava could have ever anticipated. He moved his sword up high to deflect a head chop that would have surely cut him nearly in two. His arms burned from the block, but he wasted no time in thinking about it. He kicked the axe wielder hard in the knee, bringing him down and forward - the hilt of his sword smashed into the bridge of the man's nose. It flattened it to his face, causing him to teeter back several steps. But the axe man hardly slowed - had it not been for the moon's reflection off the axe blade, Zehava would never have seen the attack that nearly took his head from his shoulders.

Shania danced her blades off the big man's sword, trying to keep him at bay until she could land a mortal blow. But the man swung feverishly at all angles with such force that most of the time it took both of her blades and all of her strength to block them. Her shoulders and wrists ached already from the repeated blocks from her attacker and she had almost lost hold of both of her weapons.

Nicolette aimed her bow, trying to find a clear target and help her friends. Finally, she let loose again striking a man who had stopped to help the first man to feel the sting of her arrows. The barbed shaft sank deep into his back, dropping him to his knees, as he tried to grab at the arrow shaft to pull it out.

Dahak watched the shadowy silhouette stalk past, the tent blade in hand. Fear knotted his insides at the sound of fighting outside, but he knew his friends needed him. Dahak lunged out of the tent, his sword leading the way - he felt the tip sink into flesh. He stood up to see his sword embedded nearly to the hilt in a stubby man's belly. The man's eyes were wide with the unpredicted pain that had found him. Dahak tore his sword out and felt a light spray of blood across his arms. The man fell to his knees, dropping his own blade, his jaw quivering in panic as he tried to stem the flow of gore slopping out of his wound. Dahak's knee connected hard with the man's face, as more men spilled into the camp.

Nicolette took aim again at one of the new men running into their camp to join the fray. She knew she was not delivering mortal blows, but if she injured them it would slow them. She fired and missed and went to reload when she saw someone to the side of her. Pain lanced through her as a spear sailed by her, cutting deeply into her side and knocking her off balance. She tried to correct her footing but her foot caught on something in the dark and she fell back. Her head cracked against a flat rock. Pain erupted through her skull blurring her vision and making her want to retch. She tried to gather her wits and push herself back up, knowing the enemy was coming in for the kill.

The axe came down again. Zehava's sword was there to block it once more. His limbs were crying out in agony after each powerful blow stopped. He cursed when he saw more men enter their camp. He pushed his attacker back, slashed for the chest and was blocked. He knew his opponent was a veteran fighter and had more years of experience, but desperation finally kicked in. He pulled his sword back and attacked high again, swinging in for an overhead chop, giving his opponent plenty of time to see it, what he did not see was one of Zehava's hands pulling a dagger. Once his sword hit the handle of the axe, his arm shot his dagger forward finding his attacker's heart through his hardened leather armor.

Shania heard Nicolette's scream - fury enraged her as she took the offensive, slashing her blades wildly, driving the man back. She spotted Dahak at the side coming to help her, her smile widened when her attacker turned his head to regard Dahak. That was all the opening she required, she brought one blade ripping to the side, knowing it would be blocked, her other blade came in from above. Her opponent's instinct had forced him to turn toward the new threat, leaving him exposed. Her curved blade sank into the side of his neck and across his jugular releasing a crimson spray as he crumpled in defeat. Shania took off toward the figure stalking toward the area where she had heard Nicolette.

Pushing past the nausea and pain, Nicolette forced herself to stand - knowing on the ground she was as good as dead. She tried to draw her sword but a meaty hand clamped over her mouth from behind. Both of her hands reached up to wretch the hand away from her mouth so she could cry out for help, but she did not have the strength to pull the powerful hand away. Desperate, she swung her hand down and connected with the man's groin. His grip loosened and she pulled herself away and turned back to face him but before she could draw her sword, his fist slammed into the side of her face sending her sprawling to the ground.

Shania was upon Nicolette's attacker before he could take a step forward to finish his job. A quick under sweep of one her deadly blades caught him across the back of the knees, and her other blade opened a long wound across his back. He cursed out as he stumbled and turned to meet his attacker, but all he glimpsed was a fading silhouette into the darkness of the jungle. He turned back to face Nicolette just as Shania's twin blade sank deep into his side passing through flesh, bone and lung. He tried to cry out, but only thick blood escaped his lips as darkness became absolute.

"You all right?" Shania asked Nicolette, helping her to her feet. When Nicolette nodded that she was fine. Shania pulled her along with her back toward the others.

Zehava and Dahak fought furiously trying to push their attackers back while Shania and Nicolette got behind them. They had landed a few minor hits that had slowed their enemy's attacks, but had also taken many wounds and were losing momentum fast.

"We cannot hold them for much longer!" Zehava yelled back, parrying a thrust for his torso.

"We have to run, but where!" Shania yelled back to him, looking for an exit, but by now, there were several men stalking in from all directions.

"You are not going to get away from us!" one of the brutes yelled.

"The river is our only hope," Zehava cried out, as a wild swing he had not seen opened up a gash across his arm and shoulder.

To try to swim the Sheeva River during the day in dry season was foolish and deadly but to try to swim the rapid flowing river during the night at the beginning of the rainy season was suicidal and they knew it. But they had little choice, if they did not, they would die here and now.

Zehava parried a vicious blow and quickly reversed his sword, the tip of his blade ripping into his attacker's forearm, forcing him to drop his sword and back away. A dagger sliced past Zehava and sunk into the abdomen of the next in line. He knew Shania had thrown the blade.

"Run!" Dahak bellowed out, grabbing Zehava as they darted into the river, ignoring the painful sensation of cold water nipping their wounded flesh.

"You cannot get away that easy - we will find you!"

Morning came and the group found themselves across the river, several miles downstream, washed up on shore. Zehava pushed himself up and looked around to see that everyone was there and alive, barely. He knew they had to get moving or they would be found, and from the looks of everyone, they would not survive another encounter.

"Come on, we have to get moving," Zehava urged.

"What, where are we?" Dahak moaned, rolling himself over and flinching at the brightness of the sun assaulting his eyes.

"Downstream a few miles, we must have passed out in the river and the current pushed us ashore," Zehava replied, looking around trying to find the best route to take.

"Are you okay?" Shania asked, helping Nicolette to her feet.

"I think so," Nicolette groaned. She was a little shaky on her feet. "My face hurts," she said, bringing her hand up to where she had taken the punch. Her cheek and right eye were swollen and bruised.

"We can tend to our injuries later. We have to get out of here before they find us," Zehava said, limping into the jungle.

They trudged along until the early afternoon. Travel was horribly slow - there was no trail or path to follow just jungle to maneuver through and around. Finally, they stopped, knowing they needed to tend to their injuries and rest their weary battered bodies.

Zehava and Dahak bit down on straps of leather while Shania cleaned, stitched and dressed their worst lacerations. Afterward, she wrapped Nicolette's gash across her side but there was nothing she could do for the bruises and swelling on her face. Shania's own wounds were minor and needed no attention.

"Who were they?" Dahak asked, resting up against a tree. "At first I thought they had to be barbarians since they attacked in the dead of night but that was not the case."

"The guards from the city, out for one last attempt to resolve their pride maybe?" Nicolette winced, her hand clutching her injured side.

"Remember the guys in the bar that the bartender was talking too who kept glancing our way? My guess is they were highwaymen, and the bartender informs them of who has worthwhile coin to go after," Zehava replied, his eyes closed as he tried to match their faces with the small glimpses he had gotten the night before.

"What is that over there?" Shania interrupted.

"What is what?" Dahak groaned, hoping it was good news.

"It looks like an old campsite." Shania called back. "Not one a barbarian would make either." She called back to them as she investigated, "tracks show three people."

18

Ursa entered the lavish study - the bright, exotic décor had been a gift from Jewel for her husband years ago, since he had to spend so much time in there. His old study had been dim and dreary with little furniture to fill and accommodate the large room and the many visitors who occupied it on a regular basis. He had been summoned by Lady Jewel and he watched her from the doorway, he was sure she was asleep, her head rested in her folded arms on top of the smooth cedar engraved desk, the rise and fall of her body was slow. He almost thought of leaving her to sleep and to find some himself, but knew important matters needed to be discussed and sleep would need to wait for the both of them.

"You summoned my Lady?" Ursa asked making his way to where she rested.

Jewel's head jerked up, a look of confusion flashing across her face, but soon disappeared. "Excuse me Ursa. I must have fallen asleep - forgive me."

Ursa smiled. "No need for forgiveness - we are all tired and would jump at the opportunity to find a few moments of rest."

"How is it looking out there?" Jewel asked, almost afraid of the answer.

Ursa let out a large sigh filled with frustration and mixed with exhaustion as he sat down on the chesterfield in front of the desk. "We have turned them back once more but I fear we are being played."

The last two days they had been at nearly constant war with the enemy. The barbarians outnumbered them greatly and more tribes swelled the enemy ranks daily making it impossible to get a tally on their true numbers. Ursa knew Dragon's Cove was too well fortified and the men defending it still too alert for concern of the enemy trying to overrun them in a full on attack, and it seemed the enemy knew this as well. The attacks that came were small contingences of a thousand warriors or so that were heavily armored with thick leather and bone gear and large wooden shields. They came in fast and for blood. Once the battle was engaged in full, they would sound a retreat and another such wave would replace them giving the defenders little time to rest.

"What do you mean?" Lady Jewel asked, unease darkening her already gaunt features.

"They are clearly trying to wear us down - keeping us on constant alert with little to no time to rest. They are hoping to run our arrows low - which is why they are sending in fully armored warriors."

"Surely they have to know we will realize this," Jewel scoffed.

"I am sure they do, but exhausted desperate men make bad decisions after a while."

"I will be sure to inform the Generals and Captains to keep an eye on our archers so we are not feeding their shields pointlessly." Jewel made a note of it so she would not forget. "What is it? There is something more you wish to tell me, I can tell by that look."

Ursa nodded in defeat at her ability to read him so easily. "I cannot be certain but I fear I spotted a Priestess among their ranks this last assault. She did not help in the attack - I believe she was there merely to observe us to find our styles and our weaknesses. If I am correct, we will be seeing more of them in the coming battles and I doubt they will be there just to observe next time."

"That is truly grave news," Jewel replied, almost in a whisper. "It has been a long time since their Gifted have believed enough in the cause to come out of their holes and join the fighting." She looked hard at Ursa, her eyes betraying all of her fears. "Tell me honestly Ursa - do we stand a chance of surviving this?"

"This battle is still young and far from over my Lady," Ursa told her, his voice full of conviction. "Talena told me as long as we made it here before the enemy did that we would save many lives."

"So we will hold the castle?" Jewel asked eagerly.

Ursa frowned with uncertainty. "I cannot say that for sure - visions can play out in so many ways. All I know is what Talena has told me."

"Will she not tell you if you ask her?"

"If she tells me too much, it may alter events that are required to happen if we are to defeat the false prince."

"How can you be so sure she can be trusted?" Jewel questioned. "How do you know for sure she is not working to her own advantage somehow?"

Ursa sighed. "In truth, I do not know for sure. Such thoughts have crossed my mind already. But my instinct tells me to trust her and so that is all I have to go by."

Jewel nodded solemnly. "I trust your instincts - they have been right far more than they have ever been wrong. How is she doing now?"

"Her voice is coming back remarkably quickly - I believe it has to do with that staff of hers. It is a very powerful weapon - more powerful than we can even begin to know. I am sure as she gains more experience with her own powers and those of the staff's, we will begin to see just how extraordinary that staff truly is."

"Until it is in the hands of the Shyroni," Jewel commented.

Ursa grimaced then sighed."Let us worry about one thing at a time." He stood from his seat, his body protesting the effort. "You should sleep my Lady - you will need your strength and your wits about you."

"I shall, but promise me you too will find rest - your wits may very well save us all."

Ursa entered his room with full intentions of going straight to sleep - he was exhausted in every sense of the word and knew that without rest he would begin to become a liability on the battlements. He and the other Wizards had been nearly overusing their Gifts, not only against the enemy but healing the many seriously wounded. He slumped down in his desk chair - if the Priests and Priestesses had joined in the fighting again, things were going to take a turn for the worse. He eyed the small leather pouch on his desk. His hand even began to reach for it but he quickly turned his attention to his bed.

He tossed and turned - his mind alive with a swirl of overwhelming thoughts and feelings. He racked his mind for ways they could better defend the castle against the hordes surrounding them, and what they might do when the inevitable happens and enemy Gifted joined the battle. Then there was Meath, who took him and why? Was he still alive or was he dead by now? He cursed himself for not bring Meath with him when he left for Solmis' Haven. Had he just done that Meath would still be safe and Nicolette and the other would still be behind these walls.

Ursa pulled himself out of bed knowing sleep was futile, his mind would not let him rest. He eyed the leather pouch again and groaned. "I did not want to have to use this again." He opened the small pouch, poured a slight amount of the powdered yellow and green herb into a cup, added water, and let the herbs release their toxicity into the water for a moment before drinking the bitter liquid down in a single swallow. Within moments, he could feel his Gift coursing through him - his senses tingled awake and alert as if he had slept for a while.

Ursa had discovered Venenum long ago in his youth. The rare drug's properties kept the mind alert and fought back the need for sleep, for a time. But when someone with the Gift used Venenum it did so much more than that, it reacted with the innate abilities, magnifying and enhancing them to new levels of strength and control. Only a handful of people knew this and for good reason too. The drug was highly addictive and continued and prolonged use would do great damage to both body and mind.

Ursa knew firsthand the additive powers of Venenum, something he had promised himself long ago he would never be trapped by again. Sometimes circumstantial necessity overruled moral reason. This was the second time he had taken the drug in the last two days. He hated it, hated the very thought of it, but he needed to be alert, he needed to be strong if they were to survive this.

Ursa held the leather pouch in his hand, feeling the weight of it estimating how many doses were left. The pouch was small, but the drug was potent and not much was needed to achieve the desired effects. Ursa had not been around the drug in nearly half a score of years and had been angry when he had discovered it in the bag that Saktas had packed for him. There had been a note inside, "*It is better to have it and never need it, than to need it and not have it. May you never need it again my friend.*" Ursa had almost dumped the herbs out when he had found it, but he had not. Something had told him to hold onto it, just in case.

Ursa's attention was pulled from his thoughts at the soft knock at his door. "Come in."

The door opened and Talena entered with a steaming cup in her hands. "Why are you not resting?" she asked, her voice still horse and gritty but fully legible now.

"My mind is a swarm of thoughts and I cannot seem to slow it long enough to find rest," he replied, slowly making no sudden movements as he tightened the drawstring and slid the pouch in a drawer. "But I could ask the same of you." He turned to face her.

"The same as you I suppose," she admitted. "So I thought I would come visit you. I had hoped to find you sleeping to be honest. I am worried about you."

"Worried about me?" Ursa asked, his body tingled with nervousness at the question. He wondered if she knew of the drug, if Solmis had foreseen its use in his vision.

"Yes, worried. You have not slept more than a few moments since the first attack came over two nights ago and you have used your powers far more than the rest of us. I know you are more powerful than the others, but even you will run yourself down without rest and that will not do any of us any good," Talena told him earnestly. "I made you this." She handed him the steaming cup. "It is the same as Solmis used to drink when his mind refused to let him sleep."

Ursa took the tin cup and inhaled the sweet aroma of the tea. "You did not need to go to the effort - I do know how to make this one myself." He smiled taking a small sip of the flavorful liquid.

"I know, but you have not yet, so I thought I would save you the effort." Talena smiled back at him.

Ursa took a deep breath and chuckled - sleep would be good for him and is the reason he sought his chambers to begin with. "You are right, thank you." He took another sip. "Can you tell me something Talena?"

"Depending on what it is you wish to know."

"Can we hold the castle against them now that their Priestesses have entered the fray?"

"I am not sure how everything works out - all I know is that we made it before the enemy did and so we will survive and we will save many lives here," she explained to him. "I would have to assume that means we hold the castle, but I cannot be sure."

Ursa nodded expecting that very response. "That does little to ease my mind, but I assumed as much. I think I am going to try to sleep now. Thank you for the tea Talena."

"You are welcome Ursa, rest well."

Ursa woke to the sound of armored men yelling and rushing past his room. He scrambled to his feet and ran into the hallway grabbing the first soldier who ran past him. "What is happening?"

"The enemy is attacking again!" The soldier explained, his nerves clearly wrought.

Ursa made his way to the battlements. *Why had not anyone roused him when this all started?* Ursa cursed himself for drinking the tea, though he had to admit he was feeling better rested. He creased the battlements - the sound of battle was absolute down the length of the wall through the foggy rain of the night.

Already the enemy was throwing grappling hooks and climbing ladders in hopes to breach the wall. But the defenders were ready, their blades slashing ropes and sinking into uncovered flesh as it creased the battlements.

A loud crackling of power turned Ursa's attention to where Antiel stood unleashing sporadic bolts of energy down into the ranks of the enemy, blasting through wooden shields and ripping through exposed flesh. Not far away stood Talena, her magical staff held high in both her arms. The obsidian orb on the end swirled violently, unable to release its potent power fast enough. The battlements trembled noticeably as a dozen bolts of lightning erupted from the enchanted weapon down into the masses of advancing savages exploding through shields, armor and bodies alike.

"That girl and staff may very well be what turns the tide of this siege." a voice said from behind Ursa and he spun around to see Lepha.

"You may very well be right," Ursa mused in awe of the enchanted staff.

"Let us send these heathens back to their holes where they belong!" Lepha roared, finding an open spot on the battlements where he could begin his own assault.

Ursa peered over the wall trying to scan the scene below but the fog and rain made it nearly impossible to make out the differences in the enemy. Ursa was just about to begin his assault down upon the enemy when he spotted what he had been looking for from the corner of his eye - a haggard, gaunt looking form pushing her way closer to the wall. Ursa could feel his Gift coursing through his body stronger than normal thanks to the Venenum in his system. Energy crackled from his hand and arced down toward the unaware priestess but a moment before it struck, a warrior pushed her hard out of the way taking the deadly blow without pause. The priestess glared up at him and summoned her own attack before Ursa could cast another, a powerful burst of wind erupted from all around her, collecting dozens of arrow shafts and spears in its violent wake.

Ursa cursed, "Get down!" But few heard him before the attack hit laying more than a handful dead or dying along the hectic battlements. Ursa peered back over the battlements, but the Priestess was already gone. He cursed again, scanning the fray below for any signs of another - he knew if there was one, there would be more.

A familiar scream pulled his attention away from his search and he turned to see Talena stagger backward, two arrows buried deep into her abdomen. Ursa was about to run to her when a thick meaty hand grabbed his shoulder and spun him around. A seven-foot giant loomed over him, a cocky grin spread across his face and a serrated bone axe in his other hand held high ready to strike. A flash of steel stole the barbarian's grin as the arm gripping Ursa fell to the stone and Rift drove his blade in the savage's chest and pushed him over the side.

"Go to her!" Rift yelled to him. "I will hold this section until you get back!"

Ursa ran to Talena's side, she was unconscious. He checked the placement of the arrows and was sure they had not punctured any vitals. He grabbed the barbed shafts and was thankful she was unconscious as he pulled the arrows clear. Thick blood spilled from the wounds quickly but soon slowed to a stop as Ursa force healed the wounds. "You there!" Ursa called to the nearest soldier. "Take her to safety and stay with her."

Ursa stormed to the wall, his hands alive with energy before he reached the edge. He wasted no time in selecting a target as several flashes of power arced from his hands into the chaotic swarm below. Ursa closed his eyes and did his best to close out the sound of battle around him so he could focus. He could feel the raw power of his innate ability tingling with anticipation as he released. The ground quaked vaguely as column after column of Wizard's fire leaped from the earth incinerating all that it touched; the fierce wavering heat blistered the flesh of anyone who got too close.

Ursa was about to release another deadly assault when a dark flash of energy caught his attention, nearly too late. The battlements around him exploded in a shower of rubble and he threw himself back, barely escaping death from the attack. The dust cleared and there was a blackened crater in the side of the wall where Ursa stood only moments before. The soldiers who had been standing near him had either fallen over or been crushed by the collapsing debris.

"Are you all right Ursa?" Lepha asked, helping him up and pulling him further from the wall's edge.

"I am fine," Ursa replied, looking down the length of the battlements. The men fought valiantly but were tiring quickly. "Get Antiel, I have a plan," Ursa urged him.

"What is your plan?" Lepha asked, turning her head to see another streak of energy explode into the wall, sending stone everywhere and muffling the sounds of dying men.

"Rift, Barkel, on my order I want all the men on the wall to stop their attacks and raise their shields above their heads. Those without will need to find cover and quickly," Ursa explained.

Both Rift and Barkel looked at each other confused. "I do not know what you are up to Wizard, but I do know better than to doubt you," Rift replied before he and Barkel left to give the orders to the men down the wall.

"What do you need us to do?" Lepha asked eagerly, hearing another blast hit the wall.

"This had better work Ursa," Lepha said looking over his shoulder at the battle raging not far away, "or you have killed us all."

Ursa knew his words to be true. If his plan did not work, Dragon's Cove would be without any magical aid, which would mean certain doom to all within its walls. Rift gave Ursa the signal that the men were ready.

"Do you really think this will work?" Antiel asked, licking her lips nervously. "I have never heard of anything like this being done before."

"It will work. It has too. It is the only chance we have," Ursa replied confidently, though his mind screamed with doubt.

The three Wizards walked to the edge of the battlements. As they did - all of the soldiers put their shields up high, covering their heads. Those who had no shields found safety behind the Wizards or under the roofs of the stairwells.

On cue, all three Wizards began summoning their innate Gifts. A fierce wind began howling out over the battlements and down into the enemy, blowing their arrows and spears back down at them. Enemies peaking the crest of the wall were met by such a force it tore them clean from the stone and threw down into the mass below.

The wind grew stronger and colder as the trio of Wizards focused their abilities. Soon, the fat drops of rain that fell into the wake of sub-zero wind began freezing solid into razor shards. The ferocious torrent of wind threw the frozen shards down into the enemy hordes with such force they penetrated through their weak leather armor and ripped through flesh like parchment. Those with shields held them high, blocking the rain of death while backing up, trying to retreat from the massacre. It did not take long for the enemy to realize their doom, those who were still alive retreated in terror, trampling over those who were too slow or already dying.

Ursa opened his eyes just in time to see the enemy fleeing and that he was the only Wizard still standing. Lepha and Antiel had already succumbed to overuse of their Gifts. Ursa grinned, glad his plan had worked, when nausea and dizziness rushed through him.

"What do you mean you retreated?" Vashina glared at the battered warrior who had informed her of the failure. "No retreat was planned - you were to take the wall!"

"We had to, Wizards too powerful, rain death down on us from sky." The barbarian explained, his voice betraying his fear for his life. "Four Wizards guard castle not two. Need better plan - too many warriors die."

"What do you mean 'rained death upon you'?" Vashina's eyes glistened with rage.

"It means we underestimated our enemy and their abilities," a commanding female voice interrupted behind them. They both turned to regard Valka the High Priestess, "and we shall not do so again."

Vashina rolled her eyes at the statement. "You and yours should have been with the army ensuring a victory and not a cowardly retreat."

Valka nodded her head to the warrior, giving him leave, which he wasted no time in using, not wanting to be caught between the two powerful women. Once he was gone, Valka's cold silver eyes shot back to Vashina. "Who are you to decide the disposal of the Goddess' servants?" Valka asked callously. "Nonetheless, several of my priestesses and priests were out there, and now most that were sent are dead."

Vashina stared hard at Valka, who seemed to glow with power and anger. Valka hardly looked like most Priestesses - who normally looked haggard or like possessed corpses. Valka was tall, slender and her womanly figure was alluring. Her silver eyes were captivatingly beautiful and her long, straight, silver hair reached past her lower back. Valka was the essence of beauty and she knew it. Vashina wanted to burn her pretty face and mar that flawless body. The thought brought an inward smile to her.

"Besides, were you not sent here to help us? I have yet to see you out on the battlefield," Valka jeered casually.

"I shall do my part when I see suitable opportunity for my talents." Vashina shot back, trying to hide her rising anger. "Not that you are one to talk. I have yet to see you out there in all your glory."

"I have other responsibilities Vashina, like keeping this army together, making battle plans with the chiefs," Valka calmly stated. "You hold neither the authority nor the power to question my actions. You would do well to remember that."

"I guess a few thousand dead warriors means nothing to you," Vashina replied snidely.

Valka smiled widely. "You guessed correctly, I have thousands more at my disposal - more join every day in our great cause of conquest for our Goddess, Zepna."

"So Valka, where is your ever-faithful lover Meshia at? It seems a little odd she is not at your heels like always," Vashina cooed, changing the subject. She wondered if Meshia had been one of the priestesses killed in the last battle.

Valka did well to hide the snarl and twist of her face at the mention of Meshia. "I sent her with the others to help see to it that the Wizards were destroyed, but she failed me and our Goddess," Valka growled, glaring bitterly at Vashina. "But that is of little matter … I have many more lovers." She turned. "I expect you out there Vashina, helping in our next attack - he would not be pleased to find you are not doing your part," she hissed, walking away.

Vashina stood in the night, glaring off at nothing. She hated that woman - she had always hated that woman. Ever since the beginning, Valka had been a thorn in her side - a thorn she could not wait to remove.

Pavilion stood a few dozen yards away, hidden behind a group of ancient cedars. He had heard the whole conversation between the High Priestess and Vashina and now he watched Vashina standing alone, cursing to herself. He could easily sense the hatred between the two and wondered where it had stemmed from.

He had followed Vashina almost the whole way from Draco Castle - nearly the entire way, neither had stopped. Vashina had used some sort of potion on her horse to make it last twice as long as any beast should have been able to run. Sadly, such potions usually resulted in the beast running itself to death. Pavilion did not have the heart to run an animal to death if he could avoid it. He had stopped at every town or village that still had people and traded his horse for a fresh one. Of course, the owner would not know about the trade until morning, when they found their horse missing and another in its place.

He had hoped the siege would not be to the extent that it was now - the enemy was dug in solidly. It would take more than the forces behind Dragon Cove's walls to dispatch this foe. Pavilion had to wonder how long they could even hold off an adversary this large. Somehow, he had to get in those walls and tell them what he knew. He wondered if what he knew would even matter anymore.

"Who is out there? Show yourself now or be killed!" Vashina ordered, staring hard in the direction where Pavilion stood hiding behind the cedar trees. "I only give one warning."

Pavilion cursed to himself. He had become so carried away with his thoughts that he had forgotten what he was doing, and that a very worthy opponent was not far off. He slowly backed away, staying in the darkest shadows, his footing flawless making not a sound, hoping she would think it was nothing. But it was too late, Vashina charged in his direction, throwing knives already in hand.

He sprang into a dead run, knowing he had to get far enough away from the barbarian camp and sentries so if things did come to blows, no one would hear them and come interfere. He weaved in and out of trees and fallen logs hoping to lose her with his speed and agility, making sure not to give her a clear shot with her deadly knifes. He made sure not to fall into a routine while he swerved and weaved in-between his surroundings, he knew that was what she was waiting for. Every few steps he could hear the thud of a blade embedding into a tree not far from where he just was or might have been.

After several minutes, she was still hard on his trail and was obviously getting frustrated, throwing more often and more randomly, knowing he would not commit to a pattern that she could exploit. He knew he would not get away from her without a fight - she was too fast and stealthy for him to just slip away.

Pavilion slowed his pace, hoping they were far enough not to be heard and to let Vashina gain some ground on him. He could hear her not far behind, gaining almost two steps for his one now. He had to admire her ability to keep up with him, not many ever could, and even after their long run, her footsteps still fell almost as silent as death. He knew she was waiting for a clear shot, now that the trees were thinning out, which is what he wanted. He faked right, hearing the predictable thud of a blade where he would have been. He dove over a fallen tree to the left, hit the ground in a roll and was back on his feet, hardly slowing his pace. He had gone left because the trees grew even thinner here, which would provide her with the clear shot he wanted her to have.

Pavilion had to rely purely on his keen senses and instincts now if he was to make this work. He heard the soft grunt from behind and knew a deadly knife was now loose in the air coming rapidly toward him. With speed faster than man was meant to achieve, Pavilion jerked slightly to the left just as the blade struck his cloak where his heart would have been. The movement was so precise that it would be impossible for anyone to know he had not really been hit. Letting his body go limp, Pavilion crumpled to the ground hard. The ruse looked perfect. He listened as his enemy approached cautiously, wondering if she would embed another knife into him just in case. No, she was too proud to believe her shot did not kill him - and she had every right to think that - she was good. She would believe her throw had slipped through the left side of his rib cage and entered his heart, killing him instantly.

She was only yards away from where his crumpled body rested - he could just see her black leather boots from the corner of his eyes. He wondered if she was going to get closer to look at his face. He always looked at the face. As if satisfied, she turned and walked away without a second glance. Pavilion grinned at his masterful ruse, his hand snatched a dagger on his belt and he sprang onto his feet, in the same motion snapping the blade toward Vashina's heart.

Vashina spun around a circle and a half, snatching his blade mere moments before it would have struck home, and was now looking back at him holding his blade as if it were a mere child's toy.

"How did you...?" Pavilion mumbled dumbfounded at what he had just witnessed.

"You underestimated me, again." She smiled arrogantly. "You would have run right into the more wooded terrain had you not been setting me up. But I must say that was a very tricky feat you tried - anyone else would have fallen for it," Vashina cooed, cleaning under her nails with his blade.

Still, Pavilion stood off guard and uneasy, not sure of what his next move would be. Never in his life had he underestimated an opponent like this. Then again, never in his life had he met someone with skills that matched his.

Starting to walk nonchalantly around him, Vashina inquired plainly, "I must ask how you became so skilled? That kind of agility and awareness does not just happen to anyone."

He followed in suit, keeping his eyes on hers and matching her step for step. "I was about to ask you the same thing," Pavilion replied, visibly unnerved by the whole situation.

"You know it is rude not to answer a lady when she asks a question. And it is a question I do ever so want to know," she mocked.

"Well I apologize - my upbringing was hardly high class," Pavilion mocked back, his adrenaline pumping hard and his unnerving feeling turning into a form of excitement.

"So why were you spying on me, stranger? Who are you and where do you fit in all of this?" Vashina asked, stabbing his dagger into a tree as she passed and pulling two of her own finely crafted blades from the sheath strapped to her upper right thigh.

"What makes you so sure I was spying? Maybe I was just passing by and you attacked me for no reason?" Pavilion replied, knowing she would hardly believe that.

Vashina stopped and let out a hearty laugh. "Tell me your name at least - I do hate to kill strangers."

"So if I do not tell you my name you will not kill me?" Pavilion asked, his tone confident.

"I am afraid not - I have to kill you either way. But I would like to know your name so I can put it on your grave," Vashina explained, beginning to stalk in a circular motion again, her knife sheath full once more.

"I underestimated you again then. I would not think you were the type to dig an enemy's grave, let alone mark it," Pavilion said to her with a hint of respect in his voice.

"Do not get me wrong - normally I would not," Vashina responded. "But you are a worthy opponent, and that is something I respect."

Pavilion smiled and nodded. "Well Vashina," he said with a wink, "My name is Pavilion." He gave a slight bow, letting his Gift flow through his body - at the ready.

"I shall tell anyone I meet who knew you where they can find you to pay their respects," she said and then launched the two blades in her hands at him.

He easily avoided the blades with a quick side step and drew both of his well-used scimitars and charged forward. His blades deflected a barrage of her viciously thrown knives as he cleared the short distance. The blades slashed in a scissor motion. Vashina jumped back, the tips of his blades missing her throat only by a finger-span. Before Pavilion could bring his blades in again, Vashina was in the opening of his arms, her knee found his groin and her elbow found his nose. He stumbled back - stunned - and again caught off guard by the attack. He had no time to react when he saw her foot kick up under his chin, lifting him off the ground and onto his back.

"Come on Pavilion - I know you can do better than that," she teased stepping away from him. "Stop underestimating me - it will get you killed!"

Pavilion got to his feet, pushing aside the pain from his groin and face, never letting his eyes stray from hers. Never in his life had something like this happened. He had underestimated her twice now and by rights should be dead had she chosen to, but she was making a point first.

He was back in his stance now and spat the blood from his mouth - putting one of his swords back in its sheath - thinking it might be wise to have a free hand with this one. He stared hard into her eyes - they were remarkably beautiful, full of energy and glimmered with life. He stepped forward in a rush, his sword down low, ready to sweep upward, his other hand slipped behind his back at the last moment, freeing one of his many hidden daggers. She stepped to the side and spun in a circle, dodging his sword and coming around hard with her own dagger in hand. She had taken her eyes off him for a second - and in that time, he had pulled his dagger. He ducked down low as her knife swung in high for a fatal blow to his neck. His dagger cut in deep on her right thigh, and the hilt of his sword slammed in hard in her abdomen sending her off balance. Soon he was behind her - he kicked his leg out, catching her in the back of the knees sending her forward to the ground.

"Well, well Pavilion, that is what I want to see," she moaned, rolling over on her back staring at him, holding her side.

Before she could make another move, he had his sword to her neck. "Do not move or I will kill you," he told her sternly.

"Come now Pavilion, do you really believe you have the upper hand yet?" Vashina laughed, throwing her hand up releasing her innate Gift, a current blasted Pavilion back into a rock face. "Did I forget to mention I had the Gift?" She laughed bitterly sweet, getting to her feet and limping over to him, healing her leg as she went. By the time she was in front of him, the gash he left on her thigh was gone.

"I knew you had the Gift," Pavilion coughed, trying to recover his breath.

"If you knew then you should have known better than to play with me," she teased.

"Why?" Pavilion remarked.

Before Vashina could even form the first word, Pavilion's hands snapped up, throwing dirt and gravel into her face and his Gift made it all the worse, blowing her back half a dozen paces. Giving her no time to recover, he focused underneath her; the ground around her turned soft and muddy and she sank down to her shoulders as if she was standing on water. The ground then firmed again before she could begin to free herself.

Pavilion's victory was short lived, before he could finish her, a handful of arrows streaked down around him from a group of sentries coming to investigate the noise.

"'Til we meet again." Pavilion yelled back to her as he ran off into the darkness of night, vanishing like a ghost.

"I said we attack shortly!" Valka screamed at the massive warrior that stood before her.

"But need supplies, need more arrows, spears and better weapons to win fight," the warrior replied hoping his life would be spared.

Valka glared into the man's eyes, anger flaring through her. She wanted nothing more than to kill this simple-minded mass of muscle and sinew. But she knew it was not his fault - he was only telling her what she already knew but did not want to admit. It was true - their supplies had not been coming in lately and what they did have was fast depleting. Their main source of strong, crafted weapons and food were from Mandrake, but the refugees and the Lord of the castle had formed an army that continued hindering the supply trains. She had not expected Dragon's Cove to hold out this long, and now it seemed like it would take another half fortnight or more to wear them down. But they did not have enough supplies, not for an army this large and growing.

"Their Wizards must be exhausted after that vast display of their powers. Now is the time to attack, when they are weak and cannot help." Valka reasoned.

"We have other problems, too many warriors die before they get to fighting. Have to climb over dead comrades to make it to walls before we can fight," the brute added, seeing that he would live another day.

Valka paced her tent for a while deep in thought, considering the brute's words. Yes, he was right, she knew better than to doubt this one, he had fought in many battles and in some, and he had even been the one to tip the scales to victory.

"I understand. How many wounded are there that cannot fight again?' Valka asked, a plan forming in her evil mind.

The warrior cocked an eye at her. "What you thinking?"

"We need time to replenish our supplies do we not? And we need to clear the field of the dead," she cooed. "And how do we dispose of the dead?" she asked.

"We burn them," the man said, his face beaming with understanding.

"Hey Dan, you think we can hold the wall and win this war now that the enemy has their Gifted involved?" a young burly soldier asked his friend while they patrolled a part of the southern side.

"I do not know Mick, I sure as hell hope—," Dan started to reply but stopped short, staring off into the night.

"What the heck is going on out there?" Mick muttered. "Are we under attack?"

"I do not know, but we had better sound the alarm - this cannot be good." Dan ran off to ring one of the large warning bells.

"How many are coming?" another soldier asked, running to the edge of the wall to see.

"I can only see a couple hundred at most, and they do not seem to be armed," Mick replied, squinting into the night.

"It has got to be some kind of trick or something," the soldier murmured, straining his eyes to see.

"What are they doing?" Mick questioned the veteran soldier. "It looks like they are throwing something every few steps."

Soon Dragon Cove's walls were alive with soldiers ready to fight back the enemy hordes once again, but battle had yet to break out.

"What in the Keeper's balls is going on out here?" Rift and Barkel both barked together.

"We do not know sir," came the reply.

"They are dumping something on all the bodies out there," Dan added.

"Maybe they are bringing their dead to life, to attack us," someone cried out, leading to whispers and murmurs from all over.

"Do not be stupid," Barkel barked out. "And even if they were bringing back the dead, we killed them once - we can do it again!" He cheered, raising a shout of appreciation from everyone, trying to keep their morale high.

"What do you make of this, Wizard?" Rift asked Antiel. Two soldiers were holding her up and bringing her to the wall to observe the oddity taking place.

"I do not know, but they are using their wounded and dying to do it. Once they are within range of our arrows, kill them," Antiel said weakly, and the two soldiers holding her up turned to bring her back to her bed. She was the only Wizard who was awake yet, but she was hardly able to help. If Dragon's Cove fell under an attack now, they would have no Wizards to help defend it for a time still.

Before Antiel had made it a few steps, the sky behind her lit up and all he could hear was the gasps and curses from everyone on the wall.

"Everyone inside! Shut and lock all doors and windows that lead outside," Rift ordered.

"Rift, what is happening out there?" Lady Jewel asked, watching people left and right stuff all the cracks and holes in the doors and windows with rags or wax.

"They had lit their dead ablaze with the aid of some sort of fuel. I think they intend to smoke us out," he informed her grimly.

"Will it work? We will be safe in here, will we not?" Jewel asked, getting a little frightened.

"As long as we can keep most of the smoke out, we should be fine," Rift replied.

"How long will it burn?" Uvael asked.

Rift stopped yelling orders for a moment and thought about it. "I do not know if you have seen the field of dead outside the castle walls, but I would say there are more than ten thousand dead out there. Most not far from the castle walls, which also means things are gonna get warm in here," Rift said.

"How long Rift?" Jewel asked.

"Well from our last reports, before the smell and smoke got too thick, they were adding to the blaze, throwing trees and anything that would burn to the pile. I would say it will burn hard and hot for two or three days, then smolder for another day or two before we could safely go out there," Rift answered, frustrated.

Jewel was now pacing the hallway, biting her lower lip. "But we will be safe in here right?'

"If we can keep the smoke out and stand the heat, then yes, I believe so," Rift said, already smelling the gut-wrenching stench of burning flesh. "They have forced us to a standstill for the time being - we cannot leave and they cannot come at us."

Talena's eyes slowly opened, and even though they were blurry, she knew the person she saw standing before her was Ursa.

"What happened to me?' she asked roughly, her throat was sore and dry.

"You almost died. That is what happened," Ursa told her. "You were hit with two arrows," he said, handing her a cup of water.

Ursa had only been awake for a little while and he still felt drained and weak - he had taken some Venenum once he had heard about what was happening outside. He wanted to be able to help if he was needed.

"All I remember is standing up there fighting, and then a wave of pain came over me so fast." She stopped and took a sip of the cool water.

"You are okay now," Ursa told her, true compassion in his voice. "You will need to be more careful out there - you are too valuable to risk like that."

Talena grimaced at the reminder. "I need to tell you something now." Ursa's brow raised in interest. "I knew Meath was taken. I am sorry I could not tell you, but you were needed here and if I had told you, you would have gone after Meath and then who knows what might have happened here." She put the water down and sat up in the soft bed.

"Why did they take him? Who took him? Where is he going?" Ursa asked, nearly pleading doing his best to suppress his rising anger.

"I truly do not know why he was taken - Solmis' vision was bleak on that. He was taken by a strong Wizard and a druid - they are from a place called Salvas, and that is where they are taking him," she finally told him, wishing she could express everything to him.

"Salvas? I have never heard of it." Ursa exclaimed, finally shaking his head as if it did not matter. "Where is Salvas?"

"To the northeast just past the boards into the wasteland not far inland from the Misty Sea," Talena told him. "I am not sure its exact location but he is still alive."

Ursa's mind raced and nearly overwhelmed him. He wanted to yell at her for not telling him earlier, yet reason held him in check. She knew things he did not and he had to trust in Solmis' plan. Meath was alive, and he now knew where he was going.

"What are you thinking, Ursa?' Talena asked, seeing his mind at work.

"We need to get out of here."

Pavilion stood perfectly still, camouflaged in a group of dark trees as a quad of scouts passed by him no more than an arm's reach away. Silent as death and as swiftly as the wind, Pavilion stepped out behind them, grabbing one that was lagging behind the others. Pavilion held his hand hard over the savage's mouth so he could not make a sound. In the same motion, he ran his dagger across the victim's throat. Before the dead barbarian hit the ground, Pavilion was gone again. The other three turned to investigate the noise of their comrade gurgling and thrashing on the ground. Before they could react, Pavilion's hand appeared out of nowhere, snatching another scout by the head and with a quick twisting motion, snapping his neck. The other two turned to see another one of their brethren fall lifelessly to the ground. They both looked around just in time to see their stalker upon them.

This was the fourth scouting party he had eliminated this night. He dragged the bodies off into the woods and did his best to hide the corpses. Day was fast approaching, and Pavilion still had much he wanted to accomplish.

He looked over to the clouds of smoke rolling to the west, though the wind was blowing east. The enemy Gifted were fuelling the flames and blowing the smoke straight at the castle.

Yes, he had a great deal to do before the sun came up. He was sure the priests and priestesses would be taking turns fueling the smoke and flames, which meant the ones who were resting would be vulnerable.

19

Prince Berrit sat in the study again, fidgeting with the gold ring on his right hand, listening to the ladies of Draco Kingdom, their eldest sons, General Miller and the castle's only remaining Wizard, Keithen. They had only just heard news of the siege that had befallen Dragon's Cove and a meeting was called to discuss reasonable a course of action. No suggestion went unscrutinized.

They had been in the study nearly half the day now and Berrit wanted nothing more than to show his true self and unleash his growing wrath upon the roomful of simple-minded fools. But no, he still had to play things with a step of caution - he could not risk such an act, not enough of the plan was in place to be so bold. He hoped Dragon's Cove would fall soon, but with there being four Wizards there to defend instead of the original two, he knew it would take longer to wear them down. It had been one of his main reason for sending Vashina, that and to ensure that conniving Priestess Valka did not betray them.

"What do you think about all this Prince Berrit?" Lady Tore asked knowing he had not being paying attention.

Berrit lifted his head and knew his expression betrayed his lack of awareness. He had been so caught up in his own thoughts that he had almost forgotten about the others around him.

"Yes, you have not made a single suggestion or comment this whole time Berrit, and we really would be interested in your opinion." Lady Angelina added.

"Well…" he started, kicking himself for not staying alert to the conversation but deciding to move forward with his plan regardless."Well, I believe we should send aid and quickly. They are in need and we have the resources to help. I still believe Lord Tundal made a horrible mistake by not sending more aid to Mandrake. Had he, it might not still be in the hands of the enemy and Dragons Cove might not be threatened now," he said with a hint of cruel intent toward Lady Tora. "It is apparent that the enemy has the means to take Dragons Cove with enough time if no outside force comes against them. If we lose two of Draco's strongholds, we will be forever weakened and may never win them back."

"Very insightful, Prince Berrit," Lady Tora replied with a bitter nip at his mention of her deceased husband.

"Do you think it wise to send our entire army to their aid leaving us vulnerable?" Lady Angelina asked. "That would make us very easy pickings."

"I agree with Prince Berrit," Ethan, Lady Angelina's eldest son piped in. "We need to send aid and fast!"

"Yes... I second that," Keithen agreed, though he doubted anyone was listening to him. "Prince Berrit knows what he is talking about."

"That would leave us defenseless!" Thoron argued.

"They would come to our aid if we needed it!" Ethan shouted across the table.

"Enough you two!" Tora barked to the two boys. "We have enough enemies. We do not need to be fighting among ourselves as well. If they take Dragon's Cove, it would only seem reasonable to assume they march for Drandor or Draco. We cannot be sure of which. My guess would be Drandor, since there has been very little enemy activity around these parts of late."

"They took Mandrake it is just a matter of time before they take Dragon's Cove if they do not get help, whether its Drandor or us next, we are in trouble," Prince Berrit replied. "If we send half our army to Dragon's Cove and messengers are sent to Drandor informing them to do likewise, as long as Dragon's Cove can hold the enemy until help arrives, the three armies should be able to crush them or in the very least force them to retreat."

"Again that leaves the problem of both strongholds weakened for invasion," General Miller stated.

"If all we do is hide behind our walls we will be no better off than Mandrake and Dragon's Cove are now, it will only be a matter of time before we too are overwhelmed. If the enemy is not opposed by a suitable army they will only grow in numbers - strength and confidence and all will be lost regardless," Berrit countered reasonably. He knew there was little hope for them now - the army that occupied Mandrake and the army that now laid siege against Dragon's Cove were in the tens of thousands. And with the Priestesses and Priests revealing themselves and taking part, the defenders were doomed.

"He is right," Angelina said, though everyone could tell it pained her to do so. "Prince Berrit is right. If we stand by and do nothing but hide in hopes to preserve our own lives, it will only be a matter of time before we too crumble against their sheer numbers. Not to mention our friends, loved ones and our countrymen need us and here we have the audacity to even think of leaving them to fend for themselves." There was a shameful silence, as her words sunk in with the bitterness of truth.

"I do not get how this is all happening? How could they possibly be doing all this? How did they know we were weak and unprepared? How did they know?" Thoron asked, frustrated.

"Turn of luck in their favor or maybe Ursa and his whelp Meath were working with them, informing them every step of the way?" Berrit answered snidely.

"That is a filthy lie!" Lady Tora screamed rising to her feet peering over the polished table at Berrit. "Ursa would never work with them, ever!"

"Is it?" Berrit replied raising an eyebrow. "Does it not strike you as odd that ever since Ursa kidnapped the Princess and escaped from the castle the enemy seems to have the upper hand? Master Ursa knows every castle's weaknesses and strengths - he also knows how many Wizards and what they are capable of doing," Berrit explained. "Do you really think those mindless savages are capable of doing what they have done without the aid of someone like that?"

Again the room was still with an awkward silence as the possibility of truth was digested from Berrit's troubling words.

"I cannot believe it," General Miller growled. "I will not believe it! You are a filthy whoreson Zandorian and the very same could be said of you. Ever since you stepped foot in these walls everything began happening..."

"General!" Lady Angelina snapped sternly stopping him in mild sentence. "Mind your tongue General." General Miller inhaled back his rage and tried to compose himself with all the strength he could muster.

"Maybe it is best if you take leave for a moment to recompose yourself General," Tora told him and he bitterly agreed, muttering curses as he went. "We do not want to believe any of it but we have to take into consideration the possibility of it being truth."

"I know you do not care to believe what I witnessed in King Borrack's bedchamber that dark night when he was murdered, but I saw what I saw," Berrit began. "Further proof, Ursa was tracked to Darnan and several of his belongings found in a man's home who has known dealings with many shady people from around the world. Who is to say some of those dealings would not be with the savages themselves? So long as they get what they seek, do you think men like that care who they deal with? I know I am Zandorian and we have been enemies for countless years in the past. But in coming here, the purpose of marrying the fair Princess Nicolette was to unite our Kingdoms and set aside our many differences. Was it not? Foul times have befallen Draco Kingdom - worse than anything we could have ever imagined - but I am only trying to help where I see reason. You hold biases against me for who I am, and that I can understand, but you are also blind to what Ursa has clearly done. The facts are in front of you - you hold your country's fate in your hands."

"We have strayed from the real issue - we need to concentrate on what we must do now, with the troubles at hand. Past transgressions will not help us with what needs to be done now," Tora reminded them all, not wanting to go down this road yet again.

"First we will need to put Draco Castle on alert and begin readying our defenses and offenses, so we will not be caught off guard like Mandrake and Dragon's Cove," General Miller interrupted as he made his way back to the table.

"Thank you Miller, that is a good place to start, we will leave that in your capable hands," Lady Angelina replied, glad to see that he had come back.

"I might be able to go one step further," General Miller added. "Send out emissaries into the city to recruit all men of age who are willing to stand with the army. In return, they and their families will be accommodated for in the army camps outside the city limits. That will lessen the hordes of refugees that plague our city streets."

"I will have emissaries sent out this very day," Lady Tora answered. "We still have heard no word back on whether Lord Dagon has been found. I suggest we send out another group to find him."

"Prince Berrit, I wonder if you would be so kind to send word to your father - King Dante - on matters regarding our troubles." Lady Angelina asked. "Any aid he could provide us in our desperate time would be forever appreciated and would greatly strengthen our bonds of friendship."

"It shall be done." Berrit nodded. "It shames me to have not done so further - my apologies."

Astaroth sat in a bath in his private quarters, irritation fumed from him like the steam from his bath. He cursed himself for not being able to make everything fall into place as he had originally planned. Ursa's interference and then his escape had forced serious alterations that were far from secure. He focused his Gift on the large brass tub he was submerged in; the water began heating up, reddening his skin to nearly an unbearable tint. He gasped in both pain and exhilaration until he could take no more, a minor alteration of thought and he cooled the water just as quickly.

He had his senses on full alert, knowing there was still another assassin out there waiting to strike. How he wanted that assassin to show himself now, so he could take his frustrations out. He hoped the assassin would follow him this night, when he went to make sure none of the messengers made it far. He hoped these would put up more of a fight than the last - how he did love it when people tried, only to fail against him. He sank down into the tub submerging his whole body, either way he would get some satisfaction out of this night.

Astaroth watched the messengers leave the city and down the eastern road toward Mandrake. He smiled wide - they were traveling together for the first part of the trip and would split in a few days when the road forked off toward Drandor. Of course, it was wise to do so - there was safety in numbers, but this night it would not serve them well.

He waited for them now in plain view on the road in the form of Prince Berrit. It would give him the element of surprise and throw his prey off until he revealed his true nature and intentions. Normally he would not be so daring as to toy with men he simply needed to kill, but this night he needed release - and how he loved to see the glistening of terror in his victim's eyes.

"Who goes there?" The lead rider called out as the group slowed their mounts. They neared the stranger and formed a semicircle across the road, their hands cautiously on their sword hilts.

"Prince Berrit, is that you?" another rider asked, walking his mount forward to get a better look.

"It is I," Berrit replied, keeping his head down.

"My Lord, what are you doing out here this late?" the lead rider asked, his voice riddled with confusion. "It is dangerous out here at night."

"There is a problem with your mission," Berrit answered, his tone hardening, "that I needed to inform you about."

"Really?" the second rider asked. "What might that be my Lord?"

Berrit lifted his head, his eyes locking with the lead rider's. "The problem is I cannot let you accomplish it!" he hissed as he revealed his true identity.

"Keeper's balls!" the lead rider cursed.

"It is a demon!" another cried out as they all drew their swords.

A sadistic smile grew on Astaroth's face as the first rider charged in, sword poised to strike. Astaroth stood perfectly calm as the rider closed the gap. Once the rider was steps away, a rocky spike shot up from the earth beneath the mount and tore into the beast's belly and back. It stopped the horse dead in its tracks, throwing its rider face first into the hard ground in front of Astaroth.

Astaroth knew he could not afford to let any of them escape now; with a mere thought, a wall of blistering flames erupted from behind the riders, blocking any thought of retreat. The rider on the ground pushed himself up to look at Astaroth just in time to witness an ice shard flying towards him, ending his life.

Three messengers dismounted and rushed Astaroth, their blades leading the way while two others fumbled loading their crossbows. The final three riders were not so courageous and searched the flaming wall frantically for a way free.

Astaroth stepped in the fray of hastily swung blades, easily sidestepping and evading the terrified men's attacks. He danced through the wild swings and mad thrusts methodically lining them up. Finally, one man rushed forward and stabbed for Astaroth's chest. Expecting the attack, Astaroth spun out of the way just in time to see the charging man impale one of his comrades. Shock stole the man's instinct to fight as he watched the life fade from his friend's eyes.

Astaroth turned back to see his plan had worked and grinned wickedly. A roar alerted him to the third attacker - he stepped into the man's high swing catching his arms before he could bring them down with any real force. Fire sprang to life in Astaroth's hands, searing and blistering the man's wrists causing him to release his sword and cry out in anguish. Astaroth kneed the man viciously in the midsection doubling him over. He wished he could see the terror on the messenger's face as an earthen spear protruded in-between them. He forced the messenger down onto it, nearly severing his head clean off.

Astaroth's keen ears heard two clicks and he knew two bolts had been released. He spun himself sideways, the first bolt shot by missing his chest by a finger's span - the second bolt tore into his cheek as it grazed by him. He stared at the wet blood that dripped into his hand and his angered flared almost uncontrollably, not because of the pain, but because they had made him bleed. He marched towards the two bowmen and stopped momentarily to snap the neck of the poor fool who had killed his comrade and nearly tore the man's head off with frightening strength. The two men threw down their crossbows knowing they would not be able to reload in time and drew their swords nervously.

The man on the right raised his sword, stepped forward a thunderous blast of power ripped him from his feet and sent him sprawling to the earth in a bloody heap of gore and twisted limbs.

The man on the left turned to the three messengers frantically trying to escape the wall of flames. "Come on you cowards, to arms!" He turned back to face his enemy just as a blade ran across his throat spilling his lifeblood onto the already crimson earth.

Two of the messengers, knowing their fate if they tried to fight their way clear, risked the Wizard's fire. Their horrific screams of agony from the other side stopped the final man from making a similar mistake. He turned to see Astaroth glaring coldly at him. He unstrapped his battle-axe from his side and tossed it to the ground knowing it would not help him - he was no fighter.

"How pathetic, you will suffer most of all!" Astaroth hissed, stepping forward, his hands alive with Wizards' fire. Before he could take another step, the ground shuddered and a rift tore open right beneath his feet - had he been any slower, he would have been swallowed up in the crevice. He scrambled frantically digging his fingers into the edge desperately.

He pulled himself out just in time to see the messenger disappear into the growth of the jungle. He rolled to his feet and made to follow when a current of air smashed into him throwing him end over end until he came to rest a dozen paces away.

The racing beat of horses' hooves grew closer and Astaroth knew he could not defeat the newcomers on these terms. He cursed in defeat as he darted into the growth after the messenger.

Astaroth sat in his chambers frustrated and angry with himself as he drained a cup of wine in a single gulp. He had not found the escaped messenger and he wondered if the man would return to the castle and reveal his secret. He would have to be fully alert of everyone now.

His powers were weakened - he had used a lot of strength this night dispatching the messengers, keeping the wall of Wizard's fire up the entire time had taken more out of him than he would have liked to admit. He hated knowing his limits and could not wait until he had none.

Astaroth fidgeted with the gold ring on his hand - he had to preserve what strength he had left in case he had to alter his features into the Prince again this night. He marveled at the enchanted ring on his finger, what a magnificent item he had acquired, even if it did have its limitations. When the ring knew the blood of someone, it allowed its Gifted wearer to alter their features into that person for as long as they had the energy to maintain the enchantment. The ring's only flaw was it could only hold the imagine of two at a time.

"Bastard rogue Wizards!" Astaroth muttered pouring himself another cup of the wine when a knock at his door interrupted his contemplations. His heart raced at the thought of who might be at his door. Had the messenger come back and exposed him? Were there a score of armed guards waiting on the other side of his chamber door? The thought unnerved him - had he not been in such a weakened state he might have enjoyed such a fight, but not now.

"Who is it?" he called out, his form altering to that of Berrit.

"It is Keithen, your Highness," a voice replied nervously.

Berrit opened the door slowly - almost expecting it to be a ruse. "What do you want?" he asked the young Wizard bitterly.

"I am sorry to disturb you, but I was sent to come inform you that your presence is requested," Keithen stuttered sheepishly.

Berrit frowned in annoyance. "Why? What is it now?" he questioned. "I am sure whatever it is can wait until morning." He began to shut the door.

"Two Wizards have shown up to the castle and they say they have important news."

Berrit's eyes lit up, pulling the door open again. "I will be down in a moment."

"I am glad you could join us Prince Berrit, and I am sorry it is such a late hour," Lady Tora said once Berrit was in his seat.

"Yes, well, I wanted to see them for myself, so I know who to watch out for," Berrit muttered, playing his Zandorian part, but really he was there to see how much they knew.

"Their names are Master Samul and Master Mervyn!" Lady Angelina snapped angrily at him.

"Yes, and they have some very interesting and could be important information," Tora cut in, not wanting those two to cause a scene in front of their newly arrived guests.

Berrit rolled his eyes, "and what is that?"

"On our way here to help at the beckon of Lord Tundal, we ran across a powerful Wizard massacring your messengers not far from the city this very night," one of the Wizards answered.

Berrit glared over at the very tall man as if annoyed that he spoke. He knew these two were going to hinder his plans a lot more than what they already had. "I see, well did you kill this Wizard and save our poor messengers?" Berrit asked snidely.

"He got away from us unfortunately and as far as we know he killed all of the messengers. We did not get there until the end and had no idea what was going on until it was too late," the other shorter and plumper Wizard put in.

"If the two of you could not even save a few simple messengers, how do you plan on helping a whole kingdom that is slipping into a chaotic war?" Berrit mocked. He was beginning to feel faint and nauseated as his powers weakened from keeping the façade of the Prince.

"Why you arrogant fool, I ought to…!" the shorter Wizard burst out in rage.

"Calm yourself Samul," Mervyn said, putting a hand on the shorter Wizard's shoulder to stop him from stepping forward.

"Are you muttering threats to a Prince?" Berrit barked, rising from his seat to look threatening.

"We cannot expect Prince Berrit to understand our full abilities in times of war," Mervyn said to Samul but his gaze was locked onto Berrit's. "I assure you good Prince that we will be of great value to Draco in this war."

"Maybe it was not wise to have woken you at such an hour Prince Berrit," Tora commented, trying hard to hold back her rising anger. "Maybe on the morrow you will remember your manners and where you stay."

Berrit glanced around the room biting back a vicious retort. Had it not been for his weakening state he would have unleashed his tongue upon them, but this provided him with means to excuse himself. "I apologize - sometimes I forget myself. I will take my leave before my lack of manners can offend further."

After the Zandorian Prince had left, Tora told them in a sympathetic and somewhat embarrassed tone, "I apologize for the way Prince Berrit acted."

"Do not apologize for the words of that man, my Lady," Master Mervyn said with a wink of understanding.

"We do appreciate your coming to our aid," Lady Angelina said earnestly.

"No need for thanks - the land is festering with enemies, our homes are in danger. The only way any of us can prevent this is to stand together," Samul replied.

"What can you tell us of this Wizard? Do you think he is still around and a threat to us? Is he a rogue just acting on his own, or is he working with the barbarians?" Lady Tora asked, getting back to the many issues.

"That is a good question my Lady," Mervyn replied. "I believe this Wizard may be a threat to us, he was indeed powerful and did not have the demeanor of a rogue. No, this one was different, I am not sure if he is working with the enemy or not or even if he was part of the Shyroni."

"Well it is late Master Mervyn and Master Samul, rooms have been made ready for you. Rest well and we will further discuss this on the morrow when we are all rested and focused," Lady Tora said with a light bow of her head.

Astaroth laid upon his silken bed, sleep eluding him as his mind raced at this new problem that had come to the castle. These two Wizards were going to make things very difficult. He needed to dispose of them before they interfered with anything more. His lust and greed for power told him to kill them and steal their Gifts. They were both skilled and powerful and would swell his own powers immensely. But they were not foolish Wizards like many he had dealt with before - no these two were hardened, well-travelled and sharp of wit. It would be no simple task to deal with them. If need be, he would send them with the army to Dragon's Cove. The thought only lasted a moment. No, Dragon's Cove should have fallen by now, but with four Wizards defending it, they had enough problems without adding two more. He would find a way—he always did.

Astaroth stretched out in the large bed, and felt a pang of loneliness at its emptiness. He wished Vashina was here with him - she had a quick wit about her and could always see flaws within his plans ...if there were any. But more so this night he relished in the thought of her warm flesh between his loins and the exotic pleasures she offered. The thought of all her sexual fetishes stirred his blood and he almost thought to go find a whore to release those stirrings, but it was much too late for that.

He slept in late the next morning, as late as he could justify without causing suspicions at his unusual tardiness to make an appearance. He needed his Gift to be replenished fully if he were to undertake this task of removing the two Wizards. He did well to find excuses for hibernating in his room for most of the day so he could stay in his true form and conserve his energies. He ventured out only a handful of times so he would be seen by others so they would not believe he had become ill and come to tend to him. He also wanted to take measure of the new guests.

Astaroth was not conceited enough to believe that he was invincible, simply because he had absorbed the essence of eight Wizards. These two Wizards were over twice his age and that meant wisdom and more battle experience and those two things were never to be taken lightly as he knew well from his youth.

Again, a knock at his door stirred him from his thoughts - he had been expecting this knock, since he had hardly been out of his room all day, they had sent someone to check on him.

Berrit opened the door to see the young Wizard Keithen standing there again. "Yes, what do you want now?" Berrit snarled, enjoying the flinch from the young Wizard.

"Sorry to bother you again, I just wanted to make sure you were all right or needed anything," Keithen stuttered nervously having a hard time making eye contact.

"What did you say?' Berrit asked off guard. "You want to know if I am all right?"

Keithen looked at him sheepishly. "Yes Highness, I know it sounds odd, but I believe you, about Ursa and Meath and all that, and I know you are the only one who can save us in this time of need," he told him with growing enthusiasm. "I know you are Zandorian and I am a Wizard, but I want you to know I am with you. Anything you need just ask and if it is within my powers it shall be done." Keithen finished with a weak smile.

A smile slithered across Berrit's face. "Yes well thank you, I think you might have helped curve my opinion of those with The Gift," he replied as his mind raced with new possibilities at this opening door. Keithen was about to walk off but Berrit stopped him in his tracks. "You know there is something you could do for me."

"Anything Highness, anything at all," Keithen replied with a big grin.

"Well I am feeling terrible about last night and how I treated those two Wizards who are only trying to help," Berrit said, trying to sound truthful. "I want you to find out what kind of wine or ale they like most. I would like to sit down with them and have a drink and apologize like a man for my impudence," He finished.

"Yes Highness!" Keithen saluted.

"Do not let them know that it is me who wants to know. I want them to be surprised," Berrit explained. After Keithen confirmed his understanding, he ran off to see it done.

Astaroth shut his door chuckling wickedly - the perfect plan played through his mind. He walked over to his desk and pulled out a pouch of rare, enchanted white powder. He had only acquired a few handfuls in his time and that was better than most ever saw - most would pay a king's ransom just for this amount. He had been saving it for when he would need it most. Now seemed that time - if he were going to make his plan work, he could not afford any more hindrances and once he had these two Wizard's Gifts, he would be that much more unstoppable.

Early the next morning, Keithen was back eagerly at his door with the information he required.

"Well Highness, I have good and bad information for you," Keithen began. "Master Samul enjoys sweet Blackberry wine, but Master Mervyn says he never drinks for it clouds one's judgments."

This did not come to much of a surprise to Astaroth - he had known many Wizards who did not drink or only drank a little because of such reasons.

"Excellent!" Berrit replied enthusiastically. "You have done me well Keithen - you have my gratitude."

"It was nothing your Highness," Keithen boasted, with pride.

Berrit mused over this prideful eagerness. "Could I trouble you for one more favor then Keithen?"

Keithen beamed with excitement. "Anything...anything at all!"

Berrit fished into his coin purse, retrieved two silver, and handed them to Keithen. "Find me a bottle of the best blackberry wine and bring it to me."

"Right away Highness!" Keithen replied gleefully as he started off.

"Keithen!" Berrit called down the hallway.

"Yes good Prince?"

"Whatever coin is left is yours to keep, for your time."

"Thank you so much," Keithen stuttered back and then took off down the hallway again.

Berrit returned to his room and locked his door, allowing his form to return to its natural state. He had expected it would not be so easy to dispose of Master Mervyn. He had a rare aura about him, a lot like Ursa, which Astaroth knew to be very dangerous. But Samul on the other hand would be easy to take care of if he could play it out appropriately. He picked up the pouch of powder again wondering how much he would need to make his plan work. He would need some left to deal with Master Mervyn when the time came.

Astaroth stood alone in one of the farthest corners of the castle's royal garden, where no one could see anything and few ever ventured. He had sent Keithen to fetch Master Samul at his request.

Now Astaroth waited in the form of Prince Berrit for Samul to arrive. He had to play the part perfectly if he was to fool the Wizard into believing his apology so he would have a drink with him. Astaroth had no true idea how much of the wine Samul would have to drink to inebriate his Gift. He had used enough of the powder he hoped to ensure that even with only a few sips, the effects would take hold.

"Prince Berrit, I would never have guessed it was you who wanted audience with me," Samul said, walking over to the bench by the small pond where Berrit stood waiting.

Berrit turned to face Samul with a shy and honest smile. "Yes well I…" Berrit coughed, playing the part flawlessly. "I wanted to… apologize for the way I acted when you first arrived," he refined and at that moment, a feather could have knocked Samul over.

"Well Prince Berrit this does come as a surprise, but you really do not need to…" Samul began but was cut off.

"No I do - I know this must come as a shock to you, a Royal Zandorian apologizing to a Wizard, but it is true. I have been under a lot of stress with the death of King Borrack and the kidnapping of my bride and now with war breaking out all over Draco Kingdom. I almost forgot what this was all about - I agreed to marry the Princess and set our old ways aside and begin a new union of trust and friendship. It is just with everything that is happening my mind had been clouded and my judgment off and for that I must apologize."

Samul listened to Berrit's words carefully and truly felt the emotion coming from the Zandorian. "I do understand your rare position - the past season has been rather vile for everyone and has everyone on edge," Samul replied. "You know Prince Berrit, I almost misjudged you, but now I see I was wrong - I accept your apology," he said with a wide, friendly smile.

"Do sit and have a glass of Blackberry wine with me Master Samul," Berrit asked, knowing if he refused, he would have to act fast. "So we may bury the old into the past and start a new kinship with similar purpose."

"Blackberry wine you say?" Samul asked, licking his lips. "Well my good Prince you have twisted my arm just right - how could I say no to my favorite drink?"

Samul sat down on the bench beside Berrit and took the cup of sweet smelling and even sweeter tasting liquor. He held it in his hands for a moment savoring the aroma and waiting for Berrit to pour his own cup.

"To new beginnings and to smiting our forever growing enemies!" Berrit toasted, bringing his cup to his lips and pretending to drink deeply from it. He did not know how the wine tasted and hoped Samul would not notice anything different.

"I will toast to that," Samul said, drinking from his cup and finishing it off in two greedy gulps. "That is mighty fine wine - might I have another good Prince?" Samul asked, holding his cup to Berrit who filled it again eagerly.

"To lasting peace between us at long last," Samul toasted, and again Berrit faked a drink while Samul downed his cup.

Berrit did not know how long it would take to dispel the Gift. He did not want to try anything until he was sure, and Samul did not seem to have a problem drinking more. After another two cups, Samul tipped his glass upside down, showing Berrit he had had enough.

"I do thank you Prince Berrit for the words and even more the wine, and I am glad you called me out here and we have resolved matters, but I must depart, there is still much Master Mervyn and I need to learn and prepare," Samul said, with a hint of a slur from the wine as its strong effects began to take effect.

"Before you go, do you think you could do me but a small favor?" Berrit asked, prepared to do what he must if his plan did not work.

"Of course I could - what do you need of me?" Samul said with a jolly smile.

"Could you light this torch for me, I think I am going to stay out here for a while and enjoy the fresh night air," Berrit said holding up a torch.

"Indeed I could," Samul said, waving his hand over the torch, his eyes bulged wide and he buckled to his knees, a groan of distress escaping his lips.

Berrit smiled wide knowing his plan had worked. "Well, seems your Gift is no longer working for you."

Samul looked up at Berrit, his eyes betraying his terror. "What is happening? What did you do to me you Zandorian cur?" he groaned out fighting back waves of pain and nausea.

Berrit grinned - his appearance shifting into his true form, "and here I thought we were becoming friends and then you have to resort to name calling."

"By all that is unholy, who are you?" Samul bellowed, trying to push himself upright. He got a hard kick to the guts for his efforts - he collapsed to the ground and vomited.

"You really should not have interfered last night, you and Mervyn allowed one of the messengers to escape," Astaroth growled, kicking Samul in the ribs flipping him over onto this back.

Samul coughed violently nearly choking on the vomit that still escaped from his mouth. "Why… why are you doing this?"

"Because I can." Astaroth's grin was full of malice as he stomped his foot down hard across Samul's face, silencing the plump Wizard. Astaroth sat down on the bench and stared down at his unconscious victim. "That was far easier then I had anticipated," he mused.

Keithen crouched behind a large rose bush many paces away, wide eyed at the treachery he had just witnessed. He watched in terror and awe as the man who was once Prince Berrit bound Master Samul's hands behind his back and carried him down a grown in path leading toward one of the lesser used cellars in the castle.

Fear coursed through every part of him - he had been so close to this man so many times and did not have the slightest clue about his true nature. But now he knew the truth - everything started to fall into place from the murder of King Borrack to Ursa, Meath and the Princess fleeing from the castle - they too must have stumbled across the truth.

Instinctively, when it was safe, he got his feet and was about to run and tell everyone, but something stopped him before he could go more than a few steps. It was not fear, it was intrigue - something told Keithen to somehow use this to his advantage. Ursa had never truly believed in him and had spent all of his time and efforts in Meath. But now, this man, this devious Wizard, obviously knew how to use the Gift better than most. He could teach Keithen everything in exchange for keeping his secret. Yes it would work - he just needed to do it right. He knew if he just strolled up to the Wizard and told him, he would be as good as dead. Keithen needed to find something to gain the Wizard's trust, or even some edge over him so this he would not be killed.

Keithen followed Astaroth from a distance making sure not to be seen or heard, which since he had spent most of his life behind these walls was not hard for him. Keithen hugged the circular stone stairwell that lead down into one of the coldest cellars, which they only used in the winter to keep wild meat frozen. He watched from around a corner as Astaroth chained Master Samul to one of the stone walls.

"What is he doing?" Keithen whispered to himself.

Astaroth paced in front of the limp form of Samul hanging from the stone wall. How pathetic he looked, so weak and meager - thankfully outward appearance had nothing to do with the strength of one's innate powers.

Astaroth snapped the riding crop across Samul's legs cutting thick lacerations into them and causing Samul to cry out at the painful awakening.

"Who are you?" Samul spat. "And what do you want with me you bastard?"

Astaroth snapped the whip across Samul's midsection causing the Wizard to wince in pain but this time he did not cry out. "That is an easy question to answer - I want your inner essence, your Gift."

Samul's eyes went wide with horror. "You are a mad man! It is not possible!"

"Are you so sure about that?" Astaroth countered.

"There are only superstitions, myths nothing more you halfwit." Samul protested. "There is no proof it is even possible."

Astaroth smirked maliciously. "I beg to differ, it is very possible - I have done it many times already."

"Why? Why would you do all of this - the King's death, the plotting and pretending to be the Prince, helping the barbarians, why?" Samul asked angrily. "What are you getting out of all this?"

"What do I get?" Astaroth cracked the whip across his victim's legs again. "I get to become the closest thing to a God this world has ever seen."

Keithen watched in utter horror and amazement for what seemed like forever while Astaroth tortured and mutilated Samul. Burning him with strange symbols and cutting other symbols into his flesh, collecting his blood and drinking it. By the end of the ritual, the stone room was alive with vivid power. Even someone without the Gift would feel the raw energy in the air if they were to stumble upon this place.

Keithen watched as Astaroth burned the last symbol into Samul's forehead, and ran a blade across his throat, filling a silver goblet with the thick blood and drinking it greedily. The goblet hit the ground, Astaroth and Samul's bodies began contorting, and thrashing violently and Keithen could see Samul's essence being pulled unwillingly from his dying body into Astaroth's. As fast as it had begun, it was over and Astaroth lay unmoving on the cold stone floor. The air shifted uncomfortably back to cold and damp, like the feeling of death.

Keithen watched as Astaroth began to get up slowly, but yet seemed stronger, firmer and more defined. Yes, Keithen could see that Astaroth had truly taken Samul's essence. This was something he wanted - this was the man he wanted as his mentor and Master.

"Teach me to be like you, I will do anything you ask of me!" Keithen blurted out stepping around the corner he had been hiding behind, catching Astaroth completely off guard.

Dagon stood on a hillside not far from where he and his men were camped - he watched the sun rise from the east. It had been almost a week since the battle he and less than half his men had escaped from and still he thought about how he could have done things differently and how they might have won that fight. Dagon knew how he could have saved more, he should have retreated as soon as he saw the ruse for what it was, but he had not, he could not - his pride had gotten the best of him. He just wanted to make those murdering bastards pay for taking his home.

"I knew I would find you out here," Jarroth called, coming up behind him. "Stop beating yourself up over the past - what has happened has happened. I do not blame you - the men do not blame you," Jarroth told him, knowing exactly what was on his friends mind. "Chances are, none of us would have retreated any sooner than we did regardless of your order."

Dagon did not say anything - he could not. He kept staring off at the sunrise.

"Our scouts have spotted a small band of enemy moving toward Mandrake castle from the northern shore. We plan on attacking them long before they can make it," Jarroth explained. "You should come with us my Lord - it would do your blade good to taste enemy blood again," he called back as he made his way back to camp.

Dagon sighed once Jarroth was gone - he knew his friend's words were true. He had lost battles before, lost many good men to war...friends and family. No it was not that - it was because of why he lost that was haunting him. His pride had gotten in the way - his pride had killed those men. Too much had happened in the last season for anyone to handle without fault.

"My Lord!" a soldier called up to him.

"What is it?" Dagon replied, not even turning to face the soldier.

"There is a Zandorian messenger here with news from the south."

"Take me to him now!" Dagon gasped.

"What news do you have from the south?" Dagon cried, not even waiting for his horse to slow before he jumped off and began running toward the messenger.

"Well my Lord, one of your messengers made it to Besha and told Lord Andras of your crisis. There is an army of six hundred hardened warriors and supplies, two or three days march away," the messenger informed him.

"Thank the Creator," Dagon gasped. "When you return to Besha, please tell your Lord I send many thanks."

"You will be able to bestow your thanks to him personally. He and his eldest son are the ones leading the army," the Zandorian informed him.

Dagon's eyes lit up with possibility. "Get this man anything he requires!" Dagon ordered, marching off with growing power in each step, something he had not had in days, but now the weight of failing was lifting with this new turn of events.

That evening, Lord Dagon and his men feasted as best they could in celebration of their small victory, which Lord Dagon had gone along for and lead his men as a true leader should always do. But they mostly celebrated because they knew in a few days an army would come to their aid. There was no ale or wine at the small feast, for alcohol was something none of them had seen in weeks. Even if there had been, not a man would have indulged - they all needed their senses at their best.

"It is good to see you again," Jarroth told Dagon as the evening began to tone down.

"I am sorry my friend for my foolishness, your words did help even if it did not look like it - thank you for not giving up on me," Dagon replied.

"I never have." Jarroth laughed clasping Dagon's hand firmly. "And I never will."

"We will see that our home is returned and force those bastards back to the wasteland where they belong," Dagon shouted, getting a cheer from everyone around him.

"An army of six hundred strong might not be enough to take our home back my Lord," Jarroth said, not wishing to kill the mood but knowing it needed to be said.

"I know, but it is a start," Dagon told him, not letting anything damper his good mood.

"Sir. Sir," a young soldier yelled running up to him.

"What is it?" Dagon asked, giving the man his full attention.

"There is another messenger here," he gasped.

"Ah, well give him food and water and a place to sleep tonight, but we have already heard the good news," Dagon said cheerfully.

"No my Lord - this man is not from the south. He says he is from Draco Castle," the soldier told him trying to keep his voice low. "He was found wandering the woods almost dead with exhaustion."

Dagon entered the small tent where the ragged man had been given quarters. Dagon could see this man had important news to tell him - he could feel it in the air, making his skin tingle with anticipation.

"What news do you bring from Draco? Do they send as army to aid us?" Dagon asked.

The messenger's eye's opened slowly to see Dagon. "No my Lord - Draco Castle is in need of you," he whispered, not able to speak any louder.

"In need of me? What for?" Confused, Dagon kneeled down closer to hear the man.

"Prince Berrit is not who he appears to be," he wheezed out. "He is a Wizard."

"What? This does not make sense; this cannot be true," Dagon muttered in disbelief. "You are tired and weak - you are talking tales not truths. Come speak with me when you are well," Dagon said, about ready to leave, but the man grabbed him.

"I know what I saw my Lord! Heed my words - Draco Castle needs you," he cried out in desperation.

"Why is not Lord Tundal doing anything about this? Why did you not tell him all this? He would be able to handle this if this heeds true," Dagon argued, beginning to think the man mad.

"Tundal is dead!" The messenger barked.

"What?" Dagon said sternly, his attention completely with the man again.

"He was murdered by an assassin, but I now believe he found out the truth of Berrit and then was killed to prevent him from telling anyone," he said slowly. "Now the ladies are trying to run the kingdom but things are just getting worse. This country is falling apart at the seams. You are the only one who can resort it."

"Rest now my good man - we will talk more tomorrow when you can tell me everything you know at length," Dagon told him, leaving the small tent.

It was almost too much for Dagon to bea - yet he knew the man was not lying. The man's eyes showed no sign of falsehoods. Dagon's family was at Draco Castle and so was the family of his dead friend, and if all of this was true, they were in danger - everyone was in danger. Dagon knew he had to return to Draco Castle and straighten this out before it was too late, the kingdom was falling apart, war was everywhere, and Draco was the only strong point left. He knew what he had to do....

20

They traveled for several long days, finding numerous signs that they were on the trail of Meath and his two Gifted captors. They had stumbled across several large old tribal camp sites. Shania was sure they were heavily armed war parties on the move, travelling west. It gave them all an ill feeling that something horrible was going to happen soon, but they were too far committed to think of turning back now.

Since their desperate death-defying swim across the Sheeva River, they had managed to avoid their attackers - they were not even sure if they were being followed or if they were thought to be dead. But on several occasions, they had to lie low while savage groups had traveled by, but they had managed to avoid all detection. With Shania along, they had little trouble finding food and fresh water, and had learned many tricks that she had when growing up in her barbarian tribe.

"Look up ahead," Dahak said, pointing to the northeast. "There is smoke coming from over there."

"Must be a town, at last," Zehava replied, relief evident in his tone. "Not many of those up this far. We had best take full advantage of it."

"Does that mean we will stay for a night?" Dahak asked, almost begging.

Zehava grinned at his friend. "That all depends on how long it takes us to get there."

"I wonder if Meath was there when they passed through here. They would have had to get supplies too. They were traveling light when they took him," Nicolette wondered aloud. "Maybe someone seen him and knows where they are heading."

"Only one way to find out," Zehava replied, altering their course so they were heading straight for the town.

"I wonder if this is where they took Meath?" Dahak questioned.

Zehava hacked several branches and vines from their path with his sword. "I doubt it, why would they take him to a small farming community?"

"I do not know - why would they take him at all?" Dahak countered.

"Dahak right," Shania cut in. "Why would they take Meath? He is just a Wizard with the Gift, plenty of them around if they just needed a Wizard, so why him? Make no senses to me."

"Well we will search the town as best we can," Zehava replied. "If he is there, we will find him!" he finished. His tone hardening as another branch fell to his sword blade.

After days of traveling through the dense thickness of the jungle, they finally make it to a lightly used road that lead to the small town ahead. Dusk was nearly upon them and the town was still a ways off. They made camp on the side of the roadway not wanting to risk traveling at night and not knowing how they would be received when they reached the town.

Shania spotted their dinner and took Nicolette off into the growth a ways to help her pick the sweet yellowy fruit that grew on several thick bushy trees near the roadway, leaving Dahak and Zehava to set up a small camp.

"You and Dahak seem to have taken a liking to one another lately," Nicolette commented as she felt the oval shaped fruit with her fingers picking only the softest ones.

Shania's hand stopped momentarily, as she was reaching up for one of the juicy fruits. She quickly turned his head to hide her quickly crimsoning cheeks. "I… he is different, funny…. I like being around him," she stuttered out timidly.

Nicolette smiled at Shania's embarrassment. She had noticed that the two were beginning to spend more and more time together and nearly leapt at any opportunity to be alone. The previous night, she had observed that by morning the two had almost closed the distance between their bedrolls. Nicolette smiled wider knowing it was growing into something more than friendship. It had been the same for her and Meath when they had been younger.

"He has a good heart," Shania said, seeing Nicolette deep in thought. "Not bull-headed letting pride get in way."

"What about Zehava?" Nicolette asked. "When you first joined us you hardly left his side."

Shania sighed. "Zehava is strong and brave, qualities I was raised to believe were most vital in a mate." She paused. "Dahak is strong and brave too, but different. He needs someone for balance. I like being needed. I like knowing I am valued. Dahak make me feel that way."

"I think I know what you mean," Nicolette told her.

"Really?" Shania asked turning to her and Nicolette nodded. "I do not know what to do, I do not want Zehava to be mad at me or hate Dahak and fight."

"Why would he be angry at either one of you or fight each other?"

"When two men share interest in a mate they fight for her," Shania replied as if it was obvious. "I do not want them to fight for me - I do not want either one getting hurt."

Nicolette nearly laughed aloud. "I do not think you have to worry about them fighting one another. They are friends and have been for a long time. Tell Zehava - he will be okay and he will understand," Nicolette assured her, knowing Zehava had likely already come to the same conclusion.

Shania smiled to herself, feeling somewhat foolish now. "Thank you for talk." Shania picked one last fruit before turning back towards the road. "But right now we need to work on finding Meath."

Nicolette followed her. "We are close. I can feel it in my heart Shania - we are close."

"Meath lucky to have such good friends that would risk their lives to search for him."

Nicolette stopped Shania. "That is what friends do - he would do it for any one of us," Nicolette explained looking deeply into Shania's glimmering eyes. "We would risk our lives to find you too Shania - you are our friend."

Shania wiped stray tears from her road-stained cheeks. "Thank you."

"No need for thanks, you are one of us now - never doubt it." Nicolette told her happily. "We should be getting back now. It is almost dark."

"Let us see if we can sneak up on Zehava and Dahak," Shania replied, a playful gleam in her eyes.

"I am not very silent when walking in this terrain - I will give us away."

Shania smiled. "I will show you how - it is easy."

"I wonder what is taking them so long," Dahak said with more than a hint of worry in his tone. "You think they are okay?"

Zehava smirked, noticing that every time Shania's name crossed his lips, it had a completely different tone than normal. "I am sure they are fine - we would know if there was trouble. They are not far away," he assured his friend.

Dahak sat uncomfortably for a moment before he spoke. "Do you really think we will find him?" he asked with a hint of doubt in his voice. "I mean it seems like a long shot. You know?"

Zehava knew this was something that was playing on everyone's mind, even his own. "I sure hope so," was all he could say.

"We will," Nicolette's voice said from behind them startling them both into nearly falling off their seats.

"How the heck did you?" Dahak stammered barely keeping his balance.

"What?" Nicolette asked casually.

"We did not even hear you coming," Zehava answered, his brow raised in wonder.

"She learn quick." Shania's voice said from near the fire and both their heads snapped around to see Shania adding wood to their small fire.

"Impressive," Zehava said, admiration showing on his face.

"I want to be able to do that!" Dahak stammered out with a childish grin.

"I will show you one day." Shania beamed.

The morning was damp, and a chilly mist glided through the jungle growth and across the dirt road, painting an eerie path to the small town ahead of them. They traveled cautiously, their hands fidgeting near their weapons the morning silence unnerving them.

They entered the non-walled town as the last of mist dissipated into the growing warmth of the day. The single sentry paid them little heed, having seen their fire burning during the night and just waved them in. Most of the town's folk were just waking up, readying themselves for the long day of work ahead of them - tending livestock or the fields. No one paid them much mind, other than a quick glance and occasionally a nod in greeting.

"We will find the market place - we can get supplies and ask some questions," Zehava told them. "Hopefully someone will know something about Meath or any travelers that have come through here recently. I have to guess that with all the barbarian activity that outside travelers would be a rare sight and easily remembered."

"Why do I get the feeling we are not going to be staying a night?" Dahak moaned. "Am I the only one who has been dreaming of a soft warm bed and not the cold stony earth?"

"We will have to see what we can find out," Zehava told him.

Nicolette was about to agree with Dahak when something caught her eye and her voice froze in her throat as she stopped.

"What is it?" Dahak asked and everyone stopped to see what was going on.

"I know that horse," Nicolette replied, her voice barely escaping her lips as she walked into the stable and right up to the old man tending the strong black and white stallion. "A fine horse you have there." She told the man, who looked up at her and beamed with pride. The horse recognized her voice and quickly nuzzled its nose under her hand for a tender scratch and soft pat.

"Thank you my lady," he replied as he continued brushing the stallion's side. "You are your friends there looking to purchase some horses maybe?"

"Possibly - what is this one's history?" Nicolette asked.

"Well, I wish I could tell you, but I only know so much about this one. Had a young man sell me this one a few days ago, all I can tell you is it is a fine animal - smart, strong and very friendly, as you can see." The old man told her.

"Can you tell me what the man who traded you this horse looked like?" Nicolette asked her voice full of hope.

The stable man thought about it for a moment then his face twisted in puzzlement. "Why do you want to know such a thing? What is all this about? You are not here to buy horses are you?"

Before Nicolette could say anything, Zehava cut in. "We believe the man who sold you this horse is the horse thief we are looking for. This horse use to belong to our Lord from Draco Castle," Zehava said, stepping beside Nicolette and standing tall, but smiled to prevent intimidating the horse dealer.

"I knew something was up with that man - he just did not seem right and all. Well I guess he was well built - dark, short hair and dark eyes and he had a bit of an odd accent not a thick one but if you listened you could tell he was not from around here," the old stable master told them.

"That is him!" Nicolette blurted out in excitement.

"I guess you are going to want to take this horse back to your Lord?" The old man muttered begrudgingly. "And the other two he sold me?"

"No, that will not be necessary," Zehava told him. "You paid good coin for these animals and your forthrightness proves your loyalties as far as I am concerned. You may keep the animals as reward for your help."

The old man beamed again. "Thank you good Sir. I do hope you catch the thief."

"You would not happen to know which way he was traveling, would you?" Zehava asked before turning to leave.

"Well he left to the west, but we had some hunters out and they saw him meet up with two others and then they head southeast on an old trail towards Drake River and the wastelands," the man replied. "Do not know why they would head that way, not much out there but trouble, but I reckon maybe they deserve what they get."

"How long ago was this?" Nicolette asked urgently.

The stable master chewed on his bottom lips for a moment in thought. "Must have been a little over half a fortnight ago now."

"Thank you for your assistance," Zehava said, nodding to the man as they walked out of the stables.

"Good luck to you!" the man called to them as he continued his work on Meath's old stallion.

They did not spend a moment longer in the town than they had to and were traveling hard northeast again. The news that they were indeed on Meath's trail was uplifting and refueled their pace. Though the time line that they were behind was disheartening it was to be expected and did not hinder their drive much.

Conversation was minimal that day as everyone seemed concentrated on the path ahead of them - their pace was nearly a jog as they all hoped to shorten their distances behind. They made Drake River before nightfall.

"So what are we going to do when we find them?" Dahak asked. The thought had been playing in his mind all day.

"Save him of course." Shania replied as if it was obvious.

"I know that, but how? I mean Nicolette said they were both highly skilled with the Gift and all." Dahak reminded them. "We do not have anyone with magic on our side."

"He is right you know," Zehava put in, catching on to what his friend was implying. "It might be difficult dealing with two Wizards."

"The Gifted die just the same as you or me if you catch them off guard," Nicolette replied in the bitterest tone any of them had ever heard from her, as she ran her fingers down the shaft of an arrow.

No one could believe what she had just said. For some reason, they all had it in their minds it would be a snatch and grab - in truth, the chances of a peaceful exchange were unlikely. It would most likely come to a fight, and a dangerous one at that.

"Well hopefully it will not escalate to that level, forcing us to prove that statement, but if it does, we will do what we must to get Meath back," Zehava said, a lot less cruelly than Nicolette.

"We do have a Gifted on our side," Shania decided to tell them. When she had their attention, she continued. "Meath, he is on our side. Once he knows we are there, he will fight with us."

"That is true," Zehava agreed. "If we can find a way to let him know we are there before we start our attack it will give him a chance to prepare."

"How would we do that without getting caught or seen?" Nicolette asked.

"I know how," Dahak boosted. "If we can get ahead of them, we can leave a message or a sign where he will see it and know it is us."

"How will he know it is for him?" Shania asked.

"We will use our army insignia," Dahak replied.

Zehava grinned in admiration to his friend. "Good thinking Dahak."

"First we need to gain ground on them - we are a long way behind them," Nicolette reminded them.

"Then I suggest we get some sleep so we can be moving again at first light," Zehava said, tossing Nicolette her bedroll.

Dawn slowly crept around the mountains and trouble crept not far away, hoping to make an easy strike. Revenge stricken, the group of cutthroats moved in eagerly for redemption of their previous failure to capture the small group. This time they had nearly doubled their numbers from before, hoping it would ensure their victory as several men moved in from the river's edge allowing no escape route this time.

Blades slid silently from scabbards and axe shafts were gripped tightly in meaty hands as the group did their best to stalk into the camp silently.

Shania crouched in a nearby tree. She was the last to stand watch and it was almost time for her to wake everyone with the rising dawn. She had caught a green viper that had been investigating the intruder occupying its home. She was about to release the deadly serpent to another tree when she noticed the dark figures below her and swarming all around the camp. Her heart skipped a beat when she counted how many there were. She knew they were sorely outnumbered and the enemy was coming in at all angles, making escape impossible.

Shania knew she had to do something and fast to try to even the odds, while she had the advantage of surprise. Without wasting another moment in thought, she jumped down from her perch and landed in front of two unsuspecting men. Before either man could react, her blade flashed across the closest one's throat opening his jugular with a spray of blood. The man dropped his weapon and gripped his throat in terror as he sank to his knees, his life already fading from his dark eyes. Before the other man even had time to think, Shania threw the deadly viper at the man's face. The irritated serpent sank its poisonous fangs deep into his cheek, releasing its burning venom. He cried out wildly as he tried to pull the reptile off him and alerted the others to the trouble surrounding them.

Zehava rushed out of their canvas tent, his sword arcing high severing clean through a man's leg. With a quick reverse, he thrust his sword behind him and embedded the tip of his blade into the toppling man's back puncturing a lung. Zehava pulled his blade clear, blocking an overhead attack and kicked up catching the bearded cutthroat in the groin. The man stumbled back in pain, his guard down as he fought to keep his footing. Zehava's blade flashed down slicing through flesh and bone decapitating his enemy in one fluent movement. His heart almost stopped when he took a moment to scan the area and just how many opponents were upon them.

Dahak scrambled out of the tent behind his friend and nearly tripped over the flailing body of a man already downed. Before Dahak could pick a target, a dagger flashed out of nowhere and embedded itself into his midsection. He did not understand what had happened - all of the sudden he was on his knees. He heard a faint cry from behind him and turned to see Nicolette, a look of panic and rage flashing across her face as an arrow released from her bow and streaked by him, he heard a grunt and the sound of a body crashing into the ground and knew she had hit her target. Dahak tried to stand but could hardly feel his legs beneath him - he looked down and saw the silver hilt of a dagger protruding from his belly. Reality crashed into his mind with stark understanding. Dahak turned back to Nicolette, who was now by his side, tears in her eyes. He tried to tell her it was okay, that he could not feel anything, but no words came out.

Shania sidestepped a wild thrust and her blades bit in deep to her attacker's overextended arms nearly causing him to drop his long sword. Nicolette's cry caught her attention and she glanced over to see Dahak slump to the earth, a blade buried into his guts. The agonizing grunt of her attacker was all that saved her as her attention returned to a clumsy, weak swing. Shania's reflexes snapped her blades up to parry the inept attack - the sheer strength of her defense caused her attacker to lose hold of his weapon, his hands no longer able to hold it securely. Rage rippled through her and her curved blades tore through the man's weak leather armor and spilled his entrails to the damp earth releasing a light steam where they landed. Shania ran towards Dahak not even taking noticing of the attacker to her side or his blade that ripped into her shoulder.

"Give up!" a black toothed brute bellowed, his meaty, scared fist connecting with Zehava's jaw with a sickening crack.

Zehava's head snapped to the side with the powerful blow and for a moment, he was sure he would lose consciousness. He managed to keep his feet beneath him and turned back to his attacker, his eyes blurred and he was no longer sure which one had hit him as several figures surrounded him.

"Drop your sword fool," the black toothed brute barked at him. "You do not need to end up like your friend over there. What a waste."

Panic surged through him. Zehava looked back to their tent and saw Nicolette trying to notch an arrow frantically as Shania huddled over Dahak's limp form.

"You do not have to die here today like this," the brute growled at him.

Zehava's attention returned to the five armed cutthroats in front of him. He did not even bother to count the others that had surrounded their small camp. Nausea flooded through him at the sight of his downed friend as he realized they would not survive this. He lifted his sword defensively in front of him - the weight of the blade impossibly heavy now as he watched crimson droplets cascade down the remaining silver of the blade.

Zehava heard someone cry out his name and watched one of the men in front of him pitch backwards as an arrow embedded into the right side of his chest.

"Tell the bitch to drop the bow!" the brute ordered him. "Or I swear to you the things I will do to her will make the Keeper himself have night terrors!"

Zehava turned back to his friends - they were surrounded. Nicolette held her bow in shaking hands unsure of where to release her next arrow as Shania held Dahak up trying to slow the flow of blood. A new fire ignited in Zehava knowing that Dahak was still alive. "What do you want from us?" Zehava hissed back, his eyes flaring with hatred.

The man grinned back at him. "The same thing all men want, wealth and power."

"You can have our coin," Zehava shot back tearing his purse from his belt and tossing it to the ground. "Take it - just leave us alone."

The man leaned down, retrieved the leather pouch, and grinned finding the weight of it satisfying. "Had this been the result of our first encounter it might have been enough." He slipped the purse into one of his pockets. "But you have cost me far too much for me to be paid off so easily and look another three of my men lay dead by your hand alone, not to mention the others," the man exclaimed, looking down at the dead men around them.

"What do you want from us?" Zehava growled, his sword gripped tightly in his hands.

A wide smile crossed his mouth, "your abilities as a fighter for starters."

"I am not a hired goon who can be bought by a cutthroat like you!" Zehava snapped back.

"Who says I was hiring?" The man replied with a menacing grin. "A shame about the other one - he would have provided some entertainment if nothing else. Now are you going to come with us peacefully or are we going to do this the hard way?"

Zehava looked back at the others - their faces were mixed with emotions. Every fiber in his body wanted to fight to the death and not give these cutthroats the satisfaction of taking them prisoner, but when his eyes fell on Nicolette…Queen Nicolette…his Queen, the only remaining heir to Draco. He knew he could not act so boldly if there was still a chance he could keep her alive.

"It is time to get moving Kara, wake up." Meath said giving her a nudge with his boot. He had been up for some time now just staring up at the night sky acting upon an old children's tale, wishing upon the fading stars that he would see his friends again. He knew dawn would not come for a while but he wanted an early start even if it meant traveling by torchlight.

"You have got to be moonstruck," Kara groaned as she struggled to sit up, her hands still tightly bound behind her back. "It is still pitch black."

"We will travel by torchlight until dawn breaks through the canopy." Meath informed her. "We have to be close to a town or village by now, and I want to reach one today. I will need food and a horse."

Kara managed to get herself to her feet. "What about me?" she asked bluntly. "You cannot believe any more than we did that you can trust me in a town."

Meath grinned. "I know - that is why I plan on leaving you tied to a tree. Do not look at me like that Kara. Of course I will tell them where to find you, but I will be long gone by then." Meath turned a stern eye on her. "And I would suggest you go back to Salvas and do not come for me again."

"Please Meath, I am begging you to reconsider this."

"And I wish you and Daden had never invaded my life, but you did. Remember?" Meath snapped back.

"But Meath you do not understand…" Kara began.

"What I understand is you abducted me, dragged me half way across the Kingdom against my will, and almost got me killed," Meath replied harshly. "But now I am in control and I am going back to my life! Now get moving."

They began traveling west once again at a slow pace due to the dim light of the torch that could only push back the darkness so far.

No conversation was made as Meath's mind was on one thing and that was finding a town and being rid of her.

Every step of the way Kara fought her better judgment about telling Meath the truth of why he needed to go to Salvas with her. But she could not - she had been ordered not to - he would not believe her now anyway.

"You cannot just leave me gagged and tied to a tree and send strangers to come fetch me," Kara insisted.

"That is the beauty of it, I can." Meath said, not even looking back to see her reaction.

"But think about what might happen to me!" Kara cried to him. "How can you be so sure they will not harm me?"

Meath pondered this thought for a moment. "I am sure I will think of something between now and then," Meath replied, wishing he had his sword with him now to help clear their path, but the magnificent blade was still with Daden and Meath would likely never see it again.

"Have you thought about how we are going to cross the river coming up?" Kara reminded him, hearing the river in the distance. "Without my powers I cannot do much to help."

Meath almost burst out laughing. "There are many ways to get across a river without the help of magic, but nice try," Meath said back to her.

"Cannot blame a girl for trying," Kara remarked.

"There is the river," Meath said, pointing straight ahead.

"Meath, I will tell you everything if you promise to..." Kara started, but Meath cut her off.

"Shhh!" Meath whispered, cupping his ears with his hands to hear better. "It sounds like there is fighting on the other side."

"We should go another way then - it is probably barbarians or highwaymen," Kara pleaded, scanning the growth around them almost expecting at ambush.

"Someone may need our help - we should check it out," Meath countered, already moving swiftly through the remaining growth towards the rivers' edge. He stopped behind several thick leafed plants not far from the bank of the river - directly across from him was a group of people. Meath watched quietly trying to decipher what was going on. It almost appeared that bounty hunters had caught a small group of thieves, but the closer Meath looked the more he could tell that was not the case. Several bodies littered the area from the fight that had ensued, but now it looked like the larger band had neutralized the smaller.

"It looks like one of them is hurt badly." Kara pointed out to the two people huddled over a moaning man.

"Something is not right here - those people are in trouble."

"How are you going to help them Meath?" Kara asked. "We are on the other side with no weapons."

Meath knew she was right, but he could not just stand by and watch as innocent people were killed by a band of cutthroats. "I can use my Gift."

"It is too far and you are not a Master Wizard - you will never be able to reach them, and even if you could make it that far you might kill someone else," Kara explained, but Meath was already inching his way closer.

Finally, Meath was as close as he could get without exposing himself in plain view. He watched for a moment longer and knew those people were in trouble as ropes were pulled out and hands were being tied. Meath took a deep breath and began to feel his innate Gift flow inside him when he heard the name Dahak from a familiar voice across the water. Meath's face went white and his legs nearly buckled beneath him as realization assaulted his every sense.

By the time Kara made it to Meath, she too recognized one of the defenders across the river - it was the Princess. "Free me Meath, and I will help save them I swear to you!" Kara pleaded to him knowing time was running out.

But Meath was not listening - he did not even realize she was behind him. Panic flashed through him when he saw one of the men backhand Zehava dropping him to the ground. Before Meath even knew what he was doing, two massive bolts of energy created from pure desperation exploded from his outstretched hands. The crackling bolts tore through the chest of a man about to bind Zehava's hands and threw him back into two others who were standing behind him.

"You are the one," Kara whispered to herself, knowing that was a distance that most experienced Wizards would be hard pressed to make with that strength and accuracy.

Meath cried out in rage as he stepped from his hiding place, deadly Wizard's fire already blossoming in his palms. He did not even hear the rustling of bushes behind him - even if he had, he would not have turned to regard it as he unleashed his fire across the river engulfing two men in an uncontrolled inferno.

"Daden NO!" Meath heard Kara scream a moment before an array of bright lights and colors erupted through his vision, overwhelming his senses, before unconsciousness embraced him.

It had been over a fortnight since Prince Kayreil and the royal family had returned to Zandor from Draco Kingdom. The affairs around the castle had been geared towards military alertness, for an eerie calm had been reported from several normally active boarder encampments.

Kayreil stood looking over his balcony into the city surrounding the castle. Boredom was consuming him more every day now that his older brother Berrit was no longer around. Not that his brother had played with him or showed much of an interest in him. However, his brother had been fun to spy upon, especially his desired fetishes with women. Kayreil had watched his brother countless times take out his abnormal sexual desires on the servant or peasant girls. At first Kayreil had been disgusted by his brother's unusual and often fatal fetishes, but after a while he had learned he too became aroused at such twisted acts.

Prince Berrit forbade anyone from entering his private chambers, unless permitted by himself. Kayreil grinned mischievously - with his brother away, he was free to snoop about and sample the many fine liqueurs and sweets he kept hidden away.

Kayreil planned his route to his brother's room strategically, not wanting anyone to know where he was going or what he planned to do. His brother's chambers were on the far northern wing of the grand castle, whereas the rest of the Royal chambers - Kayreil's included - resided in the western wing. His brother liked his privacy and made sure he got it, as most of the northern wing was empty much of the time.

Kayreil reached his brother's dark cherry wood doors and his eyes darted around making sure no one was about. He knew his brother's door would be locked tightly, but during his spying, he had seen where his brother had kept a spare key outside his room. Kayreil quickly glanced around one last time to ensure his secrecy then pushed the heavy door open, entered and quickly shut it tight once more.

The extensively lavish room was musky from nearly an entire season of inactivity but everything remained exactly the way his brother had left it. Kayreil's eyes danced with intrigue and possibility as he moved through his brother's expensive and prized possessions. The further in the room Kayreil made it, the more the musky smell became one of rot and decay. He crinkled his nose in disgust at the offensive smell, and began to wonder if his brother had left food within his chamber or possibly a body of a city whore.

Soon he was in the middle of the room, his eyes fell upon his brothers' black oak liquor cabinet, and excitement quickly overruled his sense of smell. He grabbed the polished tiger bone handles and pulled open the doors.

"My King!" A servant called, running into Dante's study. "My King, you must come with me at once!"

"What is the meaning of this?" King Dante asked clearly unimpressed with being disturbed.

"It...it is your son Highness!" the servant bellowed out, her expression distraught.

Dante sighed, his irritation - his youngest son had been nothing but a pain since their return. "What has Kayreil done now?"

The servant licked her lips nervously. "It is not Prince Kayreil.... It is Prince Berrit...."

Made in the USA
Charleston, SC
19 April 2013